Die d
Das (

C0000184322

DIE SERIE

??? »Drei Fragezeichen« – das ist das Symbol des wohl bekanntesten Junior-Detektivteams der Jugendliteratur. War die Aufklärung geheimnisvoller, oft gefährlicher Kriminalfälle für Justus, Bob und Peter aus Rocky Beach in Kalifornien zunächst nur ein Zeitvertreib, so hat sich daraus nach und nach eine ernsthafte Nebenbeschäftigung für freie Stunden und Schulferien entwickelt. Ihre Zentrale, einen ausrangierten Campingwagen, haben die drei mit Telefon, Tonbandgerät, Fotolabor, Periskop und mancherlei selbst gebastelten Apparaten eingerichtet, die ihnen modernste Ermittlungstechniken ermöglichen. Doch jeder Fall erfordert vorwiegend Köpfchen, Ausdauer und Mut – und ohne Justus' Superhirn, Bobs Forscherdrang und Peters Sportsgeist kämen die drei trotz ihrer technischen Ausrüstung nicht zum Ziel.

Von den drei ??? ist bei OMNIBUS erschienen:

Die drei ??? und der magische Kreis (20499) · **Die drei ??? und der weinende Sarg** (20471) · **Die drei ??? und der verrückte Maler** (20545) · **Die drei ??? und der Höhlenmensch** (21022) · **Die drei ??? – Der schrullige Millionär** (21759) · **Die drei ??? und die Perlenvögel** (20583) · **Die drei ??? und der gestohlene Preis** (20582) · **Die drei ??? und die Musikpiraten** (20580) · **Die drei ??? und der Schatz im Bergsee** (20713) · **Die drei ??? – Die Schattenmänner** (21751) · **Die drei ??? und der Automarder** (20765) · **Die drei ??? und das Geheimnis der Särge** (20768) · **Die drei ??? – Die singende Schlange** (21754) · **Die drei ??? und der unsichtbare Gegner** (20766) · **Die drei ??? – Späte Rache** (21752) · **Die drei ??? und der Spuk im Hotel** (20993) · **Die drei ??? und der Diamantenschmuggel** (20994) · **Die drei ??? und die Fußballgangster** (21020) · **Die drei ??? – Der rasende Löwe** (21755) · **Die drei ??? und der lachende Schatten** (21138) · **Die drei ??? und der Ameisenmensch** (21141) · **Die drei ??? und der unheimliche Drache** (21178) · **Die drei ??? und der Teufelsberg** (21180) · **Die drei ??? und der Zauberspiegel** (21181) · **Die drei ??? – Angriff der Computerviren** (21753) · **Die drei ??? und die Silbermine** (21183) · **Die drei ??? – Schüsse aus dem Dunkel** (21756) · **Die drei ??? – Geheimsache Ufo** (21185) · **Die drei ??? und der höllische Werwolf** (21186) · **Die drei ??? – Der Doppelgänger** (21858) · **Die drei ??? und der Nebelberg** (21371) · **Die drei ??? im Bann des Voodoo** (21372) · **Die drei ??? – Das Erbe des Meisterdiebs** (21373) · **Die drei ??? und die Automafia** (27979) · **Die drei ??? und die Karten des Bösen** (21370) · **Die drei ??? und die Schlucht der Dämonen** (27071) · **Die drei ??? und die Villa der Toten** (21715) · **Die drei ??? – Die bedrohte Ranch** (21760) · **Die drei ??? – Der Feuerturm** (21746)

Als OMNIBUS-Doppeldecker sind erschienen:

Die drei ??? und der Karpatenhund/Die drei ??? und das Narbengesicht (20040) · **Die drei ??? und der schrullige Millionär/Die drei ??? und der Höhlenmensch** (20390) · **Die drei ??? und die Fußballgangster/Die drei ??? und der Diamantenschmuggel** (21293)

Weitere Titel der Serie sind in Vorbereitung.

Die drei ???
Das Gold der Wikinger

Erzählt von William Arden
Nach einer Idee von Robert Arthur

Aus dem Amerikanischen
von Leonore Puschert

OMNIBUS
ist der Taschenbuchverlag für Kinder
in der Verlagsgruppe Random House

FSC
Mix
Produktgruppe aus vorbildlich
bewirtschafteten Wäldern und
anderen kontrollierten Herkünften

Zert.-Nr. SGS-COC-1940
www.fsc.org
© 1996 Forest Stewardship Council

Verlagsgruppe Random House FSC-DEU-0100
Das für dieses Buch verwendete FSC-zertifizierte
Papier *Munken Print* liefert Arctic Paper
Munkedals AB, Schweden.

1. Auflage
Neuausgabe als OMNIBUS Taschenbuch
Dezember 2007
Gesetzt nach den Regeln der Rechtschreibreform
Erstmals erschienen im OMNIBUS Taschenbuch 2005.
© 1989 der deutschsprachigen Ausgabe
Franck-Kosmos Verlags-GmbH & Co. KG, Stuttgart
© 1986 der Originalausgabe Random House, Inc.,
New York
Die Originalausgabe erschien unter dem Titel
» The Three Investigators in The Mystery of the
Wreckers' Rock«
Based on characters by Robert Arthur.
This work published by arrangement with
Random House, Inc.
Alle Rechte dieser Ausgabe vorbehalten durch
OMNIBUS, München
Übersetzung: Leonore Puschert
Umschlagbild: Thilo Krapp
Umschlaggestaltung: knaus. büro für konzeptionelle
und visuelle identitäten, Würzburg
MI · Herstellung: CZ
Satz: Uhl + Massopust, Aalen
Druck und Bindung: GGP Media GmbH, Pößneck
ISBN 978-3-570-21859-4
Printed in Germany

www.omnibus-verlag.de

Inhalt

Vorwort zu einem unfreiwilligen Abenteuer

Willkommen, Krimifreunde!

Es gibt Neues von den drei ??? und ihren Glanzleistungen zu berichten. Diesmal schlittern die eifrigen jungen Detektive ganz unfreiwillig in einen Fall hinein und dabei wollten sie doch nur harmlose Fotos von einem Familientreffen machen. Bei solchen Anlässen geht es normalerweise recht munter zu, doch diese Festlichkeit wird von rätselhaften, bedrohlichen Vorkommnissen überschattet – nachts tauchen Gespenster auf, und unheimliches Geheul ertönt. Und bestimmte Zeitgenossen haben etwas dagegen, fotografiert zu werden!

Wer die drei ??? noch nicht kennt, sei hiermit ins Bild gesetzt: Erster Detektiv ist Justus Jonas, der etwas übergewichtige Anführer des Teams, der sich durch bemerkenswerten Scharfsinn und überragenden Verstand auszeichnet. Zur Seite stehen ihm Peter Shaw, stark und sportlich, jedoch nicht völlig frei von Gespensterfurcht, und Bob Andrews mit solidem Wissen, leisem Humor und Spürsinn fürs Recherchieren.

Die drei Jungen sind an der Pazifikküste in Kalifornien zu Hause, in der kleinen Stadt Rocky Beach unweit von Hollywood. Ihre Geheimzentrale mit Detektivlabor ist in einem Campinganhänger untergebracht, der für Unbefugte unauffindbar und unzugänglich auf dem Schrottplatz des »Gebrauchtwaren-Center T. Jonas« steht. Dieses Unternehmen mit seiner einzigartigen Angebotspalette gehört Justus' Onkel und Tante, bei denen er aufgewachsen ist.

Nun aber los zum Schauplatz der Ereignisse voller Spannung und Abenteuer – auf zur Felseninsel Ragnarson Rock!

Albert Hitfield

Eine Seeschlacht

Das Boot mit dem Außenbordmotor hob und senkte sich rhythmisch in der Dünung des Pazifiks vor der kleinen Insel, an deren westlichem Ende ein gewaltiger Felsen aufragte.

»Ähnlich wie der Felsen von Gibraltar«, fand Bob Andrews.

»Entfernt ähnlich, Bob«, meinte Justus Jonas mit prüfendem Blick, »nur eben eine Idee kleiner, meinst du nicht?«

»So ungefähr tausendmal kleiner«, drückte es Peter Shaw genauer aus. »Eine Taschenausgabe des Felsens von Gibraltar!«

Das jugendliche Detektivtrio »die drei ???« war etwa zwanzig Kilometer südlich von Rocky Beach zum Fischen aufs Meer hinausgefahren. Justus mit seiner in grellen Farben fluoreszierenden Schwimmweste glich einem riesigen Ballon. Unbestritten war der Erste Detektiv ein Geistesathlet, doch andere athletische Leistungen lagen ihm weniger. Peter hingegen, der große, muskulöse Zweite Detektiv, hätte mit Schwimmweste ein prachtvolles Motiv für eine Sportwerbung abgegeben. Bob, der Mann für Recherchen und Archiv, blickte angespannt ins Wasser, als könnte er damit einen Fisch zum Auftauchen bewegen.

Die Jungen hatten Angeln mit leichten Senkbleien und fischten bei den Stellen, wo sich der Buntbarsch im Tang versteckt hielt. Bisher hatte der Buntbarsch allerdings nur wenig Interesse für ihre Bemühungen aufgebracht. Erst drei mittelgroße Fische schwammen träge im Eimer.

»Ich hab euch doch gesagt, drüben beim Genoa Reef ist es besser«, beklagte sich Peter, während er wieder einmal seine Schnur einholte, um den Köder zu wechseln. »Was sollen wir hier auf dem weiten Meer für deinen Vater eigentlich fotografieren, Bob?« Bobs Vater arbeitete als Reporter bei einer Tageszeitung in Los Angeles.

»Wollte er nicht näher erklären«, sagte Bob. Er gab etwas mehr Schnur, immer bereit für den blitzschnellen Anbiss des Barsches. »Er sagte nur, wir sollten am Dienstag hier draußen vor Ragnarson Rock fischen, und drängte mich, meine Kamera mitzunehmen. Wenn uns gute Fotos glücken, will er uns die bezahlen, aber was wir knipsen sollen, das sagte er nicht. Als ich danach fragte, lachte er nur und meinte, wenn wir es vor Augen hätten, wüssten wir dann schon Bescheid.«

»Mich interessiert an der Sache das Honorar«, erklärte Justus. »In der Kasse unseres Unternehmens herrscht beklagenswerte Ebbe. Wenn wir nicht demnächst wieder Einnahmen verbuchen können, werden wir uns wohl notgedrungen meiner Tante Mathilda als Helfer anbieten müssen.«

»Bloß das nicht…«, stöhnte Peter.

Bei der äußerst unangenehmen Vorstellung, auf dem Schrottplatz für Mrs Mathilda Jonas schuften zu müssen, ließen alle drei die Köpfe hängen. Zurzeit hatte das jugendliche Detektivteam Sommerferien und Justus' energische Tante packte des Öfteren die willkommene Gelegenheit beim Schopf und ließ die Jungen im Betrieb allerlei Extraarbeiten erledigen. Daher gaben sich die drei nun alle erdenkliche Mühe, den misstrauischen Buntbarsch aus seinem sicheren Aufenthalt im Tang zu locken, denn mit einem guten Fang würden sie sich ein schönes Taschengeld verdienen können. Nur sahen das die Fische leider nicht ein und es biss keiner mehr an. Peter gähnte und ließ den Blick über das blaue Wasser ringsum schweifen. Da bekam er plötzlich große Augen.

»Dort, seht mal!«, rief der Zweite Detektiv und zeigte auf die knapp zwei Kilometer lange Insel Ragnarson Rock.

Ein langes, niedriges Wikingerschiff kam um die östliche Spitze gesegelt. Die Nachmittagssonne spiegelte sich in den

Schilden, die längs der Bordwände aufgehängt waren. Der Bug endete in einem grimmigen, hoch erhobenen Drachenkopf, dessen weit aufgerissene Kiefer kunstvoll geschnitzte, spitze Zähne zeigten. Wilde, kriegerische Gestalten mit gehörnten Helmen, zottigen Bärten und dicken Felljacken schwangen Schwerter und Streitäxte. Vom Mast und von dem hohen Achtersteven wehten Flaggen. Raue Schlachtrufe der Krieger drangen zu den Jungen herüber.

»Das muss es sein«, stellte Justus fest. »Ganz klar!«

Bob hatte die Kamera schon schussbereit. »Mein Vater sagte, er will uns alle Bilder abkaufen, die wir machen können.«

Das Wikingerschiff näherte sich rasch. Nun sahen die Jungen, dass es sich in Wahrheit nur um ein großes Boot mit Außenbordmotor handelte, auf das man die Attrappe eines Wikingerschiffes montiert hatte. An Bord befanden sich sechs oder sieben »Krieger« mit falschen Bärten und bemalten Holzschwertern. Lachend fuchtelten die Männer mit ihren dekorativen Waffen herum, als das imitierte Langschiff am Boot der Jungen vorbeiglitt und eine kleine Bucht am Strand der Insel ansteuerte.

»Was soll denn das ganze Theater?«, rief Peter verwundert.

»Weiß ich nicht«, antwortete Bob. »Jedenfalls konnte ich ein paar gute Bilder schießen.«

»Ich vermute…«, setzte Justus an.

Weiter kam der Erste Detektiv nicht. Mit offenem Mund starrte er auf ein zweites Boot, das ebenfalls um die Ostspitze der Insel gebogen war und schnell näher kam.

»Was ist denn das nun noch?« Peter kam aus dem Staunen nicht heraus.

Das zweite Boot war lang und flach. Es war ein Zwischending aus Ruderboot und Kanu, aus massiven Planken gebaut. Bug und Heck liefen spitz zu und waren etwas hochgezogen. Und dieses eigenartige Wasserfahrzeug wurde vom rhythmischen Paddelschlag einer Mannschaft von sechs »Indianern«

in stolzem Federschmuck und ledernem Gewand vorangetrieben. Schrilles Kriegsgeheul schallte herüber.

»Das ist ein typisches Kanu der Chumash!«, erkannte Justus. »Dieser Indianerstamm war hier in der Gegend ansässig. Oben in Santa Barbara gab es einmal eine große Siedlung und man hat dort Reste ihrer seetüchtigen Kanus gefunden. Damit fuhren sie weit aufs Meer hinaus, zum Fischen und zur Jagd auf Wale und Seehunde. Sie waren ein friedfertiges Volk und manche Familien wohnten draußen auf den Kanalinseln vor Santa Barbara.«

»Nachhilfe in Geschichte brauchst du uns nicht zu geben, Justus«, meinte Peter. »Schließlich haben wir mit dir das Geheimnis des lachenden Schattens aufgeklärt, daher kennen wir ja die Chumash-Indianer.* Ich wusste nur nicht, dass sie auch hier auf Ragnarson Rock hausten.«

Justus schüttelte den Kopf. »Taten sie eben nicht, Peter. Ihre Wohnplätze lagen weiter nördlich auf den größeren Inseln.«

»Ist doch jetzt egal!«, rief Bob dazwischen. »Versucht lieber, das Boot still zu halten, damit ich besser fotografieren kann.«

Bob richtete seine Kamera auf das große Kanu mit den kriegerischen Indianern. Es hielt in schneller Fahrt auf eben jene Bucht zu, in die zuvor die Wikinger gefahren waren. Das Kanu legte auch an und speerschwingend erstürmten seine Insassen das Land. Nun entspann sich ein wildes Scheingefecht zwischen Wikingern und Indianern um den Besitz der Insel Ragnarson Rock. Heftig schwangen die Männer ihre dekorativen hölzernen Waffen. Schwerthiebe knickten den Federschmuck, Speere prallten an den Schilden der Nordmänner ab. Jeder Wikinger und jeder Indianer hatte sich ein Tuch in den Gürtel gesteckt – rot bei den Indianern, weiß bei den Wikingern. Jeder Krieger suchte solche feindlichen »Wimpel«

* Siehe »Die drei ??? und der lachende Schatten«, Omnibus Band 21138

zu erobern, während sich das Kampfgetümmel zu dem hohen Felsmassiv an der westlichen Spitze der Insel hinbewegte.

Die drei Jungen in ihrem Boot lachten und feuerten die Kämpfer mit begeisterten Rufen an. Peter und Bob hatten für die Indianer Partei ergriffen, Justus hielt es mit den Wikingern. Noch ehe die wilden Krieger den mächtigen Felsen erreicht hatten, musste Bob einen neuen Film einlegen.

»Los, fahren wir näher ran!«, forderte er die Freunde auf. »Wenn ich den ganzen Verlauf der Schlacht auf den Film bekomme, gibt das eine fantastische Bilderserie für die Zeitung, und mein Vater kauft uns bestimmt eine Menge Fotos ab.«

Sie ließen den Motor an und Peter lenkte das Boot in die Bucht hinein. Bob knipste wie besessen, bis die Schlacht entschieden war und alle Wikinger mit den erbeuteten roten Wimpeln oben auf dem Felsen standen. Diese schwenkten sie zusammen mit ihren eigenen weißen Bannern und alle Beteiligten jubelten und lachten und beglückwünschten einander.

Nun ließ Bob die Kamera sinken. Die drei Jungen hatten ihren Spaß an der turbulenten Szene auf der Insel – bis Justus zufällig über die Schulter zurückschaute.

»Bob! Peter!«

Da kam noch ein Boot an und gleich würde es krachen!

Das führerlose Boot

Das kleine Motorboot hielt direkt auf sie zu. Dann rammte es – glücklicherweise nicht stark – das Boot der Jungen, dümpelte auf den kleinen Wellen in der Bucht vor sich hin, und noch einmal gab es eine leichte Kollision.

»Das Boot treibt nur.« Peter erkannte sofort die Situation. »Der Motor läuft überhaupt nicht.«

»Und es sitzt niemand drin!«, rief Bob. »Schaut doch, das Ankertau hängt schlaff im Wasser. Das Boot muss sich irgendwo losgerissen haben.«

Peter untersuchte das zerfaserte Ende des Taues. »Nein, das wurde nicht gekappt. Sieht so aus, als hätte es sich durchgescheuert, während das Boot vor Anker lag, vielleicht an einem Felsen oder einer Kaimauer.«

Justus hatte sich noch nicht geäußert, sondern nur mit wachem Blick das leere Boot betrachtet. Nun wies der Erste Detektiv auf die Reling bei der mittleren Sitzbank. »Seht euch das an – hier, an der Riemendolle und an der Bordwand!«

Die beiden anderen schauten betroffen auf die dunklen Flecken an dem grauen Metall der Riemendolle und an der Oberkante der Bordwand. Es waren tiefrote Flecken, die im Licht der Nachmittagssonne fast schwarz wirkten.

»Das sieht ja aus wie... wie...«, stammelte Peter.

»Blut!«, vollendete Bob.

»Ja.« Justus nickte. »Als hätte sich jemand verletzt oder...« Der Anführer der drei ??? zögerte und sah seine beiden Getreuen an. »Oder als wäre jemand gestürzt und hätte sich an der Dolle den Kopf aufgeschlagen.«

Peter packte die Bordwand des leeren Bootes und zog es ganz heran. Alle drei Jungen sahen sich das Innere an. Auf dem Boden bei der mittleren Sitzbank stand ein Kasten mit Angelzubehör, daneben ein Eimer für den Köder. Ein offener Essensbehälter enthielt einige Sandwiches und einen Apfel. Dann gab es noch eine große Schwimmweste von der Art, wie sie auch die Jungen trugen.

»Alles vorhanden«, sagte Justus bedächtig, »nur die Angelrute mit der Rolle fehlt.«

»Du, Justus...«, meldete sich Bob voll Unbehagen. »Da, unter dem Sitz, schau mal – ist das ein Hut?«

Peter hielt mit einer Hand das abdriftende Boot fest und

griff mit der anderen Hand unter die Sitzbank. Er brachte einen Anglerhut mit breiter Krempe zum Vorschein. Der Hutkopf war an einer Seite aufgerissen und auf dem Ölzeug waren ebensolche dunklen Flecken wie am Boot zu sehen.

Justus war sehr ernst geworden. »In diesem Boot hatte jemand einen Unfall. Die Frage ist nun, wo befand sich das Boot, als das geschah?«

»Wie meinst du das, Justus?« Peter runzelte die Stirn. »Was spielt es für eine Rolle, wo das Boot war?«

»Justus fragt sich, ob das Boot draußen auf See war oder ob es vielleicht am Ufer vor Anker lag«, meinte Bob. »Das ist doch sicher wichtig.«

»Und war der Angler allein im Boot?«, überlegte Justus weiter. »Kam ihm vielleicht jemand aus einem anderen Boot zu Hilfe und brachte ihn an Land und hinterher riss sich das verlassene Boot los? Oder hat es sich so zugetragen, dass der Bootsführer … einfach über Bord fiel?«

Peter und Bob sahen einander erschrocken an.

»Oder«, fuhr Justus fort, »war da noch ein anderer im Boot?«

Peter wurde blass. »Du meinst, der Angler wurde vielleicht umgebracht?«

»Wir wollen keine voreiligen Schlüsse ziehen«, sagte Justus vorsichtig. »Bisher haben wir nur sehr dürftige Beweise.« Die drei Jungen saßen einen Augenblick stumm da und starrten in das leere Boot mit den dunklen Flecken. Schließlich meldete sich Bob zu Wort.

»Vielleicht gehört das Boot einem dieser Wikinger oder Indianer auf der Insel. Und wahrscheinlich hat sich jemand geschnitten oder sonstwie verletzt.«

»Immerhin möglich, Bob«, bestätigte Justus. »Das sollten wir nun herausfinden.«

Bob und Justus hielten das zerschlissene Ankertau des leeren Bootes fest und Peter startete den Motor ihres eigenen

Bootes und steuerte die Insel an. Die Wikinger und die Indianer schlenderten gerade von dem gigantischen Felsen herunter auf die Bucht zu. Noch immer schwenkten sie ihre Trophäen und schlugen sich gegenseitig begeistert auf die Schultern. Einige der triumphierenden Kämpfer erspähten Bob mit seiner Kamera. Als sich das Boot der Jungen dem Ufer näherte, wo das Wikingerschiff und das Kanu der Chumash neben einigen anderen Booten festgemacht waren, riefen die Männer herunter: »Hallo, macht mal ein paar Fotos!«

»Kommt an Land, dann gibt es bessere Bilder!«

»Fotografiert uns, die Indianer!«

»Nein, uns Wikinger! Wir sind die Sieger!«

»Kommt rüber, ihr könnt mit uns essen!«

Die drei Jungen winkten lachend ab.

»Gehört dieses Boot jemand von Ihnen?«, rief Justus dann übers Wasser.

»Nein, das ist keins von uns!«, rief ein Wikinger zurück.

»Los, kommt her und macht noch mehr Bilder!«, forderte ein Indianer die Jungen auf.

Um dem Fotografen etwas zu bieten, stellten sich einige der Wikinger und Indianer in eindrucksvoller kriegerischer Pose auf und hielten einander Speere und Äxte an die Kehlen. Bob grinste und schoss noch ein paar Bilder.

Mittlerweile ging es auf der Insel lebhaft zu. Auf einer Anhöhe über dem Strand wurden Zelte aufgeschlagen und rings um ein großes Lagerfeuer bereiteten Frauen und Kinder das Essen zu. Zum Schluss fotografierte Bob die baumlose Insel aus verschiedenen Blickwinkeln.

»Nun mach schon«, drängte ihn Peter, »sonst haben wir keine Zeit mehr zum Fischen und das soll uns doch auch was einbringen.«

»Der Film ist sowieso gleich voll«, sagte Bob.

»Tut mir Leid, Peter, aber wir sollten doch besser das leere

Boot an Land bringen«, schaltete sich Justus ein. »Es kann ja sein, dass dem Eigentümer wirklich etwas zugestoßen ist.«

»Versuchen wir doch, von hier aus die Polizei zu verständigen«, schlug Peter vor. »Das eine oder andere Boot vor der Insel hat vielleicht Bordfunk.«

»Gute Idee, Peter«, meinte Justus. Er rief zu den nun friedlich speisenden Kriegern hinüber: »Entschuldigen Sie, sind das hier am Ufer Ihre Boote?«

Ein paar Männer nickten.

»Hat jemand von Ihnen ein Funkgerät an Bord?«

»Leider nicht«, rief ein Indianer zurück.

»Ich schon, aber das ist kaputt!«, meldete sich ein Wikinger.

Bob knipste das letzte Bild. »So, nun ist der Film voll. Was machen wir jetzt, weiterfischen oder zurückfahren?«

»Ich denke, wir sollten umkehren und das Boot zurückbringen«, meinte Peter ergeben.

»Ja, unbedingt«, beschloss Justus energisch. »Es könnte sich jemand in hilfloser Lage befinden.«

Sie machten das abgerissene Ankertau des leeren Bootes an ihrem Heck fest und Peter ging auf Kurs in Richtung Heimat.

Sie waren weit hinausgefahren, und Justus sah immer wieder besorgt auf die Uhr, während Peter den Konvoi über die langen Wellen des tiefblauen Pazifiks steuerte. Sie hielten nach einem Boot mit Bordfunk Ausschau, aber einem solchen begegneten sie nicht. Bob nahm während der Fahrt die wenigen Barsche aus, die sie gefangen hatten.

»Immerhin reicht es für unser eigenes Abendessen«, meinte er optimistisch.

Der Widerstand des Bootes im Schlepptau verringerte ihre Fahrt, und es war schon vier Uhr vorbei, als sie im Bootshafen von Rocky Beach eintrafen.

»Hey«, rief Peter vom Steuerhebel am Heck. »Steht dort am Bootssteg nicht Kommissar Reynolds?«

Justus und Bob drehten sich um und sahen hin.

»Klar – und er hat ein paar seiner Leute mitgebracht!«, bestätigte Bob.

Auf den Planken des langen Stegs, der als öffentliche Bootsanlegestelle diente, konnten sie die eindrucksvolle Gestalt des Polizeichefs von Rocky Beach sehen. Zusammen mit drei uniformierten Beamten stand er bei einer schlanken Frau. Sie trug ein elegantes grünes Kleid und ihr rotes Haar leuchtete in der Abendsonne. Die Frau wirkte verstört und im Gespräch mit dem Kommissar führte sie immer wieder ein Taschentuch an die Augen und sah suchend aufs Meer hinaus.

»Wer ist denn diese Frau?«, fragte Peter verwundert.

»Keine Ahnung, ich kenn sie nicht«, sagte Bob. »Aber sie schaut so auffällig zu uns her!«

Der Blick der Frau schweifte nun nicht mehr übers Wasser, sondern war starr auf die drei Jungen gerichtet. Sie hatte ihre blauen Augen weit geöffnet.

»Nicht zu uns«, stellte Justus richtig. »Aber zu dem leeren Boot. Sie kennt es wohl.«

»Na, dann kennt sie vielleicht auch den Hut«, meinte Peter. Als die Jungen bei der Anlegestelle ankamen, griff Peter in das Boot, das sie ins Schlepptau genommen hatten, und hielt den beschädigten, blutbefleckten Anglerhut in die Höhe. Die Frau wurde kalkweiß und fiel in Ohnmacht. Hauptkommissar Reynolds konnte sie gerade noch auffangen.

 Diese Reaktion der besorgten Ehefrau ist natürlich zu verstehen. Doch wir wollen hoffen, dass der vermisste Angler noch gefunden wird – man sollte ja nicht gleich mit dem Schlimmsten rechnen.

18

Wütender Wikinger

Als der Kommissar die bleiche Frau auf einer Bank am Rand des Steges abgesetzt hatte, drängten sich die Polizisten und die drei Jungen heran.

»Nun haltet mal ein wenig Abstand, Jungs«, sagte der Polizeichef. »Und jetzt berichtet mir, wo ihr dieses Boot gefunden habt.«

Peter und Bob gaben die Ereignisse bei Ragnarson Rock in kurzen Worten wieder. Hauptkommissar Reynolds hörte aufmerksam zu, und als alles gesagt war, öffnete die Frau die Augen und machte Anstalten aufzustehen.

»Ich muss sofort hinausfahren!«, rief sie.

Ein Polizist hielt die benommene und verstörte Frau behutsam zurück und der Kommissar sprach beruhigend auf sie ein.

»In spätestens zwanzig Minuten sind wir mit einem Hubschrauber da draußen, Mrs Manning. Bleiben Sie hier sitzen und versuchen Sie, sich zu entspannen. Sie können jetzt nichts tun, wir kümmern uns um alles.«

Er lächelte und Mrs Manning ließ sich auf der Bank zurücksinken. Ihr Blick schweifte unruhig über die Umstehenden. Nun wandte sich der Kommissar an die Jungen.

»Mrs Mannings Ehemann fuhr gestern am späten Abend zum Fischen hinaus und sagte, er würde heute früh rechtzeitig zum Arbeitsbeginn um halb neun zurück sein. Das war nicht ungewöhnlich, denn er hat oft nachts gefischt. Er hatte Beleuchtung im Boot und ein Sprechfunkgerät und er fuhr nie allzu weit aufs Meer hinaus. Aber heute Morgen kam er nicht zurück und gegen Mittag meldete uns das Mrs Manning. Wir kamen hierher und stießen auf seinen abgeschlossenen Wagen, aber von ihm fanden wir keine Spur. Und niemand hatte das Boot gesehen, seit er gestern Abend hinausgefahren war. Bis ihr nun damit ankamt.«

Er sprach ganz ruhig, um Mrs Manning nicht zu erschrecken, aber er sah sehr besorgt aus, als er das leere Boot, das nun am Steg festgemacht war, ins Auge fasste.

Mrs Manning blinzelte die Jungen verwirrt an. »Was hatte Bill nur da draußen vor? Sonst war er noch nie allein so weit hinausgefahren. Er konnte ja nicht schwimmen – deshalb legte er auch immer die Schwimmweste an.«

»Wir können nicht sicher sagen, ob er so weit hinausgefahren war, Mrs Manning«, berichtete Hauptkommissar Reynolds. »Vor der Küste herrscht oft eine starke Strömung in Richtung Ragnarson Rock. Die Jungen fanden das treibende Boot am Nachmittag. In der Zwischenzeit hätte es leicht aus dem Küstenbereich dorthin abdriften können.«

»Aber«, fing die Frau wieder an, »wo ist dann Bill?«

Es entstand ein beklemmendes Schweigen.

»Das müssen wir herausfinden, Mrs Manning«, äußerte der Polizeichef in zuversichtlichem Ton. »Bestimmt wird sich alles aufklären. Vielleicht ist er zurückgefahren und hat irgendwo angelegt und später hat sich das Boot losgerissen und ist abgetrieben.«

»Aber warum ist er dann bis jetzt nicht nach Hause gekommen?«, fragte Mrs Manning. »Und warum ist er erst gar nicht ins Auto gestiegen?«

»Wir werden das aufklären«, sagte der Kommissar. »Wir haben bereits die Küstenwache mit der Suche beauftragt und alle Polizeistationen in diesem Küstenbereich suchen ihn ebenfalls. Aber es ist ja durchaus möglich, dass er sich selbst wieder hier einfindet und alles erklären kann.«

»Möglich? Und damit soll ich mich abfinden?«

Mrs Manning blickte hochgradig erregt auf die Polizisten, die Jungen und den Kommissar. Ihr Gesicht war wieder sehr blass geworden. Erst befürchteten die Jungen, die Frau würde von neuem ohnmächtig werden. Doch dann schüttelte sie langsam den Kopf. »Es ist möglich, dass er heil und gesund zurückkommt, aber sehr wahrscheinlich ist es nicht – wollen Sie das damit ausdrücken?« Plötzlich stand sie auf und nahm Peter den Fischerhut mit dem Riss aus der Hand. »Das ist sein Hut. Und es haftet Blut daran, oder etwa nicht?«

»Das könnte sein«, gab der Kommissar zu. »Ja.«

»Und hier am Boot?« Sie sah auf das leere Boot hinunter, das am Steg vertäut war. »Blut am Dollbord und an der Riemendolle. Sein Angelzeug ist nicht zusammengepackt und die Rute samt der Rolle fehlt.« Wieder schüttelte sie den Kopf. »Da draußen ist etwas passiert – ich weiß das. Irgendetwas ist passiert und Bill wird nie mehr zurückkommen.«

Sie brach in Tränen aus, ließ sich wieder auf die Bank sinken und schluchzte in ihr Taschentuch. Die drei ??? und die Polizisten standen voll Unbehagen da und wussten nichts zu sagen.

»Die Hoffnung dürfen wir nicht aufgeben, Mrs Manning«, meldete sich schließlich Justus. »Sein… seine Schwimmweste liegt noch im Boot. Da er nicht schwimmen konnte, hätte er sie sicherlich getragen, solange er sich auf See befand. Also ist es durchaus möglich, dass er irgendwo an Land ging, wie auch Kommissar Reynolds vermutete.«

»Eben«, warf Peter ein. »Vor einem Landgang hätte er die dicke, unbequeme Weste abgelegt.«

»Aber seine Angelrute hätte er wohl kaum im Boot zurückgelassen«, sagte Bob, »damit sie nicht gestohlen wird.«

Mrs Manning lächelte betrübt und schüttelte wieder den Kopf. »Ich merke schon, dass ihr Jungen es gut meint, aber beim Fischen wollte Bill die Schwimmweste grundsätzlich nicht tragen. Damit fand er sich zu stark eingeengt. Er hatte sie griffbereit neben sich, aber er wollte ungehindert mit der Angelrute umgehen und auch das Radio mit dem Funk bedienen können. Das Gerät steckte immer in einer großen Tasche in seiner Fischerjacke und beides ist ja auch weg, nicht wahr?«

Peter schluckte. »Hm ... ja, Madam, stimmt, aber ... aber ...« Entmutigt gab er es auf.

Mrs Manning schüttelte nur immer wieder den Kopf. »Nein, Bill kommt nicht mehr zu mir zurück. Da ist etwas passiert. Er muss sich bei einem Sturz den Kopf angeschlagen haben und dann ist er wahrscheinlich bewusstlos über Bord gefallen.« Sie blickte zu all den Umstehenden auf. »Ich sagte ihm immer, er sollte draußen auf See die Schwimmweste nicht auszuziehen. Aber er hörte nicht auf mich. Und nun ist er nicht mehr da.«

Wieder war es auf dem Bootssteg bedrückend still.

»Das alles tut mir sehr Leid, Mrs Manning«, sagte Hauptkommissar Reynolds. »Ich muss sagen, es sieht nicht gut aus, aber es kann sich doch noch alles zum Guten wenden.«

»Es könnte doch sein«, meinte Justus hoffnungsvoll, »dass er von einem Boot aufgefischt wurde, das keinen Funk hat und bis jetzt noch nicht an Land gekommen ist.«

»Oder dass er durch einen Schlag gegen den Kopf eine Gedächtnisstörung bekommen hat!«, setzte Peter hinzu.

»Oder dass er auf Ragnarson Rock an Land gegangen ist!«, erwog Bob.

Mrs Manning stand auf und strich ihr Kleid glatt. Sie lächelte schwach. »Vielen Dank euch Jungen und auch Ihnen, Herr Kommissar. Ich weiß, dass Sie alle es gut meinen. Aber all diese Möglichkeiten kommen nicht in Betracht, weil Bill niemals so weit hinausgefahren ist. Beim Fischen war er nie mehr als allerhöchstens eine Meile vom Ufer entfernt. Er sagte immer, eine Meile weit könnte er mit Schwimmweste im Wasser gut paddeln. Nein, er wird nicht mehr zurückkommen. Sein Boot war schon leer, ehe es zu dieser Insel hinübertrieb.

Ich fahre jetzt mit unserem Wagen nach Hause, Kommissar, und dort warte ich auf Ihren Anruf, wenn Sie seine Leiche gefunden haben.«

Mrs Manning scheint sich tatsächlich schon mit dem Schlimmsten abgefunden zu haben. Und doch sind Bobs zuvor geäußerte Worte eine Überlegung wert. Könnte sich Mr Manning wohl zu den munteren Indianern und Wikingern auf Ragnarson Rock gesellt haben? Nur – wie hätte die Gruppe sein Auftauchen wohl aufgenommen? Dass der Gestrandete auf der kleinen Insel unbemerkt blieb, ist zugegebenermaßen unwahrscheinlich und auch nicht leicht zu erklären. Nun, ich will euch jetzt noch nicht zu vorläufig müßigen Spekulationen anregen...

Langsam ging die Frau zu dem Wagen, der in der Nähe des Steges geparkt war. Der Polizeichef schickte ihr zwei seiner Männer nach. Dann wandte er sich an die Jungen.

»Gut gemacht, Jungs, das Boot sicherzustellen.«

»Gibt es... gibt es überhaupt noch eine Hoffnung, dass der Mann lebt, Herr Kommissar?«, erkundigte sich Peter.

»Es hat den Anschein, dass er sich den Kopf anschlug und über Bord ging, Peter, genau wie seine Frau es vermutet. Er war allein im Boot und es war dunkel...« Kommissar Reynolds hob die Schultern und ließ seinen Satz unvollendet. »Aber wir werden gründlich nachforschen. Habt ihr da draußen irgendetwas beobachtet, aus dem zu schließen wäre, was Mr Manning zugestoßen ist?«

»Nein, nichts, Herr Kommissar«, antwortete Peter.

»Gut. Aber gebt mir Bescheid, wenn euch noch irgendetwas einfällt.« Damit verabschiedete sich der Polizeichef. Die drei ??? hatten schon bei einer Anzahl anderer verzwickter Fälle mit der Polizei von Rocky Beach zusammengearbeitet und Samuel Reynolds wusste den scharfen Blick der Jungen zu schätzen.

Der Kommissar ging zu seinem Wagen zurück, und nachdem dieser und auch Mrs Mannings Auto weggefahren waren, vertäuten die Jungen ihr Boot sorgfältig und liefen zu ihren Rädern, die am Fahrradständer des Bootshafens angeschlossen waren.

»Hey! Ihr drei da!«

Ein kleines Boot mit Außenborder glitt auf die Anlegestelle zu. Am Steuer saß einer der kriegerischen Wikinger von Ragnarson Rock und er winkte heftig zu den Jungen herüber.

»Wartet mal – ich hab was mit euch zu reden.«

Der Wikinger bugsierte sein Boot geschickt längsseits des Steges, schlang ein Tau um einen Poller und sprang leichtfüßig an Land. Er war nicht sehr groß und sein dicker Fellüberwurf ließ ihn fast so breit wie hoch erscheinen. Seine Beine waren bis zu den Knien mit Tuch umwickelt und mit Lederriemen verschnürt. Er trug einen falschen weißblonden Bart und einen Helm mit Hörnern und einem langen Nasenschild, der sein Gesicht fast ganz verbarg. Nur seine blauen Augen waren klar zu erkennen, als er nun auf die Jungen zuschritt.

»Seid ihr die Burschen, die da heute vor Ragnarson Rock wie verrückt in der Gegend rumgeknipst haben?«

»Gibt's irgendwelche Probleme?«, erkundigte sich Bob misstrauisch.

Justus blieb ganz gelassen. »Es ist unser gutes Recht, eine in der Öffentlichkeit stattfindende Veranstaltung zu fotografieren.«

»Lass mal, ist ja schon gut«, sagte der Wikinger. »Ich möchte die Bilder kaufen. Ich nehme euch alle eure Aufnahmen ab.«

»Die hab ich ja noch gar nicht entwickelt«, erklärte Bob. »Im Übrigen hatte sie mein Vater extra bei mir bestellt.«

»Schön, dann komm ich mit euch und warte, bis du sie entwickelt hast. Mir genügen im Grunde zwei oder drei Bilder, aber die würd ich mir gern selber aussuchen.«

»Tut mir Leid, aber Bobs Vater möchte sich die Bilder sicher erst einmal selbst ansehen«, wandte Justus ein. »Und für alle, die er uns abkauft, wünscht er die Exklusivrechte. Später zeigen wir Ihnen dann gern die Fotos, die Mr Andrews nicht übernehmen möchte.«

»Ja, machen wir's so.« Bob nickte. »Morgen, wenn mein Vater die Aufnahmen für sich ausgewählt hat, überlasse ich Ihnen gern die restlichen Bilder, die Sie interessieren, Mr...«

»Sam Ragnarson«, erwiderte der Wikinger. »Hör mal, ich zahl dir einen erstklassigen Preis. Aber ihr müsst sie mich schon vorher sehen lassen.«

Bob zögerte. Immerhin konnten die drei ??? das Geld sehr gut gebrauchen. Doch dann sagte er, innerlich ganz zerknirscht: »Bedaure, Mr Ragnarson, aber mein Vater muss die Fotos unbedingt nach Los Angeles bringen, sobald ich sie entwickelt habe. Morgen könnten wir uns dann treffen.«

Sam Ragnarsons blaue Augen funkelten aufgebracht, und seine Stimme klang mit einem Mal ausgesprochen bösartig, während er mit drohender Miene näher auf die Jungen zutrat. »Ich sagte schon, ich brauch die Bilder jetzt gleich und nicht erst morgen. Wenn ihr drei Blödmänner keine Vernunft annehmen wollt, dann kann ich auch andere Saiten...«

Verdutzt und erschrocken wichen die Jungen zurück.

Da kreischten hinter ihnen Autoreifen und eine Stimme rief herüber:

»Hallo, ihr drei, ich vergaß, euch zu fragen, ob ihr in dem Boot auch bestimmt nichts angefasst habt.« Hauptkommissar

Reynolds hatte den Kopf aus dem offenen Seitenfenster seines Wagens gesteckt. Er hatte am Bordstein wenige Meter weiter hinten angehalten.

»Nur den Hut, Sir«, sagte Justus. Er lief rasch zu dem Polizeiauto hin. Dann zählte er dem Kommissar auf, was die drei ??? außerdem in dem Boot gesehen hatten.

Der Kommissar nickte und ließ den Motor wieder an und die Jungen sahen sich rasch nach Sam Ragnarson um. Der aber hatte sich in Luft aufgelöst. Samt seinem Boot war er überstürzt verschwunden.

Die Jungen liefen zu ihren Fahrrädern.

»Der hat wohl was gegen Polizisten«, sagte Peter.

»'ne ganze Menge, scheint mir«, meinte Bob dazu. »Er nahm sich nicht mal mehr die Zeit, mich nach meiner Adresse zu fragen. Na egal, dann kann er sich eben keine Bilder abholen.«

»Ich nehme den Film in die Zentrale mit«, bot Justus Bob an. »Dann kannst du gleich morgen früh herkommen und ihn entwickeln, Bob.«

Er verabschiedete sich von seinen beiden Freunden. »Und nicht vergessen: heute Abend immer wieder die Nachrichten hören. Vielleicht gibt es etwas über den bedauernswerten Mr Manning zu erfahren.«

Verfolgt!

Am nächsten Morgen kam Bob zeitig zum Frühstück herunter, um seinem Vater von den Fotos zu berichten. Am Vorabend waren seine Eltern, die nach Los Angeles ins Theater wollten, schon weggefahren, und Bob war zu müde gewesen, um bis zu ihrer Rückkehr aufzubleiben.

Mr Andrews las die Zeitung, als Bob in die Küche kam. Er

sah auf und begrüßte seinen Sohn. »Ich lese da gerade von dem traurigen Vorfall, den ihr gestern miterlebt habt.«

Bob nickte. »Hat man Mr Manning schon gefunden?«

»Weiß ich nicht, Bob. Die Zeitung wurde in der Nacht gedruckt.« Mrs Andrews schaltete das Radio ein. »Gleich müssten die Lokalnachrichten kommen.«

Der Sprecher verlas gerade die letzten überregionalen Nachrichten, dann berichtete er von einem Brand in Rocky Beach, und schließlich kam die Meldung: *»Die Küstenwache ist noch immer auf der Suche nach William Manning, einem Autohändler aus Rocky Beach. Sein führerloses Boot wurde gestern bei Ragnarson Rock von drei Jungen aus Rocky Beach gefunden: Bob Andrews, Peter Shaw und Jonathan Jonas.«*

»O nein!«, rief Bob. »Die blicken es einfach nicht, wie Justus richtig heißt!«

»Mannings Ehefrau sagte aus, dass er nicht schwimmen konnte, und so besteht wenig Hoffnung, dass der Angler noch am Leben ist.«

»Die arme Frau«, sagte Mrs Andrews mitfühlend.

»Ein großes Unglück«, bestätigte Mr Andrews. »Aber wolltest du mir nicht noch etwas anderes sagen, Bob?«

»Klar, Dad!« Eifrig berichtete Bob von den Ereignissen des Vortages bei Ragnarson Rock, während er sich über seine Cornflakes hermachte. Mr Andrews lachte. »Das hört sich ja genauso aufregend an, wie wir es uns vorgestellt hatten. Morgen werden wir einen ganzseitigen Bericht bringen.«

»Wozu denn das?«, fragte Mrs Andrews verwundert. »Mir kommen diese Burschen eher wie eine etwas angejahrte Rasselbande vor.«

»Ja, was ist so Besonderes an denen?«, fragte nun auch Bob.

»Es geht um ein Stück kalifornischer Geschichte«, erklärte Mr Andrews. »Im Jahre 1849, während des Goldfiebers, kam Knut Ragnarson, der norwegischer Abstammung war, aus Illinois hierher. Er war Schuhmacher, und der Verkauf seiner Stiefel an die Goldsucher brachte ihm mehr Geld ein, als die meisten von ihnen mit ihrer Goldwäscherei verdienten. Also ging er im folgenden Jahr in San Francisco an Bord eines Schiffes, um von Los Angeles aus in den Osten zurückzukehren und seine Familie nachzuholen. Das Schiff hatte Gold geladen und beförderte auch Passagiere. In der zweiten Nacht flutete der Kapitän absichtlich das Schiff, um es zu versenken, sicherte sich das Gold und ruderte im Beiboot zur Küste. Die meisten Passagiere gerieten in Panik und ertranken bei dem Schiffsuntergang, aber Knut Ragnarson konnte sich mithilfe eines Lukendeckels auf die kleine Insel retten. Am Ufer fand er ein Indianerkanu, das die Chumash dort hinterlassen hatten, und erreichte damit das Festland. Seither heißt diese Insel Ragnarson Rock. Alle fünf Jahre kommen die heute hier lebenden Ragnarsons und ihre Freunde zusammen, um ein Scheingefecht um den Besitz der Insel zu inszenieren. Die Leute zelten dann eine ganze Woche lang da draußen. Karl Ragnarson – euer Schulleiter – hat mir das alles erzählt.«

»Mr Karl Ragnarson?«, rief Bob. »War der etwa auch da draußen mit dabei?«

»Ganz bestimmt«, sagte Mr Andrews. »Allerdings glaube ich, dass er sich aus dem Trubel der Jüngeren ziemlich heraushält. Sein Interesse gilt vorwiegend der Familiengeschichte.«

»Apropos Geschichte«, warf Mrs Andrews ein, »was wurde denn aus dem gestohlenen Gold?«

»Und wie lange blieb Knut Ragnarson auf der Insel?«, fragte Bob.

Mr Andrews hob lachend die Hände. »Halt, halt! Mehr weiß ich zurzeit auch nicht. Wir haben einen Reporter mit Nachforschungen beauftragt. Mit Bobs Fotos gibt das einen fesselnden Bericht für unsere morgige Ausgabe.«

Bob trank sein Milchglas leer. »Justus hat den Film mitgenommen. Ich geh jetzt gleich zu ihm rüber und mache die Abzüge. Die haben wir …«

»Nun mal langsam, junger Mann«, unterbrach ihn seine Mutter. »Hast du etwa vergessen, dass im Hause Andrews heute die Fenster geputzt werden sollen?«

»Aber Mom!«, protestierte Bob. »Ich muss für Dad den Film entwickeln, das ist doch wichtig!«

»Du kennst die Regeln, Bob«, erklärte Mrs Andrews. »In den Sommerferien hilfst du mir jede Woche an einem Vormittag bei der Hausarbeit. Du hast dir dazu selbst den Mittwoch ausgesucht, weil sich das am besten mit deinen Plänen vereinbaren lässt. Und wir haben ausgemacht, dass es keine Ausnahme gibt, sonst müsste ich dir ja ständig hinterherlaufen, und es käme schließlich doch nichts zustande.«

»Ach, Mom«, bat Bob inständig, »nur dieses eine Mal! Nur heute! Ich will auch …«

»Ich nehme den Film in die Redaktion mit und lasse ihn dort entwickeln«, schlug Mr Andrews vor. »Heute Vormittag arbeite ich zu Hause. Ich fahre erst gegen Mittag zum Verlag. Dann hast du genug Zeit, deiner Mutter beim Fensterputzen zu helfen und mir später den Film zu holen.«

Widerstrebend fügte sich Bob und dann rief er in der Zentrale an. Justus seufzte, als er erfuhr, dass Bob verhindert war.

»Peter ist es auch nicht besser ergangen«, berichtete der Erste Detektiv. »Er muss sein Zimmer gründlich sauber machen. Er hat versprochen, dass er herkommt, sobald das erledigt ist. Na, dann schau, dass auch du schnellstens herkommst, Bob.«

Bob holte sich rasch den Glasreiniger und ein paar Lappen und machte sich ans Werk. Er arbeitete flink, aber es waren so viele Fenster … Es war schon fast elf, als er endlich fertig war. Er räumte das Putzzeug weg und lief zu seinem Fahrrad hinaus.

»Hör mal, Bob«, rief ihm sein Vater nach, »ich muss in einer Stunde weg!«

»Alles klar, Dad!«, rief Bob, der schon losgeradelt war.

Als er aus der Zufahrt in die Straße einbog, musste er einem zerbeulten weißen Pick-up ausweichen, der unmittelbar vor dem Haus der Familie Andrews parkte. Er war überrascht, denn kaum jemals wurde ein fremder Wagen vor dem Haus abgestellt. Seit dem Fall mit dem »Automarder«* fuhren Bobs Mutter und Vater ihre Autos immer in die Garage. Bob musste sich so sehr darauf konzentrieren, das Gleichgewicht zu halten, dass er nicht erkennen konnte, wer in dem Fahrzeug am Lenkrad saß.

Von der nächsten Ecke aus blickte er zurück. Der Pick-up war gestartet und näherte sich langsam dem Fahrrad. Bob hörte die alte Kiste ächzen und scheppern.

Er radelte schneller und bog flink um einige Ecken. Als er sich dann wieder umsah, fuhr der Pick-up noch immer gemächlich hinter ihm her. Er versuchte, das Kennzeichen zu lesen, doch vorn am Wagen war gar keines angebracht.

Mit steigender Angst trat Bob in die Pedale, so schnell er konnte, und von Zeit zu Zeit schaute er nach hinten, um nachzusehen, ob ihn der klapprige weiße Wagen nach wie vor verfolgte. Und jedes Mal war er noch da.

Bob überlegte angestrengt. Nun war er schon fast beim Schrottplatz angekommen, und wenn er tatsächlich verfolgt wurde, so hatte das wohl zu bedeuten, dass jemand in Erfahrung bringen wollte, wohin er fuhr oder wo die drei ??? ihr Hauptquartier aufgeschlagen hatten – vielleicht interessierte sich der Verfolger auch für beides. Bob beschloss, lieber nicht zum Schrottplatz zu fahren, sondern Justus und Peter telefonisch zu warnen. Er fuhr in die letzte Querstraße vor dem

* Siehe »Die drei ??? und der Automarder«, Omnibus Band 20765

Schrottplatz ein und hielt bei einer Tankstelle an, vor der ein öffentlicher Fernsprecher stand. Rasch wählte er die Nummer des privaten Anschlusses der drei ??? in der Zentrale. Aber es nahm niemand ab.

Enttäuscht legte Bob wieder auf. Peter und Justus waren also nicht da.

Er trat aus der Telefonkabine und sah in beiden Richtungen die Straße entlang. Der weiße Pick-up war nirgends zu sehen. Bob blickte sich auch auf dem Tankstellengelände gründlich um, damit er sicher sein konnte, dass der Wagen nicht mehr da war. Vielleicht war es auch gar kein Verfolger gewesen, sondern nur Zufall.

Bob bestieg wieder sein Fahrrad. Er fuhr zum Schrottplatz und an ihm vorbei bis zur nächsten Ecke. Von dem Pick-up war weit und breit nichts zu sehen. Nun konnte er wohl doch unbesorgt das Gelände der Firma Jonas betreten.

Vorsichtig radelte er zu der hinteren Umzäunung des Lagerplatzes. Die Zaunplanken zierte seit Jahren ein Kolossalgemälde von dem Brand, der 1906 in San Francisco als Folge eines Erdbebens gewütet hatte. Da waren brennende Häuser zu sehen, dazu die mit Pferden bespannten Löschfahrzeuge der Feuerwehr und flüchtende Menschen, die ihre rasch zusammengeraffte Habe auf dem Rücken trugen. Etwa fünfzehn Meter von der Ecke entfernt war ein kleiner Hund auf den Zaun gemalt. Betrübt sah er zu seinem Zuhause hin, das in Schutt und Asche lag.

Noch einmal blickte Bob wachsam in die Runde, um sich zu vergewissern, dass er von dem Pick-up nicht mehr verfolgt wurde. Dann zog er einen Stopfen aus einem Astloch, das ein Auge des kleinen Hundes bildete. Rasch steckte er den Finger hindurch und schob einen Riegel zurück und nun ließen sich drei zusammenhängende Planken aufschwenken. Das war das Rote Tor, einer der Geheimeingänge der drei ??? zum Schrottplatz. Bob war sich ganz sicher, dass niemand ihn beim Betreten des Hofes gesehen hatte.

An seinem jetzigen Standort war er vor Blicken von der Bürobaracke oder vom Einfahrtstor her zuverlässig geschützt. Er stellte sein Fahrrad ab, ging in die Hocke und kroch durch eine höhlenähnliche Öffnung in einem Stapel Baumaterial dicht vor ihm. Bob verschwand kurz unter aufgetürmtem Schrott und bewegte sich dann in einem engen Kriechgang zwischen hohen Bergen aus Altmaterial. Dieser Weg führte zu einem der vier geheimen Eingänge zur Zentrale des Detektivteams, den sie einfach »Die Tür« nannten. Der Zugang war allerdings so eng und mühsam, dass der stämmige Erste Detektiv ihn nach Möglichkeit mied. Hier könnte er nämlich durchaus irgendwann stecken bleiben!

Der Gang war kurvig und gewunden und am Ende musste Bob noch einmal einige Meter auf allen vieren krabbeln. Dann konnte er sich wieder aufrichten und klopfte an eine Schiebetür – einmal, zweimal, dreimal.

Wenn Justus und Peter drinnen waren, würde die glatte Wand zur Seite weichen. Wenn nicht...

Doch, die Schiebetür öffnete sich!

Bob betrat den alten Campinganhänger, an den sich mittlerweile außer den drei ??? niemand mehr erinnerte, denn die Detektivzentrale lag völlig versteckt inmitten gewaltiger Schrottberge. Sie war bestens ausgestattet: Dunkelkammer, Kriminallabor, Schreibtisch, Schreibmaschine, Telefon samt Anrufbeantworter, Kassettenrkorder und eine ganze Sammlung weiterer Geräte aus den Schrott- und Trödelvorräten des Lagers, die Justus repariert oder neu zusammengebaut hatte.

»Wo wart ihr beide denn? Ich habe angerufen, aber es nahm keiner ab.«

»Wir machten den Fehler, in die Werkstatt hinauszugehen«,

sagte Peter verärgert. »Dort hat uns Tante Mathilda gesehen und zum Möbelschleppen eingeteilt.«

Justus sah Bob aufmerksam an. »Was ist denn los, Bob? Warum wolltest du uns anrufen?«

Bob berichtete den Freunden von dem zerbeulten weißen Pick-up. Justus und Peter hörten gespannt zu.

»Und du weißt nicht, wer in dem Wagen saß?«, fragte Peter.

»Nein, von dem Fahrer konnte ich überhaupt nichts sehen.«

»Bist du sicher, dass er dir hinterherfuhr?«, wollte Justus wissen.

»Davon war ich überzeugt, bis ich den Umweg machte, um euch anzurufen«, erklärte Bob. »Als ich dann wieder auf dem Weg zur Zentrale war, sah ich den Wagen nicht mehr. Vielleicht hat es auch nur so ausgesehen, als verfolgte er mich.«

»Mag schon sein«, meinte Justus mit gerunzelter Stirn, »aber wir werden von jetzt an noch mehr aufpassen müssen. So, und was ist nun mit dem Film?«

»Das hatte ich doch glatt vergessen!«, rief Bob mit einem Blick auf die Uhr an der Wand. Es war schon fast halb zwölf. »In einer halben Stunde soll ich damit bei meinem Vater sein!«

»Zwei Filme können wir aber in einer halben Stunde nicht entwickeln«, stellte Peter fest.

»Dad meinte, die Filme täten es auch – er wird sie dann in der Redaktion entwickeln lassen.«

»Nur keine Aufregung«, meldete sich Justus. »Während ihr beide heute früh bei der Hausarbeit wart, entwickelte ich beide Filme. Die Negative sind inzwischen getrocknet und die bringst du eben statt der Abzüge deinem Vater.«

»Und wo sind sie?«

Justus ging in die Dunkelkammer und kam mit einem festen braunen Umschlag zurück, in dem er alle Negativstreifen verwahrt hatte. Bob nahm ihn rasch an sich und schob die Tür zum Tunnelgang wieder auf.

»Ich komm dann sofort hierher zurück, wenn das erledigt ist!« Bob wand sich behände durch den engen Gang, kroch ins Freie, lief zu seinem Fahrrad und verließ den Schrottplatz wieder durch das Rote Tor. Er bog um die Ecke und fuhr zu der Hauptstraße vor, die am Betriebsgelände vorüberführte. Als er kurz darauf links abbog, um den nächsten Weg zu seinem Haus einzuschlagen, hörte er einen Motor anspringen. Erschrocken warf er einen Blick über die Schulter.

Der weiße Pick-up war wieder aufgetaucht!

Ein bewegliches Ziel

Bob konnte gerade noch zwei Köpfe in dem weißen Pick-up wahrnehmen. Dann spurtete er los, so schnell er konnte, und hielt sich scharf rechts am Randstein.

Verflixt, der Wagen war ganz dicht hinter ihm!

Er trat wie besessen in die Pedale, aber der Verfolger kam immer näher, bis der Abstand zum Rücklicht des Fahrrads nur noch einen halben Meter betrug. Bob versuchte, den Kopf zu wenden, um vielleicht wenigstens einen der Insassen zu erkennen, aber er bekam nur den Kühler ins Blickfeld.

Der Wagen blieb nun in immer gleichem Abstand hinter dem Radfahrer und hielt strikt dessen Tempo ein, als lauerte er auf irgendetwas.

Dann lag ein unbebautes Straßenstück vor Bob. An einer Seite reihten sich Baugrundstücke aneinander, an der anderen erstreckte sich ein kleiner Park mit Bäumen, Sträuchern und gepflegten Wegen dazwischen. Plötzlich wurde es Bob klar, worauf seine Verfolger lauerten – auf einen solchen Streckenabschnitt, an dem es keine Häuser gab.

Er radelte verbissen drauflos. Da überholte ihn der Pick-up.

Er wollte sich offenbar vor ihm quer stellen, um ihm den Weg abzuschneiden!

Bob bremste ruckartig ab.

Der Wagen schleuderte noch ein Stück schräg vorwärts und wäre fast von der Straße abgekommen, ehe er mit quietschenden Reifen zum Halten kam.

Bob konnte gerade noch ein verschmutztes kalifornisches Nummernschild mit den Anfangsziffern »56« erkennen. Dann bog er rasch in die Zufahrt zum Park ein und durchquerte die Anlage auf den kurvenreichen Wegen bis zu dem anderen Ausgang an einer Parallelstraße.

Einmal blickte er sich um. Nun folgte ihm niemand mehr.

Er fuhr auf die Parallelstraße hinaus und schlug die Richtung ein, aus der er gekommen war, also zurück zum Schrottplatz.

Von hinten kam wie gerufen ein großer Lieferwagen angefahren, der vor dem Überholen kurz die Sicht auf das Fahrrad verdeckte. Bob sah wieder zurück und grinste, als der Pick-up an der hinteren Ecke des Parks auftauchte und prompt die falsche Richtung einschlug.

Als er sicher war, dass ihn die beiden Männer in dem Pick-up nicht mehr im Blick hatten, wendete er wieder und bog in eine andere Straße ein, um seinen Nachhauseweg fortzusetzen.

Und dann hörte er es. Dieses Motorgeräusch, durchsetzt von Quietschen und Scheppern! Fassungslos drehte er sich nach hinten um. Der Pick-up befand sich nun doch wieder hinter ihm! Diesmal holte das Auto schnell auf, ohne Verzögerungstaktik, und erfasste Bobs Hinterrad von der Seite. Bob geriet ins Schleudern, hielt aber mühsam das Gleichgewicht und radelte wild entschlossen weiter. Wieder berührte ihn der Kotflügel des Fahrzeugs.

Bob sah den tiefen Graben neben dem Straßenrand, spürte, wie sein Fahrrad wegrutschte, und sprang ab.

Während er schwungvoll mitten im Graben landete und

sich einmal überschlug, hörte er, wie der Pick-up stoppte. Schnell rappelte er sich hoch. Hemd und Hose waren zerrissen, Hände und Knie zerkratzt und schmutzbedeckt, aber er blieb trotzdem nicht stehen und sah auch nicht zurück. Er lief im Graben weiter und kletterte neben einem Haus heraus. Schwer atmend horchte er. Von den Verfolgern war nichts zu hören, weder Schritte noch Stimmen.

Bob blickte sich nach allen Seiten um. Auf der Zufahrt zu dem Haus, vor dem er stand, im Graben und auf der Straße war kein Mensch in Sicht. Sein Fahrrad sah er ein Stück weiter hinten am Grabenrand liegen. Das war alles. Niemand mehr wollte ihn angreifen, niemand mehr jagte ihn. Der weiße Pick-up war spurlos verschwunden!

Das kam Bob nun doch eigenartig vor. Verwirrt griff er in seine Taschen und starrte auf seine leeren Hände. Wo war der braune Umschlag?

Er sprang wieder in den Graben hinunter und schritt ihn suchend bis zu der Stelle ab, wo er vom Fahrrad gesprungen war. Nirgends fand sich der Umschlag.

Er kletterte zur Fahrbahn hinauf. Da lag sein Fahrrad.

Der Umschlag war weg.

Sie hatten all die Negative gestohlen!

Und er hätte doch wissen müssen, hinter was sie her waren! Doch es war ihm nicht ganz klar, wie er den Diebstahl hätte verhindern können. Zerknirscht hob er sein Rad auf. Dann schüttelte er die Schuldgefühle ab. Wie sagte doch Justus immer? Wenn es passiert war, half alles Jammern nichts. Bob musste nun schleunigst überlegen, wie er wieder in den Besitz der Negative kam!

Er schwang sich auf sein Fahrrad und raste zum Schrottplatz. Diesmal fuhr er gleich zum Haupteingang hinein. Sein Ziel brauchte er jetzt nicht mehr zu verheimlichen. Den weißen Pick-up war er endgültig los.

Bob ging rasch zu der Ecke des Lagerplatzes, an der Justus seine Freiluftwerkstatt errichtet hatte. Hier baute er aus Schrott und ausgedientem Material bestens funktionierende Geräte für die Detektivarbeit der drei ??? zusammen. Bob ging auf ein Stück Eisengitter zu, das wie zufällig gegen die Öffnung einer weiten Wellblechröhre lehnte. Diese Röhre war Tunnel II, ebenfalls ein geheimer Zugang der Jungen zu ihrer Zentrale. Bob schob sich durch den engen Kriechgang, so schnell es ihm seine aufgeschürften Hände und Knie erlaubten, und kam unter einem Lukendeckel im Fußboden der Zentrale heraus. Als er die Klappe hochstemmte, starrten ihn Justus und Peter verwundert an.

»Das hast du aber schnell geschafft, Bob«, meinte Peter.

Justus allerdings sah Bobs zerrissene Kleider und die verdreckten Hände. »Haben dich etwa die Kerle in dem weißen Pick-up so zugerichtet?«

»Nicht direkt, sie drängten mich nur von der Straße ab. Aber sie haben jetzt die Negative!«, stieß Bob verzweifelt hervor. »Alle!«

»Konntest du sie erkennen?«, fragte Justus rasch.

»Nun bekommen wir ja kein Geld!«, stöhnte Peter.

»Erzähl mal genau, was passiert ist«, forderte Justus Bob auf. Bob berichtete, wie er auf seinem Rad angefahren worden war. »Ich glaube, in dem Wagen saßen zwei Männer. Ich konnte sie aber nicht deutlich sehen, und vom Kennzeichen prägte ich mir nur ein, dass es aus Kalifornien war und mit sechsundfünfzig beginnt. Aber wir müssen uns die Negative wieder holen.«

»Ohne das vollständige Kennzeichen«, fragte Peter, »und ohne zu wissen, wer die Leute sind? Wie sollen wir das anstellen?«

»Na ja, das würde Tage dauern«, sagte Bob bedrückt. Er sah auf seine Uhr. »Und demnächst muss mein Vater zur Redaktion.«

Justus nickte. »Bob hat Recht. Erst muss er Mr Andrews die

Bilder bringen und dann werden wir uns mit den Dieben befassen.« Bob und Peter machten große Augen.

»A-aber Justus«, stammelte Peter, »die Bilder – die haben doch jetzt die Diebe!«

»Ja, sie sind alle geklaut, Justus«, bestätigte Bob.

Justus grinste. »Nein«, erklärte er, »eben nicht alle. Zufällig hatte ich den ganzen Vormittag nichts zu tun und da machte ich Abzüge von der ganzen Bildserie. Die Vergrößerungen waren jedoch noch nass, als du vorhin hierher kamst, Bob, und da gab ich dir nur die Negative.«

Der Erste Detektiv ging in die Dunkelkammer und kam mit den Bildern zurück. Sie waren noch feucht. Peter stieß einen Freudenschrei aus und Bob machte vor Begeisterung einen Satz. »Fantastisch! Nun aber schnell damit zu meinem Vater!«

»Halt!«, rief da Peter. »Erst schauen wir mal selbst nach, warum die Diebe so wild darauf waren!«

Er griff nach den Bildern und breitete sie rasch auf dem Schreibtisch aus. Bob und Justus traten auch heran und alle betrachteten die Aufnahmen genau. Es waren insgesamt achtundvierzig und die Tischfläche reichte knapp aus. Doch jeder der drei ??? musste den Kopf schütteln.

»Ich seh hier nur Indianer und Wikinger und wie sie aufeinander losgehen«, sagte Bob.

»Ja, und auch bei den Nahaufnahmen sind nur diese Leute beim Picknick zu erkennen«, bestätigte Peter.

Justus nickte langsam. »Angefangen bei den ersten Fotos, als wir noch draußen auf dem Meer waren, finde ich darauf nur das, was wir mit eigenen Augen sehen konnten. Aber irgendetwas muss mit auf ein Bild oder mehrere Bilder gekommen sein und das wollen die Diebe vor fremden Blicken geheim halten.«

»Etwa, was es beim Picknick zu essen gab?« Peter lachte.

»Vielleicht wollten sie ganz einfach alle Bilder für sich haben«, sagte Bob. »Zur Erinnerung.«

»Und deshalb sollten sie dich von der Straße abdrängen und dabei riskieren, dass du verletzt wirst?«, hielt der Erste Detektiv dagegen. »Das leuchtet mir nicht ein.«

»Hey, vielleicht war's auch dieser Sam Ragnarson!«, rief Bob.

»Daran dachte ich auch schon«, sagte Justus. »Aber nun bringen wir lieber erst die Aufnahmen zu deinem Vater. Wir werden ihn bitten, dass er für uns Reproduktionen machen lässt, damit wir sie in aller Ruhe betrachten können.«

»Klar, Justus«, meinte Bob. »Bis heute Abend können sie bestimmt im Labor der Redaktion die Duplikate für uns machen.«

Sie steckten die Aufnahmen in einen neuen Umschlag und krochen durch Tunnel II zu ihren Fahrrädern. Die Fahrt zum Haus der Familie Andrews verlief ohne Zwischenfall. Bobs Vater war gerade dabei, in sein Auto zu steigen.

»Ich hatte gar nicht mehr mit dir gerechnet, Bob«, sagte Mr Andrews mit einem Blick auf den Umschlag, den Justus in der Hand hielt. »Sind das die Fotos? Ich hatte doch zu Bob gesagt, ihr müsstet sie nicht erst entwickeln – fast hätten wir uns nun verfehlt.«

»Ich hatte die Abzüge schon fertig, Mr Andrews«, erklärte Justus. »Das war nicht der Grund für unsere Verspätung.«

Bob berichtete seinem Vater von der Verfolgungsjagd und den beiden Männern in dem weißen Pick-up. »Wie du siehst, sind das unsere einzigen Exemplare der Fotos. Könntest du uns in der Redaktion Repros davon machen lassen?«

»In Ordnung.« Mr Andrews nickte. »Ich verwende die Bilder für meinen Bericht und ihr bekommt je ein Repro vom Labor.«

»Dafür wären wir sehr dankbar«, sagte Justus. »Wir wollen nämlich untersuchen, warum diese beiden Männer die Bilder um jeden Preis an sich bringen wollten.«

Mr Andrews lachte. »Bob hat bei seiner Schilderung vielleicht ein wenig übertrieben, Jungs. Ihr wisst ja, dass er sich für Krimis begeistert. Diese Leute von der Insel wollten wahrscheinlich einfach die Fotos haben und versuchten, Bob darum zu bitten, und da glaubte er sich von ihnen verfolgt.«

Justus wechselte einen resignierten Blick mit den beiden anderen. Erwachsene dachten natürlich immer, die drei Jungen spielten nur Räuber und Gendarm.

»Vielleicht …«, fing der Anführer der drei ??? an.

»Sie drängten mich ab und ich flog in hohem Bogen in den Graben, Dad! Ich übertreibe gar nicht!«, fauchte Bob.

»Na ja, lassen wir das.« Nun grinste Mr Andrews auch noch boshaft. »Aber jetzt muss ich los, sonst gibt es Ärger mit dem Chefredakteur, und ich fliege in hohem Bogen raus! Eure Bilder bekommt ihr jedenfalls heute Abend.«

Mr Andrews stieg in seinen Wagen und fuhr langsam zur Straße vor. Als der Wagen auf der ruhigen Wohnstraße in der Richtung der Autobahn nach Los Angeles verschwunden war, hob Bob entnervt den Blick zum Himmel.

»Immer diese Erwachsenen!«, stieß er hervor. »Manchmal sind die richtig … Na ja, immerhin hat mir Dad einiges Interessante über Ragnarson Rock erzählt.«

Mit einem Blick auf seine Uhr wandte sich Justus an seine beiden Freunde. »Ich bin zu einigen Schlussfolgerungen gelangt«, erklärte er. »Erstens: Nach diesem albtraumhaften Vormittag hat sich Bob ein gutes Essen verdient. Zweitens: Der magere Kassenbestand unseres Detektivunternehmens gestattet uns gerade noch eine große Pizza zu dritt …«

»Nehmen wir Pepperoni, mit einer Extraportion Käse drauf?«, fiel Peter Justus ins Wort.

Der Erste Detektiv nickte und fuhr fort: »Beim Essen kann uns dann Bob über Ragnarson Rock aufklären. Und drittens: Hinterher nehmen wir uns Sam Ragnarson vor.«

Seltsame Begegnung

Es stellte sich heraus, dass Sam Ragnarson in einem baufälligen kleinen Holzhaus in Strandnähe am nördlichen Ende von Rocky Beach wohnte. Der grüne Farbanstrich war abgeblättert und durch den salzigen, feuchten Seewind und mangelnde Pflege ganz grau geworden und die kleine vorgebaute Veranda hing windschief da. Rings um das Haus wucherte ein üppiger Dschungel aus verwilderten Pflanzen – Hibiskus, Bougainvillea, Wildrebe und verschiedenen Kakteen. »Junge, Junge«, sagte Peter, »der ist wohl nicht zum Gärtner geboren.«

»Ebenso wenig wie zum sorgsamen Heimwerker«, setzte Bob hinzu.

Justus betrachtete missbilligend den heruntergewirtschafteten Bau. »Das hier ist wirklich ein Chaos. Aber hinter dem Haus scheint es so etwas wie eine Garage zu geben. Ich schlage vor, dass wir uns dort mal nach dem weißen Pick-up umsehen, ehe wir uns Sam Ragnarson vornehmen.«

Sie schlossen ihre Fahrräder an den Zaun des Nachbarhauses an und schlängelten sich flink durch das dichte Busch- und Rankenwerk am Haus entlang zu der Garage. Diese war nur eine Hütte aus roh zubehauenen, ungestrichenen, zum Teil bereits morschen Brettern und in noch üblerem Zustand als das Wohnhaus. Zwischen den Brettern klafften hier und da breite Ritzen. Die Jungen spähten durch die Lücken.

»Aha!«, rief Peter. »Ich sehe einen Pick-up! Und er ist ganz zerbeult und verrostet!«

»Stimmt, Peter.« Justus nickte. »Ist das der Wagen, der Jagd auf dich machte, Bob?«

Bob hielt wegen des hellen Sonnenscheins die Hände an die Augen und blickte lange durch eine Ritze in den dunklen Raum.

»Nein, die Farbe stimmt nicht. Dieser hier ist hellbraun, und der Wagen, der mich verfolgte, war weiß. Auch die Bauart ist anders. Und da, das Kennzeichen – es fängt nicht mit sechsundfünfzig an.«

»Na ja«, meinte Peter, noch nicht ganz überzeugt, »jedenfalls fährt er einen Pick-up. Dann hat er vielleicht auch noch einen zweiten.«

»Platz für ein zweites Fahrzeug gäbe es da drin schon«, stellte Justus nachdenklich fest. »Vielleicht hat er irgendwelche Freunde mit einem anderen Wagen losgeschickt, damit sie die Negative für ihn stehlen. Na ja, nun kommt mit.«

Sie gingen wieder vor das Haus und erstiegen die Stufen zu der wackligen Veranda. Hinter den beiden schmutzigen Fenstern vorn am Haus waren angegraute und fleckige Vorhänge zu sehen. Justus drückte auf den Klingelknopf, doch es kam kein Ton. Er versuchte es nochmals, ebenfalls vergeblich.

»Klingel kaputt.« Bob grinste. »So wie alles Übrige hier.«

»Na, wundert mich nicht«, meinte Justus dazu. Nun klopfte er an die Tür. Die Jungen warteten. Nichts rührte sich. Justus klopfte energischer.

»Der ist wohl nicht zu Hause«, sagte er. »Dann kommen wir eben ein anderes Mal wieder.«

Peter versuchte, trotz der schmutzigen Scheibe und der Vorhänge durch ein Fenster zu schauen. »Warte noch, Justus! Ich glaube, da drin bewegt sich was.«

»Meinst du wirklich, Peter?« Justus spähte auch hinein. Der dämmrige Innenraum wirkte ebenso vernachlässigt und chaotisch wie das Äußere des Hauses und die Garage. Sie sahen Sessel, deren Polsterung aufgeplatzt war. Aus einer durchgelegenen Couch stachen Sprungfedern heraus. Ein langer Tisch, einige staubige Holzstühle, verschlissene Teppiche, die achtlos zusammengeschoben in Ecken lagen – alles in diesem Halbdunkel war schmuddelig und kaputt und in Unordnung.

»Du musst mal ganz nach hinten schauen«, sagte Peter zu Justus. Hinter den schmutzigen Fenstern und Vorhängen glaubten sie, im Zwielicht des Raumes zu erkennen, wie sich jemand in einem Hinterzimmer hin- und herbewegte. Die Gestalt führte sich äußerst sonderbar auf. Sie schwenkte die Arme, erstarrte dann in der Bewegung und sah zur Seite. Dann duckte sie sich und hielt wieder Ausschau. Und nun warf sie den Oberkörper nach vorn, als wolle sie zuschlagen. Die Bewegungen waren steif und abgezirkelt, wie die ruckartigen Gesten der Schauspieler in alten Filmen.

»W-was ist denn das?«, stotterte Peter. »Mir fällt gerade ein, dass ich dringend wegmuss, sonst falle ich um vor Hunger.«

»Ist das Sam Ragnarson?«, flüsterte Bob.

Peter hielt die Hände an die Augen, weil die Scheibe spiegelte. »Keine Ahnung. Jedenfalls trägt er eine Art Uniform.«

»Im Grunde wissen wir ja gar nicht«, sagte Justus nach einem erneuten Blick in den Raum, »wie Sam Ragnarson aussieht. Wir sahen ihn nur einmal kurz und da war er richtiggehend vermummt in seinem Wikingerkostüm.«

»Ein Wikinger ist das aber nicht«, stellte Peter fest.

»Eines ist allerdings merkwürdig«, fuhr Justus fort, »warum geht er nicht an die Tür?«

»Vielleicht hört er uns gar nicht«, meinte Bob, »weil er sich ganz auf das, was er da treibt, konzentriert.«

»Oder er will uns nicht hören«, sagte Peter in einer bangen Ahnung. »Vielleicht will er einfach nicht aufmachen. Vielleicht ist das ein V-verrückter.«

»Du meinst« – Bob schluckte – »der da drin ist ausgerastet…«

Justus beschloss resolut: »Hört mal, wir gehen jetzt wieder hinters Haus und erkunden, was sich in diesem Raum abspielt.«

Alle Fenster an der Rückseite waren mit Brettern vernagelt. Nirgends konnte man hineinsehen.

»Was machen wir jetzt?«, fragte Peter.

»Na ja…« Justus blickte auf die zugenagelten Fenster und die geschlossene Hintertür. »Da bleibt uns wohl nichts anderes übrig, als so laut wie möglich an die Hintertür zu klopfen und abzuwarten, ob er darauf reagiert.«

Peter holte tief Atem. »Muss das wirklich sein?«

»Es muss sein«, entgegnete der Erste Detektiv entschlossen. »Wir müssen feststellen, ob Sam Ragnarson etwas zugestoßen ist und wo er überhaupt steckt.«

Widerstrebend pochte Peter mit den beiden anderen an die Tür. Noch immer regte sich nichts.

Justus fragte mit schallender Stimme: »Ist Mr Sam Ragnarson im Haus?«

»Wir müssen ihn sprechen, wegen der Fotos!«, rief Bob. »Wir…« Auch Peter erhob die Stimme.

Da wurde krachend die Hintertür aufgerissen. Der Mann stand im Dämmerlicht auf dem Flur dahinter und starrte die Jungen böse an. »Aufhör'n mit dem Geklingel und Gehämmer und Gebrüll, sonst bind ich euch an den Mast und lass euch auspeitschen!«

Es war ein hagerer Mann mit hoher, spöttischer Stimme und einem buschigen weißen Schnauzbart. Die blassblauen Augen blickten die Jungen unter einer marineblauen Schirmmütze mit goldenen Tressen durchdringend an. Er trug eine knapp sitzende, bis zu den Knien reichende dunkelblaue Jacke mit hohem Stehkragen und einer Reihe glänzender Messingknöpfe und dazu eine enge blaue Hose, knöchelhohe schwarze Schnürstiefel und weiße Handschuhe. In einer Hand hielt er ein Messingteleskop.

»Wir hätten gern Mr Sam Ragnarson gesprochen«, sagte Justus in gekonnt würdevollem Tonfall.

»Is' nich' da.«

Der Mann machte kehrt und wollte von der Tür weggehen.

44

»Wir müssen wissen, ob er noch einen anderen Pick-up hat!«, platzte Bob heraus.

»Einen weißen, ganz zerbeult«, setzte Peter hastig hinzu.

Der Mann drehte sich nicht einmal mehr zu den Jungen um. »Nee, hat er nich'.«

»Es ist immerhin möglich, guter Mann, dass Sam Ragnarson einige wertvolle Fotografien gestohlen hat.« Der stämmige Anführer des Trios pflegte unübertrefflich gebieterisch aufzutreten, wenn ein Erwachsener sich den Jungen gegenüber arrogant benahm. »Und wenn das zutrifft, dann sieht es sehr schlecht für ihn aus.«

Der Mann in der langen blauen Jacke blieb stehen. Ein kalter Blick über die Schulter traf die Jungen. »Nehmt euch bloß in Acht mit solchen Anschuldigungen, ihr Knirpse. Sam Ragnarson is' 'n echter Wikinger. Dem kann keiner, kapiert? Und jetzt fort mit euch oder ich lass euch kielholen!«

Der Mann trat mit drohender Miene an die Tür und schlug sie den Jungen vor der Nase zu.

»Der ist vielleicht unfreundlich.« Peter starrte auf die geschlossene Tür.

»Ja«, bestätigte Justus, »und ich frage mich, warum. Wir wollten uns doch nur ganz normal mit ihm unterhalten.«

»Und was jetzt, Justus?«, fragte Peter. »Sollen wir etwa hier auf Sam Ragnarson warten? Der ist vielleicht auf seiner Insel und bleibt noch stundenlang dort.«

»Nach meiner Ansicht«, sagte Justus, »ist es Zeit für Ermittlungen zu der Sippe Ragnarson und zu der Insel Ragnarson Rock. Peter, du gehst zur Lokalpresse und zur Handelskammer und besorgst dir möglichst viele Informationen über die Familie Ragnarson.«

»Und ich gehe ins Historische Museum und forsche dort nach Aufzeichnungen über die Ragnarsons und ihre Insel«, erbot sich Bob.

»Gut, dann gehe ich zur Bibliothek«, beschloss Justus. »Ob der Dieb unserer Negative nun Sam Ragnarson ist oder nicht, jedenfalls wollte er sie an sich bringen, und ich muss erfahren, warum.«

 Erinnert euch dieser unfreundliche Mann nicht an eine Geschichte in dieser Geschichte? Sein Beruf ließe sich aus seiner Kleidung und dem Messingteleskop erraten. Doch davon, dass es in Rocky Beach eine Zeitmaschine geben soll, habe ich allerdings noch nie gehört.

Spukt es in dem alten Haus?

Peter Shaw trat aus dem Gebäude der *Rocky Beach News*, einer kleinen Zeitung, die jeweils zum Wochenende erschien. Stöhnend rieb er sich den verkrampften Nacken. Er hatte den ganzen Nachmittag in geschlossenen Räumen zugebracht und ein solches Arbeiten widerstrebte ihm. Tief atmete er die frische Brise vom Meer her ein, während er gemächlich zum Schrottplatz radelte. Es freute ihn, nach all dem Nachschlagen in Gedrucktem und den Fragen an die Leute wieder im Freien zu sein und ein wenig Bewegung zu haben.

In der Freiluftwerkstatt stand nur Justus' Fahrrad. Peter kroch durch Tunnel II und stieg in die verborgene Zentrale hinauf.

»Ist Bob noch nicht da?«

»Er hatte bestimmt im Historischen Museum eine ganze Menge mehr nachzulesen als wir beide. Was hast denn du über die Ragnarsons herausgefunden?«

»Erst mal, dass es hier eine ganze Menge von ihnen gibt«,

antwortete Peter. »Einem George Ragnarson gehört das große Eisenwarengeschäft in der Innenstadt und Mr Karl Ragnarson ist ja unser Schulleiter. Dr. Ingmar Ragnarson hat hier eine Zahnarztpraxis. Dann gibt es noch zwei Ingenieure, die in Los Angeles arbeiten, und einen Buchhalter, der oben in Ventura beschäftigt ist. Eine ganze Anzahl weiterer Ragnarsons wohnt in anderen Orten in Kalifornien und kommt regelmäßig zu dem Familientreffen und dem Kampfspiel für eine Woche hierher. Ich habe mir von denjenigen, die in Rocky Beach wohnen, die Adressen notiert. Alle sagen, die Ragnarsons seien gute Bürger und angesehene Leute. Bis auf eine Ausnahme – Sam!«

»Was ist mit Sam?«, fragte Justus rasch.

»Er ist das schwarze Schaf der Familie. Er ging ohne Abschluss von der Schule ab und haust seither als Aussteiger am Stadtrand. Sam ist jetzt zweiundzwanzig und hat noch nie eine feste Anstellung gehabt. Ständig versucht er, sich mit zwielichtigen Geschäften zu bereichern. Ein paarmal stand er schon vor dem Jugendgericht, und einmal musste er beinahe ins Gefängnis wegen eines Betrugsmanövers, das ihm schnelles Geld bringen sollte. Alle sind sich darin einig, dass er ein Taugenichts ist, wenn nicht gar Schlimmeres. Er probiert immer wieder, ohne Arbeit zu Geld zu kommen.«

»In der Bibliothek erfuhr ich eigentlich nicht viel mehr als das, was wir schon über Bobs Vater wissen«, berichtete nun Justus. »Knut Ragnarson hatte 1849 mit dem Verkauf seiner Stiefel so viel Erfolg, dass er beschloss, seine Familie aus Illinois nachzuholen. Er buchte eine Passage auf der *Star of Panama*. Das Schiff sollte Kurs auf Panama nehmen. Dort war vorgesehen, dass die Passagiere die Landenge überqueren – den Kanal gab es damals noch nicht – und von der Atlantikküste aus mit einem anderen Schiff weiterreisen. Der Kapitän, ein Mann namens Henry Coulter, hatte allerdings andere Pläne. Auf der *Star of Panama* sollte eine Ladung Gold nach Osten verschifft werden, Münzen und Nuggets und Goldstaub. Als das Schiff von Rocky Beach abgelegt hatte, verfrachtete der Kapitän all das Gold in das große Beiboot, drehte sämtliche Bordventile auf, um das Schiff zu versenken, und ruderte mit der Mannschaft los.«

»Dann war er ja ein Dieb und ein Mörder! Wie wollte er aber sein Ziel erreichen, Justus?«, fragte Peter. »Wie wollte er sich herausreden?«

»Ich vermute, dass er behauptet hätte, das Schiff sei gesunken und all das Gold sei mit untergegangen«, sagte Justus. »Fast hätte er das auch geschafft. Die Passagiere schliefen, und nur Knut Ragnarson entging in jener Nacht dem Ertrinken. Er kam mit dem Leben davon, weil er am liebsten oben auf Deck übernachtete, und auf einem Lukendeckel konnte er sich zur Insel Ragnarson Rock retten, wie wir es schon von Bob hörten.«

»Junge, da hatte er aber Glück«, war Peters Kommentar.

Justus nickte. »Großes Glück sogar, und es verließ ihn auch nachher nicht. Die Insel ist ja nicht viel mehr als ein großer, baumloser Felsen und es gibt darauf weder Nahrung noch Tiere oder Trinkwasser. Hätte Knut Ragnarson nicht ein Kanu der Chumash-Indianer gefunden, mit dem er zum Festland paddeln konnte, wäre er auf der Felseninsel elend umgekommen. Kapitän Coulter hatte die *Star of Panama* wohlweislich weitab von den bekannten Schiffsrouten versenkt.«

»Und was wurde aus Kapitän Coulter und seinen Leuten?«, erkundigte sich Peter.

»Das weiß ich nicht. Darüber war in der Bibliothek nichts zu finden. Aber etwas anderes bekam ich heraus: dass Sven, ein Enkel des alten Knut, der in Nordkalifornien lebt, vor dreißig Jahren die Felseninsel wieder entdeckte und beschloss, die glückliche Rettung seines Großvaters alle fünf Jahre dort bei einem Familientreffen mit Picknick und lustigem Wettstreit zu feiern. Das Chumash-Kanu brachte ihn auf die Idee eines Scheinkampfes zwischen Indianern und Wikingern um den Besitz der Insel. In Wirklichkeit aber führten die Chumash niemals Kriege. Die Ragnarsons hatten allesamt Spaß an der Sache und daher wird das Treffen bis heute beibehalten.«

Plötzlich fuhr beiden der Schrecken in alle Glieder. Jemand rief laut: »Hab ich euch erwischt!«

Sie schnappten nach Luft. Bob tauchte lachend in der Bodenluke am Ende von Tunnel II auf. Sie waren so in die Geschichte der *Star of Panama* vertieft gewesen, dass sie nicht gehört hatten, wie ihr dritter Mann den Lukendeckel geöffnet hatte.

»Du spinnst wohl, Bob!«, rief Peter, als er sich wieder gefasst hatte. »Mach das bloß nicht noch mal!«

Bob stieg aus der Öffnung und schloss die Klappe. »Konntest du erfahren, was aus Kapitän Coulter geworden ist?«, fragte Justus.

»Nein«, sagte Bob. »Keiner hat ihn mitsamt der Schiffsbesatzung und dem ganzen Gold jemals wieder gesehen! Alles spurlos verschwunden.«

Bob berichtete, was er im Historischen Museum in Erfahrung gebracht hatte. Es deckte sich im Großen und Ganzen mit Justus' Erforschungen in der Bibliothek. »Als Knut Ragnarson am Festland anlegte«, fuhr Bob fort, »hatte sich die Spur des Kapitäns und des Goldes bereits verloren. Niemand hatte den Kapitän und seine Leute an Land kommen sehen oder sonst etwas beobachtet. Man einigte sich darauf, dass er wohl auf See geblieben war, bis ihn ein anderes Schiff aufnahm. Einige vermuteten sogar, er hätte sich vorübergehend auf eben jener kleinen Insel aufgehalten. Deshalb heißt sie manchmal auch Wrecker's Rock – die Insel der Schiffbrüchigen.«

Justus hatte aufmerksam zugehört. »Soll das heißen, dass Kapitän Coulter und Knut Ragnarson möglicherweise beide zur selben Zeit auf der Insel waren?«

»Genau das vermuteten damals einige Leute«, bestätigte Bob.

»Dann ist es auch möglich, dass ein Geheimnis, das der eine hatte, vom anderen entdeckt wurde«, schloss der Erste Detektiv. »Gut gemacht, Bob. Ist das alles?«

»Nein, warte mal.« Bob holte einen zusammengefalteten Zettel aus seiner Jackentasche. »Ich hab noch was anderes gefunden. Davon konnte ich mir eine Fotokopie machen.«

Er hielt die Kopie einer großen Fotografie in die Höhe, eine Aufnahme aus sehr früher Zeit, auf der ein hoch gewachsener Mann in aufrechter, steifer Haltung zu sehen war. »Das ist eine so genannte Daguerreotypie. Während der Belichtungszeit musste man sehr lange bewegungslos dastehen.«

Aber die beiden Freunde hörten gar nicht richtig zu. Mit großen Augen starrten sie das kopierte Foto an. Es zeigte einen großen, hageren Mann in knielanger dunkler Jacke mit Stehkragen und blanken Messingknöpfen. Er hatte einen buschigen weißen Schnurrbart und helle Augen unter der goldbetressten Schirmmütze eines Seeoffiziers. Und er trug enge Hosen und Schnürstiefel und weiße Handschuhe. Und ein Teleskop aus Messing. »Das ist ja der Mann, den wir...«, fing Peter an.

»– den wir in Sams Haus gesehen haben!«, schloss Justus.

»Und dieser Mann ist«, setzte Bob hinzu, »Kapitän Henry Coulter von der *Star of Panama*!«

»D-der Kapitän der *Star of P-Panama*?«, brachte Peter hervor. Justus sah Bob entgeistert an. »Stimmt das auch wirklich, Bob? Woher stammt denn dieses Bild?«

»Aus einem Buch über unaufgeklärte Verbrechen in Kalifornien. Daraus erfuhr ich, dass Kapitän Coulter und seine Mannschaft nie mehr gesehen wurden.«

»Aber«, wandte Peter beklommen ein, »das ist doch schon mehr als hundert Jahre her! Da wäre der Kapitän heute mindestens...«

»Es war vor fast hundertfünfzig Jahren, Peter.« Justus hatte rasch nachgerechnet. »Demnach wäre Kapitän Coulter mindestens hundertachtzig Jahre alt. Schiffskapitäne waren damals kaum unter dreißig.«

»Dann kann der Mann, den wir gesehen haben, unmöglich Kapitän Coulter sein!«, meinte Peter.

»Nicht zu Lebzeiten«, entgegnete Bob.

Peter stöhnte. »Mehr möchte ich gar nicht hören …«

»Bestimmt nicht zu Lebzeiten«, bestätigte Justus nachdenklich. »Daher können wir uns auf eine von drei möglichen Schlussfolgerungen einigen. Wir sahen einen Mann, der rein zufällig Ähnlichkeit mit der Gestalt auf diesem Bild hatte. Oder es tritt jemand aus irgendeinem Grund als Kapitän Coulter auf. Oder es war sein Geist.«

»Ich sagte doch, dass ich gar nichts mehr hören will!«, protestierte Peter.

Doch die beiden anderen nahmen Peters Unbehagen einfach nicht zur Kenntnis.

»Jemand, der zufällig so aussieht wie der Mann auf dem Bild, kann es nicht sein, Justus«, fand Bob. »So kleidet sich doch heute niemand mehr. Und er glich bis in jede Einzelheit diesem in dem Buch abgebildeten Kapitän. Das kann beim besten Willen kein Zufall sein.«

»Dann war es also jemand, der sich als Kapitän Coulter maskierte«, überlegte Justus.

»Oder eben ein Geist«, sagte Bob.

»Vielleicht hat Bob den Geist unwissentlich fotografiert«, vermutete Peter, »und deshalb ist Sam Ragnarson hinter unseren Negativen her. Auf der Insel geriet Sam in den Bann des Geistes und nun ist er dessen willenloses Werkzeug!«

»Ach, red keinen Unsinn«, sagte Justus ungeduldig. »Geister kann man nicht fotografieren. Außerdem gibt es keine. Es muss jemand sein, der in der Maske des Kapitäns auftritt.«

»Kann sein, dass man Geister nicht fotografieren kann«, murmelte Peter eigensinnig, »aber es gibt sie auf jeden Fall. Nur sind sie unsichtbar.«

»Wie sollte jemand ausgerechnet auf die Idee kommen, heutzutage als der Kapitän der *Star of Panama* aufzutreten?«, fragte Bob.

Justus schüttelte den Kopf. »Das weiß ich nicht. Aber wie du schon sagtest: Ein Zufall kann das nicht sein.«

»Vielleicht hat Sam Ragnarson die Negative gar nicht gestohlen«, fiel es Bob ein. »Vielleicht tat das der Mann, der sich als Kapitän Coulter verkleidet hatte.«

»Möglich, dass Sam selbst als Kapitän aufgetreten ist«, stellte Justus fest. »Aber wir wissen noch nicht genug, um diese Fragen zuverlässig beantworten zu können. Wir müssen weiterermitteln und alles Erreichbare über Sam und die anderen Ragnarsons herausfinden.«

»Und wie stellen wir das an?«, fragte Bob.

»Morgen sprechen wir mit den Ragnarsons.«

»Meinst du etwa, die stecken alle unter einer Decke, Justus?«, rief Bob.

»Bis jetzt wissen wir nur, Bob, dass Sam uns wegen der Fotos bedroht hat, dass zwei Diebe dir die Negative gestohlen haben und dass anscheinend jemand als der Kapitän der *Star of Panama* herumgeistert. Was dahinter steckt, weiß ich nicht, aber eines könnte ich mir immerhin denken. Du sagtest ja, dass der Kapitän, seine Mannschaft und auch das Gold spurlos verschwunden sind. Vielleicht liegt das Gold von der *Star of Panama* noch draußen auf Ragnarson Rock!«

Angenommen jemand hätte auf einem winzigen Eiland Gold entdeckt, das seit einem Schiffsuntergang vor langer Zeit dort lagert. Müsste der glückliche Finder denn nicht dankbar sein, wenn zufällig drei jugendliche Pressefotografen zugegen wären und mittels ihrer Schnappschüsse sein ruhmreiches Abenteuer publik machten?

Ermittlungen mit Hindernissen

Am nächsten Tag erwachte Bob erst spät. Die hektischen Fahrten durch Rocky Beach hatten ihn doch mehr ermüdet, als er wahrhaben wollte. Als er in die Küche herunterkam, fand er einen an den Kühlschrank geklebten Notizzettel:

Guten Morgen, du Faulpelz!
Gestern hatte ich bis spät in die Nacht einen Feuerwehreinsatz, ein Waldbrand oben in den Bergen. Tut mir Leid, dass wir uns nicht mehr sehen konnten, du warst schon im Bett. Kam nicht mehr zur Redaktion zurück, um eure Repros abzuholen. Heute Abend bring ich sie dir ganz bestimmt.

Gruß

Dad

PS: Mom ist im Supermarkt. Ich soll dir ausrichten:
chemische Reinigung, Rasen sprengen, dann...

Es war eine lange Liste. Ergeben machte sich Bob sein Frühstück und erledigte dann nacheinander die Botengänge und

Aufgaben. Erst gegen Mittag kam er auf dem Schrottplatz an.

Peter saß mit düsterem Blick in der Freiluftwerkstatt.

»Patrick musste zum Zahnarzt und Onkel Titus und Kenneth brauchten Justus als Helfer. Sie sind mit dem Lastwagen unterwegs.« Patrick und Kenneth waren die beiden irischen Brüder, die im Betrieb arbeiteten.

»Wir könnten es ja ohne Justus versuchen«, erwog Bob.

»Ich wüsste nicht mal, was wir überhaupt fragen sollen«, hielt Peter dagegen.

»Na, eben was es mit Ragnarson Rock auf sich hat...«

Peter zog die Brauen zusammen. »Eine innere Stimme sagt mir, dass das nicht hinhaut. Wir warten doch lieber auf Justus.«

Sie erledigten in der Werkstatt und in der Zentrale einige kleinere Reparaturen. Anschließend saßen sie in ihrem versteckten Büro müßig herum und sahen immer wieder auf die Uhr an der Wand. Bobs Blick fiel auf die Exemplare der Zeitung, die sie aufbewahren wollten, weil ihre Namen in dem Bericht über den vermissten Angler genannt worden waren.

»Oje«, meinte Bob. »Ich hatte Mr Manning ganz vergessen. Ob sie ihn inzwischen wohl gefunden haben?«

Peter schüttelte den Kopf. »Mein Vater sagte, wenn einer nicht schwimmen kann, hat er da draußen kaum eine Chance.«

Bob griff zum Telefon. »Ich rufe mal eben den Kommissar an und erkundige mich. Vielleicht ist William Manning ja doch noch wohlbehalten nach Hause gekommen.«

Er musste warten, bis Hauptkommissar Reynolds ein Gespräch auf einer anderen Leitung beendet hatte.

»Nein, Bob«, hörte er dann die ruhige Stimme des Polizeichefs. »Hier gibt es leider kaum noch Hoffnung. Die Küstenwache hat die Suche eingestellt.«

»Oh, das ist sehr traurig«, sagte Bob bedrückt.

Peter hatte am Periskop hantiert, während Bob am Telefon

war. Das Gerät bestand aus einem Stück Ofenrohr mit Spiegeln im Inneren, das durch eine Öffnung im Dach der Zentrale ausgefahren werden konnte, wenn die drei ??? den Schrottplatz überblicken wollten. Nun drehte sich Peter zu Bob um. »Der Lastwagen mit Justus ist wieder da!« Er holte das Periskop ein und beide Jungen hasteten ins Freie.

»Ihr könnt gleich mal beim Abladen helfen!«, begrüßte der Erste Detektiv keuchend seine Freunde.

Bob und Peter sprangen in die Bresche und im Nu war der Wagen leer. Onkel Titus staunte nicht schlecht über das Tempo, in dem seine Schätze auf dem Hof landeten. Als leidenschaftlicher Sammler ausgefallener Objekte hatte er auf dieser Einkaufstour einmal wieder reiche Beute gemacht. Die drei ??? entluden acht hölzerne Notenständer, fünf Klavierhocker, zwölf Hängelampen mit Seidenschirm, neun Hamsterkäfige und eine Menge Teile einer zerlegten Achterbahn. Doch schon wenige Minuten nach der Ankunft des voll beladenen Wagens hatten die Jungen die Arbeit getan und machten sich auf ihren Fahrrädern davon.

Nach kurzer Stärkung an einem Stehimbiss steuerten sie in der Innenstadt die Haushalts- und Eisenwarenhandlung an, die George Ragnarson gehörte. Das Unternehmen war gigantisch und nahm einen ganzen Häuserblock ein. Es verhielt sich zu einem normalen Ladengeschäft etwa wie die Firma »Gebrauchtwaren-Center T. Jonas« zu einem normalen Schrotthandel. George Ragnarson war gerade hinten im Lager und kontrollierte den Warenbestand. Er war ein kleiner, vierschrötiger, betriebsamer Mann, der während des Gesprächs eifrig weiterarbeitete.

»Na, womit kann ich euch Jungen behilflich sein?«

Justus meldete sich zu Wort. »Wir haben großes Interesse an der Geschichte der Insel Ragnarson Rock, Sir. Wir haben uns das Thema als Projektarbeit für die Schule vorgenommen, und wir wären Ihnen dankbar, wenn Sie uns berichten könnten, was Sie dort draußen vor kurzem entdeckt haben.«

»Entdeckt?« George Ragnarson hakte auf seinem Schreibblock wieder einige Posten ab. »Ich wüsste nicht, was wir da entdeckt haben sollten, außer dass wir alle nicht mehr die Jüngsten sind. Bei all dem Umtrieb kommt man ganz schön ins Schwitzen und spürt seine alten Knochen… na ja. Trotzdem würd ich jederzeit wieder mit den anderen da rausfahren. Aber jetzt ist wieder Arbeit angesagt.«

»Wir haben gehört, Sie hätten vielleicht etwas darüber herausgefunden, was aus Kapitän Coulter geworden ist«, fuhr Justus ganz harmlos fort.

»Wer soll das sein?« George Ragnarson sah zu seinen Regalen hinauf und schrieb emsig weiter.

»Der Kapitän der *Star of Panama*, Sir«, erläuterte Bob.

»Ach, das Schiff, auf dem sich unser alter Knut befand. Nein, über diesen Kapitän ist mir nichts bekannt.«

»Aber vielleicht Ihrem Neffen Sam?«, platzte Peter heraus.

George Ragnarson hörte auf zu schreiben und wandte sich mit unwilliger Miene den Jungen zu. »Nun ja – zu meinem Bedauern ist dieser Aussteiger mein Neffe. Aber wenn ihr Jungs was mit ihm zu schaffen habt, dann lasst mich bloß damit in Ruhe!«

»Nein, Sir«, sagte Justus rasch, »wir kennen ihn ja kaum. Wir haben nur gehört, dass er sich in letzter Zeit recht eigenartig benimmt. Hat er vielleicht irgendwelche Probleme?«

»Probleme? Mehr als ich Haare auf dem Kopf habe. Ohne Probleme geht's bei diesem großspurigen Lump überhaupt nicht ab!«

»Wir dachten eigentlich an etwas Konkreteres, Sir«, fuhr Justus fort. »Vielleicht etwas im Zusammenhang mit Ihrem Familientreffen.«

George Ragnarson schnaubte verächtlich. »Wunderte mich

ja, dass er überhaupt mit uns rausfuhr. Einmal arbeitete er den Sommer über bei mir und besaß die Unverschämtheit, sich bei allen Leuten zu beklagen, ich sei ein Geizhals. Ja, ich! Und dabei bezahlte ich ihn ordentlich, obwohl er die meiste Zeit hier hinter den Lagerregalen vor sich hindöste!«

»Dann hat er in letzter Zeit also nicht über die Stränge geschlagen?«, fragte Peter.

»Und er sitzt nicht irgendwie in der Patsche?«, hakte Bob nach.

»Über die Stränge schlägt der dauernd und aus der Patsche kommt er gar nicht mehr raus«, erklärte George Ragnarson. Doch dann knurrte er noch unwillig: »Na ja, zurzeit ist mir von speziellen Scherereien nichts bekannt.«

Die Jungen bedankten sich bei dem Geschäftsinhaber und gingen wieder, während der Mann mürrisch etwas über seinen ungeratenen Neffen vor sich hin brummelte. Draußen schlug Peter als Nächstes einen Besuch in der Zahnarztpraxis von Dr. Ingmar Ragnarson, Sams Vater, vor. Die Räume lagen in einem neuen, dreistöckigen Gebäude aus gelben Klinkersteinen in einer baumbestandenen, ruhigen Seitenstraße.

Die Empfangsdame begrüßte lächelnd die Jungen. »Nun sagt mal, ihr könnt doch nicht alle drei Zahnschmerzen haben. Wem tut's denn weh?«

»Mir nicht!«, rief Peter rasch.

»Wir kommen überhaupt nicht als Patienten«, stellte Bob richtig.

»Wir möchten den Doktor wegen seines Sohnes sprechen«, erklärte Justus. »Falls er ein paar Minuten Zeit hat.«

»Und um welchen Sohn geht es denn?«

»Um Sam«, sagte Peter.

Die junge Frau seufzte. »Das hatte ich schon befürchtet. Meistens geht es nämlich um Sam. Einen Augenblick, bitte.« Sie betätigte Knöpfe an ihrem Vermittlungsapparat, nahm einen Telefonhörer ab und sprach leise einige Worte. Gleich darauf kam ein großer blonder Mann im weißen Kittel aus dem Behandlungsraum. Er sah bekümmert aus.

»Was hat er nun wieder angestellt, Jungs?«

Sein Gesicht war gebräunt und wettergegerbt, und mit dem halblangen blonden Haar wirkte er so, als sei sein Platz eher am Ruder eines echten Wikingerschiffes.

»Wir wissen nichts, das er angestellt hätte, Dr. Ragnarson«, antwortete Justus bedächtig. »Aber vielleicht können Sie ein wenig Zeit erübrigen und uns einige Fragen beantworten.«

»Euch kenne ich doch von irgendwoher...« Der Zahnarzt musterte die drei Jungen mit fragender Miene. Dann kam ihm die Erleuchtung und er schnippte mit den Fingern. »Natürlich, ihr seid die Jungen, die draußen vor Ragnarson Rock die Fotos von uns machten! Wie sind sie denn geworden?«

»Ganz gut«, sagte Bob. »Auch dazu möchten wir Sie etwas fragen.«

»Schön, dann kommt mit rein.«

Sie betraten sein Behandlungszimmer mit Liegesessel und chromblitzendem Instrumentarium. Im Sessel saß ein ebenfalls blonder Mann, dem man zum Schutz seiner Kleidung einen weißen Latz umgehängt hatte. »Das ist mein Bruder Karl, Jungs. Er kennt sich mit Sam fast ebenso gut aus wie ich, nicht wahr, Karl?«

Die drei Jungen nickten ihrem Schulleiter zu.

»Wir kennen Mr Karl Ragnarson, Sir«, erklärte Bob dem Zahnarzt. »Wir gehen in seine Schule.«

»Dort war Sam früher auch«, meinte der Schulleiter. Er zuckte zusammen und hielt die Hand an den Unterkiefer. »Machst du dir noch lange an diesem Zahn zu schaffen, Ingmar? Ich würde nämlich ganz gern zum Abendessen wieder zur Insel rausfahren.«

»Die Jungen hier wollen was über Sam erfahren«, entgegnete Dr. Ragnarson. »Aber wir können uns ja unterhalten, während ich weiterarbeite, nicht?« Er beugte sich über seinen Bruder und fuhr mit der Zahnbehandlung fort. »Na, und woher rührt euer Interesse für Sam, ihr drei?«

Justus brachte wieder seine Version von der Projektarbeit über die Familie Ragnarson vor und erwähnte in diesem Zusammenhang, es sei ihm zu Ohren gekommen, dass Sam sich in letzter Zeit auffällig verhielte und möglicherweise irgendwelche Probleme hätte. »Auffällig verhält sich Sam eigentlich immer«, stellte Dr. Ragnarson dazu fest, »aber schwer wiegende Folgen hat das nun seit Jahren nicht mehr gehabt. Stimmt's, Karl?«

»Garrrgg-raggg«, kam es aus dem Mund des Schulleiters, in dem sich Dr. Ragnarsons Finger samt einem Spiegel und einem Instrument befanden.

»Hoppla – entschuldige, Karl«, sagte der Zahnarzt und machte den Weg frei.

Karl Ragnarson warf seinem Bruder einen warnenden Blick zu. »Ja, seit Sam zuletzt vors Jugendgericht kam, ist nichts mehr passiert. Er ist schon ein Lümmel, aber meistens schadet er sich selbst mehr als anderen.«

»Sam ist eben ein Außenseiter«, fuhr Dr. Ragnarson fort, während er eine Injektionsspritze vorbereitete. »Aber im Grunde ist er nicht bösartig, oder, Karl?«

»Darüber kann man geteilter Meinung sein.« Der Patient blickte voll Unbehagen auf die lange Kanüle. »In einem gebe ich dir allerdings Recht – sein Lästermaul ist vermutlich noch um einiges übler als seine Schandtaten.«

»Dazu hat uns auch bereits Mr George Ragnarson seine Meinung gesagt«, warf Peter ein. Dr. Ragnarson schüttelte den Kopf. »George wird es Sam sein Leben lang nachtragen, dass er sich mit seinem Sohn mal fürchterlich in die Haare gekriegt hat, als beide Jungen zehn waren. Und zu der Sache mit dem

Aushilfsjob, die George euch garantiert aufgetischt hat, kann ich nur sagen: Für die paar Kröten, die mein knickriger Vetter zahlt, würde ich mich auch jederzeit in irgendeiner Ecke aufs Ohr legen.«

Als wolle er seinen Worten Nachdruck verleihen, verabreichte der Zahnarzt dem Patienten die Injektion. Karl Ragnarson zuckte zusammen. Dann stieß er mit schmerzverzerrtem Gesicht hervor: »Ja, für Großzügigkeit ist George nicht gerade berühmt.«

»Er ist der einzige Ragnarson, der sich für unser Treffen nicht eine Woche freinimmt«, erklärte Dr. Ragnarson den Jungen. »Er kommt höchstens ein- oder zweimal zur Insel herüber.«

»Und warum sind Sie selbst nicht da draußen?«, fragte Justus.

»Ein Notfall. Während wir auf der Insel waren, bekam Karl Zahnschmerzen.«

Aus dem Vorzimmer war ein heftiger Wortwechsel zu vernehmen. Jemand stritt sich mit der Empfangsdame herum. Karl Ragnarson schien aufmerksam zu werden. Dann wandte er sich zu den Jungen. »Interessiert euch etwas Bestimmtes?«, fragte der Schulleiter langsam. Seine Aussprache war durch die Betäubungsspritze schon etwas behindert.

»Wir haben gehört, dass sich auf der Insel seltsame Dinge zutragen«, erwiderte Bob auf gut Glück.

»Wo habt ihr…?«, setzte Dr. Ragnarson an.

Da stürmte ein junger Mann mit zornigem Gesichtsausdruck in das Sprechzimmer. Er war mager und nicht viel größer als Peter, trug zerschlissene Jeans und ein schmuddeliges T-Shirt. Schuhe hatte er nicht an, rasiert war er auch nicht. »Dad…« Beim Anblick der drei ??? blieb er mit offenem Mund stehen. »Was machen denn *die* hier? Die wollen mir doch was in die Schuhe schieben! Dabei wollte ich ihnen nur die Fotos abkaufen. Wenn sie's jetzt anders hinstellen, ist das Lüge!«

»Fotos?«, wiederholte Dr. Ragnarson. »Warum wolltest du ihnen denn Fotos abkaufen, Sam?«

Der junge Mann wurde rot. »Ich – ich wollte die anderen damit überraschen. Sie sollten die Bilder als Andenken bekommen.« Ohne sein zottiges Wikingerkostüm mit dem gehörnten Helm und dem falschen Bart sah Sam Ragnarson viel jünger und längst nicht mehr so riesenhaft aus.

»Wiescho schollten die Jungen lügen?«, murmelte der Schulleiter mühsam.

»Die behaupten glatt, ich hätte sie angeblafft und zu raufen angefangen!«, fuhr Sam auf. »Ich hab denen aber überhaupt nichts getan, Onkel Karl. Ich wollte ihnen wirklich nur für all die anderen diese Fotos abkaufen.« Dazu grinste er schüchtern, als wolle er seinen Onkel für sich einnehmen.

»Na, wenn du überhaupt nichts getan hast«, sagte Dr. Ragnarson mit Nachdruck, »wie kommst du dann darauf, dass sie sich über dich zu beklagen hätten?«

Sam wurde wieder rot. »Ich... na ja... man weiß ja, wie solche Schlitzohren das drehen.«

Dr. Ragnarson seufzte. »Du warst noch nie ein geschickter Lügner, Sam. Diese Jungen haben tatsächlich nichts gegen dich vorgebracht. Doch leider scheint mir, dass du dich mit deinen Einwänden selbst beschuldigst.«

Mürrisch starrte Sam Ragnarson die drei Jungen an.

»Da gehörte esch schisch aber, dasch du disch bei den Jungen ensch-sch...«, mühte sich Karl Ragnarson trotz taub gewordener Zunge und Lippen heroisch ab.

Dr. Ragnarson griff energisch nach seinem Bohrer. »Es ist sicher besser, wenn du jetzt nicht sprichst, Karl. Mach den Mund auf, wir wollen anfangen.«

»Auf eine Entschuldigung wird dankend verzichtet, Sir«, sagte Justus sarkastisch. »Im Übrigen ist er möglicherweise noch weit übler als ein Lügner. Gestern wurden uns die Fotos gestohlen. Von zwei Männern in einem alten weißen Pick-up. Sie drängten Bob, der mit dem Fahrrad unterwegs war, von der Straße ab und rissen sich die Negative unter den Nagel.«

»Ich hab nichts gestohlen!«, wehrte sich Sam Ragnarson entrüstet.

»Sie sind aber derjenige, dem diese Fotos so wichtig waren!«, stellte Bob fest.

»Und Sie hatten es mächtig eilig«, setzte Justus hinzu.

Sam war außer sich. »Alles gelogen!«

Dr. Ragnarson sah die Jungen bekümmert an. Ebenso bekümmert blickte der Patient auf den Bohrer in der Hand seines Bruders. Der Zahnarzt wandte sich an seinen Sohn. »Stimmt das wirklich, Sam? Es sieht doch ganz so aus, als wolltest du diese Bilder haben.«

»Ich weiß ja nicht mal, wo die Burschen wohnen!«

Dazu meinte Peter: »Er hätte uns aber vorgestern Abend nachfahren können.«

»Ich sagte ihm, die Fotos seien für die Zeitung meines Vaters bestimmt«, erklärte Bob. »Und da hörte er, wie mein Vater heißt. Er hätte leicht herausfinden können, wo wir wohnen. Gestern früh lauerten mir die Diebe vor unserem Haus auf.«

Dr. Ragnarson war nun ernstlich besorgt. Der Schulleiter ließ sich im Behandlungssessel immer weiter nach unten rutschen, während er wie hypnotisiert auf die Hand des Arztes mit dem Bohrer starrte.

»Ich hab jedenfalls nichts gestohlen«, wiederholte Sam. »Wann ist es denn passiert?«

Die Jungen berichteten den Hergang.

Sam lachte triumphierend. »Da war ich ja draußen auf der Insel! Sag's ihnen, Dad!«

Dr. Ragnarson nickte. »Ja, gestern war Sam bei unserer Gruppe auf der Insel. Wir kamen gemeinsam hin, gegen elf am Vormittag, das weiß ich noch.«

Peter gab noch nicht auf. »Vielleicht hat er zwei von seinen Kumpels dazu angestiftet!«

»Also hört mal, ihr drei, das geht nun doch zu weit«, wandte Dr. Ragnarson ein. Seine Hand mit dem Bohrer hielt über dem Mund des Patienten in der Bewegung inne.

»Scho wie esch auschschieht, hat mein Neffe mit der Schache nisch schu tun«, meldete sich auch Karl Ragnarson zu Wort. »Wird mein Schahn jetsch endlisch behandelt oder nischt?«

»Sie haben vermutlich recht, Sir«, sagte Justus ganz ruhig, ohne ersichtliche Gemütsbewegung. »Es tut mir Leid, dass wir Sie bei Ihrer Zahnbehandlung aufgehalten haben. Kommt, Bob und Peter, wir müssen unseren Dieb wohl woanders suchen.«

Dr. Ragnarson schaltete den Bohrer ein.

Justus drängte Bob und Peter aus dem Raum und rasch verließen die drei ??? die Zahnarztpraxis.

Unten auf der Straße wandte sich Bob an den Ersten Detektiv. »Warum hast du denn so plötzlich nachgegeben, Justus?«

»Glaubst du wirklich, dass Sam mit dem Diebstahl unserer Fotos nichts zu tun hat?«, wollte Peter wissen.

»Das ist möglich, Peter«, gab Justus zu, »aber voll überzeugt bin ich noch nicht. Zunächst müssen wir mal ergründen, warum Sam unsere Fotos so dringend haben wollte. Und wenn Sam tatsächlich die Negative an sich gebracht hat, dann muss auf den Bildern irgendetwas sein, das er vor anderen geheim halten will.« Der Erste Detektiv sah auf die Uhr.

»Es ist kurz nach vier. Ich schlage vor, dass wir zu Bob gehen – sein Vater kann jeden Augenblick nach Hause kommen, und er wollte doch die Reproduktionen für uns mitbringen.«

Peter stieg schon aufs Fahrrad. »Dann los! Je eher wir diesen Sam Ragnarson überführen, desto besser.«

Die drei Jungen radelten die ruhige Straße entlang, Peter voran, hinter ihm Justus, und Bob bildete das Schlusslicht.

Zügig fuhren sie durch die Vorstadt zu der Gegend, in der Bobs Haus lag.

»Achtung!«, rief Bob.

Sie blickten alle nach hinten. Auf einem Motorrad kam gerade Sam Ragnarson aus einer Querstraße herangefahren. Er starrte die drei Radfahrer wütend an.

»Euch Lumpen werd ich beweisen, dass man sich nicht ungestraft mit mir anlegt!«, schrie er wütend.

Die maskierten Männer

Die drei Jungen traten in die Pedale, was das Zeug hielt, aber das Motorrad brauste heran, scherte kurz aus und streifte Bob, sodass er samt seinem Fahrrad unsanft auf dem Rasen vor einem Haus landete.

»Nicht schon wieder!«, schrie Bob.

»Nummer eins!«, rief Sam Ragnarson wild entschlossen.

Er raste an Justus und Peter vorbei, riss seine Maschine herum und brauste direkt auf die beiden zu. Justus lenkte rasch nach rechts in eine Gruppe hoher Eukalyptusbüsche und stürzte schließlich im dichten, staubigen Gestrüpp vom Fahrrad. »Nummer zwei!«, stieß Sam triumphierend hervor.

Außer sich vor Empörung, hielt Peter an, um sich Sam, der gerade mit aufheulendem Motor wieder zurücksetzen wollte, in den Weg zu stellen. Der Zweite Detektiv hob einen abgebrochenen Eukalyptusast auf und erwartete rittlings im Sattel, ein Bein auf dem Boden, Sams Angriff. In einigem Abstand vor ihm stand der wütende Motorradfahrer und musterte den dicken Ast und Peters zu allem entschlossenes Gesicht.

»He, Kleiner, was willste denn damit?«, schrie Sam herüber.

»Wirst schon sehen«, rief Peter zurück.

Sam lachte. »Na, zwei von drei ist nicht schlecht. Und ab sofort bleibt ihr schön brav zu Hause und spielt mit euren Bauklötzen, ist das klar? Sonst könnt ihr euch auf was gefasst machen!«

Mit dieser letzten Drohung wendete Sam sein Motorrad und brauste in der Richtung, aus der er gekommen war, wieder davon. Peter ließ den Ast fallen und lief zu seinen Freunden. Bob kam über den Rasen angehinkt und Justus wischte Blätter und Staub von seiner Kleidung und seinem Fahrrad.

»Ganz schön mutig, Peter«, keuchte Justus zwischen zwei Niesanfällen – kein Wunder bei all dem Staub und dem intensiven, scharfen Geruch der Eukalyptusblätter.

»Ich hab einfach rot gesehen«, erklärte Peter. »Und sonst – alles in Ordnung bei euch?«

»Mein Vorderrad ist verbogen, aber ich kann schon noch fahren. Das repariere ich zu Hause«, sagte Bob. »Diese Woche bin ich als Radfahrer anscheinend vom Pech verfolgt.«

»Ich werde noch eine Zeit lang nach Eukalyptus riechen«, bemerkte Justus, »aber passiert ist mir nichts. Hört mal, wir fahren jetzt zu Bob und … uff!«

Zum zweiten Mal stürzte der Erste Detektiv längelang in das Eukalyptusgestrüpp! Er hatte einen heftigen Schlag in den Rücken bekommen.

»Hinlegen!«, rief Peter Bob zu, und beide Jungen gingen in Deckung. »Das war schon wieder Sam!«, schrie Bob.

Justus ruderte keuchend und pustend im Dickicht der langen, staubigen Blätter, um wieder auf die Beine zu kommen. Eine gewisse Ähnlichkeit mit einem gestrandeten Wal war ihm in dieser Lage nicht abzusprechen. Peter musste sich das Lachen verbeißen, als er den Kopf hob und sich auf der Straße nach dem Angreifer umsah. Doch dann stand er auf und sagte ziemlich verdutzt: »Das war ja nur die Zeitung!«

Alle drei sahen noch, wie der junge Austräger auf der Straße weiterradelte, mit einem Grinsen und einem bedauernden Schulterzucken. Beim gewohnten schwungvollen Abwerfen seiner Zeitungen in die Vorgärten hatte er die Jungen zu spät gesehen. Bob lief zu dem Papierpaket hin.

»Das ist die Zeitung aus Dads Verlag! Mal sehen, ob die Fotos schon drin sind!«

Er hob die gefaltete, dicke Wochenendausgabe auf, die Justus als Wurfgeschoss zu Fall gebracht hatte, breitete sie auf dem Gehweg aus und blätterte hastig die Seiten um. Justus und Peter traten hinzu.

»Da ist es!«, rief Bob.

Sie beugten sich über den Bildbericht zu dem Familientreffen der Ragnarsons und dem Kampfspiel auf der Felseninsel. Der Text gab für die Jungen ja nichts Neues mehr her; dafür betrachteten sie aber umso aufmerksamer die sechs Bilder, die den Artikel illustrierten.

Sie nahmen die Fotos der als Wikinger und Chumash-Indianer verkleideten Ragnarsons so gründlich aufs Korn, als gälte es, nach dem gestohlenen Gold zu suchen. Doch schließlich schüttelte Bob den Kopf.

»Ich kann hier nichts Verdächtiges sehen. Nur diesen verrückten Verein beim Rumrennen und Blödeln.«

»Stimmt«, bestätigte Peter. »Es geht Sam doch nicht etwa um die Möwen und den dicken Seehund da links auf dem Bild? Komisch, ich selber kann mich gar nicht erinnern, dass da ein Seehund im Bild war.«

»Die Kamera fängt oft Objekte ein, die einem beim Fotografieren gar nicht auffallen. Man konzentriert sich ganz auf ein bestimmtes Motiv und übersieht dabei Dinge am Rand des Sucherbildes. Aber der Kamera entgeht nichts«, dozierte Justus, der Experte. Dann schloss er kleinlaut: »Nur kann ich hier auch nichts entdecken. Nichts als die Ragnarsons und die Insel und jede Menge Himmel und Meer.«

»Immerhin«, stellte Bob fest, »sind bei dem Artikel nur sechs Fotos abgedruckt. Ich machte aber achtundvierzig, folglich ist das, worauf es Sam Ragnarson ankommt, auf einem der übrigen zu sehen. Fahren wir doch zu mir, dann können wir alle Bilder noch einmal genau untersuchen, sobald mein Vater zurück ist.«

Bobs schlingerndes Vorderrad und Justus' Niesen – er hatte ja noch immer Staub und Eukalyptusgeruch in den Kleidern – wirkten sich hemmend auf eine zügige Fahrt zu Bob aus. Unterwegs hielten die drei ??? immer wieder Ausschau nach Sam Ragnarson, aber der böse Feind tauchte nicht wieder auf. Endlich bogen sie in die Straße ein, wo die Familie Andrews wohnte. Da hörten sie weiter vorn eine laute, aufgebrachte Stimme:

»Was wollen Sie denn von mir? Gehen Sie doch weg!«

»Das ist mein Dad!«, rief Bob.

In der Einfahrt zu seinem Haus stand Mr Andrews bei seinem Wagen und musste sich offenbar gegen zwei maskierte Männer wehren! Er hatte einen großen gelben Umschlag mit der Aufschrift FOTOLABOR in der Hand.

»Schnell hin!«, schrie Peter. »Die sind schon wieder hinter den Fotos her!«

Der Zweite Detektiv sprang vom Rad, ließ es fallen und lief zu Mr Andrews und den beiden Angreifern hin, die mit Skimützen maskiert waren. Bob kam dicht hinterher und Justus hielt in einigem Abstand wacker mit. Einer der maskierten Männer hörte die Jungen kommen und warf einen Blick über die Schulter.

»Hilfe!«, brüllte Peter beim Rennen. »Hilfe! Ein Überfall!«

»Hilfe!«, schrie auch Bob.

Mr Andrews hörte die Jungen und war für einen Augenblick abgelenkt. Da riss ihm einer der Maskierten den Umschlag mit den Fotos aus der Hand, und die beiden Männer hasteten über die Fahrbahn zu einem zerbeulten weißen Pick-up, der mit laufendem Motor wartete. Peter war ebenso nahe bei dem Pick-up wie die Angreifer. Er schlug einen Haken und stürzte sich mit einem Hechtsprung auf den Mann mit dem Umschlag. Bob tat es ihm gleich und landete auf den beiden Kämpfenden.

»Hilfe! Hilfe!«, schrie Justus.

An der ruhigen Straße öffneten sich überall Fenster und Türen. Die Nachbarn liefen aus ihren Häusern. Schnell schüttelten die maskierten Männer Peter und Bob ab, sprangen auf und liefen mit großen Sätzen zu dem Pick-up. Ehe jemand eingreifen konnte, brauste der Wagen mit kreischenden Reifen davon, schlitterte um die nächste Ecke und war verschwunden.

»Die Fotos!«, keuchte Justus.

Peter hielt triumphierend den großen gelben Umschlag in die Höhe. »Diesmal sind sie nicht drangekommen!«

Bob klopfte ihm auf die Schulter. »Gut gemacht, Peter!« Dann rief er: »Dad, ist alles in Ordnung?«, und lief zu seinem Vater hin.

»Nichts passiert«, gab Mr Andrews zurück. »Aber was zum Kuckuck soll der ganze Zirkus?«

»Das wollte ich dir ja gestern schon erklären«, sagte Bob mit einem Seufzer. »Die wollen unbedingt diese Fotos, die ich bei Ragnarson Rock machte.«

Mr Andrews nickte reuevoll. »Tut mir Leid, dass ich dir nicht gleich geglaubt habe, Bob.«

»Ach, lass mal, Dad. Aber was spielte sich denn da eigentlich ab?« Mr Andrews versuchte, die Ereignisse der letzten halben Stunde zu rekonstruieren.

»Als ich nach der Arbeit zum Haus gefahren kam, sah ich die alte Klapperkiste drüben stehen. Ich dachte mir nichts dabei. Ich trug die Reproduktionen der Fotos bei mir, die ich euch versprochen hatte. Mit den Bildern im Umschlag stieg ich aus dem Wagen und da wurde ich von diesen Rowdys überfallen. Übrigens, hat sich einer von euch das Kennzeichen gemerkt?«, fragte Mr Andrews.

»Oh, verflixt – nein, Dad«, musste Bob zugeben.

»Das Nummernschild war ganz verdreckt«, berichtete Peter, »und auch sonst konnte ich nicht viel von den beiden sehen. Aber eines fiel mir auf: Bei einem der beiden Burschen war auf dem linken Arm eine Seejungfrau tätowiert!«

»Ein brauchbares Merkmal, Peter«, meinte Justus.

Die Jungen fragten alle Nachbarn, ob jemand das Autokennzeichen notiert oder an den beiden maskierten Männern etwas Auffälliges bemerkt hatte. Aber niemand wusste etwas zu berichten, außer dass der eine größer als der andere gewesen war und dass sie alte Jeans, Arbeitshemden und schwere Stiefel getragen hatten. Durch die Skimasken waren die Gesichter völlig verhüllt, sodass niemand eine genauere Beschreibung geben konnte.

»Und sie sprachen mich auch gar nicht an«, erklärte Mr Andrews noch. »Sie sprangen nur aus dem Pick-up und versuchten, mir den Umschlag zu entreißen. Sie waren recht kräftig gebaut, aber sonst konnte ich nichts erkennen.«

Die Nachbarn zogen sich allmählich wieder zurück und die Jungen gingen ihre Fahrräder holen und folgten dann Mr Andrews ins Haus. Mrs Andrews untersuchte alle auf Schnitt- oder Schürfwunden hin, fand aber nur einen kleinen Kratzer an einem von Peters Armen. Diesen behandelte sie mit einem antiseptischen Mittel; mehr gab es nicht zu tun.

»Nun sehen wir uns aber die Bilder an«, drängte Justus.

Bob und Peter öffneten den Umschlag und legten die achtundvierzig Reproduktionen der Fotos im Wohnzimmer auf dem Sofatisch und auf Stühlen aus.

Da kam Mr Andrews herein. »Ich habe die Polizei angerufen«, sagte er, »und sie werden jemanden vorbeischicken. Wenn der Beamte die Fotos nicht unbedingt sehen muss, dann räumt sie lieber weg und sucht euch einen anderen Platz.«

»Oh, natürlich«, meinte Justus. »Wir nehmen sie in unsere Zentrale mit.«

Die Jungen sammelten die Bilder wieder ein und liefen zu ihren Fahrrädern hinaus. Bob hatte gar nicht mehr an das verbogene Vorderrad gedacht, aber zum Glück fand sich in der Garage ein Ersatzrad. Während er es montierte, fiel ihm und Peter auf, dass Justus ziemlich geistesabwesend dreinsah.

»Was passt dir denn nicht, Justus?«, fragte Peter.

»Irgendetwas stimmt hier nicht«, erwiderte der Anführer der drei ???. »Diesen beiden maskierten Männern musste klar geworden sein, dass sie uns mit den achtundvierzig Negativen eben nicht das gesamte Material gestohlen hatten – und das konnten sie nur aus der am Nachmittag erschienenen Zeitung erfahren haben. Aber Sam Ragnarson war gleichzeitig mit uns in der Praxis seines Vaters und hinterher machte er Jagd auf uns. Wie hätte er da die Zeitung durchsehen und seine Kumpane zu Bobs Haus schicken sollen, noch ehe wir selber hierher kamen?«

»Das hätte er zeitlich nicht schaffen können«, sagte Bob, während er die letzten Schrauben anzog. »Die Zeitung, die da gerade ausgefahren wurde, kam frisch aus der Druckerei. Nach seinem Drohmanöver mit dem Motorrad hätte er umgehend seine Kumpels verständigen und auf meinen Vater ansetzen müssen. Dazu hätte aber die Zeit niemals gereicht.«

»Ja, und was bedeutet das nun, Justus?«, fragte Peter.

»Das bedeutet entweder, dass Sam die Zeitung früher als die Leser zu Gesicht bekam – oder dass noch jemand anderes auf diese Fotos scharf ist!«

»Das wird ja immer schöner«, sagte Bob. »Warum sollten die sonst noch jemandem wichtig sein? Ich hab doch nur diese Zusammenkunft auf Ragnarson Rock fotografiert.«

»Eben, Bob – was steckt dahinter?« Justus runzelte nachdenklich die Stirn. Dann gab er sich einen Ruck und fuhr entschlossen fort: »Aber die Lösung verbirgt sich tatsächlich in diesen Fotos. Nur müssen wir erst draufkommen.«

Ja, was für ein Objekt hatte denn nun Bobs Kamera eingefangen? Oder geht es gar um mehrere zufällig fotografierte Motive? Schade, dass meine Leser diese vertrackten Fotos nicht ebenfalls betrachten können.

Bob war mit dem Radwechsel fertig und schob sein Fahrrad aus der Garage. »Dann wollen wir mal los und uns die Bilder genau ansehen!« Ohne weitere Zwischenfälle fuhren sie schnell zum Schrottplatz. Als sie in den Hof einbogen und ihrer Freiluftwerkstatt zustrebten, kam Tante Mathilda aus der Bürobaracke und rief ihnen zu: »Da seid ihr ja, ihr Herumtreiber! Jemand möchte euch sprechen. Diesmal geht's euch an den Kragen!«

Schreck im Dunkeln

Karl Ragnarson, ihr Schulleiter, kam hinter Tante Mathilda aus dem Büro. »Was habt ihr jetzt wieder ausgefressen, dass euer Schuldirektor euch bis hierher verfolgen muss?«, fragte Tante Mathilda. Die Worte klangen streng, aber sie zwinkerte dazu.

»Wenn Sie gestatten, Mrs Jonas«, sagte Mr Ragnarson, »würde ich gern ohne Zeugen mit den Jungen reden.«

»Aber selbstverständlich«, entgegnete Tante Mathilda mit verständnisinnigem Lächeln. »Das können Sie in der Werkstatt dort drüben tun, wo sie sich so gern verschanzen. Und sollten die Burschen etwas verbrochen haben, dann fallen Sie bloß nicht auf ihre Ausreden herein!«

Sie lachte und ging zu ihrem Büro zurück. Sorgfältig schloss sie die Tür hinter sich. Die Jungen führten Karl Ragnarson zu der Freiluftwerkstatt. Dort setzte sich der Schulleiter auf einen alten Drehstuhl aus dem Trödellager und sah sich interessiert um. Sein Lächeln wirkte noch ein wenig schief nach der Zahnbehandlung am Nachmittag.

»Entschuldigt die Geheimniskrämerei, aber ich wollte nicht, dass jemand den Grund meines Besuchs erfährt, auch nicht deine Tante, Justus.«

»Wetten, dass es um Sam geht, Mr Ragnarson?«, rief Peter etwas vorschnell.

»Ich möchte hoffen, dass es dabei nicht um Sam geht«, entgegnete Mr Ragnarson. »Aber ich muss sagen, dass ich nach unserer Unterhaltung in der Praxis meines Bruders doch etwas betroffen bin, denn draußen auf der Insel sind inzwischen tatsächlich eigenartige Dinge vorgefallen.«

»Was war denn da so eigenartig?«, erkundigte sich Justus interessiert.

»Nun, erst hörten wir vorgestern und gestern Nacht seltsame Laute, wie das Geheul eines Tieres, und irres Gelächter – aber keiner will es gewesen sein. Und dann tauchten buchstäblich aus dem Nichts Geistergestalten und gespenstisches Licht auf.«

»Wirklich... Geister, Mr Ragnarson?«, fragte Peter voll Unbehagen.

»Eine Gestalt glich einem Ertrunkenen und war über und über mit Tang behängt und die andere wirkte wie ein alter Schiffskapitän in einer langen Uniformjacke mit Messing –«

»Mit Messingknöpfen bis zu den Knien hinunter, dazu eine enge Hose und eine goldbetresste Schirmmütze!«, setzte Justus die Beschreibung fort. »Und ein Messingteleskop, stimmt's?«

»Ja, ganz genau!« Karl Ragnarson sah den Ersten Detektiv verdutzt an. »Woher weißt du denn das alles, Justus?«

»Diesen vorgeblichen Geist haben wir selbst schon gesehen, Sir«, erklärte Justus, und dann berichtete er dem Schulleiter von dem Mann in Sam Ragnarsons Haus. »Ist das alles, was Sie an außergewöhnlichen Vorfällen bemerkt haben?«

Mr Ragnarson schüttelte den Kopf. »Eben nicht. Es sind auch Sachen abhanden gekommen. Eine Stablampe, ein Jagdmesser, einige Decken, eine Daunenjacke, ein Campingkocher und eine ganze Menge Lebensmittel, auch Bierdosen. Freilich muss nicht unbedingt ein Zusammenhang zwischen den unheimlichen Lauten und Erscheinungen und den verschwundenen Sachen bestehen, aber es könnte immerhin sein.«

»Sie halten es also für möglich, dass Sam all das Zeug gestohlen hat?«, fragte Bob ahnungsvoll.

»Gestohlen, um es zu Geld zu machen.« Karl Ragnarson nickte. »Als ihr bei Ingmar wart, kam mir der Gedanke, dass ihr vielleicht mit der Kamera zufällig Sam beim Klauen erwischt habt, als wir uns alle für die Fotos in Positur stellten!«

Justus fragte: »Und warum erzählen Sie uns das alles eigentlich, Sir?«

»Die seltsamen Laute und die geisterhaften Erscheinungen machen den Kindern, aber auch den Erwachsenen allmählich Angst. Viele aus unserer Gruppe lehnen es schon ab, auf der Insel zu übernachten, wie wir alle das sonst taten. Der Spaß an der Sache ist uns für die ganze Woche vergangen. Wenn das so weitergeht, kommt ein nächstes Treffen womöglich gar nicht mehr zustande. Und noch was: Wenn Sam dieser Langfinger ist, könnt ihr Jungen da vielleicht einen Riegel vorschieben, ehe er zu unverschämt wird oder eine folgenschwere Dummheit begeht.«

Er sah die drei Jungen der Reihe nach an und lächelte kaum merklich. »Und nicht dass ich auch nur einen Augenblick an die Sache mit der Projektarbeit für die Schule geglaubt habe, klar? Mir ist genau bekannt, dass Miss Hanson, eure Geschichtslehrerin, ihren Schülern über die Sommerferien keine derartige Aufgabe gestellt hat.«

Da fühlten sich die drei ??? doch recht unbehaglich.

»Im Übrigen ist mir zu Ohren gekommen«, fuhr der Rektor

fort, »dass ihr euch erfolgreich als Detektive betätigt. Hauptkommissar Reynolds äußerte sich sehr anerkennend über euer Talent beim Aufklären von Fällen, die seinen eigenen Leuten Kopfzerbrechen machten. Da konnte ich mir leicht ausrechnen, dass ihr über Sam Ermittlungen anstellt, und so kam ich hierher.«

»Sie haben Recht, Sir«, bestätigte Justus. »Hier ist unsere Karte.« Er zog eine Visitenkarte aus der Brusttasche und gab sie Mr Ragnarson. Der gedruckte Text lautete:

Die drei Detektive
???
Wir übernehmen jeden Fall

Erster Detektiv	*Justus Jonas*
Zweiter Detektiv	*Peter Shaw*
Recherchen und Archiv	*Bob Andrews*

Der Rektor nickte befriedigt. »Ich glaube, euch kann ich ganz gut gebrauchen. Um es klar zu sagen: Ich beauftrage euch damit, die seltsamen Vorfälle auf Ragnarson Rock zu untersuchen. Vielleicht wäre ein kleiner Abschlag angebracht – damit wir richtige Vertragspartner sind«, setzte er bedeutungsvoll hinzu.

»Spitze!«, rief Peter. »Sie meinen Bares?«

»Vielen Dank, aber wir nehmen kein Honorar«, unterbrach ihn Justus. Prompt erntete er finstere Blicke von Bob und Peter. »Wegen einer für uns ungünstigen gesetzlichen Altersbeschränkung dürfen wir uns nicht als berufsmäßige Detektive verdingen«, erläuterte er, »aber wir bieten unsere Dienste mit Vergnügen unentgeltlich an. Ich möchte gleich vorschlagen, dass wir uns die reproduzierten Fotos hier in der Werkstatt gemeinsam ansehen. Vielleicht fällt Ihnen dabei etwas auf, Mr Ragnarson, das uns sonst entgehen würde.«

Der Rektor half beim Auslegen aller achtundvierzig Bilder auf Justus' Werkbank. Dann betrachteten sie jede einzelne Aufnahme ganz genau, doch es war nichts Verdächtiges zu finden. »Wie sollen wir überhaupt erkennen, welcher von diesen Wikingern Sam ist?«, fragte Peter verwirrt. »Für mich sehen die alle ziemlich gleich aus.«

Karl Ragnarson konnte helfen. »Er ist der Einzige, dessen Helm einen Nasenschild hat. Hier, das ist Sam.«

Es stellte sich heraus, dass bei sechzehn Aufnahmen Sam Ragnarson im Bild war. Die meisten zeigten ihn beim Herumalbern mit den anderen, beim Kampf gegen die Chumash auf dem Felsen, beim Essenholen, beim Grimassenschneiden vor der Kamera – alles im Rahmen des Familientreffens. Zwei Bilder unterschieden sich allerdings von den übrigen.

»Die knipste ich gleich hintereinander«, erinnerte sich Bob. Die beiden Aufnahmen zeigten Sam allein hinter der Gruppe der anderen, die beim Picknick saßen. Auf dem ersten Bild kauerte er gebückt über etwas, das nicht zu erkennen war. Das zweite zeigte ihn im Augenblick des Aufschauens, unliebsam überrascht, eine Hand angehoben, als halte er irgendetwas darin.

»Was macht er da eigentlich?«, fragte Bob.

»Eines steht jedenfalls fest«, bemerkte Peter, »nämlich dass er gerade Bob und die auf ihn gerichtete Kamera entdeckt hat.«

»Ja«, bestätigte Justus, »man sieht deutlich, dass er soeben erkannt hat, wie er fotografiert wird. Die Frage ist nur: Was machte er da, allein hinter den anderen und am Boden kauernd?«

»Wollte er vielleicht etwas verstecken?«, meinte Mr Ragnarson.

»Oder seine Diebesbeute vergraben?«, rätselte Peter.

»Oder etwas aufheben, das er gefunden hatte?«, war Bobs Vermutung.

 Verstecken, vergraben oder aufheben – was ist eure Vermutung? Doch ihr müsst euch jetzt noch nicht entscheiden. Fest steht nur, dass wir Sam im Blick behalten müssen.

Justus nickte. »All das könnte zutreffen. Ich finde, wir sollten schnellstens selbst zu der Insel hinausfahren. Dort können wir die vorgeblichen Geister und die Geräusche untersuchen, und vielleicht finden wir auch heraus, warum dort immer wieder etwas verschwindet und weshalb unsere Fotos für irgendjemanden so wichtig sind.«

»Das ist kein Problem, Justus«, sagte Karl Ragnarson. »Heute Abend wollen wir alle wieder draußen sein, jedenfalls die, die es noch nicht mit der Angst zu tun bekommen haben.«

»Aber da sieht uns doch Sam, Justus?«, wandte Peter ein. »Wenn er tatsächlich der Störenfried ist und uns zu Gesicht bekommt, hält er sich mit Tricks heute eher zurück.«

»Da weiß ich Rat«, erklärte Mr Ragnarson. »Die meisten von uns tragen auf der Insel ihr Wikinger- oder Indianerkostüm, und es sind auch immer ein paar Leute mit dabei, die nicht jeder kennt. Ich werde euch Kostüme besorgen und bei den anderen als Freunde von mir ausgeben. Ihr könnt mit uns zu Abend essen und auf der Insel übernachten.«

»Schön, abgemacht«, sagte Justus. »Wir sagen zu Hause Bescheid, dass wir über Nacht auf der Insel bleiben werden, und packen unsere Walkie-Talkies und Taschenlampen und Schlafsäcke zusammen. Und dann könnten wir uns unten bei der Bootsanlegestelle treffen – wie wäre es in einer Stunde?«

»Gut, bis dahin habe ich die Kostüme besorgt. Aber macht euch auf eine turbulente Nacht gefasst!«

Die Gestalt im Nebel

Das Motorboot durchpflügte das dunkle Wasser der kleinen Bucht. Ein gewaltiges Lagerfeuer und heller Mondschein erleuchteten das sandige Ufer und die Felsen der Insel. Die Menschen im Umkreis des lodernden Feuers wirkten wie fantastische Schattengestalten, die im Dunkeln zu schweben und zu tanzen schienen. Der Feuerschein wies Karl Ragnarson und den drei ??? den Weg zur Anlegestelle. Sie sprangen an Land und zogen das Boot auf den Strand.

»Bist du's, Karl?«, schallte Dr. Ingmar Ragnarsons dröhnende Stimme aus der bereits versammelten Gruppe herüber.

»Ja, Ingmar. Ich habe Gäste mitgebracht.«

»Sehr schön! Für Wikinger und Indianer gibt es immer noch Platz bei uns!«, sagte der Zahnarzt. Er hatte sich in einen prächtigen Wikinger verwandelt.

Die Jungen und der Schulleiter gingen auf den Lichtkreis des Feuers zu. Karl Ragnarson war mit Wams und Hose aus Ziegenleder angetan und trug den Perlenschmuck und die in dunklen Farben gehaltene Kriegsbemalung eines Chumash-Kämpfers. Bob und Peter hatten sich mit Fellen, Helmen und Bärten als Wikinger verkleidet. Sie trugen Schilde und waren bewaffnet – Bob mit einem langen Beidhänder und Peter mit einer Wurfaxt. Justus bildete die Nachhut in dem weiten, ledernen Umhang und der bemalten Holzmaske eines Schamanen der Chumash. Sehr glücklich war der Erste Detektiv nicht mit seinem Kostüm. »Ich komme mir vor«, brummelte er verdrießlich, »wie ein wandelnder Berg.«

»Es gab eben kein Wikingerkostüm, das dir passte, Justus.«
Peter grinste. »Aber wenn du dich künftig mit den Schokoladekeksen etwas zurückhältst...«

»Du siehst äußerst beeindruckend aus, Justus«, fand Karl Ragnarson. »Der Schamane war bei den Chumash wie bei allen Indianerstämmen der höchste Würdenträger.«

»Du wolltest doch schon immer mal ein Zauberer sein, Justus«, sagte Bob noch. Verstohlen grinste auch er, als Justus in dem wallenden Umhang und der grotesken Maske schwerfällig hinter ihnen herstapfte.

»Soll ich mal zaubern und euch zwei Wikingerknaben verschwinden lassen?«, drohte der Erste Detektiv. »Ihr seht in euren mottenzerfressenen Fummeln und den Blecheimern auf dem Kopf auch nicht viel besser aus.«

Da sahen Bob und Peter sich gegenseitig an und brachen in Gelächter aus. Die beiden Ragnarsons lachten auch und selbst Justus fing hinter seiner unförmigen Holzmaske das Kichern an. Dann hatten sie das prasselnde Feuer erreicht, und Dr. Ragnarson stellte die drei Neuen als Freunde seines Bruders Karl vor, die heute mit dabei sein wollten. Die beim Feuer Sitzenden – etwa fünfzehn Leute – klatschten Beifall und reichten den Ankömmlingen Pappteller mit gegrillten Steaks, gerösteten Maiskolben, dicken Bohnen und Salat.

»Haltet nach Sam Ausschau«, flüsterte Bob.

»Und nach allem, was bei dem Treiben hier irgendwie auffällig oder verdächtig wirkt«, setzte Justus hinzu. Geschickt beförderte er Fleischhappen und Bohnen durch die klaffende Mundöffnung der hölzernen Maske.

Als sie dann um das Feuer in der Runde saßen, beobachteten die drei ??? unauffällig die Anwesenden. Alle trugen Indianer- oder Wikingerkostüme und ließen es sich schmecken. Das Abendessen war über einer großen Mulde voll glühender Kohlen neben dem lodernden Feuer zubereitet worden. Auf einer

Anhöhe über dem Strand, am Rand des flackerden Lichtkreises der Flammen, war eine Reihe Zelte aufgebaut.

»Hat schon jemand Sam Ragnarson gesehen?«, flüsterte Peter.

»Bis jetzt nicht«, antwortete Bob. »Aber den Besitzer des Eisenwarengeschäfts sehe ich dort drüben.«

George Ragnarson saß auf der anderen Seite des Feuers in normaler Kleidung und aß von einem voll gehäuften Teller.

»Der Einzige, der nicht verkleidet ist«, stellte Justus fest. In der Runde ging es lebhaft und freundschaftlich zu; man unterhielt sich witzig und lachte viel. Manche hatten eine Gitarre oder ein Akkordeon bei sich und bald stimmte jemand ein Lied an. Nun wurde gesungen – alte skandinavische Lieder und amerikanische Folklore. Die Jungen sangen auch, soweit sie den Text kannten, und ansonsten summten sie eben laut und unbeschwert die Melodien mit.

Mitten in dem munteren Singen und Summen flüsterte Bob plötzlich: »Da drüben!«

Justus, Peter und Karl Ragnarson schauten hin. »Ja, das ist Sam«, flüsterte der Rektor zurück.

»Wo der wohl die ganze Zeit gesteckt hat?«, meinte Justus nachdenklich.

»Ich glaube, er kam aus der Richtung, wo die Zelte stehen«, sagte Bob.

Sam war wie bei der Begegnung vor zwei Tagen, als er die Jungen an der Bootsanlegestelle in Rocky Beach angerempelt hatte, im Wikingerkostüm. Nun hatte er sich in den Kreis um das prasselnde Feuer gesetzt und sang allem Anschein nach eifrig mit. Auch nachdem alle mit Essen fertig waren und die Pappteller und das Plastikbesteck in die Abfalleimer am Ufer geworfen hatten, ging es weiter mit Singen und Musizieren. Doch dann wurde die Abendluft merklich kühler und Nebelschwaden trieben von der See herein. Nun fuhren viele der Anwesenden zum Festland zurück, darunter auch George Ragnarson. Die Jungen harrten bei den unermüdlichen Sängern aus und beobachteten Sam Ragnarson.

»Er sitzt nur da und isst und singt«, stellte Peter fest.

»Beim Essen ist er jedenfalls ganz groß«, bemerkte Bob.

»Vielleicht ist euer Verdacht gegen Sam ganz unberechtigt«, meinte Karl Ragnarson. »Es kann ja sein, dass er gar nicht der Störenfried ist oder dass dieser üble Spuk eine ganz andere Ursache hat.«

»Ja, vielleicht steckt jemand anders dahinter«, stimmte Justus zu. »Aber das kann nur jemand hier auf der Insel sein.«

»Was meinen Sie denn mit der... anderen Ursache, Mr Ragnarson?«, fragte Peter.

»Na ja«, sagte Karl Ragnarson, »die unheimlichen Laute und die herumgeisternden Erscheinungen könnten natürlichen Ursprungs sein, optische oder akustische Täuschungen zum Beispiel, und es wäre auch nicht schwer, für die verschwundenen Gegenstände eine ganz normale Erklärung zu finden. Hier geht es ja chaotisch zu und da kann trotz der kurzen Zeit schon mal etliches abhanden kommen.«

Justus schüttelte den Kopf mit der grotesken Holzmaske. »Das wäre aber eine auffällige Häufung von Zufällen. Nein, ich bin davon überzeugt, dass all die Vorfälle planmäßig herbeigeführt wurden. Diesen Zusammenhang und die Strategie, die hinter alledem steckt, müssen wir aufdecken.«

»Justus!«, stieß da Peter hervor. Der Zweite Detektiv starrte über die Flammen hinweg zu der Stelle, an der Sam Ragnarsons Platz gewesen war.

»Weg ist er!«, rief Bob.

Außer den drei ??? und Karl Ragnarson waren nun nur noch vier Leute da und Sam hatte sich abgesetzt! Justus sprang auf, so schnell er es unter der Last seiner Maske schaffte. Er machte ein paar unbeholfene Schritte, denn der unförmige, hinderliche Schamanenumhang hing schwer auf seinen Schultern.

»Los, kommt mit«, forderte er die anderen auf. Seine Stimme klang dumpf, weil die Maske vor seinem Gesicht seitlich verrutscht war. »Nur rückt mir erst mal das verflixte Ding da gerade!«

Bob und Peter brachten die Sache belustigt in Ordnung. Dann verließen die drei Jungen die Runde beim Feuer und schritten in die dünnen Nebelschwaden, die hier und da durch die mondhelle Nacht zogen. An den Reihen der Zelte vorüber liefen sie auf das baumlose Gelände der knapp zwei Kilometer langen Insel.

Weiter vorn, wo der Nebel sich verdichtete, erspähten sie die Gestalt eines Wikingers in schnellem Lauf.

»Das ist er«, flüsterte Peter. »In genau dem Kostüm, das er vor zwei Tagen anhatte.«

Sie folgten der im Nebel verschwimmenden Schattengestalt bis zur Westspitze der Insel, wo der Fels sich wie ein riesenhaftes Tier gespenstisch ins Mondlicht reckte. An diesem Ende von Ragnarson Rock gab es nur den mächtigen Felsen und das dichte Gestrüpp, das an seinem Fuß wucherte.

»Wo geht er jetzt hin?«, fragte Bob.

»Auf alle Fälle hat er es eilig und geht geradewegs auf sein Ziel los«, meinte Justus gespannt.

So rasch und vorsichtig wie nur möglich hasteten sie hinter der vom Nebel umwölkten Gestalt her, jeden Augenblick auf der Hut, falls Sam sich umdrehen sollte. Doch das tat er kein einziges Mal. Schnurstracks lief er immer auf den großen Felsen zu, und dann…

»Jetzt ist er weg!«, rief Peter.

Weiter vorn, wo noch eine Sekunde zuvor Sam Ragnarson mit dem dicken Fellumhang und dem hörnerbewehrten Helm ausgeschritten war, konnten die drei ??? mit einem Mal nichts anderes mehr sehen als die wabernden Nebelfetzen!

Das Geisterschiff

»Urplötzlich vom Erdboden verschwunden!«, rief Bob.

»Das ist ausgeschlossen«, widersprach Justus. Aufmerksam überblickte er das mondbeschienene Gelände mit den darüber hinziehenden Nebelschwaden.

»Ja, aber wo ist er hin, Justus?«, wollte Peter wissen.

»Auf den großen Felsen kann er auf keinen Fall geklettert sein«, stellte Bob fest.

»Vielleicht ist er drübergeflogen«, witzelte Peter.

»Menschen können bekanntlich nicht fliegen, Peter, und auch nicht verschwinden«, erklärte Justus gelassen. »Hier in der Gegend muss es einen Platz geben, an dem er sich zunächst verstecken kann, um sich dann unbemerkt ganz abzusetzen.«

Justus nahm die schwere hölzerne Maske ab und umschritt gebückt in einem kleinen Kreis den Bereich, in dem Sam Ragnarson irgendwo untergetaucht sein musste. Die beiden anderen taten es ihm nach und suchten rechts und links von Justus ebenfalls das Gelände ab. Hin und wieder verhüllte eine Nebelwolke den Mond.

Dann fand Peter das Büschel Fellhaare. »Na, bringt uns das was, Justus?«

Der Zweite Detektiv stand bei einem etwa eineinhalb Meter hohen immergrünen Strauch. Solche Zederzypressen wuchsen vor der nach Osten gerichteten Steilwand des Felsens. Hier standen sie in einer kleinen Reihe. Justus zog eine Taschenlampe unter seinem Umhang hervor und richtete den Lichtstrahl auf den Strauch. Rings um die Stelle, wo das Haarbüschel hing, waren Zweige geknickt, und in geringem Abstand hinter der Gehölzreihe ragte die Felswand in die Höhe. Der Zwischenraum verlief in leichter Kurve nach links. Er sah aus wie ein von der Natur geschaffener Tunnel!

»Das wirkt ganz so, als gehörte es zu einem Wikingerkostüm«, fand Justus beim Untersuchen des Fellstückes. »Ein wenig Stoff hängt noch dran. Sicher wurde der Fetzen aus einem Wikingerumhang herausgerissen. Und es ist gut möglich, dass Sam einfach aus unserem Blickfeld verschwinden konnte – er brauchte nur zwischen zwei Sträuchern durchzuschlüpfen und in dem Gang hier weiterzulaufen.«

Die Jungen drangen in den verborgenen schmalen Raum zwischen der dichten Reihe der Zederzypressen und dem Steilhang des mächtigen Felsens ein. Justus ging voran. Nach Süden hin wich die Felswand zurück und der Weg machte eine Biegung.

In kaum zwanzig Meter Entfernung von der Stelle, wo sie das Haarbüschel gefunden hatten, erweiterten sich die Abstände zwischen den Sträuchern, und dann standen die Jungen wieder im mondhellen freien Gelände mit dem darüber hinziehenden Nebel. Ganz aus der Nähe war die Brandung zu hören.

»Tja, das war nur eine kurze Strecke«, meinte Peter. »Aber für Sam reichte es, um durchzulaufen und hier wieder aufzutauchen, wo wir ihn bei dem abbiegenden Weg am Felsen entlang nicht mehr sehen konnten. So ist er also verschwunden.«

»Aber wohin?« Ratlos sah Peter sich um.

Sie standen auf einem Streifen felsigem, mit Ginster bewachsenem Hochmoor zwischen der Südseite des aufragenden Felsmassivs und dem steinigen Ufer, das steil zur See hin abfiel. Den baumlosen Boden durchzogen schmale, tief eingeschnittene Rinnen.

»Hier gibt es eine Menge Spalten und Mulden«, stellte Bob fest. »Vielleicht hat er sich in einer davon versteckt.«

»Aber warum?«, wandte sich Peter verblüfft an Justus. »Es sah nicht so aus, als hätte er etwas weggetragen, das er beim Lagerplatz gestohlen hatte.«

»Eben, das ist die Frage, Peter.« Justus nickte. »Und er muss hier irgendwo sein. An diesem Ende der Insel kommt er ja nicht weit. Wir müssen einzeln losgehen und systematisch suchen. Seid aber vorsichtig mit euren Taschenlampen. Er darf uns nicht entdecken.«

»Justus sieht das schon richtig«, erklärte Bob. »Hier sitzt er doch sozusagen in der Falle.«

Sie trennten sich und gingen in verschiedenen Richtungen weiter, wie die Polizisten in dem alten Sherlock-Holmes-Film, die das Moor nach dem Hund von Baskerville absuchten. Der Nebel wehte noch immer über die Insel. Stellenweise verdichtete er sich, dann wieder lockerten sich die Schwaden auf, sodass sich der Mond im Wechsel verhangen und strahlend hell zeigte. Die Jungen suchten die Rinnen und Mulden im Gelände ab, bis sie zur Westspitze der Insel kamen, die an einer kleinen, verborgenen Bucht endete. Diese war im Süden durch eine Landzunge und im Norden durch einen Vorsprung des Felsmassivs gegen den offenen Pazifik geschützt.

»Nun ist er uns doch entwischt«, sagte Peter.

»So sieht es unbestreitbar aus«, bestätigte Justus bedrückt.

Die drei Jungen schritten noch die Landzunge ab, doch auch darauf hielt sich niemand versteckt.

»Was machen wir jetzt, Justus?«, fragte Bob mit einem Blick auf die stille, in Nebel gehüllte Bucht.

»Wir gehen zu der Stelle zurück, an der Sam Ragnarson verschwunden ist, und suchen nochmals nach Spuren, die uns vielleicht entgangen sind. Und wenn wir nichts finden«, fuhr der Erste Detektiv in seinem majestätischen Umhang fort, »dann gehen wir zum Feuer zurück und erkundigen uns, ob den Ragnarsons irgendetwas aufgefallen ist.«

Ehe die Jungen kehrtmachten, warfen sie noch einen letzten Blick auf die vom Mond schwach erhellte Landschaft – und plötzlich erstarrten sie.

Unten am Ufer der kleinen Bucht kauerte eine schattenhafte Gestalt und gab mit einer lichtstarken Stablampe Zeichen zur offenen See hinaus!

Die drei Jungen wagten kaum zu atmen. Sie beobachteten, wie der Lichtstrahl gleich einem langen Finger tastend den Nebel durchstreifte. Vom Meer her war Wind aufgekommen, der den Nebel in rascher Folge aufriss und wieder verdichtete. Unablässig wanderte der lange Lichtstreifen suchend über die Einmündung zu der geschützten Bucht hin.

»Da, Justus!« Bob streckte die Hand aus.

Draußen auf See war im hellen Schein der Lampe auf dem dunklen Wasser ein Schiff erschienen. Es war gespenstisch anzusehen, wie es im Nebelgewölk verschwand und wieder auftauchte, wenn eine Windbö den Schleier zerriss. Von dem einzigen Mastbaum hingen schmuddelige Segel in Fetzen herab. Eine graue Schicht schien wie ein Algenbelag über das Deck gebreitet zu sein. Immer wieder trat im Strahl der Lampe der Umriss klar hervor und verschwamm dann wieder – wie ein Geisterschiff.

»W-was ist denn das?«, stammelte Bob.

Noch während die Jungen wie gebannt hinstarrten, löste sich das gespenstische Schiff mit den zerfetzten grauen Segeln und dem algenbewachsenen Deck vor ihren Augen in nichts auf. Erst war es noch klar zu sehen, wie es sich auf einer Welle hob, dann senkte es sich, und mit einem Mal war es verschwunden! Das Licht wurde abgeschaltet.

»Kommt mit, los...« Schon stieg Peter den felsigen Abhang hinunter, um ans Ufer der Bucht zu gelangen.

Da ertönte im Dunkeln ein gedämpfter Laut wie ein Knurren. Und dann drang vom höher gelegenen Ufer der Insel über der Bucht eine drohende Stimme zu den Jungen auf der Landzunge herunter. »Keinen Schritt weiter, ihr Schurken!«

Starr vor Schrecken schauten die drei hinauf.

Dort oben stand die nebelumwallte Gestalt des Kapitän

Coulter von der *Star of Panama* und starrte finster zu ihnen herunter. Einen Augenblick sahen sie ganz deutlich die lange dunkelblaue Jacke mit den Messingknöpfen, die goldbetresste Mütze und die engen Hosen. Der Mann hob den Arm und zeigte mit einem hageren Finger auf die Jungen.

»Diebe! Unverschämte Eindringlinge!«, zischte er.

Plötzlich hatte er ein langes, bedrohliches Entermesser in der knochigen Hand und nun kam er mit schnellem Schritt durch die wirbelnden Nebelfetzen auf sie zu.

»Los, weg von hier!«, schrie Peter.

Sogar Justus ließ sich das nicht zweimal sagen.

 Wo begegneten wir diesem Kapitän Coulter zum ersten Mal? Richtig, in Sams Haus. Wer könnte also mit hoher Wahrscheinlichkeit der talentierte Schauspieler sein? Freilich wirft die Antwort hierauf gleich eine weitere Frage auf. Wer könnte denn nun jener andere Mann sein, der in der Bucht die Lichtzeichen gab?

Sam taucht wieder auf

Die drei ??? auf der vorgelagerten Landzunge liefen wie gehetzt zurück und dann auf der Insel in weitem Bogen um das Felsmassiv herum, um ihrem gespenstischen Verfolger zu entkommen und den Schutz des Lagerfeuers am anderen Ende der Insel wieder zu erreichen.

Unterwegs verlor Peter seinen Helm und Justus seine Maske, nur Bob behielt seinen Wikingerhelm auf dem Kopf. Vor der Feuerstelle kamen ihnen Karl Ragnarson und sein Bruder Ingmar mit verstörten Gesichtern entgegengelaufen.

»Sagt mal, ihr drei...«, rief der Rektor. »Wo habt ihr nur gesteckt? Wir haben euch überall gesucht!«

»Was ist denn passiert?«, forschte Dr. Ragnarson gebieterisch.

»Wir... wir waren Sam... auf der Spur«, keuchte Peter.

»Aber er ist entwischt...« Justus rang mühsam nach Atem. »Als wir einen Augenblick nicht aufpassten... und...«

»Dann sahen wir ein Schiff!«, rief Bob.

»Und einen G-Geist«, stammelte Peter.

»Und einer signalisierte mit Lichtzeichen aufs Meer hinaus«, stieß Justus hervor.

Karl Ragnarson hielt eine Hand in die Höhe. »Immer mit der Ruhe, Jungs. Berichtet von Anfang an, was passiert ist, nachdem ihr vom Feuer weggegangen wart.«

Justus' Atem ging noch immer stoßweise. »Wir merkten, dass Sam aus der Runde verschwunden war, als wir gerade mal nicht hingeschaut hatten, und da liefen wir los und sahen ihn, wie er auf das andere Ende der Insel und den großen Felsen zu rannte.« Unter Keuchen und Pusten erzählte der Erste Detektiv die Geschichte ihres Abenteuers auf dem westlichen Ende der kleinen Insel.

»Also wieder dasselbe Theater!«, rief Karl Ragnarson.

»Nur dieses ominöse Geisterschiff ist neu«, wandte Dr. Ragnarson ein.

»Ja«, bestätigte sein Bruder. »Vermutlich war das *Der fliegende Holländer.*«

»Wer soll denn das sein?«, fragte Peter verdutzt.

»*Der fliegende Holländer*«, erläuterte Justus, nicht wenig stolz auf sein enzyklopädisches Wissen, »ist eine Sagengestalt, Peter. Ein Kapitän, der ein Verbrechen begangen hatte, wurde dazu verdammt, künftig mit seinem Schiff die Meere zu befahren, ohne jemals wieder einen Hafen erreichen zu können, bis eine Frau ihm ihr Leben opfern würde. Der Kom-

ponist Richard Wagner hat den Sagenstoff zu einer Oper ver-
arbeitet.«

»Die Geschichte wurde auch verfilmt«, meldete sich Bob zu
Wort. »Vor langer Zeit habe ich den Film mal gesehen.«

Peter zuckte zusammen. »Dann war es also ein echtes Geisterschiff?«

»Karl hat nur Spaß gemacht, Peter«, klärte ihn Dr. Ragnarson auf. »Aber statt uns mit Späßen und Sagen zu befassen,
sollten wir doch lieber nachforschen, was die Jungen da eigentlich gesehen haben, Karl.«

»Ja, zeigt uns den Weg«, forderte der Schulleiter die Jungen
auf.

»Bob und Peter«, entschied Justus, »ihr geht voraus.«

»Klar«, sagte Peter unentschlossen. »Du zuerst, Bob.«

Bob warf den beiden anderen einen grimmigen Blick zu, doch
tapfer übernahm er die Vorhut.

Der Wind von der See her hatte aufgefrischt und mittlerweile fast alle Nebelschwaden weggeblasen. Im Mondlicht erreichten sie bald die Gegend am Fuß des großen Felsens, in deren Bereich Sam Ragnarson verschwunden war. Bob zeigte den
anderen, wo sie das ausgerissene Fellbüschel gefunden hatten
und wie sie durch den abgeschirmten Gang zwischen den
Zederzypressen und der Felswand auf das baumlose Hoch-
moorgelände dahinter gelangt waren.

»Sam konnte unmöglich an uns vorbei zum Lagerfeuer zu-
rückgegangen sein«, erklärte Justus. »Also liefen wir immer
weiter und suchten all die Spalten und Mulden in der Gegend
ab, aber wir fanden nichts.«

»Bis wir dann noch auf die Landzunge gingen und den
Lichtschein unten bei der Bucht sahen«, sagte Bob, »und das
Schiff draußen auf dem Meer ...«

»Und den Geist von Kapitän Coulter auf der Anhöhe am
Ufer gegenüber!«, ergänzte Peter schaudernd.

»Na schön, ihr drei«, sagte Karl Ragnarson. »Dann geht mal hier weiter, genau wie ihr es zuvor gemacht habt.«

Sie schritten durch die helle Mondnacht. Über die Uferklippen, die im Süden der Insel nicht sehr hoch waren, trieb der Wind den Sprühnebel der Brandung herauf. Als sie die Spitze der Insel erreicht hatten und die kleine verborgene Bucht vor ihnen lag, war dort unten keine Bewegung wahrzunehmen. Der Nebel hatte sich verzogen, die offene See jenseits der Bucht war ruhig und glatt und nirgends war ein Schiff zu sehen.

»Keine Positionslichter, nichts«, stellte Dr. Ragnarson fest, als er angespannt das Meer in der Ferne überblickte. »Dort draußen ist zurzeit kein Schiff, Jungs.«

Vorsichtig stiegen sie den felsigen Hang bis zu dem schmalen Strandstreifen der kleinen Bucht hinunter. Justus blickte sich nach allen Richtungen um.

»Hier ungefähr muss es gewesen sein«, meinte er. »Wir sahen, dass jemand am Boden kauerte und mit einer hellen Stablampe auf die See hinausleuchtete.«

»Da, seht euch das an!« Peter bückte sich und hob eine große Stablampe für sechs Batterien vom Boden auf.

Karl Ragnarson untersuchte das lange Ding. »Das ist tatsächlich die Lampe, die aus einem unserer Zelte abhanden kam. Ja, sie ist mit dem Namen Marcus Ragnarson gekennzeichnet.«

»Also wurde sie wirklich gestohlen!«, rief Bob aufgeregt.

»So scheint es«, äußerte Justus gemessen. »Folglich muss es eine Verbindung zwischen dem Dieb und diesem Schiff draußen auf See geben.«

»Du meinst, der gab Signale, Justus?«, fragte Bob.

»Ja, oder er lotste das Schiff in die Bucht herein«, mutmaßte Justus.

»Und was ist mit eurem Geisterspuk, dem alten Kapitän?«, wandte sich Dr. Ragnarson an die Jungen.

»Den sahen wir da oben auf der Anhöhe über dem Ufer, in

der Nähe des großen Felsens.« Bob zeigte hin. »Wir wissen nicht, ob er mit dem Burschen hier unten etwas zu tun hatte.«

»Aber auf jeden Fall wollte der Geist uns aus der Gegend um die Bucht verscheuchen«, sagte Peter.

Justus nickte. »Damit kannst du Recht haben, Peter. Ob Spukgestalt oder nicht, Kapitän Coulter wollte verhindern, dass wir der Person mit der Stablampe zu nahe kommen. Da wir den höchst geheimnisvollen Kapitän beim ersten Mal in Sam Ragnarsons Haus antrafen, hat es ganz den Anschein, als gäbe es eine Verbindung von ihm zu Sam.«

»Glaubst du, dass der dort unten mit der Lampe Sam war?«, fragte Karl Ragnarson.

»Gut möglich, Sir«, erwiderte Justus.

»Das hieße dann, dass er irgendetwas mit diesem Schiff zu schaffen hat«, setzte Dr. Ragnarson besorgt hinzu. »Und es könnte bedeuten, dass Sam in eine Schmuggelaffäre verwickelt ist, wenn nicht in Schlimmeres.«

»Das muss man leider annehmen, Sir«, bestätigte Justus.

»Was schlägst du vor, wie sollen wir weiter vorgehen?«, fragte ihn Dr. Ragnarson.

Justus überblickte gelassen die mondbeschienene kleine Bucht und sah dann in der mittlerweile ganz klaren Nacht zum höher gelegenen Inselboden hinauf.

»Der Geist jagte uns einen Schrecken ein«, sagte der Erste Detektiv, »aber ich glaube, wir erschreckten ihn ebenso. Ich nehme nicht an, dass sich heute hier noch etwas abspielen wird. Deshalb schlage ich vor, dass wir mit der Suche nach Sam weitermachen, Dr. Ragnarson. Vielleicht kann er uns mehr zu der ganzen Geschichte sagen.«

Im Gänsemarsch stiegen sie mit ihren Taschenlampen von den niedrigen Klippen des Südufers wieder hinauf zum Felsmassiv und gingen den Weg zurück. Sie machten einen Bogen um den Felsen, bis sie sich in der Mitte der Insel befanden, aber sie fanden nichts. Schließlich kamen sie wieder beim Lagerfeuer am östlichen Ende an. Einige Unermüdliche saßen noch in der Runde.

»Nun seht euch das an!«, rief Bob. Da hockte in aller Ruhe Sam Ragnarson in seinem Wikingerkostüm, lediglich ohne Helm, und unterhielt sich mit zwei Paaren. Als er die Jungen sah, grinste er breit und forderte sie mit übertrieben höflichen Gesten auf, sich ebenfalls zu setzen.

Peter und Justus hatten ihren Kopfschmuck, den sie bei der Flucht vor dem Geist verloren hatten, nicht wieder gefunden.

»Hallo, da sind ja die drei Kleinen«, lautete Sams ironische Begrüßung. »War mir ja sofort klar, dass ihr das seid, als ihr mit Onkel Karl angeschippert kamt. Der Fettwanst da ist nicht zu übersehen.«

Justus setzte zu einer heftigen Erwiderung an, aber da fragte schon Bob wütend: »Und was wissen Sie sonst noch? Vielleicht wissen Sie auch, wer hier den Kapitän Coulter von der *Star of Panama* spielt!«

»Wer soll das sein und woher kommt der?«, fragte der junge Mann mit frechem Grinsen.

»Sie wissen ganz genau, wer Kapitän Coulter ist!«, empörte sich Peter. »Den haben wir doch in Ihrem Haus gesehen! Wir redeten ja sogar mit ihm!«

Da meldete sich auch Justus zu Wort. »Natürlich kennen Sie den Kapitän, und ebenso das Schiff, von dem Ihr Vorfahr sich auf diese Insel rettete. Darum geht es schließlich hier bei dem Treffen der Ragnarsons.«

»Ich hab keine Ahnung, von was ihr da faselt. Ich fahr nur hier raus, um mit meinen Vettern ein Bier zu trinken.«

»Sam hat für Bücherwissen und Geschichte noch nie viel übrig gehabt«, kommentierte Dr. Ragnarson trocken.

»Aber wir haben doch den Kapitän in Sams Haus mit eigenen Augen gesehen«, entgegnete Bob.

Sam blickte die drei Jungen böse an. »Was hattet ihr überhaupt bei meinem Haus zu schaffen?«

»Wir kamen hin, um uns nach den Fotos zu erkundigen, die uns gestohlen wurden«, sagte Justus. »Sie waren der Einzige, der sich so auffällig dafür interessiert hatte.«

»Sonst noch was?«, wich Sam feixend aus.

»Und was ist mit dem Kerl, der bei der kleinen Bucht am anderen Ende der Insel mit einer Stablampe aufs Meer hinaus Zeichen gab?«, fragte Peter.

»Da drüben bin ich noch nie gewesen.«

»Wo haben Sie denn Ihre Lampe?«, forschte Bob skeptisch.

»Hier bei mir.« Sam holte eine große Stablampe unter seinem Umhang hervor. Sie sah fast genauso aus wie diejenige, die die Jungen bei der Bucht gefunden hatten.

»Was wissen Sie von einem Schiff, das vor kurzem auf dem Meer in die Nähe der Insel kam?«, wollte Justus wissen.

»Ich hab nirgends ein Schiff gesehen.«

Dr. Ragnarson sah seinen Sohn im Schein des Lagerfeuers aufmerksam an. Die beiden Paare, die noch auf der Insel waren, hatten sich zu ihren Zelten aufgemacht. Sam, die Jungen und die Brüder Ragnarson saßen jetzt allein beim Feuer.

»Meiner Ansicht nach ist Sam nichts vorzuwerfen«, meinte der Zahnarzt zu den Jungen. »Für all das, was hier passiert ist, muss es eine andere Erklärung geben.«

»Das nehme ich auch an«, sagte Karl Ragnarson. »Und was meint ihr drei?«

»Allem Anschein nach ist es so, Sir.« Justus nickte.

»Das ist das erste Mal, dass ich von einem dieser Bengel eine vernünftige Aussage höre«, erklärte Sam Ragnarson. Er stand auf. »Ich schlafe jetzt eine Runde, Dad. Oder ist das etwa auch nicht genehm?«

Unser Bild von Sam ist im Zuge der jüngsten Ereignisse doch etwas positiver geworden, nicht? Zumindest hat er nicht Marcus Ragnarsons Stablampe entwendet. Es wäre jedoch etwas voreilig, den jungen Tunichtgut nun gleich von allen Verdächtigungen auszunehmen.

Der junge Mann schlenderte zu den Zelten hinüber. Nachdenklich sah ihm Justus nach. Dr. Ragnarson stand auf, holte seinen Sohn ein und begann, mit leiser Stimme eindringlich auf ihn einzureden. Karl Ragnarson beobachtete die beiden, bis sie aus dem Lichtkreis des Feuers ins Dunkel verschwunden waren.

»Und was nun, Justus?«, fragte der Schulleiter.

»Wir sollten uns jetzt auch schlafen legen«, entschied Justus. »Wir drei werden uns bei der Nachtwache abwechseln, falls sich noch etwas tun sollte. Und morgen früh können wir dann die Bucht und das andere Ende der Insel gründlicher absuchen. Leute, die sich bei Nacht als Geister verkleiden und Lichtsignale in die Gegend schicken, lösen sich schließlich nicht einfach in Luft auf.«

»Ich mache bei der Wache mit«, bot Mr Ragnarson an. »Wenn es euch recht ist, übernehme ich gleich die erste Schicht.«

»Ausgezeichnet, Sir«, stimmte Justus zu. »Dann sind wir zu viert und auf jeden entfallen zwei Stunden. Unsere Walkie-Talkies bleiben eingeschaltet. Sie können das von Bob nehmen, bis er Sie dann um eins ablöst.«

Die Ragnarsons überließen den Jungen das Zelt einer der Familien, die wegen der unerklärlichen Vorfälle nicht mehr auf der Insel übernachteten. Die drei ??? besprachen noch lange die Ereignisse des Abends, ohne jedoch zu weiteren Schlussfolgerungen zu gelangen. Schließlich legten sie sich schlafen, das Rauschen der Brandung in den Ohren.

Karl Ragnarson hielt bis ein Uhr Wache und dann löste Bob ihn ab. Er wünschte dem Schulleiter Gute Nacht und setzte sich an die noch glimmenden Kohlen des Lagerfeuers. Er starrte in die rote Glut und lauschte auf Wind und Wellen.

Plötzlich ertönte durch die Nacht ein schauerliches Geheul!

Überraschende Entdeckung

Bob saß wie erstarrt vor dem erlöschenden Feuer.

Wieder kam das Geheul, wild und laut und zum Fürchten, wie das Heulen eines Werwolfs. Entsetzt flüsterte Bob in sein Walkie-Talkie:

»Justus! Peter! Aufwachen!«

Und schon wieder heulte es grauenhaft! Ein Werwolf!

Bob erschauerte und warf Holz auf die Kohlen. Er spähte in die Nacht jenseits der Feuerstelle hinaus.

»Was ist… was ist denn los?«

Peter war an das von neuem aufflackernde Feuer getreten. Gegen die nächtliche Kühle hatte er sich eine Decke umgehängt.

»Das… weiß ich nicht«, musste Bob bekennen.

Karl Ragnarson tauchte ebenfalls auf, mit hastig übergezogenem Chumash-Kittel und einem Gewehr in der Hand. Er sah sich nach allen Seiten um.

»Genau dieses Wolfsgeheul hörten wir auch in den beiden vergangenen Nächten! Könnt ihr beide feststellen, woher es kommt?« Als hätte das Unwesen die Worte gehört, übertönte das Heulen nochmals den Wind und die Brandung – eine grauenvolle Drohung, die durch Mark und Bein ging.

Bob, Peter und Mr Ragnarson fuhren herum und sahen zu dem riesenhaften Felsen an der Westspitze der Insel hin.

»Irgendwo da drüben!«, rief Bob. Er legte noch einmal Holz

nach und das Feuer loderte in der Nacht hell auf. »Es kommt immer aus der gleichen Richtung.«

»Stimmt!«, sagte Karl Ragnarson.

»Dort wo wir den Geist gesehen haben«, murmelte Peter beklommen. Justus und Dr. Ragnarson waren nun auch erschienen und standen hinter Peter und Karl Ragnarson. Der Zahnarzt, im Jogginganzug, hatte ebenfalls ein Gewehr bei sich.

»Der Geist eines Schiffskapitäns heult aber nicht wie ein Wolf, Peter«, sagte der Erste Detektiv. »Und im Übrigen wäre zu bemerken, dass es weder auf dieser Insel noch sonst irgendwo in Südkalifornien wild lebende Wölfe gibt.«

Wieder drang das Furcht einflößende Geheul zu ihnen.

»Dann ist das bestimmt eine akustische Täuschung«, scherzte Peter, wenig überzeugend.

»Es hört sich an, als wäre es in der Nähe des großen Felsens«, meinte Dr. Ragnarson.

Justus nickte. »Ja, genau von dort kommt es.«

»Bist du ganz sicher, dass es auf der Insel nicht doch Wölfe gibt, Justus?«, erkundigte sich Dr. Ragnarson. »Vielleicht hat ein Einzelner überlebt und kommt hier nicht weg?«

Justus schüttelte den Kopf. »Nein, Sir. In dieser Gegend hat es überhaupt noch nie Wölfe gegeben.«

»Keine normalen Wölfe«, wandte Peter ein. »Aber wenn das nun auch so ein Spuk ist, wie Kapitän Coulters Geist?«

»In einem Punkt gebe ich dir Recht, Peter. Ich habe den starken Verdacht, dass der Geist und der Wolf denselben Ursprung haben, wer oder was sie auch sein mögen.« Der Erste Detektiv wandte sich an Dr. Ragnarson. »Darf ich fragen, wo Ihr Sohn sich zurzeit aufhält, Sir?«

»Tja...«, sagte der Zahnarzt, »als ich ihn zuletzt sah, war er...«

»Ich bin hier, Fatso.«

Im hellen Feuerschein stand Sam Ragnarson hinter seinem

Vater und grinste. Auch die beiden Ehepaare aus der Sippe Ragnarson, die sich noch auf der Insel befanden, waren nun aus ihren Zelten gekommen. Sie erschauerten, als das fürchterliche Heulen sich wieder hören ließ. »Ich weiß nicht, was ihr vorhabt«, erklärte eine der beiden Frauen, »aber mir reicht es. Was sich da auch tut, ich will nichts mehr davon wissen.«

»Wir fahren jetzt sofort zum Festland hinüber«, beschloss ihr Mann. »Einverstanden. Wir packen unsere Sachen zusammen und gehen«, sagte die zweite Frau.

Justus hob die Hand. »Hören Sie mir bitte mal zu. Derjenige, der das Geheul veranstaltet, will damit ja gerade erreichen, Sie von der Insel zu vertreiben.«

»Na, dann hat er es jetzt geschafft«, erklärte einer der Männer. »Wir kamen hier heraus, um unseren Spaß zu haben. Diesen Terror lassen wir uns nicht bieten.«

»Wenn wir alle bis morgen früh hier bleiben«, wandte Justus eindringlich ein, »dann wird nichts mehr passieren. Und morgen werden wir aufklären, wie dieses Geheul zustande kam und was sich hinter der Spukgestalt verbirgt.«

Sam platzte heraus: »Ich mag jedenfalls nicht länger warten. Ich finde es an der Zeit, die Insel zu verlassen.«

Justus warf ihm einen überraschten Blick zu.

 Aha, Mr Sam Ragnarson gedenkt, die Insel zu verlassen. Fragen: Hat er sich inzwischen das gesichert, worauf er aus war? Schmiedet er etwa schon wieder einen neuen Plan? Oder – nicht auszuschließen – hat er es mit der Angst zu tun bekommen?

Karl Ragnarson schlug sich auf Justus' Seite. »Ich bin auch dafür, dass wir alle losgehen und ergründen, wer dieses Geheul veranstaltet. Justus hat Recht, hier gibt es keine Wölfe!«

»Außer es hat jemand einen hergebracht«, meinte Sam.

»Nein, überlegen Sie doch«, sagte Justus. »Das Heulen kommt immer aus derselben Richtung! Es wandert nicht und kommt auch nicht näher. Ein echter Wolf würde aber auf der Futtersuche umherstreifen und bestimmt fände er den Lagerplatz hier sehr verlockend.«

»Dann ist es eben kein richtiger Wolf«, sagte Sam. »Vielleicht ist es etwas anderes.«

»Ich hab jetzt genug«, stellte eine der Frauen fest. »Wir fahren los, und zwar auf der Stelle.«

»Nun gut«, meinte Karl Ragnarson dazu. »Die Jungen und ich werden losziehen und die Sache untersuchen. Warten Sie doch wenigstens noch, bis wir wieder da sind. Dr. Ragnarson ist ja bewaffnet. Er wird hier bei Ihnen bleiben, bis wir zurückkommen.«

»Falls sie überhaupt zurückkommen«, unkte Sam.

Die beiden Ehepaare äußerten sich nicht mehr. Karl Ragnarson und die Jungen holten ihre Taschenlampen und dann gingen die vier nochmals auf das Felsmassiv zu. Ein frischer Wind fegte über die schmale, kleine Insel. Die Nacht war still, bis auf das Donnern der Brandung gegen die Felsen am Südufer.

Während sie vorsichtig ausschritten, setzte das Heulen immer wieder ein.

Justus beleuchtete seine Uhr mit der Taschenlampe. »Das Heulen kommt alle zwei Minuten«, stellte er kurz darauf fest. »Viel zu regelmäßig. Kein Tier heult in sekundengenau gleich bleibenden Abständen.«

Sie gingen weiter über das baumlose Gelände und leuchteten hin und wieder mit den Taschenlampen in die Umgebung.

Schon kam das Heulen wieder.

»Da drüben ist es!« Bob zeigte auf die Nordwand des großen Felsens.

Wieder ließ sich das durchdringende Heulen hören. »Jetzt sind wir… näher dran«, sagte Peter leise.

Karl Ragnarson brachte sein Gewehr in Anschlag. Nun war das Geheul fast unmittelbar vor ihnen!

Sie blieben regungslos stehen und starrten in das Dunkel vor sich. Inzwischen waren sie bei der Nordwand des Felsens. Unter ihnen lagen ein schmaler Sandstrand und das Meer, im Hintergrund – etwa fünfzehn Kilometer entfernt – die Küste des Festlands. Das Heulen schien vom Strand her zu kommen. Den Ursprungsort konnten sie jedoch nicht genau feststellen.

»Wir müssen da runtergehen und uns teilen«, bestimmte Justus. »Das ist der einzige Weg, die Töne zu lokalisieren.«

Auf dem Sand stellten sich die vier voll Unbehagen in einigem Abstand zueinander auf und warteten auf die nächsten Heultöne. Zwei Minuten verstrichen. Diesmal hörte es sich an, als sei es mitten zwischen ihnen!

»Da!« Mr Ragnarson streckte die Hand aus.

»H-hier!«, rief Peter.

Der Zweite Detektiv stand in der Mitte des Sandstreifens, direkt unter der Steilwand des Felsmassivs. Er bückte sich und hob einen kleinen Kassettenrekorder auf.

»Es kommt vom Band!«, triumphierte Justus. »Alle zwei Minuten wird die Aufnahme abgespielt. Die Töne hallen prachtvoll von dem großen Felsen wider. Jetzt haben wir den Wolf, Sir.«

Karl Ragnarson nickte. »Sam hat einen Kassettenrekorder, der genauso aussieht.«

»Viele Modelle sind sich ganz ähnlich«, wandte Justus ein. »Ein Beweis ist das noch nicht.«

»Mag sein, aber es reicht aus, um den Jungen deshalb zur Rede zu stellen«, sagte der Schulleiter.

Eilig liefen sie wieder die schmale Insel entlang. Dr. Ragnarson saß allein am Feuer.

»Sie sind weg«, sagte der Zahnarzt. »Sie wollten nicht mehr warten.«

»Ein Kassettenrekorder, Ingmar!«, rief sein Bruder Karl. »Kein Werwolf und auch kein normaler Wolf. Ein Bluff, um die Leute von der Insel zu vertreiben, genau wie Justus vermutet hatte.«

»Aber wozu das, Karl? Was an dieser gottverlassenen Felseninsel könnte für jemanden von Interesse sein?«

»Eben das müssen wir herausfinden«, sagte Justus. Er blickte sich bei der Feuerstelle um. »Wo ist denn Sam?«

»Der ist auch mit rübergefahren«, antwortete Dr. Ragnarson.

»Er ist weg?« Bob war ganz verblüfft. »Dann ist das vielleicht doch nicht Sam, der uns von dieser Insel verjagen will! Vermutlich…«

»Da – seht euch das an!«, rief Peter. »Im Wasser!«

Der äußerste Feuerschein erreichte gerade noch das Wasser der Bucht. Und es sah so aus, als starrten von dort drei rötlich gelbe Augen herauf!

Unliebsamer Beweis

»Was ist das bloß?«, fragte Peter erschrocken.

Die Augen schienen sich zu bewegen und dann flossen sie zu langen Streifen von leuchtendem Orange auseinander. Das Ganze sah aus wie ein Rücken, mit zwei Armen…

»Das ist ja ein Mensch!«, rief Karl Ragnarson.

Der Schulleiter und der Zahnarzt hasteten zum Ufer und wateten ins Meer hinaus. Die Jungen sahen, wie sich die beiden Männer über eine bleiche Gestalt beugten, die im Wasser trieb. Dann richteten sie sich auf und kamen wieder ans Ufer. Dr. Ragnarson schleppte eine schwere Männerjacke aus Segeltuch.

»Nur eine Jacke«, erkannte Peter erleichtert. »Mit reflektierenden Aufnähern.«

»Ja, eine Jacke.« Karl Ragnarson nickte. »Aber seht sie euch an.« Die schwere Jacke war über und über zerrissen und aufgeschlitzt. Stellenweise hing der Stoff in Fetzen und an vielen Stellen wies sie dunkle Flecken auf. Der Schulleiter gab die Jacke an Bob weiter.

Bob schüttelte den Kopf. »Wer hat denn die so zugerichtet?«

»Die Flecken sehen aus wie Blut«, äußerte sich Peter. »Ich wette, das war ein Hai. Und ein großer dazu. Ein starker Weißhai, so wie es aussieht.«

»Du meinst, dass der Mann, der die Jacke anhatte, von einem Hai angegriffen wurde?« Bob schauderte es.

»Das fürchte ich auch«, sagte Dr. Ragnarson.

Bob drehte und wendete die Jacke in den Händen und untersuchte sie genau. Er zog an einer Tasche den Reißverschluss auf und holte einen silberglänzenden Gegenstand heraus. »Ein Feuerzeug. Mit einem Autoemblem drauf. Jaguar.«

»William Manning«, wusste Justus, »war Autohändler.«

»Manning?«, wiederholte Dr. Ragnarson.

»Ein Mann, dessen Boot wir fanden.« Peter musste schlucken. »Die Polizei hat ... ihn bisher nicht gefunden.«

»Das könnte seine Jacke sein, Justus«, bestätigte Bob niedergeschlagen. »Ich erinnere mich, wie Mrs Manning sagte, ihr Mann hätte ein Sprechfunkgerät in der Jackentasche bei sich gehabt.«

Justus suchte in beiden Taschen, fand aber darin sonst nichts mehr.

»Morgen bringen wir die Jacke zur Polizei«, beschloss er.

»Warum nicht noch heute Nacht, Justus?«, fragte Bob.

»Leider sieht es so aus, als wäre die Sache nicht mehr so sehr eilig.«

»Außerdem haben die anderen alle Boote außer dem meinen mitgenommen«, wandte Karl Ragnarson ein, »und wenn wir noch Ingmar mitnehmen wollten, wären wir zu viele. Zu riskant für eine Nachtfahrt. Wir bleiben besser bis zum Morgen auf der Insel.«

»Und da Sam nicht mehr hier ist«, sagte Justus noch, »sollten wir ohnehin unbedingt bleiben, um sicherzugehen, ob jetzt noch etwas geschieht oder nicht. Ich schlage vor, dass wir wieder eine Wache aufstellen. Jetzt wären Peter und ich an der Reihe.«

»Und wir anderen könnten ein wenig Schlaf gebrauchen.« Dr. Ragnarson gähnte.

Sie gingen zu den Zelten zurück. Als Justus sich noch einen Pullover übergezogen hatte und zum Feuer gehen wollte, fragte ihn Bob beklommen: »Wenn nun Sam nicht das unheimliche Geheul abspielte, wer war es dann?«

»Wer ist denn überhaupt noch auf der Insel?«, warf Peter ein. »Außer uns und ... und unserem Rektor und seinem Bruder.«

»Ja«, sagte Justus. »Nur wir und die beiden Brüder Ragnarson.«

Die drei Jungen wechselten Blicke und dann nahm Justus sein Walkie-Talkie und ging in die kalte Nacht hinaus zu dem langsam ersterbenden Feuer. Um fünf Uhr früh fing Peter gleich an zu bibbern, als er Justus ablöste.

Um sieben weckte Peter Justus und Bob.

»Das Feuer brennt wieder schön und ich hab einen Riesenhunger«, sagte der Zweite Detektiv. »Was machen wir uns zum Frühstück?« Die beiden anderen stöhnten und zogen sich die Schlafsäcke übers Gesicht hoch.

Dann erst wurde Bob bewusst, wo sie waren, und sein Kopf kam wieder zum Vorschein. »Hey – ist hier eigentlich heute Nacht noch was passiert?«

»Nicht die Spur«, erklärte Peter. »Mir war's recht so.«

»Mir ist aber was passiert«, murmelte Justus, noch ganz im Schlafsack verkrochen. »Ich war zu Eis gefroren bis auf die Knochen und erst nach zwei Stunden bin ich wieder aufgetaut und dann konnte ich nicht schlafen. Geht jetzt weg und lasst mich friedlich sterben.«

»Ich dachte, du wolltest heute früh diese Jacke zur Polizei bringen«, versuchte Bob, Justus aufzumuntern. Er schlüpfte aus seinem Schlafsack und zog sich die Schuhe an.

»Und vielleicht feststellen, ob Sam Ragnarson seinen Kassettenrekorder noch hat«, setzte Peter hinzu.

Mit dumpfem Gestöhne wälzte sich Justus aus seinem Schlafsack, wie ein Wal, der sich aus der See emporhebt. Als er auf den Beinen stand, gähnte er, reckte sich und rieb sich die Hände. »Alles klar! Aber« – er grinste – »erst wird gefrühstückt!«

»So, jetzt blickst du wieder durch«, meinte Peter.

Rasch verließen sie das Zelt und liefen zu dem hell lodernden Feuer. Schon wurde es allmählich wärmer. Wieder hatte sich ein leichter Nebelschleier über die Insel gelegt, aber die Sonne löste ihn zusehends auf, und es sah nach einem schönen Tag aus.

Karl Ragnarson saß am Feuer und begrüßte die drei ???.

»Na, was soll's denn sein, Jungs? Grillwürstchen? Oder lieber heiße Knacker? Eier? Kakao? Milch? Pfannkuchen?«

Sie stimmten einträchtig für Grillwürstchen, Pfannkuchen und Kakao und der Schulleiter setzte alte, rußgeschwärzte Töpfe und Pfannen auf den Eisengrill über den glühenden Kohlen.

»Heute Nacht hat sich nichts mehr getan?« Mr Ragnarson legte die Würstchen in die kleinere Bratpfanne.

»Nein, Sir«, antwortete Peter.

»Weil Sam gar nicht auf der Insel war«, meldete sich eine Stimme.

Dr. Ragnarson wirkte bedrückt, als er sich vor dem Feuer niederhockte und seine Hände wärmte.

»Das ist eine Erklärung«, sagte Justus, »aber nicht die einzig mögliche. Wir waren gestern Abend alle auf der Insel, und nachdem wir den Trick mit dem Kassettenrekorder aufgedeckt hatten, möchte ich bezweifeln, dass jemand Lust verspürte, uns noch in derselben Nacht von der Insel wegzuscheuchen.«

»Aber eines steht fest«, meinte der Zahnarzt, »wenn Sam nicht auf der Insel ist, dann herrscht hier Ruhe.«

»Sind Sie da ganz sicher?«, fragte Justus nachdenklich.

Die beiden Männer überlegten einen Augenblick.

»Also ich weiß bestimmt, dass er immer dann auf der Insel war, wenn jemand die Spukgestalten sah oder den Wolf hörte«, gab Karl Ragnarson zu bedenken.

»Andererseits haben wir entdeckt, dass Dinge verschwunden sind, während er nicht auf der Insel war«, musste Dr. Ragnarson einräumen.

»Das besagt nichts, denn wir wissen ja nicht, wann die Sachen gestohlen wurden«, wandte Karl Ragnarson ein. Er goss den Teig für den ersten Pfannkuchen in die größere Pfanne.

 Auf Ragnarson Rock verschwanden Gegenstände aus dem Besitz der Festgesellschaft, während ausgerechnet Sam gar nicht auf der Insel war. Telekinese? Ich denke, das sollten wir ausschließen.

Justus nickte, und alle saßen stumm in der Runde, während der Rektor die Pfannkuchen buk. Dann wandte er sich an die Jungen. »Was habt ihr nun als Nächstes vor?«

»Wir werden zum Festland fahren und dort zu ermitteln versuchen, was Sam so alles treibt«, erwiderte Justus. »Dürfte ich Sie bitten, die Jacke, die wir im Wasser fanden, zur Polizei zu bringen? Ich möchte Mrs Manning die Nachricht selbst überbringen und die Zeit drängt. Ich muss mich dringend noch einmal mit diesen Fotos befassen.«

»Das geht klar«, sagte Mr Ragnarson. »Es ist schon tragisch, wie manche Leute das Risiko auf See unterschätzen.«

Dr. Ragnarson wandte sich an Justus. »In was könnte Sam deiner Meinung nach verwickelt sein?«

Der Erste Detektiv schüttelte den Kopf. »Das weiß ich nicht, Sir, aber ich bin überzeugt, dass er alle Besucher von der Insel abhalten will.«

»Aber warum ist er dann gestern Abend selbst mit weggefahren?«, fragte Bob verwundert.

»Auch ich war sehr überrascht, als er verkündete, er wolle weg, Bob«, bestätigte Justus. »Es könnte bedeuten, dass die Umstände sich geändert haben.«

Inzwischen waren Pfannkuchen und Würstchen fertig, und alle griffen nach der ereignisreichen Nacht auf der Insel mit gutem Appetit zu, außer Dr. Ingmar Ragnarson, der sich um seinen Sohn Sorgen machte und nur wenig aß. Dann löschten sie das Feuer, erledigten mittels Sand und Seewasser den Abwasch und stiegen in Karl Ragnarsons Motorboot.

»Wir lassen mal alles hier«, beschloss der Schulleiter. »Unsere Leute kommen vielleicht noch einmal her, wenn ihr der Sache auf den Grund gegangen seid und alles aufgeklärt habt.«

Mittlerweile hatte sich der Morgennebel ganz aufgelöst und es war ein strahlender, klarer Tag geworden. Der Wind hatte sich gelegt, aber die Dünung war noch sehr bewegt. Langsam tuckerte das schwer beladene Boot aufs Festland zu. Als sie die Hafeneinfahrt in Rocky Beach erreicht hatten, zeigte Dr. Ragnarson auf die Anlegestelle für die Motorboote.

»Das da ist Sams Boot. Dann hat er sich wenigstens nicht wieder heimlich zur Insel aufgemacht.«

Die beiden Ragnarsons machten das Boot fest und die Jungen holten ihre Fahrräder aus dem Ständer am Kai.

»Was machen wir jetzt, Justus?«, fragte Peter.

»Du gehst mit Bob zu Sams Haus«, wies ihn Justus an. »Passt genau auf, was er treibt. Wenn er weggeht, dann folgt ihm.«

»Und wenn er gar nicht da ist?«, erkundigte sich Bob.

»Dann wartet auf ihn.«

»Was hast denn du vor, Justus?«, fragte Peter.

»Ich mache einen Besuch bei Mrs Manning und komme dann so bald wie möglich rüber zu euch.«

Also gingen Bob und Peter zu Sam Ragnarsons Behausung und Justus schlug im Telefonbuch Mrs Mannings Adresse nach. Sie wohnte, von Sams Wohngegend am Strand aus betrachtet, am entgegengesetzten Ende der Stadt, oben im Bergland. Der Anführer der drei ??? stöhnte innerlich – das würde eine lange, anstrengende Radfahrt werden. Und so kam es auch.

Schnaufend und ächzend strampelte der übergewichtige Erste Detektiv langsam die schmale, tief eingeschnittene Straße hinauf zu dem großzügigen Landhaus am Fuß eines kahlen braunen Berges. Das Haus selbst war von grünem Rasen und Bäumen umgeben; all dies musste freilich dauernd bewässert werden. Gerade als Justus sich keuchend auf dem letzten steilen Wegstück abmühte, kam ein Mann auf einem Motorrad im Leerlauf aus der abschüssigen Zufahrt der Mannings gerollt.

Es war Sam!

Bob und Peter werden fündig

Von der Ecke aus spähte Bob achtsam zu der Frontseite des Hauses an der Küstenstraße. Sam Ragnarsons verwahrlostes Heim lag still da. Auf der Straße war niemand zu sehen.

»Gehen wir näher ran«, meinte Peter.

Sie schlossen ihre Fahrräder ab und liefen rasch die Straße entlang zu dem kleinen Haus, das von dem dichten Dschungel aus wucherndem Grün fast zugewachsen war.

»Die Garage ist offen!«, rief Peter.

Sie hielten sich dicht an die Holzfassade mit dem abblätternden Anstrich und drangen durch den Wildwuchs vorsichtig zur Garage vor. Ein Torflügel stand offen und von der Hausecke aus konnten sie in den Garagenraum blicken. Da stand zwar der braune Pick-up, aber nicht das Motorrad.

»Sieht so aus, als wäre er mit dem Motorrad auf Achse«, vermutete Peter.

»Dann können wir ja das Haus durchsuchen!«, rief Bob. »Und dabei werden wir mit Sicherheit den Kapitän Coulter finden!«

»Wenn da drin ein Geist ist, lege ich keinen Wert auf nähere Bekanntschaft mit ihm«, sagte Peter. »Ich bleibe lieber hier draußen.«

»Ach was, ich rede doch nicht von einem Geist, Peter. Ich meine die Klamotten!«, stellte Bob richtig. »Ich vermute stark, dass sich Sam als Geistererscheinung kostümiert hatte.«

Peter machte große Augen. »Soll das heißen, dass Sam auch hinter der Maske steckte, als wir zum ersten Mal hierher kamen?«

»Ich bin fast sicher und Justus wird es wohl auch sein«, sagte Bob. »Wir brauchen jetzt nur ein Beweisstück. Wenn wir im Haus gründlich suchen, finden wir vielleicht eines.«

Peter schien noch immer Zweifel zu haben.

»Justus sagte aber, wir sollten hier Ausschau halten und warten, bis Sam zurückkommt.«

»Aber hier haben wir jetzt die Chance, auf eigene Faust herauszufinden, was er so treibt«, hielt Bob eindringlich dagegen. »Es ist doch nicht nötig, dass Justus uns jeden Schritt vorschreibt. Detektive müssen Ideen haben und beweglich sein.«

»Na ja…« Peter zögerte. »Versuchen wir's eben.«

»Komm mit, wir gehen nach vorn.«

Mit der gebotenen Umsicht schlüpften sie am Haus entlang zurück bis zu dem windschiefen Verandavorbau. Lautlos stiegen sie die Vortreppe hinauf und spähten durch die schmutzigen Scheiben. Die zerlumpten Vorhänge im Inneren waren diesmal zurückgezogen. Im Haus war niemand zu sehen und nichts rührte sich. Peter versuchte, ein Fenster hochzuschieben, aber es war verriegelt.

»Vielleicht haben wir an einem Seitenfenster Glück«, schlug Peter vor. »Sam ist nicht der Typ, der beim Weggehen immer alles abschließt und verriegelt.«

»Dann probieren wir es doch mal gleich bei der Haustür«, meinte Bob und drehte den Knauf.

Nicht abgeschlossen!

Peter war enttäuscht. »Das verdirbt einem ja den ganzen Spaß«, beklagte er sich.

Drinnen war der Fußboden des Wohnzimmers übersät mit leeren Verpackungen aus dem Schnellimbiss und mit Getränkedosen. Überall lag Staub. Schmutzige Kleidungsstücke waren achtlos auf den Boden und über die zerschrammten und beschädigten Möbel geworfen worden. Die Schubladen in einem Tisch und einer abgestoßenen Kommode waren halb herausgezogen und mit allem möglichen Zeug voll gestopft.

Im Wohnzimmer wurde ihnen somit über Sam Ragnarson vor allem eines klar: dass er ein richtiger Chaot war.

Das Esszimmer war völlig leer.

Dann gab es noch zwei Schlafzimmer. Das eine enthielt lediglich Stapel alter Autoreifen, Seiten- und Rückspiegel, Radfelgen, Türgriffe, Sitzbezüge und andere Ersatzteile, die sich vielleicht verkaufen ließen. Außerdem fanden sich hier Einkaufskarren aus Supermärkten, Messingbeschläge und etliche alte Türen.

»Wetten, dass er das Zeug zusammenklaut und dann verscherbelt?«, meinte Peter.

»Schon möglich«, bestätigte Bob. »Aber ich sehe hier nichts, was uns Aufschluss darüber geben könnte, was er auf Ragnarson Rock treibt.«

Im zweiten Schlafraum stand ein zerwühltes Bett, das muffelte, als wäre die Bettwäsche seit Monaten nicht mehr gewechselt worden, dazu eine Kommode und ein Einbauschrank.

»Hier ist auch nichts«, meldete Peter aus den Tiefen des Schrankes.

Als Letztes nahmen sie sich die Küche vor, wo sie bei ihrem vorherigen Besuch den angeblichen Kapitän Coulter gesehen hatten. Der Raum war eine schmutzstarrende Rumpelkammer; die Regale hingegen waren fast völlig ausgeplündert. Der Kühlschrank wirkte schon von außen äußerst unappetitlich.

»Das wär's dann«, sagte Bob enttäuscht. »Interessante Spuren gibt's hier nirgends.«

»Die Garage haben wir ja noch nicht durchsucht«, brachte Peter vor.

»Stimmt!«

Sie liefen hinaus zu der baufälligen Garage aus rohen Planken mit Ritzen dazwischen. Innen zeigte Peter auf einen Ölfleck, der den Abstellplatz für ein Motorrad kennzeichnete. Bob nickte. Dann sahen beide die Tür an der hinteren Garagenwand.

»Hier könnte ein Lagerraum sein«, vermutete Bob.

Die Tür war geschlossen, aber nicht abgesperrt. Dahinter befand sich ein kleiner, schmaler Raum, voll gepfropft mit Angelzeug, Surfbrettern, Fahrradzubehör, einem zerlegten Skateboard und einigen großen Stücken, die wie Teile eines großen Hängegleiters aussahen. Durch ein kleines Fenster fiel spärliches Licht ein. An der Wand gegenüber der Tür stand eine Werkbank.

»Da ist Sams Wikingerkostüm!«, rief Peter.

Der Fellüberwurf hing an einem Nagel in der Wand. Der Helm und die Stulpenstiefel mit der ledernen Verschnürung lagen auf der Werkbank. Der Schild, das Schwert und eine Beuteltasche waren auf dem Fußboden abgelegt. Peter öffnete die Tasche und sah zu Bob hoch.

»Hier haben wir unseren Geist!«

In der Tasche steckten die goldbetresste Kapitänsmütze, die lange dunkelblaue Jacke mit den Messingknöpfen, die enge Hose, die altmodischen Stiefel und das Teleskop, nicht jedoch das Entermesser. Außerdem enthielt die Tasche zerlumpte Seemannskleidung und Tang – die Ausstattung des zweiten »Geistes«, der sich den Ragnarsons auf der Insel gezeigt hatte.

»Na also!« rief Peter.

»Sam hat tatsächlich selbst die Geister gemimt, genau wie ich es mir dachte!«, triumphierte Bob. »Als wir zum ersten Mal hier waren, steckte er in diesem Kapitänskostüm!«

»Ja, und dazu verstellte er seine Stimme und machte ganz eindrucksvoll auf alt«, sagte Peter. »Wir wussten ja an dem Tag noch gar nicht, wie Sam in Wirklichkeit aussieht!«

»Nein«, bestätigte Bob. »Anscheinend hatten wir ihn dabei unterbrochen, wie er seinen Auftritt als Geist einübte. Er probierte verschiedene Haltungen und Bewegungen aus und kontrollierte sich dabei im spiegelnden Küchenfenster.«

»Hier findet sich vielleicht noch mehr, Bob.« Peter nahm sich das Chaos auf dem Fußboden des kleinen Lagerraums vor und Bob untersuchte die Werkbank. Sie gingen gründlich vor: Peter stöberte in allen Ecken herum und Bob kletterte zum Dachgebälk hinauf. Oben auf einem der Balken entdeckte er ein Kästchen. Er sprang herunter und zeigte Peter seinen Fund.

»Was ist denn das?«

»Das ist die Erklärung«, sagte Bob. »Die Erklärung dafür, dass Sam alle anderen Leute von Ragnarson Rock fern halten will.«

Peter sah sich den Inhalt des Kästchens an. Darin lagen fünf große Münzen – blanke Goldmünzen – und dazu einige goldglänzende, kleine Klumpen. Bob nahm eine der Münzen heraus. »Die ist von 1847«, stellte er fest. »Und diese Klümpchen sind bestimmt Nuggets – ebenfalls Gold.«

Die beiden Jungen wechselten einen Blick.

»Das verschollene Gold der *Star of Panama*!« Peter stieß einen leisen Pfiff aus.

»Das hat Sam auf der Insel gefunden«, ergänzte Bob.

»Und nun will er natürlich die anderen aus dem Weg haben, damit er ungestört weitersuchen kann!«, ging es Peter auf.

Das jähe Knattern eines Motorrads schien wie aus dem Nichts zu kommen. Entsetzt starrten die beiden einander an.

Spuren eines Besuchs

Vor Mrs Mannings Haus verzog sich Justus mit seinem Fahrrad blitzschnell in die Büsche am Straßenrand, als Sam Ragnarson auf seinem Motorrad aus der Einfahrt gerollt kam.

Auf der Landstraße über dem Canyon drehte der Bursche dann auf und raste an Justus vorüber, ohne ihn zu sehen. Das Motorgeräusch verhallte und wieder war alles still.

Justus richtete sich langsam auf und schob sein Rad die steile Zufahrt zu dem großen, weitläufigen Landhaus hinauf.

Er lehnte das Fahrrad an die Hausmauer und klopfte an der Eingangstür. Darauf erschien ein großer Mann mit ernstem Gesicht, der einen dunklen Anzug mit Krawatte trug.

»Könnte ich bitte Mrs Manning sprechen?«, fragte Justus.

»Sie ist gerade in der Küche und macht Kaffee. Du kannst hereinkommen und bei mir warten.«

Im Wohnzimmer setzte sich der Mann hin und lächelte Justus melancholisch zu. Nachdenklich sah er auf seine Uhr.

»Wollte der andere Mann auch zu Mrs Manning?«, erkundigte sich Justus.

»Welcher andere Mann?«

»Sam Ragnarson. Ich sah ihn eben wegfahren.«

»Ich bin hier niemand anderem begegnet, mein Junge.«

Da setzte sich auch Justus und sah sich bewundernd die teure Einrichtung und die modernen Gemälde an den Wänden an. Die großen Fenster ermöglichten nach allen Richtungen den Ausblick auf die Bergwelt. Von einer Fensterfront aus bot sich ein malerisches Panorama des Meeres im Hintergrund. Auf einem Tisch sah Justus die gerahmte Fotografie eines kleinen, stämmigen Mannes in mittleren Jahren, der vor einem großen Reklameschild stand: MANNING AUTOMOBILE – JAGUAR UND TOYOTA.

»Tut mir Leid, Steven, aber … Oh?«

Mrs Manning stand im Türrahmen und trocknete sich die Hände an ihrer Schürze ab. Die schlanke rothaarige Frau trug nun ein einfaches schwarzes Kleid und sah blass und verhärmt aus. Sie richtete die müden blauen Augen auf Justus.

»Dich kenne ich doch, junger Mann, oder nicht?«

»Ja, Madam, wir sind uns am Bootshafen begegnet, als meine Freunde und ich das Boot Ihres Mannes gefunden hatten.«

Die Frau starrte ihn ausdruckslos an, als wollte sie nicht an jenen Tag und an das leere Boot erinnert werden. Dann seufzte sie bedrückt.

»Natürlich. Du bist…?«

»Justus Jonas, Madam.«

»Ja.« Sie nickte, als wäre der Name irgendwie wichtig. Dann wandte sie sich an den ernsten Mann. »Das ist einer der Jungen, die Williams Boot fanden, Steven.« Zu Justus sagte sie: »Steven ist der Bruder meines Mannes. Er weiß ebenso zu schätzen wie ich, was ihr getan habt. Allerdings habe ich mich bei euch noch gar nicht für die Bergung des Bootes bedankt. Ohne das hätte ich vielleicht niemals erfahren, was… meinem armen Bill zugestoßen ist.«

Justus erkannte plötzlich, dass er Scheu davor hatte, Mrs Manning von dem neuen Fund der drei ??? zu berichten. Doch tapfer fing er an: »Meine Freunde und ich waren über Nacht auf Ragnarson Rock und entdeckten dort etwas, das vielleicht Ihrem Mann gehört.«

Mrs Manning sah Justus starr und gespannt an.

»Es ist eine schwere Segeltuchjacke«, fuhr der Erste Detektiv fort, »mit reflektierenden Streifen auf Rücken und Ärmeln, und in einer Tasche steckte ein Feuerzeug mit einem Jaguar-Emblem.«

»Das ist Bills Jacke!«, rief Mrs Manning. »Kann ich sie bitte sehen?«

»Leider nein«, sagte Justus. »Sie ist nämlich zurzeit auf dem Polizeirevier. Aber dort können Sie sie sicherlich ansehen.«

»War sie… noch heil?«, fragte die Frau zögernd. »Ich meine, war Bills Jacke unbeschädigt?«

Justus blickte auf seine Füße. »Nein, sie war überall zerrissen und zerfetzt und voller dunkler Flecken.«

Mrs Mannings Gesicht verzog sich schmerzlich. »Was…?«

»Haie«, sagte Steven Manning grimmig. »Schrecklich. Nun wissen wir ja Bescheid. Wenigstens haben wir Klarheit.«

Mrs Manning begann zu weinen. Sie setzte sich auf ein langes weißes Sofa und schluchzte in ein kleines Taschentuch. Steven Manning trat zu ihr und berührte sie sacht am Arm.

»Es tut mir ja so Leid, Phyllis. Ich werde zur Polizei gehen und die Jacke identifizieren und dann komme ich heute Abend wieder her. Immerhin wird das die Versicherung davon überzeugen, dass der arme Bill tot ist und dass sie seine Lebensversicherung auszahlen müssen. Kommst du allein zurecht?«

Die schluchzende Frau nickte so heftig, dass ihre roten Haare in der Morgensonne, die durch die Fenster schien, aufleuchteten.

»Es war sehr klug von Bill, dass er mit dieser Versicherung Vorsorge für dich getroffen hat«, sagte Steven Manning noch. »Dafür sollten wir dankbar sein.«

Er nickte Justus zu und ging dann. Der Erste Detektiv hörte, wie er vor dem Haus seinen Wagen anließ und die abschüssige Zufahrt hinunterfuhr.

»Hm ... Mrs Manning?«, meldete er sich behutsam.

Die schlanke Frau schluchzte nur immerzu in ihr Taschentuch. Justus änderte seine Sitzhaltung und räusperte sich. »Ja, also könnte ich wohl ganz kurz mit Ihnen reden, Mrs Manning?« Die rothaarige Frau stöhnte vernehmlich und hob dann den Kopf. Sie trocknete sich die Augen und rang sich für Justus ein schwaches Lächeln ab.

»Entschuldige, Justus. Die Nachricht hat mir all das Furchtbare wieder frisch ins Bewusstsein gebracht. Aber das Leben muss dennoch weitergehen, nicht wahr? Was wolltest du mir denn noch sagen?«

»Als ich zu Ihrem Haus radelte, sah ich einen Motorradfahrer aus Ihrer Einfahrt rollen. Können Sie mir sagen, was dieser Mann hier wollte?«

»Ein Mann? Mit einem Motorrad? Ich habe hier kein Motorrad gehört.« Sie schüttelte den Kopf. »Ich kann mir nicht vorstellen, wovon du redest, Justus. Ich habe keinen Mann gesehen.«

»Er heißt Sam Ragnarson«, fuhr Justus fort. »Sagt Ihnen dieser Name etwas?«

Wieder schüttelte Mrs Manning den Kopf. »Nein, überhaupt nichts.«

»Vielleicht hat ihn Ihr Mann gekannt?« So schnell ließ Justus nicht locker.

Sie zog die Brauen zusammen und betupfte sich wieder die Augen.

»Das glaube ich nicht. Einen Mann namens Ragnarson hat Bill nie erwähnt.«

»Dann haben Sie also bestimmt nicht kurz vor meinem Kommen mit einem Motorradfahrer gesprochen?«

»Nein, ich merkte ja gar nicht, dass da einer hier war. Was meinst denn du – was suchte der? Was wollte er? Kam er etwa hierher, um mit Steven zu reden?«

Nun musste Justus den Kopf schütteln. »Nein, Madam. Ihr Schwager sagte nur, er hätte ihn nicht gesehen.«

»Dann weiß ich auch nicht, was dieser Mensch hier wollte.«

Justus verabschiedete sich kurz und ließ Mrs Manning allein auf dem Sofa zurück, wo sie auf ihre Hände starrte. Draußen ging der Erste Detektiv zur Seitenmauer des Hauses, an der er sein Rad abgestellt hatte.

Sobald er von den Wohnzimmerfenstern aus nicht mehr gesehen werden konnte, schob er das Fahrrad vorsichtig auf die Zufahrt zur Garage und zum hinteren Bereich des Hauses. Die Garage war riesig und für mindestens drei Fahrzeuge gebaut.

Beim Gehen betrachtete Justus genau den Boden. Er fand aber nichts, bis er zu der Treppe vor dem hinteren Eingang kam.

Die Treppe führte zur Küche hinauf. Im Erdreich einer Blumenrabatte neben den Stufen sah er dann eine eindeutige Spur – den Abdruck eines Motorradreifens! Auf den Treppenstufen selbst, oben bei der Hintertür, lagen Erdkrumen, zweifellos aus dem Blumenbeet. Sie waren noch feucht.

Sam Ragnarson musste an diese Tür gekommen sein und Mrs Manning war bei Justus' Ankunft in der Küche gewesen. Nun blieb nur die Frage, ob sie sich beide an der Küchentür begegnet waren. Und was war eigentlich aus dem Kaffee geworden, für dessen Zubereitung Phyllis Manning so lange gebraucht hatte? Justus überlegte scharf. Er war so in Gedanken, dass er die beiden Männer überhörte, die auf ihn zukamen, bis sie dicht hinter ihm standen.

Zwei Männer mit Skimasken. Und einer der beiden hatte eine tätowierte Seejungfrau auf dem Unterarm! Justus versuchte wegzulaufen, aber die Männer waren schneller. Sie packten ihn und eine harte, schmutzige Hand verschloss ihm den Mund.

 Psst! In einigen Sätzen, die Steven Manning zu seiner Schwägerin sagte, steckt ein ganz heißer Tipp. Doch diesmal kein Wort mehr von mir...

Einer benimmt sich seltsam

Bob und Peter hörten, wie das Motorrad vor der Garage mit laufendem Motor stehen blieb. »Das Fenster!«, flüsterte Peter. Sie prüften, ob sich das einzige schmale Fenster in dem Lagerraum öffnen ließ. Es klappte. Vorsichtig schoben sie es höher. Ein lautes Quietschen war zu hören!

Die Jungen hielten den Atem an.

Zum Glück hatte der Motor das Geräusch übertönt. Dann wurde er abgestellt, aber vorläufig hörten die beiden keine Schritte in ihrer Richtung näher kommen. Flugs zwängten sich Bob und Peter durch die Fensteröffnung und landeten draußen im Schutz des dschungelähnlichen Gartens, von wo aus sie das Haus und die Garage beobachten konnten.

»Gut, dass Justus nicht dabei ist«, flüsterte Peter in dem sicheren Versteck. »Er hätte niemals durch das Fenster gepasst.«

»Psst«, machte Bob warnend. Dann grinste er und zeigte zur Garage hin. Sam Ragnarson, barfuß und in abgeschnittenen alten Jeans und zerrissenem T-Shirt, schob gerade mit munterem Pfeifen sein Motorrad in die Garage. Danach stieß er beide Torflügel weit auf. Bob und Peter sahen, wie er in den braunen Pick-up stieg, den Motor anließ und rückwärts aus der Garage fuhr.

»Er fährt wieder weg!«, flüsterte Peter ganz enttäuscht.

»Wir müssen versuchen, ihm zu folgen!« Bob richtete sich aus dem Gestrüpp auf.

»Halt, warte!« Peter hielt seinen Freund am Arm zurück. Der Wagen hatte auf der Zufahrt nochmals angehalten. Sam sprang heraus, lief zur Garage zurück und öffnete eine der Packtaschen seines Motorrads. Wieder pfiff er vor sich hin, während er eine Flasche aus der Tasche holte und sie neben dem Pick-up hinstellte. Dann stieg er auf die Ladefläche, hob dort eine große Plane an und sprang mit einem leeren 20-Liter-Plastikkanister und einem Trichter wieder herunter.

Aus ihrem Versteck beobachteten Bob und Peter, wie Sam die Flasche öffnete, den Trichter in die Einfüllöffnung des Kanisters steckte und den Flascheninhalt in den Kanister goss. Mit äußerst zufriedener Miene kickte er die leere Flasche ins Gebüsch, schraubte den Kanister zu und schob ihn wieder unter die Plane. Er schien einen Augenblick zu überlegen, dann ging er noch einmal in die Garage.

»Der hat doch was vor mit diesem Kanister«, rief Peter.

»Und wir müssen hinterher! Aber wie stellen wir das an?«

»Hinten im Laderaum könnten wir uns vielleicht verstecken«, schlug Peter vor.

»Ja, unter dieser Plane!«

Peter biss sich auf die Lippe. »Aber Sam kann jeden Moment wieder herauskommen und uns erwischen.«

»Einer von uns muss eben aufpassen, während der andere unter die Plane kriecht.«

»Eben, deshalb kann es nur einer schaffen, in den Pick-up zu kommen.«

»Und der andere muss sowieso auf Justus warten oder ihn suchen gehen«, meinte Bob.

»Pssst!«

Sam kam grinsend wieder aus der Garage. Diesmal hatte er das Holzkästchen bei sich, in dem die Jungen die Goldmünzen entdeckt hatten. Er legte das Kästchen auf den Beifahrersitz und blieb wiederum überlegend stehen. Dann nickte er kaum merklich und ging um den Pick-up herum zum Hintereingang seines Hauses. Die Tür erwies sich als verschlossen. Er suchte in seinen Taschen, fand aber nichts. Mit unwirschem Gemurmel machte er sich auf den Weg zur vorderen Haustür.

»Jetzt oder nie!«, rief Peter.

»Ich leg mich unter die Plane«, sagte Bob. »Ich bin der Kleinere.«

Das musste Peter anerkennen. »Also gut, ich warte dann hier noch eine Weile auf Justus, und wenn er nicht kommt, mache ich mich auf die Suche. Beeil dich. Wenn ich abwinke, dann kommt Sam!«

Bob kroch aus dem dichten Gestrüpp und lief zum Heck des alten braunen Pick-ups. Peter behielt die vordere Hausecke im Blick. Bob kletterte auf die Pritsche, schlüpfte rasch unter die schwere Plane und zog sie über sich, bis sie ihn völlig zudeckte und von außen nichts Verräterisches zu bemerken war.

Sekunden danach kam Sam aus der Hintertür und lief zum Wagen. Mit befriedigtem Grinsen stieg er ins Führerhaus, ohne hinten an der Pritsche nochmals nachzusehen. Im Rückwärtsgang lenkte er den Wagen aus der Zufahrt und fuhr weg. Peter sah ein wenig beklommen zu, bis der Pick-up um die nächste Ecke bog und verschwand. Er wartete eine Zeit lang auf Justus. Dann holte er sein Fahrrad, ließ Bobs Rad am Zaun angekettet stehen und flitzte zu einer Telefonzelle. Vielleicht hatte Justus sein Vorhaben bei Mrs Manning schon erledigt und war zur Zentrale gefahren, um vor dem Treffen mit Bob und Peter noch weiteres Zubehör zu holen. Ihre Walkie-Talkies hatten alle drei bei sich, aber noch lieber wäre es Peter gewesen, wenn sie auch die Peil- und Signalgeräte für den Notfall zur Hand gehabt hätten, falls Bob in einer Falle landete oder gar geschnappt wurde. Justus hatte möglicherweise dieselbe Idee gehabt. In der Zentrale meldete sich niemand. Hastig schlug Peter Mrs Mannings Adresse im Telefonbuch nach.

Der Zweite Detektiv radelte, so schnell er es schaffte, in das Hügelland vor der Stadt und zu dem Canyon, in dessen Nähe das Haus der Mannings stand. Bald hatte er das Stadtgebiet hinter sich gelassen und die Landstraße erreicht, die sich über dem Canyon in stetiger Steigung kurvenreich in die Berge wand. Die scharfen Kurven nahm er auf den Pedalen stehend. Schließlich war er an der steilen Zufahrt zum Haus der Mannings angelangt.

Er sah sich überall nach Justus' Fahrrad um, fand es jedoch nicht. Mrs Manning kam auf sein Klopfen hin selbst an die Tür. »Oh, du bist ja auch einer von diesen Jungen!«

»Ja, Madam«, bestätigte Peter. »Ist Justus da?«

»Er war hier, ja. Es war so aufmerksam von ihm, mir persönlich die Sache mit… der Jacke meines armen Bill zu berichten. Ich bin euch Jungen sehr zu Dank verpflichtet. Denn wenn ihr drei nicht…«

Peter fiel der Frau ins Wort. »Ist Justus nicht mehr da?«

»Nein, eben nicht... hm – wie heißt du noch gleich?«

»Peter«, sagte der Zweite Detektiv. »Wann genau ist Justus denn weggefahren?«

Mrs Manning blickte auf das Zifferblatt der hohen, alten Standuhr in der Diele. »Na, also mindestens vor einer Stunde. Ist was nicht in Ordnung?«

»Das weiß ich nicht, Madam«, erwiderte Peter voll Unbehagen. »Hat er vielleicht erwähnt, wohin er wollte?«

»Tut mir Leid, nein.«

»Ist etwas vorgefallen, während er hier war? Irgendetwas Ungewöhnliches, etwas außer der Reihe?«

»Nicht dass ich wüsste.« Peter bedankte sich und ging zu seinem Fahrrad zurück, das er seitlich am Haus abgestellt hatte. Was war Justus nur zugestoßen? Er untersuchte den Boden vor der Hausmauer, fand aber nichts außer dem Abdruck eines Motorradreifens im Erdreich einer Blumenrabatte bei den Stufen zum Hintereingang. Doch das hatte wohl nichts zu bedeuten. Die Spur eines Fahrradreifens war jedenfalls nirgends zu sehen.

Wo steckte der Erste Detektiv? Warum war er nicht wie abgemacht zu Sams Haus gekommen? Es sah ihm gar nicht ähnlich, ohne Vorankündigung einfach zu verschwinden. Und es war nun schon zwei Stunden her, seit die Freunde ihn zuletzt gesehen hatten.

In großer Sorge schob Peter sein Fahrrad langsam die abschüssige Zufahrt hinunter bis zu der gewundenen Straße beim Canyon. Und da sah er das Fragezeichen.

Es war an einem Telefonmast rechts neben der Straße! Ein hastig mit weißer Kreide hingekritzeltes Fragezeichen.

Schon vor langer Zeit hatten sich die drei ??? dieses System zum Markieren einer Fährte ausgedacht. Es sollte jeweils den anderen die Verfolgung und das Aufspüren ermöglichen, falls alle sonstigen Wege zur Verständigung blockiert waren. Im Übrigen stellte das Fragezeichen das Symbol der drei ??? dar und jedem der Freunde war eine Farbe zugeordnet. Weiß war Justus' Farbe.

Justus hatte also auf dem Telefonmast sein Fragezeichen hinterlassen! Peter suchte systematisch die Umgebung ab. Und da sah er die flachen Reifeneindrücke eines leichten Lastwagens und die schmale Fahrradspur!

Die Fährten kreuzen sich

Unter der Plane klammerte sich Bob an die Seitenwand der Pritsche, wenn der Wagen mit quietschenden Reifen um Straßenecken raste. Vorn auf dem Fahrersitz drückte Sam ausgelassen auf die Hupe und lachte dazu wie ein Irrer. Was auch immer Sam Ragnarson vorhatte, es musste ihm diebisches Vergnügen bereiten.

Einmal hielt der Wagen an und Sam stieg aus und unterhielt sich mit jemandem. Bob hob eine Ecke der Plane an, um zu sehen, wer das war, aber der andere war nicht in seinem Blickfeld. Bob konnte lediglich erkennen, dass sie vor dem Haus standen, in dem sich die Zahnarztpraxis von Dr. Ragnarson befand.

Sam fuhr weiter, und als das schlecht gefederte Fahrzeug endlich wieder zum Stehen kam, roch Bob die salzige Seeluft und vernahm die Geräusche vom Hafen her. Dann hörte er Sam hinten auf die Pritsche steigen. Bestimmt wollte er jetzt den Plastikkanister holen, der gleich neben Bob unter der Plane lag!

Der Kleinste der drei ??? machte sich noch kleiner. Vorsichtig rückte er so weit von dem Kanister ab, wie es ohne verräterische Geräusche und Bewegungen abging. Wenn nur Sam die Plane nicht ganz zurückschlug!

Bob hielt den Atem an. Eine Hand griff unter die Plane, tastete nach dem Kanister – und fand ihn nicht!

Bob atmete lautlos.

Die Hand tastete weiter herum, bekam aber nur einen kleinen Spaten zu fassen!

Bob hörte, wie Sam etwas vor sich hin knurrte und den Spaten auf die Straße warf. Nun konnte er jeden Augenblick die Plane hochheben, um den Kanister zu suchen! Wieder streckte sich die tastende Hand im Dunkeln aus. Bob holte tief Atem und schob den Kanister mit dem Fuß nach vorne, bis er nur noch eine Handbreit von Sams Fingern entfernt war. Und dann die letzten Zentimeter!

Sam grunzte zufrieden, packte den Kanister, zog ihn an sich und sprang von der Pritsche herunter. Bob lauschte auf Sams Schritte, die sich auf dem Asphalt entfernten und dann hohl auf den Planken eines Bootssteges widerhallten.

Mit äußerster Vorsicht spähte er ins Freie hinaus. Er konnte die Hafenanlagen und Gebäude sehen und den Verkehrslärm auf der Küstenstraße hören. Schnell wälzte er sich unter der Plane hervor und blickte über die Seitenwand des Wagens. Auf dem Steg, bei dem alle Boote der Ragnarsons vertäut waren, hatte sich Sam über Karl Ragnarsons Boot gebeugt.

Bob sprang rasch entschlossen über die hintere Ladeklappe und kauerte sich im Schutz eines der Hinterräder auf den Boden. Auf dem Steg war Sam unterdessen zu einem anderen Boot gegangen. Der 20-Liter-Kanister stand vor seinen Füßen.

Bob sah sich nach einem geeigneteren Versteck um. Gleich gegenüber der Anlegestelle war ein Restaurant mit Terrasse. Bob lief rasch zu einem der Tische im Freien hin, setzte sich hinter eine große Kübelpalme und sah zu, wie Sam drüben von Boot zu Boot ging.

Plötzlich sprang Sam in sein eigenes Boot, machte es los und ließ den Motor an. Hilflos und verzweifelt stand Bob auf, während Sam das Boot vom Steg weg und durch das Hafenbecken lenkte. Dann sah er das Boot abbiegen und auf einen langen Pier weiter unten am Hafen zuhalten. Bob rannte auf dem Fußgängerweg zu dem entfernten Pier hin.

 Ist das nicht aufmerksam von Sam, wie er bei jedem Boot seiner Verwandtschaft dafür Sorge trägt, dass für die nächste Fahrt nach Ragnarson Rock auch genügend Treibstoff im Tank ist?

Peter radelte die kurvenreiche Canyonstraße in Richtung Rocky Beach hinunter und hielt dabei auf der Fahrbahn und an Bäumen und Sträuchern nach weiteren Zeichen von Justus Ausschau. Dann kam er an eine Wegkreuzung. Wo ging es nun weiter?

Mitten auf der Straße, die zur Stadt führte, lag eine orangefarbene Korkscheibe. Darauf war mit weißer Kreide ein Fragezeichen gemalt! Peter grinste. Justus wusste sich doch immer zu helfen, wenn eine Fährte zu hinterlassen war!

Peter behielt die Straße aufmerksam im Auge. Doch erst bei der nächsten Kreuzung fand er wieder ein Zeichen. Wieder lag da eine orangefarbene Korkscheibe mit einem kleinen weißen Fragezeichen, um ihm den richtigen Weg zu weisen.

Peter strampelte noch eifriger, bis er an eine Gabelung kam. Er sah sich nach einer neuen leuchtenden Korkscheibe um. Aber es lag keine da.

Diesmal gab es rein gar nichts, worauf sich ein weißes Fragezeichen fand!

Peter wusste, dass Justus seine Spur markieren würde, wo immer dies möglich war. Als der Wagen an diese Gabelung gekommen war, hatte man Justus sicherlich beobachtet. Peter

122

blieb nichts anderes übrig, als sich für einen der beiden Wege zu entscheiden und ihn abzufahren, bis er wieder eine Markierung fand oder bis die Strecke endete. Wenn er dann noch kein Zeichen entdeckt hatte, musste er eben umkehren und den anderen Weg verfolgen. Er entschied sich für den Weg nach rechts, denn bisher hatte ihn die Fährte immerzu in die Richtung des Industrie- und Hafengebiets von Rocky Beach geleitet. Schon nach knapp einem Kilometer Fahrt sah er ein Stück Holz nahe der Fahrbahnmitte liegen. Ein Stück dunkles, glatt geschliffenes Treibholz mit einem weißen Fragezeichen! Peter hatte den richtigen Weg gewählt.

Die Spur führte Peter eindeutig zum Hafen. Nun erstreckte sich vor ihm die Küstenstraße, die am Hafen und den Piers entlangführte. Doch an welchem Pier, bei welchem der vielen Boote sollte er Justus suchen? Im ersten Augenblick war Peter ganz mutlos und wusste nicht weiter. Dann überlegte er scharf. Die orangefarbenen Korkscheiben waren Schwimmer – sie dienten dazu, ein Schleppnetz für die Fischerei an der Wasseroberfläche zu markieren. Vielleicht war Justus im Wagen eines Fischers, der zu seinem Boot fuhr. Also musste Peter die Piers systematisch absuchen.

Langsam fuhr er auf dem Uferweg für Fußgänger entlang, der den Hafen umrundete. Da – an einem Telefonmast fand sich wieder ein kleines weißes Fragezeichen. Der Mast befand sich genau an der Stelle, wo eine Zufahrt von der Küstenstraße abzweigte und zum Parkplatz vor dem privaten Pier einer Firma führte. Dort standen auch mehrere Betriebsgebäude. Peter schloss sein Rad am Fahrradständer an und ging zum Parkplatz. Das letzte weiße Kreidezeichen fand sich auf dem Reifen eines zerbeulten weißen Pick-ups mit kalifornischem Kennzeichen, das mit den Ziffern 56 begann. Das war der Wagen der Männer, die gegen Bob und auch seinen Vater handgreiflich geworden waren, um die Fotos zu erbeuten!

Peter sah sich um. Als Versteck kam nur eines der Gebäude auf dem Firmenpier infrage.

Er lief über den Parkplatz zum Pier vor und sah sich jedes Gebäude aufmerksam an. Es handelte sich um Lagerhäuser eines Fischfangbetriebs; überall waren Fässer und Netze und Taurollen gestapelt. Menschen konnte er nirgends entdecken.

Mittlerweile war es Nachmittag geworden und viele Mitarbeiter waren wegen des bevorstehenden Wochenendes wohl schon weggegangen. Peter suchte die schmutzigen Fensterscheiben nach einem Zeichen von Justus ab. Auch an den verschlossenen Türen und den Hauswänden fahndete er nach dem weißen Fragezeichen. Doch es war nichts zu finden.

Am Ende des Piers, beim letzten der Häuser, war ein Trawler für die Schleppnetzfischerei festgemacht. An dem einzigen Mast und dem am Mastfuß befestigten, schräg aufwärts führenden Spriet hingen Netze. Mit orangefarbenen Korkschwimmern!

Da bewegte sich jemand im Schatten zwischen den hohen Wänden der beiden letzten, zweigeschossigen Gebäude. Peter vernahm verstohlene Geräusche.

Er schlich näher heran und sah jemanden kauern, der sich offensichtlich zu verbergen trachtete. Nun hatte er Peter gehört und drehte sich um.

»Peter!«

»Bob, du?«

Die beiden Freunde liefen aufeinander zu.

»Was machst du denn hier?«, flüsterte Peter. »Du solltest doch Sam Ragnarson beschatten.«

»Hab ich doch gemacht. Er fuhr mit seinem Boot hierher, zu dem letzten Haus, und blieb eine Weile drinnen. Dann stieg er wieder ins Boot und fuhr aus dem Hafen! Da war nichts mehr zu machen«, erklärte Bob. »Aber was tust du hier? Und wo ist Justus?«

Peter berichtete von seinem Besuch bei Mrs Manning, von Justus' rätselhaftem Verschwinden und von der Fährte, die ihn hergeführt hatte.

»Er steckt sicher ganz schön in der Klemme«, schloss Peter. »Sonst hätte er unterwegs nicht all die Fragezeichen hinterlassen.«

Bob nickte. »Jedenfalls muss er hier sein. Aber wo?«

Beide Jungen überblickten die Reihe verlassener Bauten am Ende des Hafens. Es schien ganz so, als hätte sich der kompakte Erste Detektiv in Luft aufgelöst!

Gefangen!

Justus warf wütende Blicke auf die beiden maskierten Männer vor ihm. Er war in einer kleinen Dachkammer mit einem einzigen hoch gelegenen Fenster an einen unbequemen Stuhl gefesselt. Weit unten hörte er die Wellen an die Verankerung des Piers anschlagen und die Luft roch nach Fisch und Teer.

»Ich empfehle Ihnen dringend, mich freizulassen, sonst nimmt es für Sie ein böses Ende«, drohte der Erste Detektiv.

»Der hat ja 'ne große Klappe«, knurrte der größere Mann, der sich eine braune Skimaske mit Augenlöchern über das Gesicht gezogen hatte.

»Diese naseweisen Lümmel. Schnüffeln überall rum, wo sie nichts verloren haben«, bemerkte der Kleinere mit der tätowierten Seejungfrau auf dem Arm.

»Sie können sicher sein, dass meine Freunde mich aufstöbern«, warnte Justus die beiden. »Sie werden mit der Polizei herkommen. Entführung ist eine schwer wiegende Straftat.«

»'ne ganz große Klappe, Walt«, wiederholte der Große.

»Wenn du deine Freunde wiedersehen willst, Kleiner«, sagte der Tätowierte, »dann pack lieber jetzt aus und sag uns, wo die Fotos sind, die ihr gemacht habt.«

»Da sind Sie leider einen Tag zu spät dran«, entgegnete Justus unnachgiebig. »Mr Andrews hat die Bilder gestern in seiner Zeitung abgedruckt.«

»He, Ted, nimm den Dicken mal in die Mangel«, feixte Walt. »Was hier zu spät ist, das entscheiden wir. Im Übrigen reden wir von den anderen Bildern, ist das klar?«

Ted trat bedrohlich nahe an Justus heran. »Wir wollen alle Fotos, die noch übrig sind, Fatso – und zwar sofort!«

Justus beschloss, auf den Busch zu klopfen. »Was treiben Sie und Sam Ragnarson auf Ragnarson Rock? Was wird da geschmuggelt?«

»Wer soll 'n das sein – Sam Ragnarson?«

»Wie kommt ihr Jungs auf die Idee, dass wir auf der Insel was treiben?«

»Da machen wir lieber 'n großen Bogen drum.«

»Is' viel zu riskant, was, Ted?«

»Aber immer.«

»Wir haben Sie gestern Nacht dort draußen gesehen!«, versuchte es Justus auf gut Glück.

Die beiden vermummten Männer in dem kleinen Raum sahen Justus stumm und lauernd an. Umso lauter hörte man jetzt unten die Wellen gegen den Pier schlagen.

Schließlich sagte der Tätowierte: »Solche Knirpse spielen sich manchmal schlauer auf, als für sie gut is', meinste nich', Ted?«

»Viel zu schlau«, antwortete der Große.

»Und dann findet man sie vielleicht im Hafenbecken.«

»Wenn man sie überhaupt findet ...«

Justus auf seinem Stuhl wurde es ziemlich mulmig, doch er ließ sich nichts anmerken. »Mich können Sie nicht einschüch-

126

tern«, sagte er ganz ruhig. »Wenn es Ihnen um diese Fotos geht, dann können Sie es sich gar nicht leisten, mir was anzutun, ehe Sie die Bilder haben!«

»Da sei mal nich' so sicher, Junge«, knurrte Walt.

»Ihr seid zu dritt«, sagte Ted. »Wenn deine Kumpels dich mucksmäuschenstill im Wasser treiben sehen, dann geben die uns die Fotos vielleicht doch ruck, zuck.«

Justus wurde blass, wahrte aber die Fassung. Was die maskierten Männer auch mit ihm vorhaben mochten – ihm würde es nichts nützen, Furcht oder Panik zu zeigen. Stattdessen steigerte er sich nun in Zorn, ja in kalte Wut hinein.

»Was haben wir schon getan – Sie etwa bei einer Schmuggelaktion fotografiert?«, redete sich der Erste Detektiv in Harnisch. »Na, und um was geht's? Um Gold? Illegale Einwanderer? Drogen?«

»Schmuggel?«, wiederholte Ted. »Der Knabe hält uns für Schmuggler.«

»Der Bursche hat wirklich was drauf«, sagte Walt.

»Der is' ja doch ganz schön schlau«, bestätigte Ted.

»Wenn wir Schmuggler sind, dann müssen wir echt gefährlich sein. Stimmt's, Junge?«, meinte Walt. »Nun sag uns schon, wie wir an diese Fotos rankommen.«

»Gib uns die Bilder«, war Teds Angebot, »und du landest wieder zu Hause. Mit heiler Haut und mit deinem ganzen Lebendgewicht.« Er grinste hämisch.

»Na, dann rufste jetzt am besten deine Freunde an und sagst denen, sie sollen die Bilder herbringen«, forderte Walt barsch. »Los, Junge, mach schon.«

»Solang du noch kannst.«

»Du willst doch wohl nach Hause, oder nich'?«

Justus schluckte, dann nickte er. »Also gut. Ich werde anrufen.«

»Brav. Kluges Kind«, lobte Ted.

»Aber keine Tricks, Kleiner«, riet Walt. »Wir haben in deiner Jacke eure Karte gefunden und wissen eure Telefonnummer. Also mach keine Zicken.«

Ted ging aus der Kammer und kam mit einem Telefon wieder. Er stöpselte es in eine Dose an der Wand neben Justus ein und wählte nach ausgiebigem Studium der Visitenkarte der drei ??? die Nummer der Zentrale. Dann hielt er Justus den Hörer vors Gesicht.

»Sag denen, du bist da auf 'ne Idee gekommen«, befahl Ted. »Du musst dir dringend hier unten all die Fotos ansehen, weil du wissen willst, ob du Recht gehabt hast. Sag ihnen, sie sollen sich beeilen.«

»Und denk dran, was dir passieren könnte«, warnte Walt. »Keine Tricks.«

Justus nickte. Es war ja möglich, dass Peter oder auch Bob zur Zentrale zurückgefahren war, um auf seinen Anruf zu warten. Sollte einer von beiden dort sein, würde er eine verschlüsselte Mitteilung durchgeben, aus der sein Freund erkennen konnte, dass der Erste Detektiv in Gefangenschaft geraten war.

Das Telefon klingelte. Immer wieder. Niemand nahm ab. Ted knallte den Hörer wieder auf den Apparat. »Wir warten. Dann versuchen wir es noch mal.«

Vom Eingang unten war ganz schwach ein Klopfen an der Tür zu hören. Die beiden maskierten Halunken erstarrten.

»Geh mal nachsehen«, sagte Ted.

Walt, der Kleine, verließ den Raum und zog sich dabei die Maske herunter. Justus hörte ihn treppab gehen. Erst blieb alles still, dann rief Walt herauf:

»Hey, Ted, das is' der neue Chef vom Fischmarkt! Komm mal eben runter.«

»Keinen Mucks«, schärfte Ted dem Gefangenen ein. Dann ging er auch.

Gesetzt den Fall, die Brüder Ted & Walt sind so etwas wie Schmuggler. Da sie auf die Fotos so scharf sind, musste es sich bei dem Schmuggelgut – sofern irgendetwas davon zufällig vor Bobs Objektiv gekommen ist – um etwas ganz Brisantes handeln. Ja, warum nicht ein praller Beutel mit Nuggets? Oder warum nicht eine Reihe Päckchen mit Drogen? Oder...

Justus hörte, wie die Kammertür von außen abgeschlossen wurde. Er zerrte an den Stricken, mit denen seine Arme und Beine an den Stuhl gefesselt waren. Sie gaben ein wenig nach, lockerten sich aber nicht. Verzweifelt sah er sich in dem kleinen Raum nach etwas um, das ihm zur Befreiung verhelfen konnte. Aber es gab nichts. Das Fenster war einen Spalt hochgeschoben, doch selbst wenn Justus mitsamt dem Stuhl dorthin zu hoppeln vermochte, lag es in unerreichbarer Höhe.

Für ihn stand fest, dass Peter oder Bob sich auf die Suche nach ihm gemacht und die Fährte seiner Fragezeichen aufgespürt hatte. Die erste Markierung an dem Telefonmast gleich bei der Zufahrt der Mannings war ihm leicht gefallen. Justus hatte vor dem Mast den beiden Entführern gegenübergestanden, während sie sein Fahrrad in den Pick-up hievten. Die Hände hinter dem Rücken, hatte er rasch und unbemerkt das Fragezeichen hingekritzelt.

Danach war es freilich schwierig gewesen, weitere Spuren zu legen. Immerhin hatte er es geschafft, die Korkschwimmer und ein Stück Treibholz aus dem Wagen mit Fragezeichen zu versehen und das Zeug immer dann abzuwerfen, wenn Walt, der mit ihm hinten auf der Pritsche saß, gerade nach vorn blickte.

Das letzte Signal war am einfachsten gewesen; er hatte sich nämlich vor einem Hinterrad auf den Boden hocken müssen, während Ted bei dem Gebäude am Ende des Piers prüfte, ob die Luft rein war, und Walt nach dem Zeichen von Ted ausschaute, damit er Justus in das Haus bringen konnte.

Mit ein wenig Glück hätte es Bob oder Peter gelingen können, die Spur aufzunehmen und zu verfolgen. Doch falls er sich nicht befreien konnte, war es ihm unmöglich, sich bemerkbar zu machen. Noch einmal spannte er sich energisch, aber vergeblich gegen seine Fesseln. Dann ließ er sich wieder zurücksinken, heftig atmend und mit schwindender Hoffnung, doch weiterhin hielt er nach irgendetwas Ausschau, das ihm nützen konnte.

Er sah nur sein Fahrrad.

Eine Weile starrte er auf die Packtaschen am Gepäckträger. Darin steckte sein Walkie-Talkie, sofern die maskierten Entführer es nicht herausgenommen hatten! Am Morgen, nach der Rückkehr von Ragnarson Rock, hatte er es eingepackt.

Mit äußerster Anstrengung richtete sich Justus mitsamt dem Stuhl, an den er gefesselt war, auf und stellte sich auf die Füße. Gehen konnte er nicht, da seine Beine fest zusammengebunden waren, aber er konnte hüpfen, bis er bei seinem Fahrrad war. Dort ließ er sich vornüber auf die Knie fallen und tastete mit der Nase eine der Packtaschen ab.

Das Walkie-Talkie war noch da!

Mit den Zähnen zerrte er die Schnalle auf, hob die Klappe und hielt sie mit dem Kopf offen. Dann nahm er das kleine Gerät in den Mund und zog es vorsichtig aus der Tasche. Er konnte es nicht richtig festhalten, es entglitt ihm … Plötzlich fiel es klappernd zu Boden.

Justus hielt den Atem an.

Er lauschte. Unten blieb es ruhig, bis auf das Klatschen der Wellen gegen die Stützpfeiler des Piers und die hin und wieder schwach vernehmlichen Stimmen. Doch niemand kam herauf. Justus ließ sich zur Seite kippen, schob das Walkie-Talkie gegen eine Wand und drückte die Nase auf den Einschaltknopf.

»Hallo!«, stieß er in seiner unbequemen Lage mühsam und gepresst hervor. »Bob! Peter! Hört ihr mich? Bitte kommen, Bob und Peter ...«

Kühne Rettungsaktion

»Bob! Peter! Hört ihr mich? Bitte kommen, Bob und Peter ...«
Bob und Peter kauerten hinter einigen Kisten neben dem zweigeschossigen Holzbau am Ende des Piers. Gerade hatten sie beobachtet, wie ein Mann an die Eingangstür klopfte und dann hineinging. Und nun schien die Stimme ihres Freundes geradewegs vom Pier her zu ihnen zu dringen.

»Das ist Justus!«, rief Peter. »Mein Walkie-Talkie!« Bob griff nach seiner Tasche. Rasch zog er das kleine Gerät hervor, das Justus gebaut hatte, und drückte auf den Knopf »Senden«.

»Justus! Wo bist du? Ist alles in Ordnung?«

Justus' Stimme aus dem Gerät klang so, als halte er sich die Nase zu. »Bob? Ich bin in irgendeinem Gebäude am Ende eines privaten Firmenpiers am Hafen. Die gleichen beiden Männer, die dir die Negative abgenommen hatten, haben mich vor Mrs Mannings Haus entführt. Wo seid ihr denn?«

»Vor genau diesem Haus!«, sagte Peter eifrig in sein Walkie-Talkie. »Ich habe deine Spur verfolgt!«

»Und ich bin auch dorthin ...«, fing Bob an.

Justus schaltete sich rasch dazwischen. »Ihr müsst mich hier rausholen. Ich bin gerade allein, sie besprechen unten was mit dem Chef vom Fischmarkt und sind damit sicher eine Weile beschäftigt. Aber es muss schnell gehen!«

Bob sagte: »Sag uns erst mal, wo du genau bist, Justus.«

»In einem kleinen Raum, ich glaube ganz oben im letzten Gebäude auf dem Pier. Ich bin an einen Stuhl gefesselt. Es gibt nur ein kleines Fenster, das einen Spalt offen ist, aber es ist zu hoch, und ich komm nicht ran.«

»Was siehst du denn durch das Fenster?«

»Nur den Himmel, Bob.«

»Und was hörst du?«

»Wellen, die an die Stützpfeiler des Piers schlagen. Und irgendwelche dumpfen, schweren Stöße gegen das Haus.«

Peter machte Bob ein Zeichen und wies auf das Fischerboot, das im Rhythmus der Brandung gegen die Verankerung des Piers vor dem Gebäude stieß. »Kannst du sonst irgendwas von deinem Fenster aus sehen, Justus?«, fragte Peter.

Kurz blieb es still. Dann kam Justus' Stimme wieder, ganz leise: »Eine Wolke, fast kreisförmig.«

Auch Peter und Bob sahen die kleine, runde Wolke im Westen. Sie liefen hinter das Haus zum westlichen Ende des Piers, drehten sich um und blickten in die Höhe. Das einzige kleine Fenster in der Westmauer des Gebäudes lag hoch oben, zum Wasser hinaus. Zwischen der Hauswand und dem Hafenbecken war auf dieser Seite nur ein ganz schmaler Weg.

»Alles klar, Justus, ich glaube, wir haben dein Fenster entdeckt«, meldete Peter. »Kannst du irgendetwas unternehmen, um wegzukommen?«

»Gar nichts«, kam Justus' Stimme aus dem Walkie-Talkie. »Ich bin an einen Stuhl gebunden und kann die Stricke nicht zerreißen oder durchtrennen.«

Bob und Peter standen dicht an der Mauer des verlassenen Gebäudes und überlegten. Immer wieder stieß der Trawler knarrend und ächzend gegen den Pier. Auf der weiten Wasserfläche des Hafens jenseits des Piers tummelten sich Paddler, Wasserskiläufer und Surfer.

»Wenn Justus nicht wegkann«, sagte Peter zu Bob, »dann müssen wir eben zu ihm rauf.«

Bob sah zu dem kleinen Fenster im Obergeschoss hinauf. »Ja, aber wie?«

Peter dachte einen Augenblick nach. Dann schlenderte er bedächtig um das zweigeschossige Haus herum und sah auf das Deck des Trawlers hinunter, der auf dem bewegten Wasser des Hafenbeckens dümpelte. »Da! Auf dem Deck liegt ein langes Tau! Wir müssten doch das Boot so rangieren können, dass einer von uns über das Spriet durch das Fenster ins Haus einsteigen kann!«

Bob blickte am Bootsmast hinauf und dann zu dem kleinen Fenster hoch. »Einer von uns – na, wer wohl? Lass mal, ich weiß schon.« Er schnitt eine Grimasse.

»Heute ist dein Glückstag!«, spottete Peter gutmütig. »Den Kleineren und Leichteren trifft es eben, Bob. Wir wissen ja nicht, was das Tau und das Spriet aushalten, und wenn du wieder unten bist, müssen wir noch Justus abseilen!«

Die beiden Jungen sprangen vom Pier auf das Bootsdeck hinunter und Peter nahm das eine Ende der dicken Taurolle auf. Er machte es um Bobs Mitte fest und erklärte ihm sein Vorhaben. »Du kletterst am Netz hoch bis zum Ende des Spriets, und das schwenke ich dann mit der Leine herum, bis du vor dem Fenster bist. Du steigst durch und ich gebe mit dem Tau nach, bis du auf dem Fußboden stehst. Dann schneidest du bei Justus die Stricke durch und ich ziehe euch zwei zum Fenster hoch, einzeln natürlich. Und dann haltet ihr euch wieder am Spriet fest, ich schwenke es herum und ihr könnt am Netz herunterklettern.«

Bob schien Zweifel zu haben. »Ich weiß nicht recht, Peter. Das alles hört sich ja ziemlich riskant an.«

»Riskant ist höchstens, dass wir womöglich von den Burschen, die Justus verschleppt haben, erwischt werden, also muss es jetzt ganz fix gehen. Hier hast du mein Taschenmesser, damit befreist du Justus. Wenn ihr so weit seid und beide vom Haus wegkönnt, dann ziehst du am Tau.«

Mittlerweile war Bob fachkundig angeseilt und kletterte am Netz hoch. Das war einfacher, als er erwartet hatte – es ging genauso leicht wie an einer Leiter. Als er am Ende des langen Spriets angekommen war, das vom Mastfuß aus schräg aufragte, zog Peter an der Leine und schwenkte das Spriet herum, bis Bob sich am Fensterrahmen festhalten konnte. Es gelang ihm, das Fenster vollends hochzuschieben und auf dem Sims Fuß zu fassen.

An Deck des Trawlers brasste Peter die Sprietleine und hielt sie fest, bis Bob die Beine über den Sims geschwungen hatte. Dann ließ der Zweite Detektiv Bobs Tau allmählich nach und Bob tauchte hinter dem Fenster im Raum unter.

Drinnen lag Justus noch auf der Seite am Boden. Er sah auf und grinste, als Bob an dem Tau zu ihm heruntergelassen wurde. Sobald Bobs Füße den Boden berührten, löste er sich aus der Schlinge und lief zu Justus hin.

»Los, mach schnell!«, sagte Justus. »Die können jeden Augenblick wieder hier sein!«

Bob nahm sein Taschenmesser und durchtrennte die Stricke, mit denen Justus an den Stuhl gefesselt war, mit einigen raschen Schnitten. Dann liefen Bob und Justus zum Fenster. Den Stuhl nahmen sie mit. Erst stellte sich Bob auf den Stuhl und zog sich zu dem Fenstersims hoch.

Dann kam Justus an die Reihe. Er bestieg den Stuhl, packte Bobs Hand und schaffte es unter Ächzen und Stöhnen schließlich auch bis hinauf zum Sims. Das schmale Fenster erwies sich für den gewichtigen Ersten Detektiv als hinderlicher Engpass.

Zuletzt zwängte er sich wie ein Korken im Flaschenhals mit einem gewaltigen Ruck hindurch und bekam das Netz am

Ende des Spriets zu fassen. Als Bob und Justus sich am Netz sicheren Halt verschafft hatten, holte Peter die Sprietleine dicht, um das Spriet vom Fenster wieder wegzuschwenken.

Doch er hatte die Belastung durch Justus' zusätzliches Gewicht unterschätzt. Als das Spriet vom Fenster zur Seite kurvte, rutschte ihm die Leine aus den Händen, und das Spriet glitt im Bogen weiter weg, bis es über dem Wasser war. Am Ende seines Schwenkbereichs wurde es mit einem Ruck abgebremst. Justus und Bob verloren den Halt, segelten hilflos zappelnd durch die Luft und platschten ins Wasser des Hafenbeckens.

Schnappend und prustend wie Delfine tauchten die beiden wieder auf.

»Wirf eine Leine runter!«, keuchte Justus.

Peter an Deck des Trawlers wollte sich halb totlachen. Doch dann hörte er hinter sich zorniges Gebrüll. Er fuhr herum. Die beiden maskierten Männer kamen auf ihn zugelaufen! »Schwimmt ans Ufer!«, schrie Peter. Dann stürzte er sich selbst ins Wasser.

Die drei Jungen schwammen zum flachen Strand am Beginn des Piers. Bald hatten sie Grund unter den Füßen und wateten klitschnass an Land. Sie mischten sich unter die anderen Leute am Ufer und tauchten in den Massen der Spaziergänger auf der Strandpromenade unter.

»So, die wären wir los«, sagte Peter. »Mit den Masken kommen sie uns nicht nach.«

»Wir nehmen rasch einen Bus und machen, dass wir hier wegkommen!«, drängte Justus.

»Und was wird aus meinem Fahrrad?«, fragte Peter.

»Die Räder holen wir später ab«, entschied Justus.

Im Bus nahmen die drei ??? ganz hinten Platz, denn ihre nassen Sachen tropften noch immer. Sie handelten sich von den Mitfahrern erstaunte Blicke ein, aber das kümmerte sie nicht, und außerdem waren sie eifrig mit dem Austausch ihrer Erfahrungen beschäftigt. Bob und Peter erzählten Justus, was sie in dem kleinen Lagerraum in Sam Ragnarsons Garage entdeckt hatten und wobei sie Sam am Hafen beobachtet hatten.

»Dann spielte also Sam den Geist des Kapitän Coulter und den Geist des ertrunkenen Seemanns und wahrscheinlich obendrein noch den Wolf. Und das alles deshalb, weil er draußen auf Ragnarson Rock Gold von der *Star of Panama* gefunden hatte!«, schloss Bob seinen Bericht.

»Ja, und die beiden maskierten Männer müssen seine Komplizen sein«, ergänzte Peter.

»Deshalb hat er sich auch mit denen getroffen!«, fuhr Bob fort. »Ich möchte wetten, dass einer von ihnen gestern Nacht draußen auf dem Schiff war und dass der andere ihm vom Ufer aus mit seiner Taschenlampe Signale gab. Und Sam versuchte, uns im Kostüm des Kapitän Coulter zu verscheuchen. Mit dem Schiff sollte das Gold abtransportiert werden!«

»Das ist schon möglich, Bob«, meinte Justus nachdenklich, »aber irgendwie will mir nicht ganz einleuchten, warum Sam auf die Hilfe der beiden angewiesen sein sollte, um sich das Gold zu holen.«

»Aber was hatten sie dann dort draußen zu schaffen, und warum kam Sam heute zum Pier, um mit ihnen zu sprechen?«, fragte Peter.

»Nun ja, es sieht ganz danach aus, als machten sie gemeinsame Sache«, räumte Justus ein. »Bestimmt hat mich Sam oben bei Mrs Mannings Haus erspäht, und da schickte er sie mir auf den Hals, damit sie mich entführen.«

»Ach, Sam war also oben beim Haus der Mannings?«, fragte Bob.

»Ja. Wahrscheinlich hatte er von seinem Vater gehört, dass ich einen Besuch bei Mrs Manning machen wollte, und da setzte er sich auf sein Motorrad, um vor mir da zu sein.«

Peter blickte nicht ganz durch. »Aber warum hätte er den ganzen Weg da rausfahren sollen?«

Justus hob die Schultern. »Vielleicht will er uns eben die ganze Zeit im Auge behalten. Jedenfalls fragte ich Mrs Manning, ob sie mit Sam gesprochen hatte, aber weder ihr noch ihrem Schwager war er zu Gesicht gekommen. Er hatte sich wohl irgendwo im Freien versteckt. Halt, Augenblick mal… Ein Reifenabdruck seines Motorrads war ja in der Erde vor dem Küchenausgang zu sehen. Also muss er sich wohl doch nicht versteckt haben. Aber warum hat ihn niemand gesehen?«

Der Erste Detektiv hielt verwirrt inne.

»Das alles scheint mir nicht so ganz zusammenzupassen«, meinte er schließlich. »Na, gehen wir zur Zentrale zurück und denken den Fall nochmals durch!«

 Wieder einmal bieten sich fürs Kombinieren mehrere Möglichkeiten.
Sam und die beiden Maskierten könnten sein:
1. Komplizen
2. Rivalen
3. Zwei Parteien mit jeweils eigenem Ziel

Sam und seine Intrigen

Im Versteck ihrer Zentrale legten die drei Jungen nochmals die achtundvierzig Bilder auf Schreibtisch, Tischen und Aktenschrank aus. Rasch hatten Peter und Bob die Aufnahmen ausgesucht, auf denen Sam Ragnarson zu sehen war.

»Das ist er«, stellte Peter fest, »wie er sich im Gelände hinter den anderen Leuten zum Boden bückt. Bestimmt war er da gerade auf die Goldmünzen und Nuggets gestoßen.«

»Und dabei hat er gemerkt, wie ich Fotos machte«, sagte Bob, »und deshalb wollte er die Bilder an sich bringen.«

Justus schritt langsam im Raum hin und her, und während sie gemeinsam den Fall von neuem aufrollten, betrachtete er die Bilder sorgfältig, eines nach dem anderen.

»Ja, das müssen die Aufnahmen sein, um die es Sam geht«, bestätigte der Anführer der drei ???. »Man kann nicht erkennen, was er da gerade macht. Allerdings weiß er das nicht, und er will nicht riskieren, dass jemand anders auf den Fotos etwa die Münzen entdeckt. Er will jetzt ungestört allein auf der Insel sein, damit er weiter nach Gold suchen kann. Deshalb versuchte er, mit dem Wolfsgeheul auf seinem Band und seiner Verkleidung als Geist die Menschen dort zu vertreiben.«

Justus trat vor die nächste Bilderserie. »Und die beiden Männer mit den Gesichtsmasken arbeiten mit ihm zusammen. Sie haben in seinem Auftrag unsere Negative gestohlen und wollten dann auch noch die Reproduktionen erbeuten«, fasste Bob nochmals die Ereignisse zusammen. »Sam schickte sie los, um dich zu entführen, Justus, und dann fuhr er selbst hin, um sie zu fragen, ob sie die Bilder nun hatten. Auf keinen Fall sollten andere erfahren, dass er Gold gefunden hat.«

»Vielleicht ist er inzwischen auch schon auf den Rest gestoßen«, mutmaßte Peter. »Er hat alles irgendwo auf der Insel versteckt und die anderen beiden Ganoven sollen es nun mit dem Fischerboot abholen und an einen sicheren Ort schaffen.«

»Deshalb wollten sie bestimmt gestern Nacht im Nebel los«, erkannte Bob, »aber wir haben sie dabei aufgestört. Sicherlich probierten sie es gestern, gerade weil es neblig war, obwohl sich noch einige Leute auf der Insel aufhielten!«

»Ja.« Justus nickte nachdenklich. »Das wäre eine logische Erklärung. Aber unser Problem ist damit noch nicht gelöst. Wozu brauchte denn Sam die beiden Männer? Warum sollte er andere an seinem Goldfund beteiligen? Draußen auf der Insel hätte er doch leicht ein Versteck finden können. Dann wäre es auch nicht schwer gewesen, das Gold in kleinen Partien zum Festland mitzunehmen, solange niemand davon wusste.«

»Vielleicht war er auf die beiden angewiesen, weil er sein Spiel anhand unserer Fotos bereits durchschaut glaubte und uns misstraute«, meinte Peter. »Nun wollte er all das Gold möglichst schnell wegschaffen.«

»Das könnte sein, Peter«, bestätigte Justus stirnrunzelnd. »Und doch erscheint es mir nicht logisch, dass Sam die beiden Burschen gestern Mr Andrews auf den Hals schickte, noch ehe er in der Zeitung die sechs Fotos überhaupt gesehen hatte. Und wir dürfen nicht vergessen, dass Dr. Ragnarson selbst bestätigte, Sam sei genau zu diesem Zeitpunkt draußen auf der Insel gewesen, als die Männer am Mittwoch Bob überfielen und sich die Negative schnappten.«

»Aber wenn es nicht Sam war, der die beiden mit dem Diebstahl der Fotos beauftragte, Justus«, sagte Bob verwundert, »wer war es dann?«

»Und außerdem«, wandte Peter noch ein, »hat Bob ja gesehen, wie Sam auf dem Pier mit den beiden redete!«

»Alles richtig«, musste Justus zugeben. »Sie arbeiten mit Sicherheit zusammen.«

»Sollten wir denn nicht nun Dr. Ragnarson und Mr Karl Ragnarson verständigen?«, fragte Bob. »Und vielleicht auch die Polizei?«

Justus knetete seine Unterlippe zwischen den Fingern – ein Anzeichen dafür, dass er konzentriert überlegte. Lange sah er auf die Reihen der Fotos herunter. »Wir haben keinen stichhaltigen Beweis dafür, dass Sam das Gold hat, mindestens solange wir die Münzen nicht vorweisen können. Und ich bin eben nicht so sicher, ob die Sache mit dem Goldfund alles ist, was sich da draußen womöglich abspielt. Die einzige Straftat, von der wir berichten könnten, ist die Entführung, und die können wir Sam nicht ohne konkrete Beweise anlasten. Nein, ich bin der Meinung, dass wir Sam auf frischer Tat ertappen und überführen müssen, ehe wir uns an die Polizei wenden können. Und das muss auf Ragnarson Rock geschehen. Heute Abend werden wir mit Sams Vater und seinem Onkel noch einmal zur Insel hinausfahren. Ich schlage vor, dass wir uns zu Hause warme Sachen holen und Bescheid sagen, dass wir vielleicht noch einmal über Nacht dort bleiben.«

Sie verließen die Zentrale durch Tunnel II und Bob und Peter marschierten zu Fuß los. Als Bob zu Hause ankam, war es schon fünf Uhr vorüber, und sein Vater saß im Wohnzimmer.

»Na, Bob, gibt es was Neues von den beiden Männern, die euch die Fotos abnehmen wollten?«

»Wir glauben, dass sie mit Sam Ragnarson gemeinsame Sache machen, Dad. Er hat auf der Insel das Gold von der *Star of Panama* gefunden und das will er natürlich geheim halten.«

»Dann hast du also ganz zufällig Fotos von diesem Goldfund gemacht?«

»So oder ähnlich müssen wir es uns zusammenreimen.«

Bob lief in sein Zimmer, um seine Jacke zu holen, kam aber gleich wieder herunter.

»Dad, richte bitte Mom aus, dass ich zum Abendessen nicht da bin. Wir fahren nämlich noch mal raus nach Ragnarson Rock. Vielleicht bleiben wir auch über Nacht.«

»Ist gut, Bob.«

Bob lief in der warmen Abendsonne zum Schrottplatz zurück und kam dort gleichzeitig mit Peter an. Justus hatte schon gewartet. Der Erste Detektiv war sichtlich aufgeregt.

»Los, kommt, ihr beiden, Patrick sitzt schon im Lastwagen! Wir müssen sofort losfahren zum Hafen, damit wir bestimmt auf der Insel sind, ehe es Nacht wird!«

»Was ist denn los, Justus?«, rief Peter. »Ist was passiert?«

»Im Augenblick sehe ich noch nicht klar, Peter«, erklärte Justus rasch, »aber ich habe mir all die Fotos noch mal angesehen, und wenn ich mich nicht täusche, geht da draußen auf Ragnarson Rock etwas viel Folgenschwereres vor sich, als wir uns das bisher vorstellen konnten!«

»Aber warum so überstürzt?«, erkundigte sich Bob, als sie zum Lastwagen trabten, in dem Patrick wartete.

»Weil Sam schon auf der Insel ist und weil es nach Einbruch der Dunkelheit zu spät sein könnte.«

»Und die beiden Herren Ragnarson?«, fragte Bob verwundert.

»Die sind schon unten am Hafen«, sagte Justus. »Ich rief sie an, als ihr weggegangen wart. Sie wollen um sechs ablegen, mit allen, die noch einmal Lust zu einer Überfahrt haben.«

»Wie kommen wir zu unseren Kostümen?«, wollte Peter wissen.

»Darum brauchen wir uns jetzt nicht mehr zu sorgen«, meinte Justus erleichtert. »Sam weiß ohnehin, wer wir sind und was wir vorhaben.«

 Wer von meinen Lesern mittlerweile auch so zweifelsfrei Bescheid weiß wie der Erste Detektiv, hat wahrhaftig ein großes Lob verdient. Und wer – wie Bob und Peter – noch nicht so ganz klar sieht, darf sich auf einen spannenden Endspurt und eine große Überraschung gefasst machen.

Sie stiegen hinten auf die Pritsche und Patrick fuhr los zum Hafen. Die holprige Fahrt in dem schlecht gefederten alten Vehikel verhinderte unterwegs eine vernünftige Unterhaltung, aber Bob und Peter fragten sich insgeheim, was Justus diesmal für Pläne geschmiedet hatte. Bald erreichten sie die Schnell-straße längs der Küste, und dann kamen sie an dem Pier vorüber, auf dem Justus eingesperrt gewesen war.

»Mein Rad ist zum Glück noch da«, sagte Peter erleichtert. Er zeigte auf den Fahrradständer, wo es angeschlossen war.

»Da steht noch ein anderes Fahrrad, Peter«, stellte Bob fest. Auch Peter hatte es gesehen.

»Das ist deins, Justus!«, rief er.

»Patrick, lass uns mal eben aussteigen«, rief Justus. Der Wagen hielt an und die Jungen untersuchten Justus' Fahrrad. Es war offenbar unbeschädigt. Jemand hatte es einfach gegen Peters Rad gelehnt. Die Packtaschen waren auch noch daran.

»Die beiden maskierten Männer befürchteten wahrscheinlich, dass ich die Polizei hierher mitbringe!«, sagte Justus. »Also schafften sie mein Rad samt Gepäck herunter und stellten es zu deinem hin. Ein Glück, dass es inzwischen keiner geklaut hat.«

»Und wie können wir jetzt beweisen, dass sie dich entführt haben?«, ging es Bob auf.

»Können wir eben nicht«, sagte Justus verärgert. »Das war doch der Sinn der Aktion. Da es keinen Beweis gibt, würde mir die Polizei meine Darstellung vielleicht gar nicht abnehmen.«

Sie hoben die Fahrräder auf die Pritsche, und Patrick fuhr weiter zu dem Pier mit der öffentlichen Anlegestelle, wo auch die Boote der Ragnarsons festgemacht waren. Eine kleine Gruppe Inselfahrer stand wartend bei den Booten. Karl Ragnarson und Dr. Ingmar Ragnarson gingen auf die Jungen zu.

»Da scheint mit allen Booten was nicht in Ordnung zu sein!«, rief der Schulleiter ärgerlich. »Kein Einziges lässt sich starten!«

»Das war gezielte Sabotage!« Dr. Ragnarson hatte es erkannt.

Zurück zur Insel

»Also das hat Sam angestellt!«, rief Bob. Er berichtete den anderen von dem großen Plastikkanister, der vermutlich eine Chemikalie enthalten hatte. »Der hat irgendwas in die Benzintanks gegossen, das den Kraftstoff verunreinigt, damit die Motoren nicht anspringen! Für etwaige Zuschauer sah das natürlich so aus, als wollte er Benzin nachfüllen!«

»Dann ist er jetzt allein auf der Insel«, erkannte Peter.

»Haben Sie nicht noch andere Boote, Sir?«, erkundigte sich Bob bei Karl Ragnarson.

»Sam hat jedes Einzelne unserer Fahrzeuge außer Betrieb gesetzt!«, sagte dieser wütend. »Ich begreife einfach nicht, was mein Neffe da treibt und was er sich dabei denkt.«

»Jedenfalls trat er als Geist auf und ließ das Wolfsgeheul ertönen – das reicht ja wohl«, erklärte Peter.

»Er hatte nämlich das verschollene Gold gefunden!«, platzte Bob heraus.

»Gold?« Karl Ragnarson begriff nicht gleich.

»Ja, Sir«, berichtete Justus. »Ihr Ahnherr Knut Ragnarson konnte sich bekanntlich von der sinkenden *Star of Panama* retten und fand Zuflucht auf der Insel. Dort strandeten möglicherweise auch der Kapitän und die Besatzung samt der Ladung Gold – wenn auch vielleicht nur vorübergehend. Wir wissen inzwischen, dass zumindest ein Teil des Goldes, möglicherweise aber auch alles, auf der Insel liegen blieb und dass Sam darauf stieß, als er in diesem Jahr zum Familientreffen mit hinausfuhr. Natürlich wollte er seinen Fund nicht mit der Sippschaft teilen, und deshalb hat er immer wieder versucht, Sie und alle anderen Ragnarsons von der Insel zu vergraulen.«

»Und gestern Nacht wäre er fast ans Ziel gekommen«, fuhr Bob fort. »Er hatte allen außer Ihnen beiden und uns dreien die Insel gründlich vermiest. Heute beschloss er nun, die Boote lahm zu legen, damit nun wirklich niemand mehr hinfahren konnte.«

»Außer vielleicht diesen beiden Fischern«, meinte Peter.

»Dann mieten wir uns eben ein Boot!«, erklärte Karl Ragnarson.

»Das können wir uns sparen«, sagte Justus. »Wenn mich mein Verdacht nicht trügt, ist Sam jetzt da draußen, zusammen mit zwei gefährlichen Burschen, die uns die Negative gestohlen und mich entführt haben.«

Justus berichtete kurz von den beiden maskierten Männern, ihren Angriffen auf die drei ??? und seiner Entführung. »Ich befürchte, Sam ist außer seiner Goldsuche auch in eine andere Sache verwickelt und macht sich noch gar nicht klar, dass die beiden kriminelle Diebe und Entführer sind. Egal was Sam auf dem Kerbholz hat, jetzt ist er wahrscheinlich selbst in großer Gefahr. Wir müssen Kommissar Reynolds verständigen und erreichen, dass die Polizei schleunigst mit uns zur Insel hinausfährt.«

»Gut, fahren wir zum Polizeichef«, sagte Dr. Ragnarson.

»Nehmen wir meinen Wagen, der ist am schnellsten greifbar«, bot Mr Karl Ragnarson an.

Die Jungen schickten Patrick nach Hause und alle fünf stiegen in den Wagen des Schulleiters und fuhren schnurstracks zum Polizeipräsidium. Dr. Ragnarson meldete sie beim Schalterbeamten an, und Hauptkommissar Reynolds kam selbst herunter, um sie in sein Amtszimmer zu führen. Justus unterrichtete ihn kurz über den Fall.

»Ich weiß nicht, wie mein Sohn an diese beiden Männer geraten ist, die sich mit den Jungen anlegten und Justus entführten«, sagte Dr. Ragnarson, »aber nach dem Vorgefallenen könnte Sam diesmal wirklich in Gefahr sein, Kommissar. Wir sollten sofort hinfahren!«

Der Polizeichef stand auf. »Leider muss ich Ihnen beipflichten, Ingmar. Nach der Beschreibung durch die Jungen handelt es sich bei den beiden um die Brüder Ted und Walt Greene, zwei Fischer aus dem Ort, die schon zuvor mit dem Gesetz in Konflikt gekommen sind. Die Polizeibarkasse wird am Hafen auf uns warten. Gehen wir also.«

Karl Ragnarson fuhr die vier zum Hafen zurück und der Kommissar kam bald darauf mit drei Beamten nach. Alle gingen an Bord des Polizeiboots und die Besatzung legte sofort ab. Es war kurz nach sieben Uhr und die Sonne stand schon tief am Horizont. Justus stand am Bug, den Blick auf die klar sichtbare Silhouette von Ragnarson Rock gerichtet.

»Hoffentlich schaffen wir es noch rechtzeitig, Herr Kommissar«, meinte der Erste Detektiv mit einer Spur Besorgnis.

»Warum meinst du denn, Sam könnte in Gefahr sein, Justus?«, fragte Dr. Ragnarson.

»Es ist nur so eine Vorahnung«, sagte der Anführer der drei ???. »Aber wenn ich damit Recht habe, sollten wir möglichst bald nach Einbruch der Dunkelheit auf der Insel sein.«

Der Kommissar sah nach dem Sonnenstand. »Das wird knapp, Justus. Vor Sonnenuntergang kommen wir wohl kaum hin.«

»Gut, das wird genau richtig«, stellte Justus fest. »Wenn es bei unserer Ankunft gerade dunkelt, ist das von Vorteil, denn dann können wir ungesehen an Land gehen. Falls es allerdings schon längere Zeit dunkel ist, kommen wir vielleicht zu spät. Wenn wir dann kurz vor der Insel sind, sollten wir die Motoren so weit wie möglich drosseln und ohne Beleuchtung anlegen.«

Der Kommissar war einverstanden. »Ich sage der Besatzung Bescheid.« Er sollte Recht behalten – die Dunkelheit hatte sich gerade über Ragnarson Rock gesenkt, als das Patrouillenboot die Insel erreichte. Die Motoren wurden fast ganz gedrosselt, sodass das Boot nahezu lautlos in die Bucht glitt. Die noch aufgebauten Zelte der Ragnarsons waren als schattenhafte Umrisse auf der Anhöhe über dem Strand zu sehen.

Das große Polizeiboot musste mitten in der dunklen Bucht vor Anker gehen und die Jungen, die beiden Ragnarsons, der Kommissar und seine Leute ruderten im Rettungsboot und in zwei Schlauchbooten an Land. Geräuschlos zogen sie die Boote aus dem Wasser auf den verlassenen Strand.

»Da, seht mal«, flüsterte Peter.

»Das ist Sams Boot«, erkannte Dr. Ragnarson.

Das kleine Motorboot mit dem Außenborder war auf den Sand hochgezogen. Sonst befand sich in der Bucht kein Boot.

»Ich sehe keine anderen Boote, Justus«, bemerkte der Kommissar ruhig nach einem Blick zurück aufs Meer.

»Nein, Sir, hier noch nicht.« Der Erste Detektiv sah sich in der zunehmenden Dunkelheit auf der Insel um. »Wenn meine Vermutung über Sams Vorhaben mit den beiden Fischern stimmt, dann sollten wir am anderen Ende der Insel in der Nähe des großen Felsens nachforschen.«

»Gut, machen wir«, sagte der Polizeichef. »Ich schlage vor, dass wir uns über die ganze Insel verteilen.«

Er gab seinen Beamten die entsprechende Anweisung. Schließlich startete Bob ganz außen an der Nordseite und Mr Karl Ragnarson ging am Fuß der niedrigen Hügel im Süden entlang. Die Übrigen teilten sich das dazwischenliegende Gelände auf, wobei die Polizisten sich in regelmäßigen Abständen einreihten, um rasch eingreifen zu können, falls jemand Hilfe brauchen sollte. Langsam schritten sie über die kleine Insel bis zu dem hoch aufragenden Felsen am westlichen Ende.

Als sie die Zederzypressen am Fuß des Felsmassivs erreicht hatten, schlugen sie alle die Richtung nach Süden ein und durchquerten den moorigen Geländestreifen zwischen dem großen Felsen und dem offenen Meer.

Und da stolperte Peter über den kleinen Holzkasten, der auf dem unebenen Boden lag. Der Deckel sprang auf und Goldmünzen und Nuggets rieselten heraus.

»Hier irgendwo in der Nähe muss Sam sein«, sagte der Zweite Detektiv leise. »Seine Schatzkiste hat er anscheinend unterwegs verloren.«

Doch abgesehen von dem Kästchen, gab es weit und breit keine Spur von Sam Ragnarson.

»Wir müssen eben weiter nach ihm suchen«, sagte Hauptkommissar Reynolds.

»Herr Kommissar, ich glaube, ich hab eine Idee, wie wir ihn finden können!«, kam Justus mit einem Vorschlag.

Justus deckt den Schwindel auf

»Und das wäre, Justus?«, fragte der Polizeichef.

»Kommen Sie nur mit, Herr Kommissar«, sagte Justus. »Ich werde es Ihnen zeigen. Die anderen verhalten sich bitte ganz ruhig und schalten keine Taschenlampen ein.«

Der Erste Detektiv ging los und betrat die schmale Landzunge, die vor der kleinen Bucht am äußersten Ende der Insel lag. Lautlos folgten ihm die anderen. Es war zwar nicht neblig, aber der Mond war noch nicht aufgegangen, und sie mussten gut auf den Weg achten.

»Hier ist uns der ... der Geist begegnet«, flüsterte Peter.

»Ach, Unsinn«, tat Bob dies ab. »Das war doch Sam, als Kapitän Coulter verkleidet.«

»Bist du da so sicher?«, meinte Peter zweifelnd.

Justus legte den Finger an die Lippen und kauerte sich nieder. Aufmerksam betrachtete er den jenseits der Bucht in die Höhe ragenden Felsen, das Gelände der Insel und das Wasser.

»Was suchst du denn da, Justus?«, flüsterte der Kommissar.

»Ich glaube, Sir…«, fing Justus an.

Unten am Ufer der kleinen Bucht hatte es zu blinken begonnen. Der Lichtstrahl war aufs Meer hinaus gerichtet.

»Ist das Sam?«, fragte der Kommissar leise.

Ehe Justus antworten konnte, flüsterte Peter impulsiv mit heiserer Stimme dazwischen: »Da! Schaut mal!«

Draußen auf dem Meer waren Positionslichter aufgetaucht und ein Schiff näherte sich rasch der Insel. Es glitt durch die schmale Einfahrt in die Bucht und warf den Anker aus. Eine helle Lampe am Ruderhaus erleuchtete die ganze Bucht.

»Das ist das Geisterschiff!«, rief Bob mit gedämpfter Stimme. Es war der Einmaster mit den »zerfetzten« grauen Segeln, den sie im Nebel gesehen hatten. Nun konnten sie erkennen, dass es sich bei den »Segeln« um Netze handelte, die von dem langen Spriet hingen. Das »Geisterschiff« war nichts anderes als der Trawler, der vor dem Gebäude, in dem Justus gefangen gesessen hatte, festgemacht gewesen war. An Bord hielten sich zwei Männer auf.

»Das sind die zwei Greenes, kein Zweifel«, sagte Hauptkommissar Reynolds. »Bist du sicher, dass sie deine beiden Entführer waren, Justus?«

»Es sieht ganz so aus«, fand Justus. »Einer groß, einer klein und stämmig. Wenn wir sie zu Gesicht bekamen, trugen sie allerdings immer diese Masken.«

Gespannt verfolgten die Zuschauer auf der Landzunge, wie das Paar ein Schlauchboot zu Wasser ließ. Der größere Mann stieg ein und paddelte ans Ufer. Er sprang heraus und zog das Schlauchboot auf den Strand. Dann stand er vor der kleinen Bucht, als wartete er auf etwas.

»Worauf wartet der wohl?«, fragte Karl Ragnarson.

»Vermutlich auf Sam«, sagte sein Bruder beklommen.

Der einsame Schiffer am Inselstrand sah auf seine Uhr.

Justus blickte wieder zum Felsen hinüber. »Aha«, sagte er leise und befriedigt. Die anderen schauten ebenfalls hin.

Da standen plötzlich zwei Männer, als seien sie eben aus dem Felsmassiv aufgetaucht.

Der eine war Sam Ragnarson.

Der andere war ein kleiner, kräftig gebauter Mann mittleren Alters, der eine helle Hose und eine Daunenjacke trug.

»Die Jacke!«, flüsterte Karl Ragnarson. »Genauso eine ist aus unseren Zelten verschwunden!«

Es hatte den Anschein, als drängte der kräftige Mann Sam vor sich her den Hang hinunter und dann über den Sandstrand der Bucht, wo der Schiffer bei dem Schlauchboot wartete. Sam ging stolpernd und schleppend, als sträubte er sich, den Weg zum Schlauchboot zu gehen.

In der Hand seines Begleiters blinkte etwas auf.

»Das ist ja ein Messer«, sagte Dr. Ragnarson entsetzt. »Er hat Sam in seiner Gewalt!«

Der Kommissar stand auf. »Halt! Polizei! Sie sind alle festgenommen! Messer fallen lassen und Hände hoch!«

Die Polizisten richteten ihre Stablampen und Dienstwaffen auf den kräftigen Mann, Sam und den großen Kerl beim Boot. Ein Beamter war zur Spitze der Landzunge gegangen und hielt den Mann auf dem Trawler mit Pistole und Licht in Schach.

»Sein Arm!«, rief Peter und zeigte auf den Mann an Bord. »Darauf ist eine Seejungfrau tätowiert!«

»Dann waren es also eindeutig die Brüder Greene, die mich überfallen haben«, erkannte Justus grimmig.

Der Mann mit dem Messer und die beiden Fischer schienen einige Sekunden lang von dem direkt auf ihre Gesichter fallenden Licht der Stablampen geblendet zu sein. Dann ließ der stämmige Mann am Strand sein Messer fallen und hob die Hände. Alle außer dem Polizisten bei der Einfahrt zur Bucht gingen zum Ufer hinunter. Sam wischte sich den Schweiß von der Stirn. Zerknirscht nickte er seinem Vater und den drei ??? zu.

»Hätte ich mir nie träumen lassen, dass ich mich mal über euren Anblick so freuen könnte, Jungs«, bekannte der junge Mann. »Wie seid ihr nur dahinter gekommen?«

»Ja, nun red mal, Justus«, forderte der Polizeichef den Ersten Detektiv auf. »Was geht hier eigentlich vor sich? Und wer ist dieser Mann?«

Er wies auf den stämmigen Mann in der hellen Hose und der gestohlenen Jacke, der Justus wütend anstarrte.

»Darf ich vorstellen, Herr Kommissar – Mr William Manning«, sagte Justus. »Mit den Meldungen über sein tragisches Ableben war man ein klein wenig zu voreilig!«

»Manning?« Hauptkommissar Reynolds war bass erstaunt.

»Ja, Sir«, sagte Justus. »Der Mann, der allem Anschein nach ertrunken ist. Allerdings war das nur ein simples Betrugsmanöver zum Schaden der Versicherung. Manning wollte seinen Tod bei einem Bootsunglück vortäuschen und sich dann draußen auf Ragnarson Rock verstecken. Seine Freunde, die beiden Fischer, sollten ihn später dort abholen und außer Landes bringen. Seine – hm – Witwe hätte dann die Lebensversicherung kassiert, die nach meiner Vermutung nicht gering ist, wie Sie sicher ermitteln werden. Und dann wäre sie in seinem neuen Versteck irgendwo im Ausland wieder zu ihm gestoßen.«

William Manning stieß einige saftige Flüche aus, die an den Anführer der drei ??? gerichtet waren.

Unbeirrt fuhr Justus fort: »Ein unglücklicher Zufall wollte es, dass die Ragnarsons gleich nach Mr Mannings Ankunft zu ihrem Fest auf der Insel eintrafen. So konnte er es nicht riskieren, sich dort abholen zu lassen. Erst gestern Abend erschien ihm das günstig, als die meisten Ragnarsons die Insel verlassen hatten und starker Nebel aufgezogen war. Er dachte, der Nebel würde ihm Schutz bieten, aber wir machten ihm einen Strich durch die Rechnung.«

»Nichts davon kannst du beweisen, du Lümmel!«, schrie William Manning. »Ich hatte einen Unfall mit dem Boot und dabei verlor ich das Gedächtnis und die Orientierung. Erst jetzt kann ich wieder klar denken!«

Justus lachte. »Jedes Schulkind würde sich eine pfiffigere Ausrede einfallen lassen!«

Der Autohändler bedachte ihn mit wütenden Blicken.

»Sie werden uns einiges zu erklären haben, Mr Manning«, äußerte Hauptkommissar Reynolds.

»Sein Plan war im Übrigen wirklich ganz schlau«, meinte Justus noch. »Ich denke, die Sache hätte funktioniert, wenn nicht die Ragnarsons dazwischengekommen wären.«

»Und unsere drei Juniordetektive!«, setzte der Kommissar anerkennend hinzu.

Albert Hitfield ist im Bilde

»Wann kam dir zum ersten Mal der Verdacht, dass William Manning gar nicht ins nasse Seemannsgrab gesunken ist, Justus?«, fragte Albert Hitfield.

Eine Woche war vergangen und die drei ??? waren nach Hollywood gefahren und saßen nun dem berühmten Filmregisseur an seinem Schreibtisch im Universum-Studio gegenüber. Gerade hatte Mr Hitfield Bobs Niederschrift zu den Ereignissen auf und um Ragnarson Rock gelesen und aus der Hand gelegt.

»Im Grunde war das erst in dem Augenblick, als ich Sam Ragnarson bei Mrs Mannings Haus gesehen hatte und die Dame des Hauses steif und fest behauptete, ihn nicht getroffen zu haben«, erklärte Justus. »Das hörte sich bei näherer Betrachtung ziemlich unglaubwürdig an. Aber auch schon vorher hatte ich mich gefragt, ob es eigentlich noch jemand außer Sam auf unsere Fotos abgesehen hatte. Als Mr Andrews überfallen wurde, konnte Sam nämlich die Bilder in der Zeitung noch gar nicht zu Gesicht bekommen haben. Im Übrigen hätte er es zeitlich nicht geschafft, nun auch noch schnell den beiden maskierten Männern Beine zu machen.

Mir drängte sich immer stärker die Vermutung auf, dass Sams Wunsch, seinen Goldfund geheim zu halten, für ein solch auffälliges Interesse an unseren Fotos keine ausreichende Erklärung lieferte. Als Bob und Peter die Zentrale verließen, um für unsere zweite Nacht auf der Insel warme Kleider zu holen, sah ich mir alle Aufnahmen noch einmal ganz gründlich an.«

Justus zog vier Fotos aus einem Umschlag und legte sie vor Albert Hitfield auf dem Tisch aus. »Das sind Bilder von der Siegesszene der Ragnarsons nach ihrem Kampfspiel auf der Insel. Wenn Sie genau hinschauen, dann können Sie unten vor dem großen Felsen ein Gesicht erkennen.«

Albert Hitfield nahm die Fotos in Augenschein, griff dann zu einer Lupe und betrachtete sie lange und aufmerksam. »Es fällt einem nur bei äußerst gründlichem Hinsehen auf. Aber da lässt sich tatsächlich ein Gesicht erkennen – jemand, der ganz überrascht hinter einem Strauch hervorspäht!«

»Genau«, sagte Justus. »Und da kam mir plötzlich ein Gedanke – wenn nun Mr Manning am Leben wäre und sich auf Ragnarson Rock aufhielte? Wenn er Bob beim Fotografieren beobachtet hätte? Und wenn er nun darauf bedacht sein müsste, dass niemand – schon gar nicht die Leute von seiner Lebensversicherung – diese Fotos zu Gesicht bekommen durfte, weil sie daraus entnehmen konnten, dass er noch am Leben war? Das würde für vieles, was hier vorgefallen ist, die Erklärung liefern.«

Peter stöhnte. »Mir ist immer schleierhaft, wozu eine Lebensversicherung eigentlich gut sein soll.«

»Sie dient der Unterstützung der Angehörigen für den Fall, dass der Versicherte stirbt«, erklärte Mr Hitfield. »Zu Lebzeiten zahlt er allmonatlich eine verhältnismäßig geringe Prämie an die Versicherungsgesellschaft. Beim Tod des Versicherten zahlt die Gesellschaft den Hinterbliebenen die Versicherungssumme aus – das kann beim Todesfall in jungen Jahren weit mehr Geld sein, als an Prämien einbezahlt wurde. Die Höhe dieser Auszahlung wird nämlich im Voraus bei Vertragsabschluss vereinbart.«

»Für Mr Manning war das eine halbe Million Dollar«, bemerkte Bob dazu.

»Unglaublich!«, rief Peter. »Das ist ja wie ein Glücksspiel, oder? Nur muss man sterben, um auf seine Kosten zu kommen.«

»Du drückst das etwas drastisch aus«, meinte Mr Hitfield, »aber man könnte es durchaus so sehen, dass beide Seiten ein Risiko nach Art eines Glücksspiels eingehen. Die Versicherungsgesellschaft rechnet damit, dass der Versicherte ein hohes Alter erreicht – nach der Statistik trifft das für die meisten Menschen zu – und dass sie Monat für Monat die Beiträge erhält. Der Versicherte seinerseits hat die Gewissheit, dass seine Familie im Fall seines vorzeitigen Todes finanziell abgesichert ist. Mr Manning allerdings wollte die Versicherungssumme kassieren, ohne dabei ans Sterben zu denken. Es ist wohl anzunehmen, dass er in finanziellen Schwierigkeiten war?«

»Ja«, erwiderte Justus. »Das Ehepaar Manning lebte auf großem Fuße, doch das Geschäft mit dem Autohandel war in den vergangenen Jahren nicht mehr so gut gelaufen. Da schmiedeten sie einen im Grunde recht einfachen Plan. Es musste lediglich ein Unglück auf See mit Blutspuren am Boot und an einem Hut vorgetäuscht und eine zerfetzte und blutbefleckte Jacke ins Wasser geworfen werden. Dann sollte sich Mr Manning bis zum Abend auf Ragnarson Rock verstecken, wo ihn die beiden Greenes abholen wollten.«

»Aber das Familientreffen der Ragnarsons und Bobs Fotos machten ihm dann einen Strich durch die Rechnung«, warf Peter schadenfroh ein.

»Manning beobachtete Bob dabei, wie er auf der Insel fotografierte«, fuhr Justus fort, »und daher gab er über das Funkgerät aus seinem Boot den Brüdern Greene Bescheid, sie sollten uns diese Fotos abjagen. Er sagte ihnen auch, er könnte nicht von der Insel weg, solange die Ragnarsons sich dort aufhielten. Nun war er ja auf einen längeren Aufenthalt im Freien nicht eingerichtet, und so stahl er aus den Zelten der Ragnarsons Essen und Kleidungsstücke, um über die Runden zu kommen.«

»Warum schafften es die Greenes nicht früher, ihn von der Insel wegzubringen?«, fragte Albert Hitfield.

»In den beiden ersten Nächten war es klar und mondhell«, erwiderte Peter, »und sie wollten das Risiko vermeiden, dass sie von den Ragnarsons gesehen wurden.«

»Aber in der dritten Nacht«, fuhr Bob fort, »war das Wetter neblig und die meisten Ragnarsons waren ohnehin durch Sams Machenschaften verscheucht worden. Also riskierte es Manning, seinen Freunden, die schon mit ihrem Boot hergekommen waren, mit einer Stablampe Lichtzeichen zu geben. Das war allerdings ein Fehler. Wir beobachteten das Manöver und auch Sam entging es nicht.«

»O ja, nun kommen wir zu diesem Sam«, sagte der Regisseur. »War er auch in den Versicherungsbetrug verwickelt?«

»Nein, das nicht«, antwortete Justus, »zumindest nicht von Anfang an. Ursprünglich wollte er nur alle anderen von der Insel vertreiben, damit er ungestört nach Gold suchen konnte.

Deshalb trat er als Geist in Erscheinung und spielte die Kassette mit dem Wolfsgeheul ab. Dann aber sah er zufällig William Manning auf der Insel und machte sich einen Reim darauf, wer dieser Mann war. Sam sagte sich, dass er mit einer Erpressung eher zu Geld kommen könnte als mit der Goldsuche. Er fuhr aufs Festland zurück und machte einen Besuch bei Mrs Manning. Das war unmittelbar, bevor ich selbst dort hinkam. Mrs Manning sah sich gezwungen, Sams Forderungen zu erfüllen, und er tat sich mit den beiden Greenes zusammen, damit Mr Mannings Abtransport von der Insel glatt vonstatten gehen würde. Dazu sollte auch Sams Sabotagemanöver an den Booten der Ragnarsons beitragen. Später fuhr er dann mit den Greenes zur Insel zurück.«

»Die Habgier hat diesen jungen Mann zu äußerst törichtem Vorgehen getrieben«, stellte Mr Hitfield fest.

»Na und ob!«, rief Peter. »Manning und den beiden Greenes war ein Mitwisser und Hintendraufsteher wie Sam denkbar lästig, und deshalb wollten sie ihn zuletzt auch mit Gewalt von der Insel wegschaffen, um ihn los zu sein. Wer weiß – die hätten ihn vielleicht an die Haie verfüttert!«

»Und entsprechend erleichtert war er dann, als ihr auf der Insel auftauchtet«, sagte Albert Hitfield. »Wo ist übrigens der Amateur-Goldgräber jetzt?«

Justus grinste. »Der sitzt zu Hause und dreht Däumchen. Das Gericht hat ihn wegen Beihilfe im Fall Manning verurteilt, die Strafe aber zur Bewährung ausgesetzt. Allerdings hat er die Auflage erhalten, nicht mehr zur Insel Ragnarson Rock hinauszufahren.«

»Alle anderen Ragnarsons sind seit Tagen dort und wühlen das Gelände um«, setzte Peter lachend hinzu. »Und von dem, was sie finden, kriegt Sam kein Stäubchen ab. Das macht ihn garantiert total fertig.«

»Viel haben die Leute bisher allerdings nicht mehr gefunden«, erklärte Bob. »Nur ein paar Münzen, und damit hatte es sich.«

»Dann stimmt es also, dass Kapitän Coulter und seine Schiffsbesatzung sich vorübergehend auf der Insel aufhielten und einen Teil des Goldes dort zurückließen«, meinte Mr Hitfield. »Doch was aus ihnen und dem Rest des Goldes geworden ist, bleibt nach wie vor das Geheimnis des Meeres um Ragnarson Rock.« Die drei ??? nickten.

»Und die Mannings und die Greenes – was erwartete diese Herrschaften?«

»Das stand inzwischen alles in der Zeitung«, sagte Justus. »Sie wurden allesamt in Haft genommen, unter der Anklage des Betrugs, der Körperverletzung, der Planung einer Straftat und der Entführung. Sie werden noch recht lange Zeit mit Anwälten und Gerichten zu tun haben. Der Einzige, der nichts zu befürchten hat, ist Steven, Mr Mannings Bruder. Er wusste nämlich nichts von dem betrügerischen Plan und glaubte wirklich, William Manning sei tot. Er nimmt den Mannings die Sache noch mehr übel als die Versicherungsgesellschaft.«

»Also hat das Gute wieder einmal den Sieg davongetragen«, sagte der große Regisseur. Dann erkundigte er sich noch augenzwinkernd: »Und welche Belohnung habt ihr drei nun von Karl Ragnarson für die erfolgreiche Aufklärung des Falles bekommen? Sein ursprüngliches Angebot über eine Honorarzahlung hattest du ja abgelehnt, Justus, wie ich vorhin las.«

Der Erste Detektiv wurde ganz unvermittelt und ungewohnt hochrot. »Ja, Sir, das ist schon richtig. Na ja … Mr Karl Ragnarson war sehr angetan von dem guten Ausgang der Sache. Sein Bruder brauchte sich keine Sorgen mehr zu machen, die Insel konnte wieder zum ungestörten Tummelplatz der Ragnarsons werden und sein Neffe Sam war mit einem blauen Auge davongekommen.«

»Und da ist nun anscheinend etwas, das dir gar nicht passt, Justus, wie?«, fragte Mr Hitfield mit forschendem Blick.

»Tja … Mr Ragnarson wollte uns unbedingt ein Zeichen seiner Anerkennung zukommen lassen, da wir ja kein Geld annehmen können.« Justus fummelte an seiner Sporttasche herum, die er vorher neben seinem Stuhl abgestellt hatte. Bob und Peter tauschten mit diebischem Vergnügen vielsagende Blicke.

»Und das hier ist es.« Justus beförderte einen großen, schweren Gegenstand ans Tageslicht: ausgerechnet die Schamanenmaske der Chumash-Indianer, die zu seinem Kostüm auf Ragnarson Rock gehört hatte – jene klobige Holzmaske, die ihn auf Schritt und Tritt behindert und gestört hatte!

Peter und Bob brachen in schallendes Gelächter aus. Albert Hitfield hielt sich diskret die Hand vor den Mund, weil er es sichtlich schwer hatte, ernst zu bleiben.

Dann räusperte er sich und sah die drei ??? der Reihe nach an. »Auch ich habe mir erlaubt, euch für euer erfolgreiches Wirken mit einer Überraschung zu bedenken. Indessen handelt es sich ebenfalls nicht um einen materiellen Wert. Ihr habt doch noch eine Viertelstunde Zeit?«

Die Jungen nickten gespannt. Albert Hitfield teilte seiner Sekretärin über das Telefon mit, er habe nun Zeit für Mr Steadfast und das Kamerateam.

Mr Leonard Steadfast, der gleich darauf eintrat, stellte sich den drei ??? als Detektiv des Versicherungsunternehmens vor, das beinahe das Opfer des Manning'schen Betrugsmanövers geworden wäre. Verblüffend war der Kontrast zwischen seiner leisen, bedächtigen Sprechweise und dem strengen, durchdringenden Blick der dunklen Augen hinter den dicken Brillengläsern.

»Ich hatte einen Unfall und lag monatelang im Krankenhaus«, berichtete er. »Als die Sache Manning zu untersuchen war, musste sich mein junger, noch nicht sehr erfahrener Kollege allein darum kümmern. Nun habt ihr drei ihm ja mit euren eigenständigen Ermittlungen gewissermaßen unter die Arme gegriffen. Unsere Gesellschaft ist euch zu Dank verpflichtet und das soll die Öffentlichkeit auch erfahren.«

In kurzer Zeit hatten Fernsehtechniker in Albert Hitfields Büro ihre Kameras aufgebaut und dann wurde ein Bericht für den Regionalsender gedreht. Der große Filmregisseur hielt sich dabei ganz zurück. Einmal ging er im Hintergrund quer durch den Raum – ein kurzer, unauffälliger Auftritt »inkognito«, wie er ihn in seinen Filmen zu praktizieren pflegte. Der Freund und Berater der drei ???, die wieder einmal einen Fall erfolgreich gelöst hatten, war wie immer im Bilde.

Alfred Hitchcock
Die drei ???

www.omnibus-verlag.de

The elder woman reached forward and, ~~~~ aside the shield with its strange device, drew the girl into the other chamber and sat her down.

'I told you that the strangers came here for a purpose; that they appeared to be looking for something . . . or someone. Years ago, when you were cast upon the seas in that casket, you were clearly meant to die. Eola and I found the casket by the will of the ocean god. The triskele symbol, carved on that casket, and on the medallion which you now wear, my child, is the only clue as to the land of your origin. And now, from the sea, strange warriors arrive with their shields bearing the same symbol. They search and destroy. I believe that those who sought to put you to death as a baby have now learnt that you still live. They were sent to kill you, Scáthach.'

By the same author
available from Mandarin Paperbacks

Ravenmoon
Raven of Destiny

Peter Tremayne

ISLAND OF SHADOWS

Mandarin

A Mandarin Paperback

ISLAND OF SHADOWS

First published in Great Britain 1991
by Mandarin Paperbacks
Michelin House, 81 Fulham Road, London SW3 6RB

Mandarin is an imprint of the Octopus Publishing Group,
a division of Reed International Books Limited

Copyright © Peter Tremayne 1991

A CIP catalogue record for this title
is available from the British Library
ISBN 0 7493 0907 5

Typeset by Falcon Typographic Art Ltd,
Edinburgh & London
Printed and bound in Great Britain
by Cox & Wyman Ltd, Reading, Berks

Her skin, like chalk.
Her cheek, a rose.
While clear and bright her watchful eyes.
Dexterous as a wind-blown hawk.
Agile in the hunt.
In combat – invincible,
For she is the raven's daughter.
Wise beyond a druid's wisdom.
Champions tremble at her coming,
Praising the gods for her leaving.
Such is the mighty Scáthach
of the Island of Shadows!

–Maelsuthan Ua Cerbaill
d. AD 1010

One

The sun was high in the cloudless heavens. It was a hot day with just the faintest of breezes to shift the listless canvas which hung from the tall masts of the ship, pushing it reluctantly over the calm, flat waters, on which a myriad gold and silver lights sparkled in the noonday brilliance. The forward motion of the vessel was scarcely discernible.

Rónán Mac Méin stood on the stern deck and surveyed the blue stretches of the ocean around him with deep green eyes which reflected the changing moods of the sea. He was a short, stocky man, with greying, close-cropped hair; a grizzled veteran of forty years of sea-faring. His skin was brown, tanned by the sea winds almost to the colour of nut except where a scar spread from the corner of his left eye across his cheek to his thin, grim mouth; a livid scar, lending a fearsome feature to his unsmiling countenance. Rónán Mac Méin was captain of the squat merchant ship, the *Cáoc*, whose black, ponderous lines bore no resemblance to the jackdaw after which it was named. More was it like a lumbering porpoise than a sleek bird as it bobbed and drifted before the faint winds. Twice that morning Rónán Mac Méin had ordered his men to wet the sails in order to coax more leeway out of the wind. But it was a hot day and the sails quickly dried.

The *Cáoc* was a full day out from the coast of Gallia bearing a cargo of wines for the merchants of the kingdom of Mumhan in Éireann. A full day out and the ship was barely halfway to the southern coastline of Mumhan so slow were the winds, so calm the seas. The *Cáoc* seemed to drift aimlessly.

Rónán Mac Méin squinted his sea-green eyes into the golden brightness of the hanging orb and sighed.

It was to be expected. After all, this was the day of the sun-standing, the *grian-tairisem*, or the summer solstice. Sometimes a ship could be becalmed for days in the breezeless periods. And yet the auguries had shown that it was an auspicious time to make the voyage. Rónán Mac Méin compressed his lips and his eyes darted to the straight-backed figure of the woman who stood in the well of the ship, hands on the rail, staring northwards as if expecting to catch sight of the distant shadowy coastline of Éireann. Yes, it had been Buimech herself who had pronounced the augury two nights ago, calculating the age of the moon and the position of the stars in their girdle around the sun. And was not Buimech the Learned renowned for her wisdom throughout the entire land of Éireann? Buimech who had once faulted the chief druid of Éireann before the High King himself! If Buimech the Learned declared the auguries to be favourable, who was Rónán Mac Méin, a simple mariner, to argue with her?

Yet the breezes were becoming negligible, the forward motion of the ship was imperceptible. The *Cáoc* was truly becalmed.

Once again, the ageing captain let out a deep sigh.

Better it might have been had he refused to allow Buimech and her husband, Eola, to take passage on his ship. Who knew what ill-fortune a female druid could bring on shipboard? A few more days in Gallia would have ensured the tide and winds. Yet Buimech had said it was an auspicious time to start the voyage. If only he had been possessed of the courage to refuse Buimech passage; if only he had made some excuse. But what excuse could he have given which the all-seeing eye of

8

a druid would not see through and realise the fear which lurked in his mind?

Even if the pragmatic Rónán Mac Méin was not in awe of the druidic powers and knowledge of Buimech, he was in awe of her husband Eola for Eola's academy of martial arts at Uibh Rathach was famous throughout the world. Not only did the great champions of the Fianna, the High King's bodyguard, go to Eola for their tuition but champions and would-be champions from many lands took the voyage to Mumhan in search of Uibh Rathach. Eola, with his tall, sinewy frame, and stern, unmoving eyes, was one to put fear in the cowardly and respect in the brave. When Eola made a request, it was an order to lesser men.

Even Ablach, the mate of the *Cáoc*, who had been against taking Buimech and Eola aboard from the start, was afraid of them and from his fear sprang forth hatred.

In the well of the ship Buimech turned and glanced at Rónán Mac Méin. The grizzled captain of the *Cáoc* stood staring into her eyes for a moment. In spite of the fact that Buimech was beyond her middle years, the face was strikingly attractive, a face beyond mere beauty with its white skin and splattering of freckles, the tinge of red on the cheek bones, bright blue eyes, and flaming red hair matching the redness of her mouth. Those bright blue eyes stared straight into those of Rónán Mac Méin and held his gaze. Softly a smile, a secret smile of knowledge, turned the corners of the woman's mouth; a smile as if Buimech knew what manner of thoughts echoed in the captain's mind.

Rónán Mac Méin bit his lip and dropped his gaze in embarrassment.

Buimech turned with her soft smile to continue gazing at the sea's endless vista.

A moment later there was a soft footfall behind her.

Buimech did not turn.

'A gentle day, husband,' she said quietly.

'Too gentle for the likes of our captain and his crew,' replied a strong male voice. 'They grow impatient for the wind.'

'They will have it soon, Eola,' Buimech replied confidently, turning to meet the gaze of her husband.

Eola was a tall man, above six feet in height, with dark, shoulder-length hair, greying at the temples. On his forehead was the golden circlet of a hero which the High King, Baitin Mac Tigernma, had fixed there with his own hand when Eola had become chieftain of the Fianna at Teamhair. Eola was now approaching two score and ten years and was over a score of years older than when he had resigned from the leadership of the High King's bodyguard. A score of years older than the time he had set up his academy of martial arts at Uibh Rathach. Even though most regarded him as being beyond military age, yet there was not a champion in all Éireann, not in the world beyond, who could best Eola at any weapon – not sword, javelin nor bow. Eola was their master and he could cast a spear from a galloping horse or a rocking chariot at full speed and still expect to find a bull's-eye nineteen times out of twenty. He was still a handsome man, with a broad forehead and warm brown eyes, whose well-muscled frame bore itself with a noble dignity. A figure which put to shame many young men half his age and less.

Eola smiled at his wife.

'Are you certain the wind will come?'

'As certain as the moon will rise. But the moon does not rise before the appointed hour and neither will the wind come before the appointed time.'

Eola knew better than to question his wife further. Had they not been man and wife for thirty years and had he not seen enough examples of her druidic craft to know that when she said a thing was to be then it would be so?

The hours passed, weary and breathless.

The crew, with nothing to do until the wind came up, sat on the deck, some playing *brandubh*, the board game of black raven, while others spoke together nervously, as if they were conscious of their voices disturbing the midday quiet. Rónán Mac Méin had ordered the sails to be soaked again but there was no wind, not even a breath now. The ship was totally still.

'Ho, the deck!'

The cry of the lookout at the mainmast caused eyes to be turned upward in his direction. The man had flung an outstretched hand to the west. Eyes turned to follow it.

'What do you see?' demanded Rónán Mac Méin, his voice grating like an ancient capstan in the quiet.

'A cloud! A cloud which speeds over the ocean!'

There was a murmuring as the sailors ran for the port rail of the ship, eyes staring towards the western horizon.

It was but a moment before they saw what the lookout, from his higher elevation, had spotted.

It looked as if there was a great white cloud billowing and rolling towards them at sea level.

Rónán Mac Méin drew his breath sharply. Never in all his years at sea had he witnessed such a phenomenon. The murmuring among the sailors was growing now and one or two of them were looking anxiously towards the druidess, Buimech. The grizzled captain joined with furtive gaze the anxious glances. Buimech had crossed the well of the ship with her husband and together they stood calmly, examining the oncoming white cloud.

'What manner of misfortune is this?' demanded one of the sailors, calling out to Rónán Mac Méin.

The grizzled captain forced a smile.

'By the gods! Have you never seen a heat cloud before?

Have you never seen the haze rise over a meadow on a summer's morning?'

'That I have,' replied Ablach, the mate, before the sailor could answer. 'But not such a haze as this which moves in such a manner without the wind.'

'But it means that the wind is coming,' insisted Rónán, with more confidence in his voice than he felt.

Again he glanced at Buimech, hoping to have some confirmation of his assertion. The druidess stood ignoring the consternation of the crew, standing with folded arms watching the approaching cloud with a faint smile on her lips.

The white billows grew closer, stretching well up above the height of the main mast and spreading a great distance across the sea, rolling inexorably forward like the waves of the restless ocean.

'Hands to quarters!' yelled Rónán MacMéin. 'Stand by to wear the ship!'

It was wise to prepare for any contingency.

The cloud rolled forward, bursting over the ship like a great tidal wave, rolling over and encompassing it. It seemed suddenly that the great orb of the sun was blotted out, and the *Cáoc* was enveloped in a cold, clinging dampness which caused its captain to shiver. The ship was entrapped in a dense mist of milky whiteness, so thick was it that it was painful to take a breath. Visibility became confined to simply a yard or two.

'Break out the torches!' cried Rónán Mac Méin, but his voice seemed muffled in the surrounding gloom.

He heard voices calling but they, too, were faint and muffled. No one acknowledged his command.

He cursed softly and began to stumble forward to the locker in search of tinder, flint and steel.

Then he halted. A strange smell began to pervade the ship. A sickly sweet smell of rotting seaweed, a strong pungent odour which caused him to catch his breath and retch at the putrefaction. Then he heard a low rumbling noise, like the sound of far-off thunder.

Abruptly, the mist was gone. The cloud that had passed over the *Cáoc* was sweeping away.

Rónán Mac Méin stood staring after it, hardly believing the evidence of his own eyes. The great bank of mist was rolling in a circle, sweeping around the ship and then turning back to the west in the direction in which it had come.

The strangest aspect of this was that not once had he felt the hint of a wind, not once had there been the touch of a breeze. The *Cáoc* stood just as becalmed as it had been before. Within minutes, the great white cloud had disappeared beyond the sea's western rim. The grizzled captain stood staring after it, still as a statue. Finally, slowly, he licked his lips and whispered: 'May all the gods of the Dé Danaan stand between me and evil!'

'Deck ho! Something in the sea.'

The cry of the lookout at the mainmast was sharpened with fear,

'Where away?' demanded Rónán, drawing himself together.

'Port side. Something in the water!'

The captain hurried to the port rail and stared down at the calm blue waters. A dark, rectangular object was bobbing on the sea. His eyes narrowed. It was like a casket of some sort, about four feet in length and two feet in width and perhaps two feet in depth, though part of it was under the water so that it was difficult to assess the exact measurement.

The casket seemed to be drifting towards the *Cáoc*.

'Haul it in,' ordered Rónán, returning his wondering gaze to the western horizon.

There was now no sign of the cloud; no sign of anything disturbing the hot, breathless day.

It took a while before the casket was drawn up

over the side of the *Cáoc* and deposited in the well of the ship.

Rónán came down from the stern deck to where his crewmen had surrounded the object.

His expert seaman's eyes had been accurate as to its dimensions and closer examination showed it to be a casket of carved wood, a wood the like of which he had never encountered before; a black, shiny wood, which seemed as light as cork. Strange whorls and circles were inscribed all over the box while on its lid stood a strange triskele-shaped design.

'There is a gold latch here, Rónán,' muttered one of the sailors, pointing to the clasp which seemed to keep the lid in its place.

'Could it be a casket of treasure?' muttered Ablach, a greed entering his speculative gaze.

Another member of the crew laughed sharply. 'Is there no sense in you? With the lightness of the box, how do you expect a great treasure to be stowed inside?'

'Let's open it,' Ablach suggested.

Rónán Mac Méin moved forward, shouldering the others aside, and reached down, flicking back the latch. Then, pausing momentarily, he lifted up the lid which fell back on hinges.

Inside was a bed of silken cushions of bright colours. Lying wrapped in a long green shawl, fringed with golden threads and tassels, was a small baby which opened its wide light green eyes and chuckled at their staring faces. It was no more than a few weeks old, with a faint covering of red hair on its pink scalp. It gurgled contentedly there, both little hands clenched into fists. In one fist it held a small golden chain to which was attached a medallion. Even without picking it up, Rónán could see that it was a reflection of the triskele symbol borne on the lid of the casket.

14

'By the gods of the Dé Danaan!' whispered Rónán softly.

For a long while no one spoke as they stood in a stupefied circle gazing down at the chuckling child.

'This is a bad omen,' declared Ablach. 'First we are becalmed, then came that awesome cloud and now we find a child in the middle of the ocean, far away from landfall. The child must be some spirit of ill-fortune.'

'Throw it back whence it came!' another seaman suggested in agreement.

'No! That you shall not do.'

The soft yet commanding tone of Buimech cut through the sullen murmurs of agreement which echoed from the crew.

Rónán stared at the druidess.

'Do you have knowledge of this?' he asked, gesturing at the casket.

'I have,' replied Buimech, ignoring Eola's worried frown as he stood at her side.

'Knowledge or not,' cried Ablach, 'the child will be sent back to the place whence it came. We want nothing of sorcery or evil!'

Buimech raised a slender hand to quell the muttering of their discordant voices.

'You will not throw the child back. That much is written in the sky as surely as you can tell the ages of the moon at night.'

'What would you have us do, Buimech?' asked the grizzled captain with reluctance in his voice.

'Give the child to me and proceed on your way to Mumhan.'

Rónán laughed sourly.

'One task is easy, but the other . . . how will we proceed when there is no wind?'

'The wind will come,' Buimech assured him.

Ablach stood scowling at the druidess.

15

'I say the wind will only come when we have thrown this child of ill-omen back to the waves and appeased the anger of Manánnan Mac Lir, the ocean god, who will then cause the wind to blow for us!'

He took a pace forward, a gnarled hand on a wicked looking knife in his belt. His face showed his evil intent.

'It shall be as I say,' Buimech insisted without raising her voice.

'Then I say you shall be given the child and both of you shall be cast over the side,' sneered Ablach, drawing the knife.

'Sheath the knife, sailor, or you will never see the green shores of Éireann again.'

Eola stepped forward before his wife. He spoke measuredly and softly. His stern eyes gazed reflectively at the seaman. The man blinked at the tall warrior. He stood uncertainly. Yet what had he to fear? Eola was unarmed. No sword nor knife was carried in his belt. And Ablach was far younger than the man. True he had heard that the man had once been a warrior but that was long ago. Yet why did the old man seem so confident? Ablach hesitated and licked his lips. A soft smile hovered on Eola's lips; the smile of hidden knowledge, for in that moment the sailor had given away his hesitation, his uncertainty. And in uncertainty there was defeat.

'Put that knife away,' Eola repeated. There was utmost confidence in his voice as if he were speaking to a recalcitrant child.

Rónán Mac Méin moved forward and grabbed the sailor's shoulder in a huge, calloused hand, spinning him round roughly.

'I am captain of this ship, Ablach. I will say what is to be done. You have sailed your last voyage with me. Now sheath your knife and get to the masthead. You'll not come down before we reach the coast of Mumhan.'

Ablach paused only a second but, at the fierce light

in the captain's eyes, he sheathed his knife sullenly and strode off towards the rigging.

Rónán Mac Méin glared after him for a second or two and then turned to Buimech and Eola.

'You may have this child into your care, Buimech, if that is your wish,' he said. 'My wish is that a wind will blow that will take us to the shores of Éireann.'

'The wind will come. Be patient,' replied Buimech, moving to the casket and lifting the baby from the silken cushions. She turned with a smile of joy to her husband, holding the infant in her arms and crooning softly to it. It chuckled and held out its little hands to her.

The sailors began to disperse with uneasy mutterings. Rónán Mac Méin returned scowling to the stern deck.

Eola watched them disperse with a cautious eye. He glanced aloft to where the figure of Ablach was ascending the rigging. Then he turned to his wife.

'Is there meaning to this, Buimech?' he asked.

'Manánnan Mac Lir, god of the oceans, has brought this child to us so that she may be taught our skills and wisdom.'

'She?'

Eola stared down at the child nestling in his wife's arms. He had no knowledge to make out whether the child was girl or boy as it lay wrapped in the green silken shawl.

'She,' confirmed Buimech. 'She has been sent to us to be raised as our own.'

Eola stared at his wife. It was true that the one sadness in both their lives was their lack of children. Yet they had both accepted it as the will of the gods and were content with their love for each other. Now his wife had spoken and he was willing to accept this strange child from the sea as a gift from the gods. Yet . . . and yet, if only the child had been a boy. A boy he might have instructed in his skills so that the child would become the mightiest warrior in all Éireann.

17

Buimech smiled at her husband as if reading his thoughts.

'Have no worry. She is destined for greatness. Thousands of years hence, the children of Éireann will still be talking of her before their fires at night. Her name will be forever on the lips of heroes. This I know, Eola. She will be the mother of champions and the teacher of champions. And even the greatest champion in all Éireann will one day bow before her and humbly ask for her wisdom and knowledge.'

Eola raised his eyebrows in astonishment.

'How can such a prophecy be?'

'It can be because it is, Eola.' She smiled down at the infant, still clinging fiercely to the golden medallion. She is now our child . . . our daughter.'

'But where did the child come from? Who gave it birth?' demanded Eola.

'That is not for us to ask,' his wife replied. 'But one day this child will search for the answers to those questions. That will be her trial. But it is not our concern. Our task is to nurture, love and train her. And we must guard these symbols . . .' She nodded to the medallion and to the intricately designed casket. 'One day they will help her in her task.'

Buimech suddenly raised her face and turned westward.

Was there a faint haze there? A faint haze low down on the horizon?

She raised the child in her arms, holding her up at the full length of her reach, stretching towards the horizon.

'We accept the task,' she whispered. 'Now you may send the wind.'

Eola shivered slightly. A moment passed before he realised that the cause of the reaction was not superstition but a sudden coolness in the temperature. A soft breeze was blowing on his cheek. The flat blue level of the sea was breaking up into a series of little white crests. There came an abrupt crack of canvas.

'The wind! The wind!' cried a sailor.

Suddenly there was a stampede of bare feet on the sanded wooden boards of the ship and the sailors raced to their stations.

Rónán Mac Méin's voice grated across the decks.

'Stand by! Stand by to turn her into the wind!'

Buimech chuckled in delight.

'So it is written in the sky. So shall it be.'

Eola sighed. 'Such knowledge is beyond my understanding.'

'Each to their own craft, Eola,' replied his wife. 'Our task will be to ensure this child has knowledge and understanding from both of us.'

The great sail was cracking now as the *Cáoc* was turned skilfully into the wind and began to race towards the distant coast of Éireann, beyond the northern horizon.

The baby in Buimech's arms gurgled happily as if it knew that it had passed through some danger and was now heading homewards.

Even Eola smiled at the baby's infectious laughter.

'The child has no name,' he said. 'We should name her.'

Buimech nodded thoughtfully and was silent for a moment or two.

'She has emerged from the shadow of death with her origins shrouded in mystery,' she observed. 'Then let her name be called "Shadow". Yes, that is a good name for her. Henceforth, we shall call her Scáthach.'

Two

The girl crouched behind a clump of whitethorn and dog-brier at the edge of a forest clearing, beside the bend of a stream. Here the stream eddied to provide a drinking pool where, for time beyond counting, numerous species of forest animal had worn a path down its bank – the majestic buck deer, the timid fawn, the cunning fox, the fearless wolf and the ferocious boar. Large and small, all the wild beasts came along that path to satiate their thirst at the pool. And this the girl knew as she relaxed on her heels behind her thorn bush hide, a bow held loosely across her knees, an arrow already half slung.

She was tall, her long limbs supple and well-shaped, yet, on closer inspection, the muscles were well developed, though not disproportionately so, implying a strength unusual in someone of her sex and age – an age which was scarcely more than a score of years. The skin was fair yet tanned as one used to a life in the open. Her face was oval in shape with a broad forehead. The eyes seemed at first glance to be deep green in colour, although a second glance showed them changeable in tone, as if reflecting her variable moods. Her face was not one of beauty but it was a face which made people look twice. It reflected a certain humour and vitality which bore a distinction of character, of perception and intelligence. Most striking of all was her hair: flaming red which, when caught by the sun's rays, glittered and flickered as if a million tiny flames danced in it. She wore it unbraided, falling to her shoulders and down to her waist. The only adornment was her *minn n-óir*, a small diadem of gold with its colour-enamelled centre-piece which was worn around the forehead to denote that she was of no mean rank in society.

She wore a cloak of deep yellow hue which fell from her shoulders to her knees and which was edged with otter-fur. Beneath the cloak she was clad in a collarless tight-fitting jacket with short sleeves with a matching short skirt that reached just above the knee. Both were of linen dyed saffron in colour. At her waist was a leather *criss* studded with bosses of silver and bronze from which hung a *bossan*, a purse of elaborate ornamentation. From the *criss*, at her left side, hung a short sword and hunting knife in a double-sheath of workmanlike leather. A quiver full of arrows hung from her right. Her shoes were of half-tanned hide, free from hair but retaining the pliability of rawhide.

The girl's hands were noteworthy by their delicacy, with their slender, tapering fingers and carefully manicured nails, which seemed to be incongruous to the bow in her hand as if she clutched some alien instrument. Such well groomed hands and her long unbraided hair were hallmarks of beauty and held in great esteem by the people of Éireann.

The girl sat back on her heels, her eyes half closed, yet there was a marked attention in her stance as her keen ears listened carefully to the sounds of the forest around her, picking out each sound and carefully categorising it. She could hear the movement of deer not far away, a buck and a roe. A boar was snuffling through the undergrowth on the far side of the stream. She could also hear a scampering of hares followed by the soft growling of an over-optimistic wolf as it trotted after them in search of a meal. All this the girl could make out against the windy rustling of the

21

trees and the constant chorus of numerous species of birds.

Time passed yet the girl made no movement in her position. She was like a statue, moulded firmly into the forest environment as if she had been carved out of granite. Even when a flying insect alighted on her face, she made no move to brush the irritant aside.

Eventually she heard the sound she was hoping for.

Only an almost imperceptible tightening of the muscles in her arms and legs showed an acknowledgement of the sound.

Along the well-worn trail to the watering hole came a sturdy red roe which paused every so often to sniff suspiciously at the air and listen in order to ensure its natural enemies were not within close proximity. It reached the pool and lowered its head to the water.

The girl now rose swiftly to her full height in one flowing motion; at the same time her delicate hands strung the arrow to the bow, drawing back the string to her shoulder and releasing it almost, or so it seemed, without aiming. Miraculously a second arrow appeared strung to the bow before the first was scarcely on its way. Then the second arrow was speeding after the first and yet a third arrow was strung already.

The roe leapt as the first arrow caught it, entering almost to the flight of the feather, and the beast was falling lifeless by the pool by the time the second arrow embedded itself within an inch of the first arrow.

There was no sound. The death had come so quickly and quietly that not even the bird song was disturbed in the clearing.

The girl stood quietly for a moment, all senses alert for any danger. When she perceived that all was well she unstrung the third arrow and replaced it in the quiver at her side. She moved quietly but quickly forward and knelt beside the carcass of the deer. Her mouth turned down briefly as she gazed on the creature's beautiful red hair and symmetrical lines.

'Forgive me, Os, god of the deer folk,' she whispered. It was a formula all hunters repeated on the killing of such an animal, for they, like all animals, were slaughtered from necessity, for food, or warm clothing. In return their spirits were propitiated by the hunters so that man and beast could live in harmony. For in the philosophies of the people of Éireann, all creatures were related, all were possessed of an indwelling spirit, even the tall trees and granite rocks. Thus humankind was but a part of nature and must coexist in amity with it in all its aspects. The wild beast supplied food and clothing and the gods must be thanked for that. Nothing was to be taken for granted by man.

And in the killing of a deer, above all creatures, one had to be careful; for had not Fionn Mac Cumhail, the captain of the Fianna, bodyguard to the High King, come across a deer near this very spot and been about to slaughter it when that very deer spoke to him: Had it not been Sadbh, the goddess, who had been turned into a deer for refusing to marry an evil, powerful druid? And was not Fionn's famous son Oisin, the 'little deer', born out of a union between Fionn and Sadbh? Yes; deer were mystical creatures whose hunting was carried out with due reverence.

The girl carefully cut her arrows from its heart and threw them into the water as an offering to appease the spirit of Os, god of the deer-folk.

When due ceremony was ended, the girl hooked the bow over her shoulder and bent down to seize the roe by its front legs with one hand and the hind legs with the other, swinging it up onto her shoulders as if it had been some light weight. Having settled her burden, she began to stride easily along the forest path. She paused once to gaze at the position of the sun. It lacked a short while until noonday and she calculated that she would be able to reach her father's fortress at Uibh Rathach, on the other side of the mountain, by early afternoon. She smiled happily for he would be well pleased with the results of her morning's hunting. He it was who had suggested that she return with a deer for the feasting table that evening. She had not protested for she had known it was another of his tests to see whether she was fit to wear the champion's torc that he promised would one day be hers.

She journeyed easily through the forest until the ground began to rise and the trees gave way to shrub and then the shrub gave way to low-lying gorse and the bald rocks of the granite mountains which surrounded Uibh Rathach. The hills were wild and rough with many rock precipices swept by the winds. She paused and shifted the weight of the slaughtered animal on her shoulders before starting her ascent up the stony path which would lead her over the shoulder of the mountain to within sight of her father's fortress, standing at the head of a horse valley within sight of the sea.

She had hardly begun the upward climb when there was a strange croaking cry in the sky above her and a black object hurtled out of the sky at her feet. She took an involuntary step backwards, one hand sliding to the short sword at her side.

At her feet lay a dead crow, its wings outstretched and twisted.

The girl gave a sharp intake of breath.

'Gods of the Dé Danaan between me and all evil!' she whispered.

The crow was the symbol of death and battles whose black shape was often used by the Mórrígú, goddess of death and slaughter. For a dead crow to fall out of the sky was an omen of evil. It sent a shiver through the supple frame of the girl.

For a moment she peered down at the carcass, as if

seeking a reason for the death of the bird in flight. Then, hesitantly, she skirted the creature and began to hurry on, climbing swiftly now along the path. Trying to suppress the unease which she now felt, the girl was alert, her eyes moving rapidly from side to side, seeking danger, as she continued the climb.

At last she reached the shoulder of the mountain and moved around it into the valley which was dominated by the fortress of Uibh Rathach.

Her anxious gaze surveyed the valley and once again the breath was caught within her.

A black pall of smoke was rising from Uibh Rathach. It was not the single thin stream from a cooking fire but a large black billow rising from the buildings within the great stone walls. Even from this distance her narrowed eyes could see flames leaping and see what appeared to be bundles of rags, which she knew to be bodies, lying around the walls.

With a sudden cry, she flung aside the burden of game, and began to run forward down the mountain path towards the fortress.

As Scáthach entered the smashed, burning gates of the fortress, she saw several of the household of Uibh Rathach had fallen trying to defend themselves against the raiders. But when she saw Buimech with the fallen Eola her eyes took in nothing else. She ran to them and fell on her knees.

Eola of Uibh Rathach had sold his life dearly. Five strange warriors lay stretched in death around him, terrible wounds bearing witness to the old warrior's battle fury. By his side knelt Buimech, cradling Eola's head in her lap. Her eyes were beyond tears. They were wide and disbelieving, the skin stretched tautly around them, the mouth set grimly.

She had no need to ask whether Eola was dead.

'Who did this evil deed, my mother?' she whispered,

25

her emotions filled with a mixture of horror and outrage.

Buimech raised her eyes to her adopted daughter.

'Alas, this was written in the heavens, my child. The prophecy is fulfilled.'

'Prophecy?'

Buimech sighed.

'It is a story that will be long in the telling, child.'

Scáthach shook her head impatiently.

'Tell me who did this and let me attempt to overtake them while their trail is still fresh.'

Buimech shook her head.

'No, child. They have fled across the seas. The day will come when you exact vengeance for this deed but first you must be armed with knowledge.'

'But what happened?' demanded the girl.

'This morning, while you were hunting, a strange vessel arrived in the bay below here. Eola and I offered hospitality to the captain and his crew. The hospitality was abused. They turned on us, slaughtering Eola and sacking the fortress.'

'But why?'

'Let me tell you all in the time appointed.'

Gently, Buimech laid Eola's head down, and rose to her feet, gazing around. She was not one to demonstrate her emotions and she seemed cold and detached to the young girl, who was fighting desperately to keep her sorrow in check for it was unseemly to display it while her mother displayed none.

'Come, child,' Buimech said at last, 'let us gather our household and prepare Eola's pyre.'

It was dawn, the exact moment when the sun's extremity began to emerge over the eastern horizon, that Buimech, acting as both wife and druid, lit the funeral pyre of her husband. All the rituals had been observed. Buimech and

26

Scáthach had washed the body of the fallen warrior and dressed it in the finest clothes, together with armour, shield, sword and spears. Then the body was placed on the *fuat*, a bier, laden with the bushy branches of the common birch. Buimech had cut the traditional *fé*, a rod of aspen, with the name and station of Eola in Ogham characters, and laid it alongside him, so that his name and deeds would accompany him into the Otherworld. The *fuat* was placed on a wheeled cart which was drawn by two oxen to the place of burning, a spot high up on the mountainside above Uibh Rathach.

The removal of the body to the site, which was done just before the dusk of evening, was accompanied by the survivors of the household of Eola who, as tradition prescribed, accompanied the body with great cries of lamentation and wailing and the clapping of hands in sorrow. Words expressive of their sorrow and praise of the dead – the *nuall-guba*, or lamentation of sorrow – echoed across the mountainside. All night this act of the *caoineadh*, the keening, was carried on, for this was the time of watching and all around the body torches blazed so that the Evil Ones, the misshapen Fomorii, gods of corruption and harm, could not come near to claim a soul.

Then, at the moment of dawn, Buimech took the torch and moved forward to stand at the foot of the pyre. She called in a loud voice filled with genuine anguish.

'Sorrowful to me to be in life after my husband, Eola, has gone on to the Otherworld. Sad my eye and withered my clay since we have watched at his funeral bed.'

Then she plunged the torch into the birch scrub and each mourner came forward, a small bunch of twigs held in their left hand which they threw onto the funeral pyre in token gesture, before returning to their place and giving voice to a soft wailing, rising and falling, falling and rising as they marked the passing of Eola to the Otherworld.

Behind Buimech, Scáthach shivered softly. Since she was a child she had always had a fear of death. Not of meeting death in battle but of the place of the dead to which her father's ashes would soon be transported. It conjured up the unpleasant visions of dark, brooding forests, and rotting vegetation, of dank-smelling earth and the scurry of half-unseen creatures of the night. Yet the girl fought back her fears, just as she had fought them back all her childhood for she knew that both Eola and Buimech would scold her for them. So she stood silently, with lips compressed, by the bier whose eager flames were consuming her father's mortal remains, suppressing the fearfulness that was in her heart.

It was evening at Uibh Rathach when Buimech led her adopted daughter to a special room in which Scáthach had never been before. It was a room which had its only entrance from the sleeping chamber of Eola and Buimech.

Buimech smiled sadly at the girl.

'The time has come when I must tell you of what I know of your origins, my daughter.'

Scáthach was puzzled.

'What has that to do with the assassins of my father?' she demanded. 'Rather than listen to such stories, I should be leading a troop of warriors in chasing those assassins and exacting retribution for what they have done.'

Buimech shook her head.

'Time for that.'

'But they fly farther away with each moment,' the girl insisted. 'The sooner I start, the sooner will I have a chance to catch up with them.'

'There is much you must know first,' Buimech said evenly, unlocking the door to the side chamber and, taking a lighted torch, ushering the girl inside.

The chamber was a simple store room. Some of Eola's favourite weapons hung around the walls, while boxes stood here and there. At one end of the room was an ornately decorated casket. It was to this object that Buimech moved.

'Mother!' There was exasperation in Scáthach's voice. 'This is nothing but a delay. I am losing precious time.'

Buimech did not respond to the girl's irritation, instead she simply pointed to the casket.

'Look!' she commanded softly.

Scáthach bent forward and peered at the box. It was rectangular and of carved wood but a wood such as she had never seen before; a black, shining wood. And it was covered with strange whorls and circles incised over its surface and on the centre of the lid was a curious triskele design.

'What is it?' demanded the girl.

'That was the casket in which Eola and I found you.'

Scáthach frowned. Eola and Buimech had made no secret of the fact that she was their adopted daughter. Buimech had always told her that when the time was opportune she would reveal all she knew of the girl's background. But why now? Why now, when every minute was valuable in tracking down the slayers of her father?

Buimech took from the cask a golden medallion on which the same triskele design was engraved.

'You were clutching this in your hand when we found you,' she said quietly. 'It bears the same symbol as that which was on the box. Take it now and wear it. It will mean much to you.'

'But why tell me this now?' Scáthach asked, taking the medallion and placing it around her neck, hardly noticing it.

Buimech turned aside and took a shield which was leaning against the wall.

'Eola slew several of his enemies before he died. Each

of them bore a shield, this is one of them. Look at it, my daughter.'

Scáthach gazed on it; her eyes widened slightly.

It bore the same curious triskele design as on the casket and the medallion at her neck.

'What does this mean?' she whispered.

Buimech sighed softly.

'What it means, my child, is that I think the assassins came in search of you.'

Scáthach stared at Buimech, hearing the words but not quite taking in their meaning.

The elder woman reached forward and, setting aside the shield with its strange device, drew the girl into the other chamber and sat her down.

'I told you that the strangers came here for a purpose; that they appeared to be looking for something . . . or someone. Years ago, when you were cast upon the seas in that casket, you were clearly meant to die. Eola and I found the casket by the will of the ocean god. The triskele symbol, carved on that casket, and on the medallion which you now wear, my child, is the only clue as to the land of your origin. And now, from the sea, strange warriors arrive with their shields bearing the same symbol. They search and destroy. I believe that those who sought to put you to death as a baby have now learnt that you still live. They were sent to kill you, Scáthach.'

The girl gazed up at Buimech, still scarcely comprehending what she heard.

After a while she said: 'Tell me how you found me and what you know of my origins.'

It was a while before Buimech finished her account.

'Such is the story of your coming, Scáthach,' she ended with eyes unnaturally bright. 'All this was written in the heavens at the time. I knew it. Yet I thought there was still time, time for you to grow a little more before your destiny took charge.'

The girl regarded her step-mother sadly.

'It is sad that I have caused the death of Eola.'

Buimech shrugged.

'It was written,' she repeated, but the indifference she tried to display was betrayed by the uneven tone of her voice. 'Now it means that you must begin to tread the path the heavens have set out for you. You must leave Uibh Rathach and seek the land whence those marauders came. You must learn the meaning of the triskele symbol and how you are connected with it. You must find out why you were cast away to die on the high seas, why the warriors who bear the triskele symbol are still afraid of you, so afraid that they must search you out to kill you.'

Scáthach pursed her lips in perplexity.

'I do not understand.'

'Understanding will only come when you have learnt the meaning of the symbol.'

'But how am I to find out where these assassins came from?' protested the girl. 'Had I left at once, while their trail was fresh . . .' She shrugged helplessly as she realised the futility of the task. 'Ships leave no trails to follow across the sea.'

A soft smile crossed Buimech's face.

'Nevertheless, you will follow them. And you must set out from Uibh Rathach alone.'

'Alone?' the girl protested. 'But there are many who would volunteer to accompany me from Uibh Rathach to avenge Eola's death.'

'Nevertheless, it is your destiny to go alone.'

'I . . . I do not think I am ready,' Scáthach said.

'Not ready?' smiled Buimech sadly.

'I am ready in arms but I still retain the fears of my youth, my mother.'

'Then you must find ways to discard them.'

'How?'

'What causes you fear?'

The girl hesitated.

'I am afraid of the place of the dead ones . . .'

'That is natural, my daughter. But one day you will learn that death is simply part of life.'

'I fear my inabilities: I fear that powerful monsters lurk in the shadows against which my sword is powerless.'

Buimech sighed.

'One day you will learn to meet the monsters from the shadows and slay them. Then you will truly be the champion of Uibh Rathach. You are ready, Scáthach. You are ready to commence your journey and go in search of your destiny and let us pray to the gods that you will find yourself along the road.'

For a few moments Scáthach was silent and then she bowed her head to her mother.

'There is none wiser than my mother, Buimech,' she said softly. 'Tell me what path I must tread.'

'Your first step on this path, my daughter, is to find a sailor . . . he must be an old man now. Seek out Rónán Mac Méin. He was the captain of the ship called the *Cáoc* in which Eola and I were travelling when we found you.'

'How could he help?' frowned the girl.

'By his knowledge of the tides and currents of the sea. From such knowledge he might be able to tell you at what spot the casket was placed in the sea. By following the tides and currents you will discover the shore of the land of your birth and thence the meaning of the symbol and why death is stalking your path.'

'Where can I find this Rónán Mac Méin?'

'You must ask for him in the taverns of the sea-ports of Mumhan.'

Buimech reached forward and drew the girl to her in one long, hard embrace.

32

'Go now, my child. Begin to tread your allotted path. This is where I must stop. For it is written.'

'I will go,' Scáthach said, fighting back the tears. 'But I will return having taken vengeance on those who slew Eola. I will bring you back their heads so that you may display them as a warning to any who would slay by treachery.'

Buimech shook her head, holding the girl by the shoulders at arm's length.

'No. You will not return. Neither will I be here. For this much is written. I cannot see whether you will succeed or fail. The gifts that were given me by the gods are finite. But this much I know: Eola's death was an act to shame both the gods and men. His was an unlawful slaughter and therefore there is only one form of protest open to me. Soon I will follow Eola to the Otherworld.'

Scáthach opened her mouth to object but snapped it shut again. She knew that such a protest was useless. Buimech was choosing the ancient form of protest, a ritual as old as Éireann itself − a ritual fast to the death so that the whole world might know and be shamed by the unlawful killing of her husband. She knew that nothing she could say would dissuade Buimech from her intention.

'Burn the memory of the triskele symbol into your memory, my daughter,' whispered Buimech. 'Remember its every curve and line, lest you lose that medallion. Then take your weapons and go and may the gods that brought you safely to Eola and me guide your footsteps in your quest.'

Scáthach drew herself up to her full height and gazed softly into the face of her step-mother. Her mouth was compressed tightly and she blinked back the tears that threatened to flood down her cheeks. She knew now that it would be for the last time that she beheld Buimech's features.

33

'May the gods be with you, mother . . . my mother.'

Then she turned away, full of grief and controlled fury, her mouth set into a thin narrow line. Already the triskele symbol was engraved vividly upon her memory. She did not need the piece of gold metal around her neck to remind her. Every detail, every line, was as sharp in her mind's eye as if she had the object before her. She took up her weapons, her sword, spear and shield, and strode through the still smoking ruins of Uibh Rathach. It had been the only world she had ever known, a world of kindliness and comfort. Now it was no more. Gone were those she had loved as her only parents. Who would comfort her now when she feared the shadows of the night and the terrors of the place of the dead, when she feared the shadows of her own mind? Now she had no one, no one but herself on whom to rely. The survivors of Eola's household stood watching her go in silence. She walked with her shoulders back, head high, looking neither to right nor left, not acknowledging them. But they knew. They could see the tears streaming from her eyes in spite of the firm set of her jaw. She turned out of the gates of the great fortress and marched down the valley road towards the seashore.

Three

The sun was high in the heavens as Scáthach reached the crossroads. She halted and gazed around her. The main road, the one which she had been following, led from the west due eastward in a straight line. It was a long, uninterrupted and uninteresting track; mile after mile of predictability. But at this juncture another roadway turned off to the south into a wild and desolate countryside, a grey, stony land of granite and jagged hills. Desolate, yes; but with the sun shining on the land, it seemed possessed of a fierce beauty.

For four days now Scáthach had travelled along the coastline of Mumhan, one of the great kingdoms of the land of Éireann. Four days inquiring at each port for news of the ancient sailor, Rónán Mac Méin. Several people had heard of him, for apparently his name was renowned among the sea-ports, but it had only been at the last village that the keeper of the local hostel had definite news.

'Take the road to Dún na Séad, the fort of jewels, and you will find him there.'

'Where is this place?' Scáthach had demanded.

'It lies on the tip of one of the remote peninsulas of the country,' the hosteler had replied. 'It is a port, a small port at the end of a remote road. It is there, at the fort of jewels, that you will find Rónán Mac Méin for he was born there and he has returned to die there.'

The girl had pressed for further directions and finally set off with light enough heart, swinging along the road, blood tingling in anticipation of the nearness of the object of her search. Finally, she had come to the crossroads from where the roadway to Dún na Séad left the main highway and swung southwards down the peninsula towards its furthest tip.

She paused and sat for a moment on a roadside boulder which obviously marked the boundary division of a clan land. She could not interpret the Ogham which marked the territorial division for the characters were worn and faded with age. For a while she rested in the gentle heat of the sun, eyes closed as she relaxed in its comfort. She had scarcely slept these last four days. She felt exhausted. Four days and nights she had existed on nervous energy, her mind too active to succumb to sleep. But now, now her body was demanding what her mind had refused to give. Sleep. She needed sleep. She felt herself drifting. Then she shook herself, realising that it would not do to tarry for long. She must reach the port before dark and she had not been able to ascertain exactly how long it would take to travel the roadway into Dún na Séad.

She stood up, stretched a moment and set out again, moving away from the main highway and following the road among the granite hills.

For the last four days her mind had been filled with thoughts and memories of Eola and Buimech. Above all, she kept going over the story of how Eola and Buimech found her cast away in a casket on the high seas. Ever since she was old enough to understand, Eola and Buimech had not kept from her the fact that she was not their own child. That had not mattered to her. Eola and Buimech had expended on her all the love and care that any natural parents could. She had wanted for nothing. But that was not to say that she had been spoilt or pandered to.

Both Eola and Buimech had always been there to comfort her in times of need but they had also taught her to stand on her own two feet, to be independent in all things. And they had imparted many of their skills to the girl. From Eola had come the skill of how to handle weapons, of how to defend oneself with minimal injury to one's opponents. For the true code of a champion was not to inflict injury but to defend oneself and others from hurt. From Eola had also come the skills of the hunt. Buimech had taught her the reflective side of human nature, and how to cure pain and sickness with a druid's skills, and to understand and live at one with nature instead of seeking to dominate it. Indeed, from both her foster parents had come the philosophy of the great harmony of the universe. That everything was related and needed to be treated with respect. For out of disharmony comes crisis and destruction.

36

Scáthach hoped that Eola and Buimech had taught her well for she would have need of their skills before her journey was through; of that she was sure. She worried as she thought more, for deep within her she was afraid that she was not entirely at one with herself and nature. From her childhood she had possessed fears of shadows, of things intangible and unseen and, in spite of Eola and Buimech, they remained with her. She hoped, desperately, that she would overcome those fears as Buimech said she would, but . . .

The raucous laughter halted her in her tracks. Her day-dream shattered as she beheld the broad, stocky figure of a man in her path. He was an ugly man, bearded, with bulbous nose and a sneering expression on his dirty features. His clothes were ill-cared for. He wore a tarnished helmet, carried a buckler on one arm and an impressive workmanlike sword in his right hand. The girl's eyes narrowed. The man was clearly no warrior.

'Well, well,' the man's voice was as ugly as his appearance. 'What have we here? A little girl, but finely dressed and with shield, sword and spear as if she were a champion?' The man seemed seized by laughter again. 'Champion?' The idea apparently amused him. 'Champion of what, my little maiden?'

Scáthach frowned in annoyance.

'You are blocking my path.'

Once more the man guffawed.

'You are perceptive in your youth, little girl. You wear the clothes of one used to the comfort of life. Therefore, my understanding of it is that you carry a fine purse as well. It is only your purse I want . . . for the moment.' Then the man caught sight of the gold medallion around her neck and pointed to it with the tip of his sword. 'And I'll take that as well.'

The girl's eyes now narrowed.

Robbers. She had heard from Eola that such creatures

haunted the coastal roads; evil men, aye, and women, thrown out of the society of their clans, outcasts who had transgressed the laws with no thought of compensating those they harmed. By no tension of her muscles did she betray her sense of readiness as she eyed her opponent, weighing up his grasp on his sword, the way he carried it and his shield, in an assessment of what type of fighting man he might be. In fact, it seemed she made no move at all as she stood there, feet wide apart, her shield slung on her back in the carrying position, her sword in her scabbard hung from her left shoulder while in her right she carried her two javelins. Her bow and sling of arrows were also slung. To one whose eyesight was untrained it seemed that she was simply encumbered by the weapons she carried.

The ugly man was still chuckling as he blocked her path.

'Come on, girl. I haven't all day to exchange pleasantries.'

'No more than I, you fat fox whelp,' she replied. 'Stand aside.'

The man stopped laughing, his eyes suddenly wide in astonishment.

'What did you say?' he said slowly, not believing his ears.

'I said, stand aside.'

The man suddenly roared with laughter again and shook his head.

'My, but you are a playful little wench.'

It was the flicker of his eyes that gave away his companions. Scáthach saw the shadows creeping up behind her and knew that she must act at once. She spun round, using the length of her javelins like a long club, and smashing them against the head of the man who was creeping up at her right shoulder. He grunted and dropped to his knees. Without pausing, she reversed the javelins, spinning round, and thrusting their butts into the stomach of the other man moving to her left. They caught him full in the solar plexus, knocking him backward into a sitting position on the path with a grunt of surprise. Then Scáthach had discarded the javelins and unsheathed her sword and was moving towards the ugly man, crouched ready for the conflict, her sword point performing short circling motions as she came.

The ugly man stared at her in astonishment, his eyes moving quickly towards his disabled companions. Then he swore unpleasantly and rushed upon the girl, his great sword slashing into the air.

It was all too easy. The man clearly had no training in weaponry at all. The girl moved easily under his guard, knocking aside his shield with a blow from her own and stabbing her sword into the upper muscle of the arm. It was a classic counter the like of which she had practised numerous times with Eola. She was almost surprised at how easily the movement worked. The ugly man grunted in pain and his sword dropped from his nerveless fingers. For a second or two he stood staring at the blood staining his arm. Then he gave a howl of anguish.

Scáthach took a couple of steps back and frowned at the man. Then she shrugged. He was clearly in a state of shock at the swiftness of his defeat. She turned to view his two companions, men as ugly and as ill-clothed as their leader. They were still in the position they had fallen, one on his knees, holding the side of his head where the javelins had struck him like a club, the other seated, almost comically, on the pathway, still clutching his stomach and blowing for want of breath.

She sheathed her sword and bent to pick up her javelins. Then she turned to the ugly man.

'What name are you known by?' she snapped.

The man blinked.

'I am Éccneid.'

'Then you are well-named for you are, indeed, foolish.'

'What do you want of us?' the man replied gruffly.

'Nothing, save that you leave here, for when I reach the *dún* of the next chieftain I will tell him that I have met you and your companions and woe betide you if you remain in this territory.'

Éccneid nodded slowly. If the warriors of the local chieftain came searching for him, he would be taken before the clan assembly and his fate would be assured. For those outcasts who refused to reform, a fate of exile on a lonely inhospitable island awaited. Such was the punishment of those who transgressed the laws of the society and who refused to compensate for their wrongdoing.

Scáthach thrust out her hand holding her javelins, pointing back along the path she had come.

'Go!'

The three robbers said nothing but drew themselves up and began to walk along the path. It was Éccneid who suddenly halted and turned back. His ugly features were split by what was meant to be an obsequious expression.

'May I ask what champion we have been defeated by?'

The girl thrust out her chin.

'Defeated? The word implies a combat of equals.'

'Nevertheless, what name is given to a girl of such tender years who can vanquish grown men in the blink of an eye.'

'I am called Scáthach of Uibh Rathach.'

Éccneid smiled and bowed.

'We shall remember that name,' he said.

The girl frowned a moment. Was there some other meaning to the man's words?

She watched the three men walk off, watching them until they were almost out of sight before she continued her journey. Even then, she kept herself alert in case they tried to return and outflank her to take their vengeance. But as the time passed and as she moved through low-lying, almost flat country, bounded on the south-eastern side by the sea's long dim level, she relaxed. There was no one in sight and the country was such that not even the cleverest rogues could attempt to hide themselves in it, let alone prepare an ambush.

It was dusk when Scáthach came to the outskirts of Dún na Séad and she was now weary from the long day's journey. She heard the breakers crashing on the granite rocks somewhere ahead and smelled the salt brine of the ocean. Here, too, the air was chill from the breeze that blew from the sea. She paused, glimpsing the lights of the little port below the road nestling in a small cove. However, just a little way ahead on the road, she saw a closer glimmer of light. She was tired, thirsty and hungry. She hoped that it was a *bruden*, a public hostel. Moments later her expectation was fulfilled when she saw, by the side of the road, a lantern flickering from a tall post on the *faitche*, or lawn, which led to the stone building. By the light of the lantern she saw, incised in Ogham script on the wooden name-board below, the name '*Bruden na Rialtais*', hostel of the stars. She walked up to the building and pushed open the heavy oak door.

The place seemed deserted at first. A log fire was crackling in the huge fireplace in which a great cauldron of aromatic broth simmered gently, its perfume permeating the place. It was warm and comforting. The lights were lit and flickering against the polished oak and red deal panels of the room.

The girl hesitated. She had never been in such a place before. Then, fighting down her sense of awkwardness, she called: 'Ho, there!'

A moment passed before there was a movement somewhere in the building and then a door creaked open.

A short, silver-haired man emerged, florid of face, with deep-set eyes that reflected the fire of the torches, causing them to sparkle in the light. His movements were jerky and appeared almost clumsy. His eyes narrowed when he saw his customer. He came forward with a frown and a growl in his voice.

'What is it you seek?' he demanded, with none of the tone one would expect in a hosteler wishing to fulfil the wishers of his clients.

Scáthach sniffed in displeasure.

'What else would I be seeking but food, drink and a place to pass the night?' she snapped.

The hosteler's eyes took in her weaponry, carried as if by one who was used to wielding it, and the richness of her garments. He hesitated.

'It is strange for a young girl to be travelling alone in this country . . .'

He paused as he saw the blaze of anger in the girl's eyes.

'Do you question all your customers in this fashion, hostel-keeper?' she demanded.

The man lifted a shoulder and let it fall.

'I just remark that it is unusual, that is all. In that, where is the offence?'

'The offence, man, is not attending to the duties of your office!' she replied.

The man bit his lip as he realised that here was one used to being obeyed. Young and slight as this slip of a girl was, she carried herself with the demeanour of a seasoned warrior.

'May I ask,' his tone was a little less rough now, 'who graces my Hostel of the Stars?'

'I am Scáthach of Uibh Rathach.'

The man's eyes widened.

'Of Uibh Rathach, you say?' He sounded surprised. 'Are you kin to Eola of Uibh Rathach?'

She nodded.

'He was my father.'

The hostel-keeper's eyes widened even further.

'Was? Has his grave been measured?'

'He died five days since.'

'Alas, then Éireann lacks a great hero.'

The man's sadness seemed genuine. He bowed his head for a moment and then raised it to stare at the girl.

'Are you then his daughter?'

'By fosterage,' she confirmed. 'I am daughter of Eola and Buimech.'

'Welcome to my poor hostel, Scáthach of Uibh Rathach. Come freely. Go safely; and leave something of the happiness you bring.'

The man inclined his head in a bow.

'What is your name?' asked the girl with a frown of surprise at this new courtesy.

'I am Brosc.'

Scáthach inclined her head in acknowledgement at the extravagance of his welcome.

'Come, be seated, daughter of Eola. Let me prepare a meal for you.'

The girl allowed herself to be led to a table near the fire and divested herself of her shield and weapons. She stretched luxuriously in its warmth while Brosc, the hostel-keeper, busied himself laying a place.

'I had the privilege to know your father when he was captain of the Fianna, the bodyguard of the High King,' he explained, as he brought platter and bowl to the table. 'I was once a bowman in the High King's retinue and when I grew too old to carry my bow in his service, I returned to my clan lands and sought to end my days peacefully as a hostel-keeper.'

He took her bowl.

'A dish of broth for you, daughter of Eola? It is a broth

made of leek and oats, mixed with cream and seasoned with parsley.'

She nodded absently.

'Whose clan lands are these?'

Brosc smiled.

'These are the lands of the Eidersceoil.'

'Where would I find the chieftain?'

'At the fort of jewels. Why do you seek him?'

Scáthach explained how she had been set on by three robbers on the road.

Brosc whistled softly.

'By Éccneid, no less! He may have the name of a fool but he is not a man to be crossed. Take warning, daughter of Eola. He is a man with a long memory and with it a balance for measuring wrong done to him. He will seek vengeance.'

Scáthach shrugged.

'He is a rogue and a foolish rogue. His sort I could defeat if they came in their legions.'

She said it without boasting for it was a simple statement of fact.

Brosc considered her for a moment and saw the truth of it in her demeanour.

'You are the daughter of Eola,' he sighed. 'Nevertheless, be warned. Champions are taught truth and honour. That is not the way of Éccneid. Watch your back while you are in this country.'

Scáthach smiled thinly.

'I hope that I will have no need to for it will be the duty of the Eidersceoil to seize the man and his companions, if they are still here, and bring them before the judges to be heard.'

'That is so. But take heed of my warning, daughter of Eola.'

The girl fell to her broth, which she ate with a slice of good bread, while Brosc filled a cup with mead and

44

proceeded to bring her a plate of sliced pork with a salad of meadow trefoil and scullions.

'As you know this area well, Brosc,' the girl remarked at length, resting back pleasantly from her meal and sipping the honey-flavoured mead, 'you may know a man whom I am seeking.'

Brosc came forward eagerly.

'Perhaps. If he is in this area, then I shall know him.'

Scáthach nodded.

'I am seeking an old mariner, Rónán Mac Méin. He was captain of a ship called the *Cáoc*.'

Brosc's face broke into a broad smile.

'I know him well. But he has retired from the sea now. As you say, he has many years behind him. And the *Cáoc* has long since rotted its timbers.'

'But he still lives here?' pressed the girl, eagerly.

'Indeed, he does.'

'Then tell me where I may find him.'

Brosc's eyes suddenly narrowed suspiciously.

'He is friend to many here, daughter of Eola. Many would wish no harm to befall him.'

There was an implied question in the statement.

Scáthach smiled.

'I seek him not with any intention of harm. He has information which might help me. That is all.'

Brosc relaxed.

'In that case, daughter of Eola, you have no need to stir. Every evening old Rónán comes to the Hostel of Stars to take a cup of mead. He will be here soon.'

'That is good news to my ears, Brosc,' smiled the girl. 'It has been a long journey searching for him.'

Brosc looked at her curiously.

'Your business with the old captain must be important then?'

'Important to me,' she replied shortly.

45

Brosc hesitated and then shrugged. Curiosity was written all over his features but he contained it.

The door of the *bruden* opened and new customers entered, sailors by the look of them. Britons, with their curious accents. The girl sat back sipping her mead as she watched Brosc serve the newcomers, burly men with the sea, sun and wind tanning their faces and muscular forearms. They sat talking loudly in a corner, a great flagon of ale between them. Then more customers came in, a local farmer, a man and his wife, two women on their own whose profession grew obvious and who cast suspicious and angry glances in the direction of Scáthach until Brosc made a whispered explanation to them and thus they lost interest. Within a short time, the hostel had filled. An old man entered, and for a moment or two, Scáthach thought that this might be the old sailor whom she sought. But the old man was obviously the local story-teller for he made his way to a special stool, set to one side of the room, raised on a small dais, and someone plied him with ale and demanded a tale.

People crowded round to shout out suggestions as to what the tale should be. Someone wanted to hear the story of Durbhola, a daughter of a king of the merfolk who married a human. Brosc intervened to demand the story of Búanann who was 'the mother of heroes' and taught the martial arts to the ancient heroes of Éireann. In making the request, Brosc grinned in the direction of Scáthach. Perhaps he meant it as a compliment but the girl was too tired to care. The lack of sleep over the last four days was catching up with her. Every time she closed her eyes she found it almost impossible to reopen them. And, in addition, the good food, mead and the heat of the fire overcame her and her eyelids were drooping. Sleep crept up over her although she fought to keep awake, to listen to the rise and fall of the old man's voice as he made his recitation. Sleep conquered.

It seemed an age before she fought her way out of it, blinking and forcing herself awake.

The room was quiet, a little chill for she saw that the fire had died to embers. She blinked again and glanced round. There was no one about. The hostel was deserted. She lay on a bench with a blanket covering her. But her weapons were gone. She was alone.

Four

Scáthach leapt to her feet, all senses tuned for danger. She made her way to the door of the hostel, half expecting it to be barred, but it was not. She flung it open. It was morning. The bright light of day spilled into the hostel causing her to blink while she attempted to adjust her eyes to the light. She had been more exhausted than she had imagined. The long walk of the last four days had caught up with her. To have fallen into such a deep sleep, not to be disturbed by the carousing of the tavern, the departure of the guests, was a new experience. She stood blinking at the early dawn sunlight, the sharp blue sky and crystal air.

She half-turned back into the hostel in search of Brosc when a heavy masculine voice hailed her.

'Good morning, daughter of Eola.'

She turned back.

Just outside the door, seated on a wooden bench, sat an old man with grey-grizzled hair and a leathery weather-beaten face. His pale, sea-green eyes held her in their amused light.

Scáthach frowned.

'Who are you? How do you know me?'

The old man chuckled deeply.

'Easy to say. My friend Brosc tells me that you were searching for me.'

Her eyes widened.

'Are you Rónán Mac Méin?'

'I am he,' the other acknowledged. 'When I came to the hostel last night and Brosc told me who you were and who you sought, we went to where you lay. You have come a long journey. You were dead to this world. So we felt it better to leave you undisturbed. I came here this morning to break my fast and see if you were awake.'

The girl smiled a little ashamedly.

'I cannot understand how I could sleep so long and so deeply.'

The old sailor grinned.

'Then you don't know what true exhaustion is, I'm thinking. Why, I've known men who have had to stay on their feet for three or four days at a time, weathering a storm on board ship, dropped at the end of it and be dead to the world for two days and more. You have come a long way. It must have been a hard journey.'

The girl nodded.

'I have come from Uibh Rathach.'

'And Eola is dead. Brosc has told me this.'

'May he be reborn with health and good fortune in the Otherworld,' said Scáthach.

'And does your mother, Buimech, live?'

'In body only,' replied the girl. 'She makes the ritual fast in protest at the unlawful slaying of Eola.'

Rónán Mac Méin sighed deeply.

'Unlawful? That is bad. And your mother on a ritual fast? That I can understand. She was a powerful woman, your mother. Powerful and wise beyond understanding.'

He gazed at the girl.

'Why have you come to seek me out?'

The girl went and sat down by the old sea-farer.

'Because Buimech told me to, and said that you might help me.'

Rónán Mac Méin scratched his chin thoughtfully.

'And how might that be?'

'My parents told me that I was fostered by them. Buimech told me the story of my finding, cast adrift in the sea in a casket.'

'Ah,' said the old man, as if he suddenly understood everything.

There was a scuffling noise from the door of the hostel and the sleepy face of Brosc looked out. He saw them seated together and smiled.

'It is good. I will bring you breakfast.'

He was about to duck back inside when Scáthach motioned him to stay.

'Where are my weapons?'

Brosc bobbed back again.

'Why, put in a place of safety while you slept in case they were . . .' he hesitated.

'Stolen?'

The girl supplied the word.

The hostel-keeper nodded.

'The Hostel of the Stars is sited by a sea-port. Sometimes we get strangers staying and sometimes strangers have odd codes of hospitality.'

'Well,' said the girl sharply, 'I thank you for your solicitude but never take my weapons again without my knowledge or approval. It may be that I have need of them.'

Brosc looked unhappy.

The old sailor shook his head gently.

'You have no need to mistrust Brosc. He would have protected you with his life.'

Scáthach felt uncomfortable at the rebuke and coloured a little.

'I doubt it not, but a warrior without weapons is as a ship without sails.'

'I'll fetch them now, daughter of Eola,' said the hosteler, his face red with mortification, and disappeared to suit the word with action.

The old man shook his head.

'He was once a great bowman. He served the High King when Eola was captain of the Fianna. Trust him.'

She turned to meet his bantering sea-green eyes.

'And can I trust you?'

Rónán Mac Méin chuckled in amusement.

'I suppose, if I wore your shoes, daughter of Eola, I would be suspicious of everyone. Trust is an instinctive thing. Maybe only experience makes one trust or distrust.'

She nodded, thoughtfully, and then said: 'I will trust you for I have no other choice.'

Brosc came hurrying out of the hostel carrying her weapons and shield and placed them by her side. He turned back to the hostel again but she reached and placed a restraining hand on his arm.

'I am sorry that I was churlish and insulted your hospitality, Brosc. Can you forgive one who is an innocent in the world and fearful of that which she does not know?'

Brosc hesitated and gazed down at her artless face; then he smiled.

'Daughter of Eola, I thought to do what was best. There is nothing to forgive. Let me bring you breakfast.'

He turned back into the hostel.

Rónán Mac Méin smiled approvingly.

'You are a true daughter of Eola and Buimech.'

Scáthach's lips drooped.

'Not so and we know it,' she replied. 'I was but a child fostered. And you must help me trace my origins.'

The old sea-captain scratched the bridge of his nose reflectively for a moment or two and then shrugged.

'I guessed that was the reason for your coming. But all I know is what Eola and Buimech must have told you. You were found cast away on the seas in a casket which, by the will of the ocean god, floated until we were able to pull it from the sea. But what else can be told?'

'One thing more, which only you can tell me.'

'And what is that?'

'You must dredge your knowledge of the tides and currents of the sea, consider the spot where I was found and tell me where it was likely that the casket in which I was found was placed in the waters.'

Rónán Mac Méin sat back and stared thoughtfully at the girl.

'It is a long time ago.'

'Please try to recall.'

The old sailor chewed his lower lip in thought.

'Well, the currents in that spot wash from the coast of Gallia . . . but it is a long, long coastline. Let me think now . . .'

Brosc returned with dishes of cold meat and drinks made from the infusion of herbs.

Rónán Mac Méin was still sunk in thought. The girl sat quietly. Then the old seaman's brow cleared.

'Surely,' he said, as if confirming his thought verbally. 'Yes, in that sea where you were found, the main current washes up from the coast of Gallia which is the country of Lethra.'

'Lethra?' frowned the Scáthach. 'What place is that?'

The old man shrugged.

'In all my days I never travelled there. It is a strange country about which little is known. It is a land which does not encourage merchants.'

'But it was from there that the casket, placed in the sea, would travel to the point where you picked it up.'

'If the casket travelled by the currents.'

Scáthach drew her brows together.

'How else would it have travelled?'

The old sailor raised his shoulders and let them fall in a helpless gesture.

'Who knows? At the time many of my men saw the work of Otherworld forces in the finding of the casket.'

The girl gave a merry peel of laughter.

'Do I appear as a creature from the Otherworld?'

Rónán Mac Méin shook his head.

'And if so,' went on the girl, 'then I should look to this land of Lethra for the solution to the mystery.' She hesitated, one hand going to finger the gold medallion at her neck and then she said: 'Tell me, do the warriors of this land of Lethra bear a strange triskele device on their shields?'

'That I would not know, daughter of Eola. As I have said, I have never visited that country nor seen anyone who claimed to have been there or from there.'

Scáthach sighed.

'Then I must find a ship to take me there.'

'Easier said than done.'

'But our ships trade regularly with Gallia and with Britain.'

'Yet not one do I know that would make the voyage to Lethra.'

The girl jerked up her chin in confidence.

'I will find a ship.'

The old sea-captain smiled at her youthful assurance.

'And mayhap if I were forty years younger, nay, even twenty years, I would be your captain.'

The girl smiled.

'I will find a ship,' she repeated.

Brosc came to clear away the remains of their breakfast and overheard her.

'Well, if it is a ship you need, then Dún na Séad is the place. It is one of the busiest ports of Mumhan. Why, there are a dozen vessels there.'

It was the first time that Scáthach turned her gaze down the hill to the bay below. She had arrived at the Hostel of the Stars at dusk and so had not seen anything but the winking lights of the seaport, nestling in a cove below. Now she saw the numerous buildings of the port stretched by a long low silvery strand. Beyond the surrounding cliffs and headlands there stretched numerous islands which afforded protection to the little harbour and there was little reason to ask why the place had been chosen as a trading port. Indeed, she could see many big ships at anchor off the coast, large ships from Gallia, with their heavy oak timbers, leather sails and great chains to pull them with. There were lighter vessels from Britain, the big island to the east of Éireann, whose ships were almost similar in design and size.

Scáthach nodded and smiled.

'Yes; there must surely be one ship here which will take me to Lethra.'

'Lethra?'

Brosc frowned at the name.

The girl turned to him.

'Yes. Do you know of it?'

Brosc shook his head and she saw him exchange a quick glance with Rónán Mac Méin.

'I only know of it by the tales and gossip of the sailors which frequent here, daughter of Eola. It is a land in Gallia which does not encourage travellers.'

Scáthach stood up and smiled.

'Then it is high time this strange land had visitors.'

She gathered her weapons and reached for her purse.

Brosc saw the gesture and shook his head vehemently.

'My house is your house, daughter of Eola. My life was frequently bought by the concern and courage of your father.'

'You place me in debt, Brosc,' protested the girl.

'No, no. I am already in the debt of Uibh Rathach.

Should you ever wish for a place to sleep free from the care of treachery and attack, should you ever seek food or even one that was once a good bowman, then come to the Hostel of the Stars.'

Scáthach reached out a hand and smiled at the hosteler.

'Then should you, Brosc, ever require a service that I can render, do not hesitate to call on the name of Scáthach of Uibh Rathach.'

She turned to Rónán Mac Méin and likewise held out a hand to the old seafarer.

'I am also in your debt. Perhaps more than I can say at this time.'

The old sailor smiled awkwardly at the young girl.

'I hope that you go safely to Lethra, and return safely. The gods go with you.'

She smiled again.

'If you can find no passage by nightfall,' called Brosc, as she turned away down the road to Dún na Séad, 'return here.'

She raised a hand in acknowledgement and strode with a light step down the roadway. The sun was climbing high into the heavens now, pouring down its warmth on her body, and encouraging the fragrance of wild herbs, the roadside shrubs and flowers, to assail her nostrils. The fragrance intermingled with the faint odour of the sea as a gentle sea-breeze rolled over the shore.

As she walked into the township, curious glances were cast in her direction. It was obviously a market day for the place was crowded. Country folk herding cows, dragging goats, carrying squawking chickens by the legs, prodding donkeys on which were loaded the fruits of the countryside, blocking the narrow streets of the sea-port. Weather-beaten sailors were everywhere, purchasing goods from stalls set up in the main square of the town, obviously seeking provisions for their various ships.

Here and there the girl saw men of haughty authority

54

who, by their garb, she took to be captains of the numerous ships which lay offshore. She accosted one, who looked less formidable than the others, a stocky, dark-haired man, whose clothing and manner proclaimed him as a Briton.

'Are you the captain of one of the ships?' she asked.

The man halted and gazed at her for several seconds. She did not like the speculative gleam in his eyes and drew herself up, the muscles of her face tightening.

'Captain? No,' replied the man. 'But I am mate on one of the traders. Why?'

'I am seeking a passage to Gallia.'

The Briton pursed his lips regretfully.

'Ah, but we are bound for the country of the Silures in Britain. A passage there you could have had and welcome.'

The girl shook her head.

'Do you know where I could find some of the captains of the ships from Gallia?'

The Briton turned and called in his own language to a tall, sandy-haired man, whose rolling gait and sturdy linen clothes identified him as a sea-farer. The sandy-haired man halted and turned.

'Here is Vercarnrix,' the Briton said. 'He's a Gaulish merchant captain. Try your luck with him.'

The Briton muttered something to the seaman called Vercarnrix and went on his way into the throng.

The Gaul came up to the girl and stood frowning at her.

'You seek passage to Gallia?'

He spoke in the language of the people of Éireann but his voice was heavy with the accents of his own land.

'I do,' replied Scáthach eagerly. 'Are you bound there?'

'I am so,' replied the man. 'We ship goods to the country of the Trinovantes in Britain and then go on to the country of the Belgae in Gallia.'

The girl frowned.

'I have little knowledge of the country. Is the country of the Belgae near the land of Lethra?'

A strange look came over the seaman's face.

'Lethra? What makes you ask about Lethra?'

'It is to Lethra that I ultimately seek passage,' replied Scáthach.

Vercarnrix stared curiously at her for a moment or so.

'Why would you, a young girl of Éireann, want to go to Lethra?'

Scáthach felt a little annoyed at the man's questioning.

'That is my business,' she said waspishly.

'And the business of those who are stupid enough to give you passage there,' replied the Gaul.

'What do you mean?'

'Mean? That the land of Lethra is an accursed place and the gods between it and my soul, today and nine times nine years from this day.'

She stared at him in amazement.

'What do you know of this land of Lethra?' she pressed. 'What do you know that it puts such fear in you?'

Vercarnrix stood gazing at her and shaking his head.

'Better you know not. You'll get no passage from me to take you towards Lethra.'

He turned into the crowd but she chased after him and caught his arm.

'I must know.'

He turned back to her.

'If you do not know about Lethra, why do you seek it out?' he demanded.

'I know nothing about it . . . only that I need to go there to fulfil a task imposed on me. I can say no more.'

The sailor hesitated and then shook his head again.

'I will tell you this, and no more can I tell you. Beware of the misty land of Lethra. Evil dwells in its valleys and cloaks its mountains. No one goes there willingly and those who go never return. I will not help you on your journey.'

With that, the man turned and was soon lost in the crowded the market place.

Frowning at the man's words, Scáthach stood among the crowds brooding silently for a moment or two. It seemed that Lethra had a bad reputation among the traders and seafarers. Well, there was surely someone who would take her. She turned to the crowd to search out new prospects. However, her next contact was with a young master of a coastal vessel who was of little help although he recommended her to a tavern on the quayside where, he assured her, captains gathered.

Of the four burly sea-captains who were gathered in the smoky inn, all had the same reaction when she stated her destination. Only two of the captains were taking their ships to Gaul and one was heading for the far reaches of Iberia, a country to the south where it was said that the children of Éireann had originally come from; a magical land from where Mil, his wife Scota, daughter of the Egyptian Pharaoh Nectanebes, and their sons, the ancestors of the Gaels, had arrived to defeat the gods of the Dé Danaan and drive them underground. The other captains were bound for Britain. None would help her on her way to the land of Lethra and all were of one voice in warning her of a terrible fate if she saw the shores of the strange country.

For most of the morning and afternoon, Scáthach wandered the smoky taverns and quays of Dún na Séad searching for a passage to Gallia and growing more and more despondent as she met refusal after refusal.

Dusk crept on and she began to reconcile herself to the fact that she would have to retrace her footsteps to the Hostel of the Stars and confess her failure to Brosc and Rónán Mac Méin. She felt angry and her pride was a little hurt, although the teachings of Buimech had always taught that pride blinded truth; that there was but a step between pride and disgrace for pride destroyed all symmetry and grace. Pride should not enter the soul of a true warrior.

She sighed and turned through the narrow alleyways of the port, now abruptly emptied of people who had hurried back to their homes with the gathering dusk. She sought to get away from the quayside, back to the main square from which she could find the main road back to the Hostel of the Stars. She found herself in a dark alley which turned at an awkward angle and seemed to led nowhere in particular. Annoyed at taking a wrong turn, she made to retrace her steps and found her way barred by two dark shadows.

She halted, her hand slipping automatically to her sword hilt.

Before she could move, her arms were pinioned at her sides in a hard grasp by someone who had slipped up unseen behind her.

One of the figures chuckled softly.

The sound was familiar. It belonged to a wheezy and ugly voice

'Éccneid,' whispered Scáthach.

The burlier shadow of the two moved forward a step or so. Even in the gloom she could see that his sword arm hung uselessly at his side.

'I am glad you recognise me, Scáthach of Uibh Rathach. You will now know why you must die.'

There was a coldness in his voice which sent a shiver down the girl's back.

She twisted and tried to pull loose from the grip which held her arms tightly to her sides. Almost at once she realised that the powerful grasp of the man behind her could not be broken by her lithe form twisting and struggling.

'I will have vengeance for what you did to me, you whelp of a wolf-bitch!'

58

Scáthach saw the man raise his left arm to its full height and glimpsed the dark object held there. She braced herself for the swift descent of the dagger.

Five

'What manner of knavery is this?' demanded a firm masculine voice.

Out of the shadows of the alley there emerged a tall figure.

Éccneid swung round in surprise.

Scáthach felt the surprise also in the man who had held her in a vice-like grip. For a split second she felt his grip relax and she twisted and lunged, succeeding in wrenching herself free.

'Help me!' she called. 'These thieves mean to kill me!'

There was a gasp of astonishment from the newcomer and abruptly a glint of something shiny in his hand.

'Kill the interloper!' yelled Éccneid, his voice contorted in fury. 'But leave the girl to me!'

One of his companions sprang forward, only to give a shrill shriek of agony and collapse to the ground.

The burly figure of Éccneid paused.

Scáthach, finding herself free, swung round on the attacker behind her, and drawing her sword, thrust at him. She aimed for his shoulder and felt the blade make contact. A second yell of anguish in as many seconds split the quiet of the alley. Then the burly figure of Éccneid, the thief, was lumbering out of the alley leaving his companions to fend for themselves. A moment later, the man whom Scáthach had struck also fled from the alley.

The tall figure of her rescuer moved closer in the shadows.

'Are you hurt?' the voice demanded.

Scáthach could not distinguish the man's features but the voice was soft and pleasant enough.

'I think so. Did you kill one of them?' she asked, indicating the body which lay on the ground.

She saw the man's head shake in the darkness.

'No. There was no need. I merely pricked the man's arm at which he seemed to be disagreeably surprised. He seems to have fainted. Who are they?'

'Thieves,' replied the girl. 'I encountered them yesterday and wounded one. They came to take vengeance on me.'

'You wounded one?' the man's voice was surprised.

Scáthach bit her lip in annoyance. Why should the man be astonished? Did he not think a woman capable of performing such a feat?

There was a groan as the remaining thief stirred.

The tall man went to stand over him, sword at the man's throat.

'We can turn this jackal over to the watch,' he said. 'Rise, creature.'

'Mercy,' groaned the other. 'I beg you, mercy.'

The thief slowly rose to his feet.

'Precede us from the alley,' commanded the man.

He was obeyed with reluctance.

They moved back onto the quay of the old port where burning brand torches now lighted the area which also showed the lights of several taverns.

'Let's find the watch,' the tall man said.

Scáthach frowned thoughtfully. Then she placed a hand on his arm.

'If we do, it would mean that we would have to attend the hearing before the Brehon and give evidence.

That might take a week or more. I cannot delay my journey long.'

The man bit his lip.

'And I, I too sail on the morning tide. There is but one choice.'

He turned to the cowering wounded thief and prodded him with the point of his blade.

The man growled.

'This is your lucky day, my friend. You may go and rejoin your misbegotten companions. But tell them this ... if I see you again in this region, if you attempt to waylay this girl again, then I shall not be lenient, nor will it be a Brehon who will judge. I shall be the one who will despatch you to your rebirth in the Otherworld.'

He prodded the man again and the thief closed his eyes and groaned as he felt the sharp point of the blade pricking his flesh.

'Go!' snapped the tall man.

The thief turned and shambled off into the darkness, clutching his arm.

The tall man turned, sheathing his sword, and looked down at the girl.

'A bad experience,' he said.

Scáthach disliked the superiority in his voice as if he were talking to a child.

'Not as bad as some I have had,' she replied as if bored by the matter.

'Well, let me take you into a tavern and buy you a cup of mead.'

She was about to refuse when she remembered the man had said he was sailing that morning. Was he captain of some ship? Perhaps she might persuade him to take her; even if she could get to Gallia it would be better than being stuck in Éireann.

'Very well,' she said.

He turned and led the way to a nearby tavern. It was

one of the less crowded, and so less noisy, of the quayside taverns. It was a well-lit place with a friendly fire and a smiling hosteler to greet them. The tall man ordered some mead and turned to bid his guest be seated. He paused in some surprise as his gaze took in the slight form of the girl, her curious, engaging beauty, but, more astonishing, her business-like weaponry and shield, which she carried with the air of one accustomed to them.

On her part, Scáthach was also able to see her rescuer for the first time. He could not have been more than a few years older than she; he had finely chiselled features, with a high forehead, a shock of fair hair and light grey eyes that seemed to twinkle with permanent amusement. She found his features attractive and comforting. He wore a hero's torc around his neck, and carried the weapons of a warrior. She glanced at the quality of his accoutrements and realised that here was a scion of a house of substance.

The tall youth, for he was scarcely more, gave a curious half bow.

'I am Flann Mac Fraech. May I be permitted to know your name?'

She answered his smile and said: 'I am Scáthach of Uibh Rathach.'

A puzzled frown crossed his features.

' . . . *of* Uibh Rathach?' he repeated, with emphasis. To use such a title meant one was chieftain of the *dún*. 'I know only of Eola of Uibh Rathach, who is renowned throughout all Éireann.'

The girl nodded slowly.

'I am Scáthach, daughter of Eola, may he be reborn well in the Otherworld.'

The warrior bit his lip.

'Sad it is to hear of the death of so great a champion. Did age overtake him?'

The hosteler came forward with their mead and after he had left Scáthach shrugged.

62

'He was treacherously slain by vermin who gained entrance to his *dún* under the laws of hospitality and who then profaned those laws. Now Buimech, my mother, makes ritual atonement.'

Flann Mac Fraech pursed his lips uncomfortably. He knew what that meant. A ritual fast to the death in protest at the injustice.

'And what do you seek here in Dún na Séad?' he pressed.

'I seek those who killed my father. I seek to follow them to Gallia, where I believe they came from.'

The young warrior raised his brows.

'Gallia?'

Scáthach nodded.

'Alas, I was hoping that you were a captain of a vessel, since you said you were sailing on the morning tide. I am searching for a passage to Gallia.'

Flann shrugged.

'Alas, I am no seaman but a warrior although my journey takes me to Gallia on the morrow. I must shake the dust of Éireann from my shoes.'

'You say that with regret,' observed the girl.

'Indeed. I am now merely a soldier of fortune, a warrior who can only hire his services to others and who can no longer fight for his own kin.'

'Why is that?'

'I am Flann Mac Fraech,' he repeated with a sad note of resignation in his voice. 'My people are . . . were . . . the Cruithne. Our clan were ruled by a petty tyrant Aintiarna who laid heavy taxes upon us and levied the clansmen to make war upon our neighbours with whom we had long lived in amity. I tried to lead our people in an attempt to overthrow Aintiarna. I failed. Aintiarna would have had me slain had it not been for the intervention of our druids who forbade it. Instead I was outcast and must never return while Aintiarna lives.'

There was a silence between them.

'A sad tale,' observed Scáthach after a while.

'And one with which I shall have to live,' replied the young man, the corners of his mouth turning down. 'But tell me more of your tale and why you think the assassins of your father are from Gallia?'

Scáthach hesitated. She found herself curiously drawn to the young warrior, as if there were a warmth of friendship between them, and that coupled with the need she felt to confide her problems to someone of her own age made her respond to his sympathetic inquiry. Soon she was telling the story in the fullness of its detail, from the mysteries of her birth to the riddle of the triskele motif which was leading her to Lethra.

It was a long time before she sat back and paused.

Flann sat silently for a while, as if deep in thought.

Eventually he raised his eyes and gazed at Scáthach. They were shining with an eagerness.

'I have passage on a ship sailing to Gallia on the morning tide. Let me intercede with the captain to take you also to my port of disembarkation. From there, if you will have me as your companion, we will both proceed to Lethra.'

The girl stared curiously at the young warrior.

'Why would you wish to go to Lethra?'

Flann raised his voice and laughed.

'And why not? I have told you my circumstances. I am but a soldier of fortune. The world is mine to wander where I choose. Lethra has an air of mystery to it. Maybe I will find adventure there which is denied me elsewhere. Maybe I will come with you because Eola of Uibh Rathach was a great champion of Éireann and his blood cries out for justice. Maybe.'

'Do you know what port in Gallia your ship is headed.'

Flann shook his head.

'Once in Gallia we will seek out this kingdom of Lethra wherever it is,' he said with assurance.

Scáthach hesitated for a moment and then she smiled. She liked the impetuous and pleasant young warrior and it was a truism that two were better than one when faced with the hazards of the unknown.

'Very well, Flann Mac Fraech. If you can persuade the captain of your vessel to take me, we will make the journey to Lethra together.'

The young warrior slapped his knee and grinned with enthusiasm.

'Already there is adventure awaiting us. What more can we ask for? Come, let us seek out the captain of the vessel.'

Goll was a swarthy-complexioned man with a shock of black hair that almost hid his face. He wore an eye-patch over his left eye which, presumably, he had lost. Scáthach's first reaction to his sharp, almost ugly features, his cunning appraisal, his sneering, thin mouth, was of dislike. Then she remembered Buimech's teaching that the succulence of a nut is not judged by the attractiveness of its shell, therefore a person cannot be judged by their outward appearance. Nevertheless, she felt that she would not be able to bring herself to like the ill-favoured sea-captain.

Flann had tracked the man down in one of the other quayside taverns. He was drinking with another, who was, so Scáthach later learnt, the mate on the ship. He was a fleshy faced, moon-featured individual with a tendency to smile too readily, showing ill-kept teeth.

'Lethra?'

Goll stared at them, his one eye winking in amazement in the flickering lights of the tavern.

Flann nodded.

'Surely it is not far from the port in Gallia to which we sail?'

'Far enough. I will not risk my ship to sail to Lethra. Sooner I would sail my ship in the waters of the Fomorii, the Evil Ones who dwell beneath the waves in the northern seas.'

Flann heaved a sigh and glanced at the girl.

'Then will you give passage to Gallia for Scáthach? Then we can proceed to Lethra by land ourselves.'

Goll grinned speculatively.

'Surely. There is always room for passengers . . . for a price.'

Scáthach drew herself up and gazed steadily at the man.

'How much is your price for a passage to Gallia?' she demanded.

Goll pursed his lips thoughtfully.

'Nine gold pieces,' he said after a moment.

Flann gasped.

'But that is twice the sum you asked for me.'

Goll smiled and scratched his nose.

'It is simply a matter of supply and demand,' he replied. 'The girl wants to go to Gallia. If she wants to go that badly, she will pay the price.'

'But . . .' began Flann. However, Scáthach reached forward and silenced him with a pressure of her hand on his arm,

'You are discerning, Goll. I will pay you your price.'

Goll chuckled and reached out a gnarled hand.

Scáthach continued to smile into his ugly features.

'I will pay one third now, one third when we are at sea and the remainder when we make landfall in Gallia. Those are my terms.'

Goll's humorous expression vanished. He stared hard at the girl seeing the determination in the line of her jaw and the steely quality of her eyes. He read resolution and strength in her expression and knew there would be no bargaining. Goll was a pragmatist.

'Very well,' he said sullenly. 'It is agreed. A third now.'

She handed him the three gold pieces.

'We sail on the morning tide,' said Goll. 'Our ship is the *Nemhain*. If you are not on board, we shall not wait.'

'I'll be on board.'

She turned and left the tavern followed by Flann. Outside she said:

'Your captain does not inspire confidence in his integrity.'

Flann shrugged in the darkness.

'It is hard to be fastidious when you are in need. I ask no more of Goll than that he put me on the shore of Gallia in safety.'

The girl had to admit that the young warrior was right.

'The morning tide is eight hours away,' she observed. 'I will eat and get some sleep before we sail. There is a hostel just above the port called the Hostel of the Stars. I shall stay there.'

Flann was hesitant.

'Are you not worried in case Éccneid is still lurking in the vicinity?'

She shook her head.

'I'll meet you on the quay at dawn.'

'I'll be there,' Flann confirmed.

With a light step she turned into the darkness and, for the second time that evening, began to retrace her steps through the gloom through Dún na Séad towards the Hostel of Stars.

It did not take her long to return to the hostel. Brosc seemed pleased to see her.

'What luck, daughter of Eola?' he said as he showed her to a table before the fire.

There were only a few other people in the hostel.

'I have a passage to Gallia,' smiled Scáthach. 'I sail with

67

the morning tide so I need to be awakened in the hour before dawn.'

'That I shall do. What ship do you sail in?'

'The *Nemhain*.'

The hosteler's eyes widened.

'Not Goll's ship?' he asked sharply.

'You know Goll?'

'I know nothing good of the man,' replied Brosc. 'Among the sea ports there is much gossip. It is said that Goll has been known not to forsake piracy in pursuit of money. I would have a care of him and his crew. He and Éccneid were spawned from the same egg.'

'The daughter of Eola can look after herself,' Scáthach replied. 'But do you mean that Goll and Éccneid are brothers?'

Brosc shook his head.

'I only meant they were brothers in spirit and not in flesh. Evil, the both of them.'

'I can take care of myself,' repeated the girl.

'I have no doubt. But Goll is not an honourable man. Remember that.'

'Don't worry. I will remember. Now let me have food and rest, Brosc, for I must make an early start in the morning.'

'Have no fear. I shall awake you in time for the tide.'

Brosc was as good as his word, for it was still dark when he shook the girl awake. While she performed her toilet he prepared breakfast and within half an hour bade the man farewell and started down the darkened path towards the still sleeping seaport.

There was a faint light in the eastern sky when she reached the quay. There were several people about for it seemed several of the ships were preparing to leave with the morning tide. However, the first person she saw was the figure of Flann Mac Fraech. He came to her, his face wreathed in smiles.

'Have you rested well?' he asked.

'Yes. And you?'

'I was worried in case Éccneid was still bent on revenge. It is good to see you safe.'

She shrugged.

'I doubt whether he is within a mile of Dún na Séad. He has twice learnt a lesson from my sword.'

A short, stocky seaman approached them.

'Are you for the *Nemhain*?'

'We are,' confirmed Flann.

'Pick up your dunnage and follow me.'

They presumed that 'dunnage' referred to their belongings and they turned to follow the little man to the steps of the quayside. He went down with dexterity into a small skiff which was tied below and stood, balanced comfortably in the rocking craft, waiting for them to join him. Flann helped Scáthach into the craft and when she was seated safely in the stern, he followed her. The seaman took the oars and propelled the skiff forward into the curious half-light of dawn towards a sleek black vessel, swinging round her stern until he came alongside to where a rope-ladder was slung.

Again, Flann helped the girl from the skiff, although she swung up the ladder agilely enough. Flann followed and they found themselves on the deck of the *Nemhain* where Goll was standing, feet apart, hands on hips. He leered towards the girl.

'A third when you are aboard,' he said shortly by way of greeting.

Scáthach shook her head with a thin smile.

'The bargain was one third when we are at sea,' she corrected. Being a few yards off-shore is scarcely being at sea.'

Goll drew his brows together in anger, hesitated and then shrugged.

'Very well. We set sail now to catch the tide. Do not get in the way of my seamen.'

He turned brusquely and stalked off towards the stern.

Flann gave a wry grimace in Scáthach's direction.

'Come on, let's find a place on the lee of the ship, out of the way.'

'The lee?'

Flann grinned.

'Easy to see that you haven't been to sea before.'

The girl shook her head.

'I only sailed to the small islands off the coast of Éireann but I have never sailed on big ocean vessels such as the *Nemhain* before.'

Flann guided her across the deck to the farther side of the ship out of the blustery breeze which was now blowing from the shore.

'The lee of a vessel is its sheltered side, the quarter towards which the wind blows,' he explained.

Men were scurrying about the ship now, hauling on lines, scampering up the rigging. To Scáthach, all seemed confusion. Yet, she felt, there must be a method in it all, some purpose to the frenzied activity which her untrained eye could not discern.

The tip of the sun was now just above the eastern horizon, the gusting breeze began to crack at the canvas of the sails while a myriad wavelets hit and thumped at the wooden planks of the vessel. Around the ship there wheeled large gulls with their plaintive cries.

Goll, from the stern deck, was bellowing orders. There was a scampering of bare feet on the sanded boards of the vessel as half a dozen men bounded into the bows and began to throw their weight against a wheel-like object, grunting in the exertion of moving it in an easy rhythm. Then one set up a cry, echoed in chorus by the others; it was a strange weird chant which seemed to give impetus to the motion of the men against the wheel.

Flann leant forward towards the girl.

'That's called the capstan. They are winding in the anchor. Then we'll be off.'

The ship was shuddering now, the wind filling her sails. She seemed to shake with eagerness, like a terrier just about to be unleashed in search of game.

Then the anchor was up and the vessel dipped and began to glide towards the open sea.

Scáthach caught the tang of salt as the sea breeze struck her face. It was a pleasant aroma and the motion of the vessel as it dipped and rose before the winds was exhilarating.

'Well,' smiled Flann, 'the journey has begun.'

Scáthach breathed deeply of the pungent odours of the sea.

'Now I know why it is some men and women make their lives upon the seas,' she smiled.

Flann chuckled.

'You won't say that when we are hit by a squall or a storm.'

She turned to gaze at his humorous face.

'You have been to sea lots of times before, then?'

He shook his head.

'No. But I have been across the sea to the land of Alba for many of my tribe have settled there. I have sailed the stormy straits from Ulaidh to the shores of Airer Ghàidheal. That is enough experience of the sea for me. Each time I crossed we encountered huge squalls and storms and each time I vowed never to set foot on shipboard again. So much for one's intentions and vows.'

Scáthach pursed her lips.

'Why is it that you decided to cross the sea to Gallia when, as you say, most travellers from the north simply cross the strait to Alba?'

Flann chuckled.

'You have answered your own question. I did not want to follow where others go. Besides,' and here his young face took on a serious expression, 'I wanted to put a good distance between myself and Aintiarna, the chieftain of the Cruithne. For good reason, too: I fear that Aintiarna would send assassins to destroy me.'

'But that would be against the law,' breathed the girl.

Flann's lips turned down in a cynical expression.

'Ah, daughter of Eola, you should know that humankind are not a perfect species. They make fine laws and set high moral standards but constantly fail to live up to them. The law says that the people elect chieftains to carry out their wishes. Remember the saying? – Why is a people stronger than a king? Because it is the people who ordain the king, the king does not ordain the people.'

The girl made a slight gesture of impatience.

'I know the law.'

'Alas, kings and chieftains sometimes forget the law. They hold themselves above the law instead of being subservient to it. Do not think that all chieftains are wise and honourable. Aintiarna is one such who murdered to ensure his succession and repressed to ensure he stayed in office. Sadly my people put their faith in me to overthrow the petty tyranny of Aintiarna. I failed them and Aintiarna wanted me slain. His Brehons forbade it, for such is the law, and told him that he could only banish me. That he did. But he would rather have me slain in case I became a threat to him again.'

Scáthach did not say anything and after a while Flann went on.

'Maybe one of these fine days I shall return to the land of the Cruithne. In the meantime, I have to survive. That was why I put it about that I was sailing for Alba when, in reality, I took a horse and rode southwards . . . and took a ship for Gallia. I am ready for what adventures come.'

72

'How long will it take us to reach Gallia?' asked the girl after a while as they leant side by side against the rail of the ship, watching the bobbing horizon as the sun rose majestically and blood red over its rim.

'Depends on the weather,' replied Flann. 'I have no knowledge of the ocean here but the sailors were saying that we could make landfall at our port of destination in two and a half days.'

'That's a long time to be journeying on the sea.'

She peered around the ship.

'Do we get offered cabins?'

'Cabins can be dark and smelly places. The air is stuffy and makes one prone to sickness. The deck is a much more comfortable place to sleep during the night.'

Flann came to a halt and a red flush tinged his face.

'Of course,' he muttered, abruptly realising that there were times when a woman needed privacy in the company of men. He cursed himself for a fool. 'I will go to see Goll or his mate.'

Scáthach smiled her gratitude as she stretched at the railing.

She felt a confidence now. Lethra held the answer to the mystery of her birth and Eola's murder. Of that she was sure. And now her journey to Lethra had begun. Unconsciously she fingered the gold medallion at her neck. She had no need to examine its triskele symbol for that was burnt sharply into her memory. She watched Flann Mac Fraech moving across the deck, walking uneasily as he tried to find his sea-legs. She felt pleased that he had joined her quest. She did not feel so alone in the world. There was something warm and comforting about the young warrior with his honesty and strength. *And* his handsomeness; she found herself smiling gently at the thought.

Then she drew her brows together in annoyance. That was a conceited thing to think. Had Eola and Buimech

73

fostered and trained her to be a simpering maid who smiled with downcast eyes at the first man who came along? She had been trained for a purpose. She had not been made privy to the secrets of Buimech nor the artistry of warrior craft in order to waste it. Eola had scarcely begun his journey to the Otherworld and Buimech was even now making her ritual fast to seek atonement for his unlawful slaughter and here she was simpering after a young warrior. She felt a shame as she thought about it. She reminded herself that she had a task to fulfil. She was in control, in command of this quest – indeed, it was her quest. If Flann Mac Fraech wished to accompany her on that journey then she would welcome him. But she was in charge. She must not resign any decision making to him, nor seek comfort from him simply because he was a male. After all, she was Scáthach, daughter of Eola of Uibh Rathach, and she was entitled to wear the golden hero's torc.

She felt annoyance at the litany of self-justification which drifted through her thoughts. Buimech's gentle voice echoed in her mind. 'Come child, those who seek nothing but faults will see nothing else. It is easier to confess one's faults than to search for the qualities in one's nature.' Maybe Buimech was right. Maybe she was being too hard on herself. She sighed and gave herself to the spectacular scene that was opening before her, with the sun now standing above the horizon lighting the sea's long expanse in a breathtaking blue, causing a myriad lights to sparkle and dance across its surface. The canvas was tight-stretched above her as the winds whispered and chattered through the rigging. High above the gulls still circled the vessel giving vent to their lonely wild cries.

Six

The weather continued fine with blue, cloudless skies and a firm breeze from the north-west which caused the *Nemhain* to glide gently through calm waters. It was a pleasant enough voyage, thought Scáthach, as she rested in the bow of the ship, gazing southward for any sign of approaching land. It was now just after noon on the second day of the journey. She had no complaints at the way the villainous looking Goll and his men treated her. She had been given a cabin for her privacy and Flann had been attentive enough . . . in fact, too attentive if anything.

She pursed her lips. She did like the eager young warrior and, if she admitted it, she felt comfort in his companionship. A long voyage into the unknown when one was alone was a depressing experience and she was grateful he had joined her on her quest. Yet she did not want to place too much reliance on his companionship. She had to be her own person. What was it that Buimech used to say? A tub must stand on its own bottom. Indeed. She must first rely on herself as Buimech had taught. 'A wise woman will never lose anything if she possesses herself.'

She frowned in annoyance, realising that it was not the first time that her thoughts had run on such matters. In fact, several times she found herself secretly admitting her like of Flann and then trying to seek refuge in self-justification.

She turned at the sound of a footfall behind her and found Flann standing there. She was about to make a pleasant greeting but hesitated when she saw his face was white and etched with worry.

'What is the matter?' she demanded.

He glanced around conspiratorially.

'Scáthach,' he had lowered his voice to a whisper, 'go to your cabin and collect your weapons. Do so casually, so as not to arouse curiosity. When you have done so, join me on the stern deck.

She stared at him in astonishment.

'Why?' she demanded.

'Why, because I have overheard a conversation between Goll and his mate which was not intended for my ears.'

Scáthach suppressed a sigh of impatience.

'Tell me,' she demanded.

Flann came to lean on the railing, keeping his gaze out to sea. The girl also leant against the rail next to him.

'Well?' she prompted.

'I was lying on some rope at the stern of the ship, behind some boxes. I'd gone there to nap in the midday sun. I became aware of Goll and his mate standing not far away. They did not see me. They began to speak about how they would rob us and then throw us overboard before we reached Gallia tomorrow.'

Scáthach felt a chill course through her body.

'They said this? You heard them correctly?'

Flann nodded.

'But why? I don't carry sufficient gold to make it worth their while.'

'Nor I,' agreed Flann. 'But I am afraid that our unlamented mutual friend Éccneid has a hand in this affair.'

Scáthach breathed hard.

'Éccneid? How does he enter this matter?'

'Éccneid must have followed us, saw us bargaining with

Goll for a passage. He approached Goll later and made his own bargain. Goll will pick up a nice sum from Éccneid if you and I do not set foot in Gallia. Whatever Goll can pick up from us before we are tossed into the sea is merely a bonus.'

'And how does Éccneid know that Goll will keep his bargain? He could just as easily take Eccneid's gold and let us go as take the gold and kill us.'

'Apparently Éccneid is not that trusting. He is hiding below decks for he wants to witness your death for he believes in the sweetness of revenge.'

Scáthach let out a long incredulous sigh.

'And this will happen before we sight Gallia tomorrow morning?'

Flann nodded.

'What do you propose we do?'

'Arm ourselves and be prepared to sell our lives dearly. We cannot swim to Gallia from here, so we must hold off Goll and his crew until we come close inshore. That is why I suggest you get your arms and join me at the stern deck at the tiller. That position will give us control of the ship.'

The girl was silent.

'And you say that Éccneid is aboard? That he is hidden below?'

Flann made an affirmative gesture.

'Do you know where?'

'I would imagine he hides in Goll's cabin at the stern. But where he is does not really matter so long as we are ready for him and his cut-throats.'

Scáthach stretched up, reaching a decision.

'I will join you on the stern deck as soon as possible,' she said. 'Be ready.'

Flann cast a worried look in her direction.

'Be sure to attract no suspicion that we know their plan,' he said quietly.

The girl turned casually from the rail and began to

thread her way across the deck to the entrance to the bow cabins where she had been allotted an accommodation. She entered her cabin without challenge. Now her pulse began to quicken. She seized and buckled on her weapons and turned out of the cabin again. However, she did not return immediately to the deck but moved down a narrow, dark and stinking passageway which ran throughout the length of the ship to the stern cabins. The passageway passed between the crew's quarters and the storage areas before entering the area in which Goll and his mate had their cabins.

Moving stealthily, Scáthach hauled herself along in the swaying semi-darkness, trying to ignore the nauseous stench. Thankfully she encountered no one as she traversed the length of the ship.

She knew her purpose and her mind had no qualms as she determined its execution.

She entered the main stern cabin complex and found there were two side cabins and one main cabin, the main cabin being clearly Goll's personal domain. She hesitated before the door and then drew her sword. She swung into the cabin and halted, her eyes searching it in the gloomy light. It was empty.

She paused, intently examining the cabin. It was small and crowded with bric-a-brac. In fact, every part of Goll's cabin was littered with booty of some kind or another, every corner except one where part of the wooden panelling of the cabin stood free from any obstruction. Scáthach gazed at it a moment. Then she moved quietly aside from the door and closed it shut behind her with a sharp click. She had only to wait for a moment before the panel began to swing slowly aside. Someone stirred in the dark recess beyond.

Like a stealthy cat, the girl was across the cabin with her sword raised.

Éccneid stared at her in the gloom. There was fear written on his features.

'You were warned twice, Éccneid,' the girl said softly. 'Twice you went unpunished. Now your crime cannot be ignored. You have murder in your heart.'

Éccneid made to draw his sword, fumbling in the narrow confines of his hiding place. His mouth opened to cry for assistance.

Scáthach drove her blade straight through his heart.

The man's eyes widened and stared, as if in disbelief, as the life sped from him.

As the girl drew out her blade, the man slumped to the floor, spilling into the cabin.

Her face showing no emotion, Scáthach bent forward and wiped the blade of her sword on the man's clothes. Then she sheathed the weapon, bent forward and heaved the carcass back into the secret recess and pushed the door shut. Goll would be in for a surprise when he opened that door, she thought grimly.

Then she left the cabin as silently as she came, making her way back through the passageway to the bow cabins and thence on deck. She stared about her. The sailors were continuing to carry on with their tasks. It seemed all was normal. She could see Goll in the well of the ship supervising some task and her eyes sought out the mate. He did not appear on the decks. She strolled easily along the deck, keeping to the far side, away from Goll and hoping that he was so distracted by his task that he would not see that she had her weapons with her and leap to conclusions.

Flann was already standing near the sailor who manned the tiller. She swung up the steps which ascended to the stern deck, about six feet above the main deck. Only Flann and the tiller man were on this deck. Scáthach smiled grimly towards Flann and went straight to the tiller man.

'Do you value your life, sailor?' she demanded without preamble.

The man looked startled.

The girl smiled tightly into his weather-beaten face. Sometimes her smile could convey more menace than the smile from features more uglier than her usually attractive face.

'If you wish to live, you will stay by that tiller and keep this ship on course no matter what may befall. Do you understand?'

Her voice was soft and easy, as if she were discussing the weather prospects.

The man swallowed hard and nodded, not daring to speak lest his voice betrayed his fear.

'If you do not keep your hands on the tiller and steer towards the coast of Gallia then you will die. And your death will be without worth.'

The sailor tried to find his voice.

'I swear by the gods that I . . .' he began.

But Scáthach had turned away.

Flann moved across to her with a worried expression.

'Is it wise to precipitate their attack now?' he asked.

She shrugged.

'They will soon find Éccneid and when they do . . .' She made a dismissive gesture.

He stared at her in astonishment.

'Éccneid?'

For a moment or two he gazed on her calm features reading the meaning in her steady eyes. Here was no faint hearted girl but a decisive warrior who had taken the war to the heart of the enemy. For the first time since he had heard of Goll's plot Flann began to wonder whether the two of them might be able to hold off an attack from Goll's seamen.

The girl was already busy examining the defensive qualities of their position.

'You take a stand at the starboard side,' she instructed,

observing that entrance to the stern deck was gained by two companionways, one on either side of the ship. 'I'll take the other side.'

'Agreed,' called Flann cheerfully, moving to the position and making himself ready.

Scáthach had suddenly noticed the ship's mate scuttling down the main deck towards his captain. He bent over Goll and whispered in his ear. Goll straightened up with abruptness and stared around. After a few moments his dark eyes caught sight of the girl and he glared balefully in her direction. Then she saw he had spotted Flann. A look of understanding crossed his features as he saw their weapons ready.

He shouted orders; Scáthach could not hear what they were from the distance she stood, but the crew hurried in several directions almost immediately appearing with various villainous-looking weapons.

Scáthach cast a glance over her shoulder towards the plainly nervous tiller man.

'Remember what I said. Leave your tiller and you are a dead man.'

'I swear by the gods,' the man began to wail again, but the girl turned back. One man was already running for the companionway at whose top she stood. Without challenging the man, she released the arrow she had strung in her bow and he went crashing back on the deck, the feathered shaft sticking out of his chest.

There was a stillness on board.

Goll gazed at the dead sailor in disbelief.

The lines had been drawn. Goll abruptly realised that he was not facing some simpering woman but a determined foe. A warrior who was stubborn and as resolute as he was. Nevertheless, he made an effort to persuade her to surrender.

'You are outnumbered, woman!' He called. 'Put up your weapons. Your resistance is useless.'

81

'You forget that I control this ship, Goll,' replied Scáthach, waving one arm towards the tiller. 'Perhaps it is your men who should put up their weapons?'

Goll was stung to anger by what he saw as the insolence of the girl's reply. He turned to his mate.

'Take some of the men and storm the companionway. I'll take the rest and keep that young whelp busy.' He gestured to where Flann stood ready with his sword.

The mate hesitated. After all, Goll was sending him against someone armed with a bow.

'What are you waiting for?' Goll snapped.

The mate sighed and gestured to a few of the men.

'Follow me,' he said, moving cautiously forward.

The next moment he was on the ground clutching at the shaft which had embedded itself in his shoulder and cursing the gods. His men hesitated and then another arrow sped from the girl's bow and embedded itself into the thigh of another of the sailors.

'Haul back!' yelled Goll furiously, easing himself behind the mainmast for cover.

He looked about for some means of retrieving the situation. He was being made to look incompetent by a mere girl in front of his crew.

'With me!' he growled to his men and broke into a shambling run towards the companionway which Flann held. Goll, while leading the charge, did not attempt to clamber up the steps first but stood aside to allow the men following him to do so.

Flann stood carefully poised, sword point flickering as the first man tried to scramble upwards. He lunged quickly and, with a cry, the man toppled backwards into his companions behind him, blood oozing from his shoulder.

'Up! Up!' Goll cried.

His men went up unwillingly only to fall back before the young warrior's expertly handled weapons.

82

Eventually the captain of the *Nemhain* drew his men back to the well of the ship.

From her position, Scáthach grinned at Flann.

'That's taught these dogs a lesson,' she said triumphantly.

Flann gave an answering smile, but shrugged.

'They'll be back.'

The girl glanced at the white-faced tiller man who had stood watching the fight, clutching at his tiller in obedience to the girl's instructions.

'I hope there is no need to remind you of your course?' she said.

The man swallowed and licked his dry lips nervously.

'By the gods, lady . . .'

She gestured him to silence.

'How far are we from the coast of Gallia?'

'With these winds, lady, we will sight the coastline at dawn tomorrow. We shall make landfall about midday.'

Scáthach bit her lip thoughtfully.

'What are you thinking?' asked Flann.

'I am trying to place myself in the mind of Goll in order to see how he would overcome us.'

Flann compressed his lips a moment and glanced at the sky.

'He has time enough. I would be inclined to wait until nightfall.'

The girl frowned.

'You are right. When darkness falls, then he will make his attack for he knows that I will not be able to use my bow. If I were him, I would launch another attack directly on our front and while we are thus engaged, he could send men around to take us in the rear.'

'How so?' demanded Flann. 'The only way onto the stern deck is up these stairways we defend.'

'Under cover of darkness a good seaman could surely

climb along the outside of the ship and come up over the stern-rail,' replied Scáthach.

Flann moved to the side of the ship and glanced over. The girl was right. An agile man could easily swing along the side of the ship while their attention was diverted and come over the stern rail. He turned back to the girl.

'What can we do?' he asked.

Scáthach turned to the steersman.

'Do we touch no other land before tomorrow?'

The man shook his head.

'No small islands?'

'None on this course, lady,' he said.

She turned with interest.

'None on this course,' she repeated with emphasis, 'but some that are near?'

The steersman hesitated and then shrugged. He had already committed himself.

'South, south-west lies an island but no one lives on it nor does anyone make landfall there. It is a desolate place where they say the Fomorii, the gods of the abyss, dwell. The place is dangerous for it is surrounded by great jagged rocks.'

'And when could we make landfall there?'

The steersman looked startled.

'Speak!' snapped the girl irritably.

'Why, I suppose we could reach there by dusk this evening but it is dangerous what with the rocks. We could not get close to the island before dawn.'

Scáthach chuckled.

'It sounds just the place.'

Flann was puzzled.

'Look,' Scáthach moved across to him, for Goll and his men still remained down in the well of the ship, and there seemed no danger of an imminent attack. 'It is useless heading for Gallia. We will never get there with what remains of today and then a full night and half a day between us and landfall. If we bring the ship close to the islands, Goll may be worried less about overcoming us than ensuring that the *Nemhain* doesn't splinter itself to pieces on the rocks.'

'But how does that help to extricate us? If the island is deserted and inhospitable . . .?'

Scáthach shrugged.

'One problem at a time. I believe in providence.'

Flann pulled a face.

'And I in our own ingenuity,' he countered.

The girl grinned.

'I will not argue, Flann. But changing course towards the island holds out more hope than keeping on to Gallia. When darkness comes we have little chance of maintaining our defences.'

Flann heaved a sigh.

'Very well. I suppose it might present a diversion for Goll and his men,' he said grudgingly.

Scáthach turned to the steersman.

'Change your course for the island.'

'But . . .'

The steersman looked decidedly unhappy.

Scáthach went to his side and laid her hand at the sword in her belt.

'I hope you will not object too strongly,' she said softly.

The steersman swallowed and nodded.

'South, south-west it is, lady,' he muttered and swung at the wheel.

Apparently, in the well of the ship, Goll and the rest of his crew had not noticed the change of course. And, as time passed, it became obvious that Scáthach had been correct. Goll was obviously waiting for nightfall before he recommenced his attempt to overpower them.

Indeed, the sun was low on the horizon and dusk was

creeping up from the east when the steersman, now tired and haggard looking, sung out.

'The rocks are away to our starboard bow, lady.'

Scáthach moved forward, eyes screwed up to focus.

'The island is just behind that barrier.'

Flann from his position braced himself.

'What now?'

He had an answer for Goll had suddenly realised the change of course by noticing the position of the setting sun and hearing the harsh slap of waves from the rocks that protruded from the sea away to the east.

He gave a roar of anger and began to coax his men closer to the stern deck again.

Scáthach immediately strung her bow and sent out a warning arrow which caused the sailors to halt again by the mainmast, using it as a shield.

'What now?' repeated Flann, preparing himself for the inevitable change.

'Trust to providence until we can give providence a hand,' replied the girl.

The light was fading rapidly now as the sun slid below the horizon. It was then that Goll decided to launch his attack. Scáthach managed to use her bow twice more in the shadows before having to discard it and resort to her sword. There were now half a dozen unwounded crewmen who were goaded on by Goll to attack the stairways to the stern deck. As she had anticipated, Scáthach saw one man slip over the rail of the ship, trying not to be noticed. However, her attention was fully occupied by the group at the foot of the companionway trying to push their way up towards her.

Another man was making his way along the side of the ship and Flann was now hard pressed, falling back a few places from the top of the companionway and thus allowing a couple of men to ascend to the stern deck.

Goll, sensing victory close at hand, urged his remaining men forward and took the lead.

'Where is providence now?' cried Flann, irony in his voice rather than bitterness.

The girl was too busy to answer as she fended and parried her attackers.

The steersman still clung firmly to the tiller, his face white, watching the tumult of the struggle swaying this way and that.

A terrible crunching sound suddenly drowned out the noise of the struggle and the forward glide of the vessel halted so that everyone was thrown off balance. The deck of the ship heaved upwards almost at an angle of forty-five degrees. Then there was chaos, cries of alarm and anger.

Slipping across the deck, her sword knocked from her grasp, Scáthach struck a rail and halted. She paused trying to recover her breath.

The ship must have struck a rock.

She peered around for Flann. He was struggling down the deck, trying to disengage himself from a seaman, and making his way towards her.

There came a grinding of timbers and the ship lurched ominously. Some cried out with fear.

Flann reached her. He was grinning in spite of a cut on his face.

'Is this your providence?'

The girl pulled a face.

'We will have to see,' she replied, gasping a little as the vessel gave another lurch.

Flann peered around into the gloom.

'Can you swim?'

She nodded.

'Then I suggest we vacate this vessel. Her bottom is probably ripped open and she will slip off these rocks any moment.'

As if in agreement with him, the *Nemhain* gave

another shudder and her timbers cracked and splintered in protest.

'Which way is the island?' asked Flann, as they clutched the side rail of the dangerously pitching vessel.

'It must lie in that direction,' the girl replied, indicating the direction with a jerk of her head.

There was more splintering of wood followed by cries of fear from the crew, clinging precariously to the wreck.

Flann reached out to the girl and took her hand.

'Ready?'

She smiled quickly and nodded.

Together they scrambled over the rail of the ship and jumped off into the sea.

It was dark and the waves were choppy.

'We must try to keep together,' yelled Flann above the smack of the water on the nearby rocks.

He began to swim slowly, using easy strokes, and Scáthach fell into his rhythm. They swam for a while silently until they could no longer hear the sound of the sea breaking over the rocks nor the creak of the ship's timbers. It was black now for it was a cloudy night and there was no moon nor stars to guide them. They just swam on hoping that they were heading in the right direction.

Then a faint sea breeze began to create little foam caps on the waves, the breeze seemed to grow stronger and stronger until the waves grew in size and force. They began to be tossed hither and thither.

Flann struggled to keep close to the girl. Scáthach was weakening against the tumultuous waves. He tried to catch her but a wave, larger than the rest, suddenly swept her away and he was hard pressed to keep himself afloat.

Scáthach tried desperately to catch Flann's hand but the large wave pulled her away. Suddenly she realised, with a cold terror, that she was alone in the ocean with large crashing waves breaking around her.

'Oh god of the ocean!' she began to pray silently. 'Oh great Manánnan Mac Lir, help me. Help us. You who protected me while I was a babe, cast adrift on the ocean, and brought me safe to the arms of Eola and Buimech, help me now!'

There was no answer to her pleas and the sea, if anything, began to increase in ferocity. The waves and winds screamed in her ears. She was hard pressed to keep herself from going under. The water was pounding her relentlessly, its giant hands slapping at her until her senses began to grow numb. She began to think: 'So this is what drowning is like.' Then she was drifting, drifting into insensibility. A silent blackness shut out the icy waters and the pounding waves.

Seven

Scáthach came to with the sound of the sea in her ears. Yet it was not the fierce fury of the pounding waves which had carried her into unconsciousness but the gentle lapping of the tide on the shallow sandy seashore. She also became aware of the warmth of the sun on her face and a gentle breeze tugging at her hair. A further sound caught her attention. The snap and crackle of a fire and a sensation of heat on one side of her body. She lay a moment drinking in the realisation that she had not drowned. This much was clear. She blinked a moment and opened her eyes to gaze on a blue expanse of sky in which a few white clouds drifted. Then she made the mistake of trying to sit up and a groan escaped her lips as a wave of dizziness and nausea overcame her.

A shadow fell across her and she tried to focus her eyes on it.

An old man crouched beside her. He had an ancient, weather-beaten face, lined as the granite lines the western cliffs. Bright blue eyes twinkled at her. His tough brown skin was surrounded by a shock of white hair. His face bore a kindly, concerned expression. He wore a druid's tonsure on the crown of his head and his flowing saffron robe confirmed that he was of that priestly calling.

She tried to sit up again and once more the dizziness seized her.

'Careful, my child,' the old man intoned softly. A gentle hand on her shoulder pushed her back. 'Lie still a moment until you recover your senses.'

Scáthach's mouth was very dry and, as if he discerned her desire, the old man raised a golden bowl of clear water to her lips. He raised her head with one hand. She swallowed gratefully and eagerly but the old man did not allow her more than one swallow.

'It is not wise, my child.'

She stared up at him mutely. She trusted his benign expression, the gentle concern.

She tried to form words. They seemed an age in coming.

'Flann!' she managed to gasp, at last.

The old man smiled and nodded.

'Your young companion? He is safe. But he has grazed his head on a rock and has not recovered consciousness yet. But have no fear for him.'

Scáthach continued to stare up at the old man.

'Who . . . who are you?' she managed to get out.

'I? I am called Ruacán the Wizened.'

'And where am I?'

'You are getting better by the moment to ask such questions,' smiled the old man.

Scáthach pushed herself into a sitting position, fighting back the dizziness. Her warrior's training under Eola had made her tough and determined enough to withstand what would lay others low in sickness for days. She shook her head from side to side in an effort to shake the dizziness from it and looked about her.

She was on a sandy beach, on a rocky shore, not far from the mild blue waters of the sea. An open fire on which a medium-sized cauldron steamed crackled on the beach. On the other side of the fire was stretched the prone figure of Flann Mac Fraech. He looked pale as he lay there and above his left eye was a bluish bruise.

Ruacán saw her sudden look of anxiety.

'I have said, do not worry. He will be all right after a while. Come, my child, take some more water and if you feel better then you may take a little of the herb broth that I have made.'

Silently, Scáthach reached out for the cup of water and took a swallow.

'How did we come to this place:' she asked.

The druid nodded towards the sea.

'You were both borne ashore in the arms of Manánnan Mac Lir, the ocean god, or else how would the sea give you up?' he said enigmatically.

'We were washed ashore?' the girl demanded. 'Then what of the ship?'

The bright eyes of the druid gazed at her. She suddenly shivered as if she felt the strange mystical aura of the man. It was as if he could read her mind as another might look at the sky and discern the weather.

'Ship? Alas your ship has gone down.'

He turned to the cauldron and began to fill a bowl with the aromatic brew.

'Sip this, my child, and you will soon feel fully recovered.'

'And did you find us lying on the seashore?' pressed Scáthach.

'I found you, yes.'

'And so we owe our lives to you.'

The old man chuckled.

'You owe your lives to providence.'

Scáthach glared at him sharply. Did he know more than he was saying? Why, oh why, did druids never say what they meant directly?

'But your mother was a druid,' the old man suddenly said.

Scáthach stared at him for a moment in startled wonder.

'What did you say?' she whispered. How could he have read her mind so well.

'Have no fear, Scáthach of Uibh Rathach,' the old man went on. 'It is simply a sleight of hand which makes me appear to know more than I know.'

'Then how do you know who I am?' demanded the girl.

The bright eyes twinkled.

'How? Easy to tell. You wear the torc of a hero, and the patterns tell me that it is the torc of Eola of Uibh Rathach. I have heard tell that Eola adopted a child, a girl child, named Scáthach. It is logical that you are therefore that person. And being that person, your mother was of equal fame – Buimech the druidess.'

She continued to gaze at him but she felt slightly disappointed. It was so easy as the old man told it. Merely a question of logic and deduction.

'You are disappointed,' observed the old man. 'You expected some gift of the supernatural. Alas, I am but an old man skilled in many things. Yet I am now just a conjurer of magic. To everything in life there is a logic, a reason, and when we do not understand it we tend to dismiss it as magic and supernatural.'

Scáthach shrugged ruefully.

'My mother passed on much of the philosophy of the druids but I confess that I have learnt little.'

The old man, Ruacán, chuckled. It was a rather high-pitched sound.

'You have imbibed more than you think, my child. It needs only the right moment to emerge; the right stimulus and then wisdom is yours.'

There came a groan from Flann and the young warrior began to stir.

At once Scáthach and Ruacán were by his side.

'Flann, it's all right. We are safe.'

Flann blinked and stared up at the girl. He tried to speak but his lips and mouth were dry. As he had with Scáthach, the druid gave the young man a little to drink.

'My head hurts,' Flann said after a moment. He sounded slightly surprised.

The old druid chuckled.

'Then you are getting better. Had your head not hurt then that would be a cause for worry. Lay awhile and rest. Your questions will be answered later.'

Scáthach sat beside Flann sipping at the herbal broth the druid had prepared. She was growing stronger and her faculties were coming back. She was recalling the teachings of Buimech and the ways of the druids but from what little she knew she began to realise that Ruacán the Wizened was on a higher plane of advancement than most she had encountered.

He sat by the fire examining her under large shaggy white eyebrows, his bright eyes still twinkling.

'There is much that disturbs you, Scáthach,' he said after a while.

The girl saw no reason to waste words.

'Much.'

'And you are even now wondering whether I am friend or foe?'

'I think you are a friend,' replied the girl carefully. 'A foe would not save us from the sea merely to destroy us.'

The old man nodded gravely.

'There is none can fault your logic, daughter of Eola.'

There was a pause.

'You wonder whether you should tell me about your quest,' he went on.

This time Scáthach gasped a little. Automatically, her hand went to the gold medallion at her neck.

Flann was easing himself up on one elbow and, shaking his head as if to clear it, beginning to take in his surroundings.

'How do you know that I am on a quest?'

This time Ruacán the Wizened laughed outright.

'Use your own powers of deduction, daughter of Buimech, for surely your mother taught you something of our reasoning.'

Scáthach sighed.

'I am wearing the hero's torc of Eola. I am alone on the high seas with a young warrior for companion. What else would I be doing so far from home and thus accoutred if I were not on some journey in search of something?'

The old man slapped his thigh.

'You might make a druid yet. Yes, your logic is without fault.'

'No. I am no druid nor wish to be,' replied the girl.

Ruacán was suddenly serious and nodded.

'Indeed. You are destined for other things, daughter of Eola and Buimech.'

Flann had been following this conversation, frowning for a while.

'Will someone tell me what has happened? How did we get here? And where is "here"?'

Ruacán gestured at the girl.

94

'She will tell you while I gather our breakfast. Take of the broth. It will make you well.' He rose. 'I shall return shortly.'

They watched him walk off along the beach.

Swiftly, Scáthach narrated what she knew. Flann shook his head, groaning a little at the pain.

'It seems a wondrous thing, Scáthach,' he said softly. 'My last thoughts in that tempest were of the futility of our deaths in the waves.'

'Well, the ocean god must have heard us for we were not consumed by the seas.'

'But who is this man Ruacán?' demanded Flann. 'A druid, yes; but what manner of man and can he be trusted?'

'That he can,' replied the girl. 'I feel that strongly. He might be able to help us reach Lethra.'

'And so you will tell him about your quest?'

'I shall.'

A moment later the old druid returned along the beach with a large sea trout which he gutted and skewered over the fire.

'As we eat, you shall tell me of your quest,' he said, as he settled himself down again.

Scáthach frowned.

'You seem certain that I had made up my mind to tell you?'

The druid smiled and said nothing.

After some hesitation, Scáthach recounted her story until the moment of leaping into the sea from the floundering *Nemhain*. Flann broke in once or twice to explain a detail, such as his part in the affair and his background.

After they finished the story the druid said nothing. He bent to the fish and judged it to be ready to eat and prepared it. They watched him in silence.

'Well?' demanded Flann, not able to conceal his impatience any more.

The twinkling eyes of Ruacán stared back at him.

'That is hardly a question, young man.'

'Can you place us in the direction of Lethra by telling us what island this is and how far off the shore of Gallia it is?'

The druid prodded at his fish.

'Eat,' he commanded, 'and you will grow strong. Strong enough to continue your journey.'

'Then you will help us with directions?' pressed the girl.

Ruacán smiled, his bright eyes glistening.

'First let me help you with some advice. You have powerful enemies, daughter of Eola. More powerful than you have ever dreamt. They are possessed of powers that would make even the heroic sons of Míle Easpain, who wrested Éireann from the gods, think twice before pursuing the path which you intend to follow and pitting their prowess against such enemies.'

Flann gave a snort of laughter but Scáthach signalled him to silence.

'Do you think to turn me aside from my path, Ruacán?' she questioned quietly.

The old man shook his head.

'I have no power to change what is in your heart, Scáthach. Yet I am duty bound by my honour and knowledge to warn you of the dangers you will encounter.'

'That I have enemies who must be powerful was revealed to me by the fact that they sent a raiding party to kill me at Uibh Rathach. Instead of killing me, they killed my father, Eola. They forced my mother, Buimech, to make the ritual fast at his unlawful death. I know enough to say that those powerful enemies went in search of me. They learnt that I had escaped their sentence of death placed on me as a child. For they must have cast me into the seas to die. Thanks to Eola and Buimech, I was saved. All this I have known a long time since, Ruacán. I knew the dangers before I made the first footsteps on this path.'

Ruacán watched her proud defiance of fear with a smiling face.

'And you, Flann Mac Fraech, one time of the Cruithne? Do you scorn the dangers too?'

Flann raised his chin stubbornly.

'I do.'

Scáthach and he exchanged a quick smile, a look of something which was not lost on the druid.

'Then know this, the both of you: to fight such enemies you will need to equip yourselves with weapons more skilfully crafted than any made by ordinary, mortal hands.'

They stared at him for a moment. Scáthach made an impatient gesture.

'Are you saying such weapons exist?'

'And where are such weapons to be found?' demanded Flann.

Ruacán gazed into the girl's eyes.

'There are such weapons,' he said softly. 'But they are only for you, Scáthach of Uibh Rathach.'

Flann pursed his lips, trying to hide the blow he felt to his warrior's pride.

'Come, druid,' he forced himself to say, sneering a little, 'are you saying that there are weapons fashioned by the gods for the asking?'

Ruacán's quiet gaze did not leave the girl's face but he addressed his reply to Flann.

'Did I say that they were to be had for the asking? Courage and skill are needed to obtain them.'

'Then I will get them for Scáthach,' said Flann, rising.

'No!' Ruacán's reply was sharp. 'Only Scáthach of Uibh Rathach can obtain what are rightfully hers.'

Scáthach leant forward towards the druid.

'Enough games of words, Ruacán.' she said. 'Speak plainly.'

The corners of Ruacán's mouth turned down but his face was still full of quiet humour.

'Then plain it shall be, Scáthach. On the far side of this island is a deep pool. At the bottom of the pool is an underwater cave in which is stored a shield and a javelin. They belong to the ocean god, Manánnan Mac Lir. If you are without fear and confident in your skill and honour, you can seek to obtain that shield and javelin. With such weapons you will become invincible to your enemies.'

Flann was staring at the old druid in outright disbelief.

'And how can you know such things?' he snapped.

The old man's bright eyes flickered up to the young warrior.

'I am of the knowledge. I know. She is partly of the knowledge,' he nodded to the girl. 'She will tell you that I speak of what I know.'

Flann glanced at Scáthach. She was biting her lip. She cast him a quick look and nodded.

Flann coloured a little. He knew that to question a druid was a social transgression and yet the scepticism in his mind was strong.

Scáthach examined the old man's face closely.

'What you are saying is that if one dives into the pool, to the underwater cave, one can have this shield and javelin?' She grimaced. 'Then if this is such a simple task, why has no one taken the property of the ocean god before?'

'Did I say it was simple?' reflected Ruacán. 'There is a guardian of the cave to overcome.'

'Ah! A warrior?' asked Flann.

'A warrior of the deep; a warrior of the oceans. Not a warrior in the sense you might accept.'

Flann looked perplexed.

'In what sense then?'

'That is not for me to say.'

98

'You seem to claim much but venture little,' grunted Flann.

'I am claiming nothing and saying only what must be said,' retorted the druid.

Scáthach stood up. She felt strong and fit as if the events of the last twelve hours were of no consequence.

'The weapons are in the cave? You are sure of this?'

The old man nodded.

'Then I will retrieve them,' Scáthach said with a tone of simple finality.

'But what of this guardian?' protested Flann. 'How can we trust this old one? He may not be telling the truth. It may be some trap.'

The old man rose.

'She will know, young man. She will know if she is the person it was ordained she should be.

He began to stride away.

Scáthach took a hesitant step after him.

'Where is this pool?' she called out.

The old man did not stop but called across his shoulder.

'On the far side of the island. You will know it when you see it.'

Flann frowned.

'I do not like this, Scáthach.'

The girl turned to him with a smile.

'It is a test. Of that I am sure. Well, we must be equal to it. Come, let us find this pool and the underwater cave.'

She turned and began to pick her way across the rocky terrain of the island.

It was midday when they came to a small rocky cover on the far side of the island. Ruacán had been right. The pool was easily discernible for two lines of rocky causeway encircled it like the outstretched claws of a crab, leaving only a small, narrow channel through which the sea could gush at high tide. But now the waters within the

99

encompassing arms were still, the still waters of a deep sea-pool.

Scáthach paused. She felt alert and astonishingly fit. She put it down to no other reason than the herbal broth which the druid had prepared for she felt no ill-effects at all from the adventures of the last twelve hours. Nor apparently did Flann who stood at her side. She surveyed the pool with a critical eye.

'This must be Ruacán's pool,' Flann said unnecessarily.

She did not reply.

'I do not like it, Scáthach,' the young warrior continued as he gazed uneasily at the darkened waters. 'I have been thinking. If there are weapons here and they do belong to the ocean god, better leave them for fear of his anger.'

The girl smiled at her companion.

'I did not think you were of faint heart, Flann,' she said in amusement.

The young man flushed.

'Nor am I when it comes to fighting men!' he protested. 'But if we are to believe the words of the druid, then some immortal guards those weapons . . .'

'He did not say that,' rebuked the girl. 'He simply said there was a guardian. Anyway, didn't our ancestors, the children of Míle Easpain, go to the land of Éireann when it was peopled with none but the gods and drive them to the low places beneath the hills? We have conquered the gods before and we shall do so again. The gods are immortal and powerful only so long as they fulfil the desires of humankind. When they do not do so, then the gods die.'

Flann licked his lips nervously. While part of his mind admitted shame before the courage of the girl, another part admired her confidence and steadfastness, while a third part urged him to quit this place.

'The druid ought to be with us to guide us.'

Scáthach shook her head.

'I shall dive into the pool and search for these weapons,' she said firmly.

She strode forward to an outcrop of rock overlooking the natural sea pool and stared down into the blackness. Then, without a second glance at Flann, she stripped off, keeping only her belt from which hung her hunting knife, the only weapon saved from the wreck of the *Nemhain*.

'Take care!' muttered Flann as the girl took a step forward to the edge of the outcrop, stood stretched on tiptoe, hands reaching before her. Then the muscles in the backs of her legs tensed as she gathered her energy and pushed off into a graceful dive hitting the blackness of the waters below with scarcely a ripple.

Flann moved to the outcrop and stared down, his brow creased in lines of worry.

The dark waters closed over Scáthach, turning rapidly from dark green into inky blackness.

By Dana, mother of the gods, how could anyone see in such blackness?

She swam instinctively through the darkness towards the shoreline, under the underhang of rocks, the only logical direction in which the entrance to a cave might be.

Strangely, as she swam, she became aware of the water growing lighter. It puzzled her. At the same time she realised that any moment she would have to fight her way to the surface unless she found the cave and a source of air in it. It was difficult to breathe now, her lungs were hurting and she was dying to open her mouth. In the eerie light she caught a glimpse of a black aperture and then she was pushing up to the surface. She broke through the waters and floated a moment or so on her back, gasping and recovering her breath.

'Do you see anything?' called Flann from the rocky overhang.

'I think I see the entrance to the cave,' she replied, having recovered. 'I'm going into it.'

With a wave of her hand, she drew in breath again, and sped downwards through the blackness and back to the eerie glow in the water, a form of light which seemed to have no source. She saw the dark opening and swam for it. A moment later she was in a cavern which glowed with the same strange light. A water passage had taken her into a pool which emerged in the cavern which seemed to act as an airlock to the waters outside. She broke the surface and involuntarily opened her mouth. She gasped at the icy cold air. It was slightly musty but good enough to breathe. She trod water, lying slightly on her back, and breathed deeply at the same time staring around the cavern in which she had surfaced.

It was then that she realised the cause of the light. It was a natural phenomenon, a phosphorus for the cavern walls seemed to be covered in a yellow translucent substance which glowed luminous in what would have been total darkness.

Scáthach turned slowly, moved to a rocky ledge and began to pull herself up. As she did so she became aware of a constriction around her ankle, as if someone had tied a rope around it. A powerful tug jerked her backwards. Then she had time to gain one lungful of air before a second, sharper tug dragged her back into the water. She turned, pulling and tugging at her trapped legs.

In the phosphorescent waters she saw a dark shadow nearby. It was huge. Her heart lurched as she saw giant tentacles slicing through the water around it and realised that one of those sinewy limbs had wrapped itself around her foot. For a moment she felt utter panic and her fear paralysed her. Creatures from the shadows, the old nightmare of her childhood. She was alone and helpless, without weapons, and the creature was powerful and irresistible. She could not fight it. It was invincible. It was supreme. And who was she? Then she thought she heard, from within the deep recesses of her mind, the chiding tones of Eola and Buimech. Immediately she sought to calm her fears. She became aware that Eola and Buimech had taught her well.

She arched her lithe body over, bending double towards her ankles while, at the same time, reaching for her hunting knife at her side. The waters around her were threshing with the muscular energy of the terrible creature of the deep. Amidst the waving limbs, she caught sight of a single baleful eye and a terrible beak-like mouth which kept opening and snapping shut. She reached forward again, slashing with her knife at the limb which had wound itself around her ankle. Even as she did so another tentacle slithered through the waters and wrapped itself around her waist and a third caught her left arm.

She did not panic but continued to hack at the limb, slicing through it until the water was mingled with an inky black substance which trickled from the severed flesh. Then, at last, her ankle was free, but her lungs were bursting for air. There would be no time to hack at the other limbs which held her fast. The giant creature was drawing her slowly towards its baleful eye and snapping jaw. Its wicked malevolent eye continued staring at her struggling form without blinking. A few seconds more and she would either drown or be crushed in that terrible maw.

Caught between desperation and resignation, Scáthach drew back her right arm and hurled her hunting knife through the swirling waters towards the terrible staring eye.

A moment later the waters erupted into a furious whirlpool. The girl found herself moving through the water which such speed that, for a moment or so, she lost consciousness. Then she found herself free of the entwining limbs and she was shot upwards with an incredible momentum which caused her to erupt into the cavern again with such a force that she was thrown clear of the water for a moment. Then she dropped back. Gasping for breath, she turned and struggled towards the rocky floor of the cave and fear of the creature gave her enough strength to pull herself from the water and move a sufficient distance away from the swirling pool. The water was still bubbling with a froth caused by the threshing of the thing below. Then the foamy whirlpool subsided. All was quiet.

It was a long while before Scáthach found enough breath to stir. She glanced towards the now still pool. There was no sign of the creature. The creature of the shadows had gone. She felt a sense of inward satisfaction. She had faced her childhood nightmare and overcome it. It was she who had emerged supreme.

Slowly she stood up and took stock of the cavern. The luminescent substance was like a wax covering everywhere on the jagged walls and the light it provided was good enough to make out the details. The main chamber of the cave was about fifteen feet in height and little passageways and caves seemed to lead off from it. By the time she had visually examined her surroundings she had recovered her strength and breath.

The terrible creature must have been the guardian of the cave which Ruacán had warned against. Well, it was blind now . . . blind or dying for her hunting knife must have surely found its mark in the eye and the eye was often as not a short way to the brain.

She stared about. But if this cave was the one in which the ocean god, Manánnan Mac Lir, had chosen to hide his shield and javelin, where would they be?

She began to explore each separate cave carefully.

It was not long before she came on the right one, a medium-sized cave leading off from the main cavern. In the cave was a flat granite slab on which were spread the pelts of several animals whose identity she could not even begin to guess at. On the pelts lay a large oval shield and by it a slim handled javelin of some six feet in length.

The girl stared at the shield with some degree of awe. It was four feet in length and twenty inches wide at its broadest point. Unlike the usual round shields of wicker or yew, covered with hide, or strips of decorative metal, this shield was of bronze ornamented with silver and with two silver bosses surrounded by intricate pattern-work consisting mainly of concentric circles and inlaid with enamel.

She hesitated a moment and then bent down and picked it up. In spite of the metals of which it was made, it was light to hold as if it had been tailor-made for her. She held it easily in her left hand by the looped leather handle. There was another leather strap, the *sciathrach*, which would hang the shield across the shoulder in case two hands were needed in battle or, when it was not being used, would carry the shield slung over the shoulder.

A smile of delight spread across her features. This, indeed, was a shield fit for a warrior.

She turned her attention to the javelin. She had seen many javelins before, their heads either hammered from iron or cast in bronze. This one carried an extraordinary beauty in its crafting. Its head was slim and fluted and cast in bronze, fixed on a long handle of oak by means of a socket into which the end of the shaft was thrust and kept in place by rivets. The point was sharp and highly polished and was six inches in length. On the shaft, where a warrior would hold it for casting, was a winding of silk and a hook in which the thrower inserted a forefinger to help gain an extra impetus for the cast.

Something odd struck her as she stared at both javelin and shield. They were still brightly polished and yet for how many years had they reposed in this cave? She cast a nervous glance around, as if someone would materialise to claim them as their possessions. Then she shook herself. If they were truly the weapons of Manánnan Mac Lir, then keeping them polished and bright would be a small achievement for a god.

Scáthach picked up the javelin, testing its balance cautiously, and weighing it in her hand.

Shield and javelin possessed a vibrancy in her hands. It was if they throbbed softly in her grasp like living things. She felt a surge of confidence as she held them. They belonged to her and were part of her. She suddenly felt laughter welling in her and gave vent to a chuckle. She stood and beat the shield rim with the metal of the javelin, issuing the time-honoured challenge to the world at large. The noise reverberated throughout the cavern.

Above it came an answering sound. Abruptly the laughter went from her face as she realised the noise was that of disturbed water from the main cavern.

Was the terrible water-creature still alive?

She moved quickly from the small cave into the main cavern with shield and javelin at the ready.

From the water pool, which was both only entrance and only exit to the outside world, she could see the movement of the black waters. She tensed expectantly and drew back her throwing hand. Curiously, she found the weapon shuddering slightly in her hand with a quivering motion of its own volition, as if eager to be cast, eager to get at the enemy.

Thus poised, Scáthach stood waiting.

The waters suddenly parted and a figure swam up. For a moment it lay, head thrown back, gasping for breath.

The girl's eyes widened and she dropped the point of her javelin.

'Flann!'

The young man stared at her briefly and then swam to the side of the pool, heaving himself up on the rocky floor. He crouched a moment, breathing deeply, before standing up and gazing at her. There was relief in his face.

'Scáthach! Are you safe?'

The girl smiled broadly.

'As you see. Why did you follow me?'

Flann's anxious gaze wandered over her figure, taking in the red weals on her right arm and lower leg where she had been seized by the denizen of the deep.

'A short while after you dived,' he began, 'I saw a commotion in the water and then blood came to the surface. I dived in to come to your aid. As I did so, the most terrifying creature emerged threshing in its death agony. A frightening sea beast with eight long limbs. I have never seen its like before.'

'But you had no weapon,' observed the girl softly.

'I was frightened for you, Scáthach. It took me three dives to find the entrance to this cavern.'

'Is the creature dead?'

'Dead indeed,' affirmed Flann.

Scáthach gazed into the eyes of the young warrior for a moment, changing the javelin to her left hand. Then, on impulse, she reached up and kissed him full on the lips. Then she backed away and sought to hide her confusion in a smile.

'I am safe enough,' she sighed. 'Come, let us be gone from this place. Are you recovered to swim back?'

Flann, his face more crimson than usual, nodded silently.

Together they climbed back into the pool and dived into its depths seeking the exit. It was a few moments before they were treading water in the sea-pool. There was no sign of the tentacled creature. Its carcass must have sunk to the depths of the waters. They swam easily towards the rocks and heaved themselves up, Scáthach handling the shield and javelin with ease, as though they were extensions of herself. They made their way to the spot where they had left their clothes and lay down in the hot sun's rays, exhausted. Soon the midday sun had dried the water from their bodies and then they dressed.

They were just finishing dressing when a dry cough sounded behind them.

Ruacán the Wizened stood there. His bright eyes were fastened on the shield and javelin. In the sunlight they shone with dazzling beauty.

'So?' he smiled.

Scáthach returned his smile.

'So . . . you were right, Ruacán. These are weapons fit for a great warrior.'

The old man nodded.

'And a great warrior you shall be, Scáthach of Uibh Rathach. Your name will be on the lips of people when the gods who made those weapons are forgotten.'

'Truly, did the gods make these weapons?' demanded Flann, gazing sceptically for the first time on the prizes which the girl had taken from the cave.

Ruacán nodded gravely.

'The shield is called *An Seancholl Snidheach* – the strong ridged hazel – which was given to the ocean god, Manánnan Mac Lir, by The Dagda, father of the gods. It is said that the shield will shriek a warning when its owner is in danger.'

Scáthach examined the bronze and silver shield with its intricate mystical patterning, its peculiar brilliance, and once more felt an unfathomable awe.

'And the javelin?' asked Flann, not hiding the cynicism in his voice. 'Does that have magic properties, too?'

'Indeed, my son. That is the *Corr-Bholg*, the sharp spear, of Manánnan Mac Lir, with which he slew many of the Fomorii, the gods of darkness.'

'Then I am well armed,' said the girl softly.

Ruacán gave a slight nod.

'Yet your best armament is in your heart, Scáthach.'

'What do you mean?'

The druid shook his head.

'You will know when the time comes. But, until then, you may continue your journey to Lethra.'

Flann scowled.

'Easier said than done, Ruacán. We are cast ashore on this island and perhaps a day's sail from the coast of Gallia. Where do we get a ship?'

'Did I say that I was cast ashore?' queried the old druid.

Flann shot him a glance of annoyance.

'Are you saying that you have a ship here?'

'A ship? No. But I have a small *curragh*, a skiff which is big enough to take us to Gallia.'

Scáthach met the gaze of the druid's bright eyes.

'Are you saying that you will help us reach the borders of Lethra?'

'You will need advice on this journey of yours, Scáthach of Uibh Rathach. You have a strong right arm in young Flann of the Cruithne there. I am old and somewhat bent, but the ages have not diminished my learning or judgement. I would come with you and give you freely of my advice if you would hear it.'

Scáthach did not hesitate.

'I will hear it, Ruacán. You have spoken the truth so far.' She turned to Flann. 'Do you agree?'

The young man pursed his lips and thought for a moment.

'I have little use for magic and less for druids. When I see the druids who surround the tyrant Aintiarna of the Cruithne and fawn and dote on his every word, then I say to myself – how can we trust such who claim to be enlightened when they lead us into servitude?'

Ruacán gazed sadly at the young man.

'I can only say that we are human and humankind have faults. Do not blame the singers for the song.'

Flann shrugged.

'It matters not to me whether you come or stay. If Scáthach needs your advice, who am I to object?'

The girl looked troubled but decided not to press the matter other than say: 'I wish Ruacán to come with us, Flann.'

Flann gave a gesture of indifference.

'So be it,' he said.

The old man pretended not to notice his surliness but turned and said: 'Let us eat, for it is well past the midday sun. When we have done so, we may continue to the coast of Gallia. From the coast, Lethra is but three days' journey.'

Scáthach started at the information.

'You know your way to Lethra?'

'I would be a poor traveller if I did not. This island is less than one day's journey from that part of the shore of Gallia which is the easy path to the land of Lethra.'

Even Flann expressed surprise.

'Then we are close by?'

'Close, but far,' the druid replied. 'There are several things to be accomplished, many dangers to be overcome before you will stand at the gates of the capital of Lethra where the answer to Scáthach's riddle lies.'

'Even so,' smiled the girl, 'we are closer than I dared imagine. Do you truly know the way to Lethra?'

'I have told you so,' the old man answered. 'But I say again, it is not an easy road. So let us prepare and be on our way before it grows too dark to start our journey.'

Eight

They had been journeying for three days since they had
set foot on the rocky shore of Gallia. Three days from
the open, rolling hills of the coastal plain into the dark
oak forests which lay beyond. Ruacán led the way with
easy confidence, sometimes striding ahead in spite of
his age, his robe flowing, his long oak-staff as his aid.
Scáthach and Flann followed more leisurely, examining
the unfamiliar countryside with interest. It was a terrain
that was like the lush green of Éireann and yet somehow
alien to it, not quite as green and fresh. And, along the
way, there were far fewer hostels and inns for travellers.
Indeed, they met with very few people on the roads at
all. Only the occasional merchant passed them by with a
curious look when they declared they were on the road
to Lethra.

On the morning of the third day they came to the
entrance of a long, narrow valley, thickly carpeted with
oak, hazel and pine. The path was so narrow through the
woods that in some places they were forced to go in single
file and several times Flann demanded whether the old
druid had been led astray from the main road. However,
Ruacán insisted that he knew the path and that they were
heading in the right direction.

After an hour or so pressing through the thickly
growing wood and underbrush, Scáthach paused and
sniffed the air.

'What is it?' asked Flann.

'I smell a fire.'

Almost at that moment they heard the clang of metal on metal some way ahead of them.

'A smithy,' Flann cried with a grin.

Ruacán smiled at him.

'An accurate deduction, my son.'

Flann's eyes narrowed at the gentle irony in the old man's voice. He still did not trust the old man. Nor did he not feel comfortable with him. There was something mysterious about him and Flann was a practical person who disliked mysteries. He had learnt never to trust druids as a group of people. He had seen them betray his people, the Cruithne, into the hands of a petty tyrant for their own glory. No one could persuade him that there was integrity among them. They merely wanted power over people and sought to gain it by preying on their superstitions. This old man was no different. He had persuaded Scáthach to trust him but that was no reason for Flann to follow suit.

Ruacán was pressing along the path and eventually came into a large clearing. Flann had been right. A large wooden cabin stood in the clearing alongside which was a forge. A fire was glowing there before which a giant of a man stood in the soiled leather apron of a smithy, his biceps rippling as he heaved a heavy length of iron from it with one hand while the other lifted a heavy hammer to shape it.

The giant was over six feet in height, broad and muscular beyond anyone Scáthach and Flann had seen before. He had a shock of red hair, wide blue eyes and a humorous face. He raised his head and regarded them quizzically as they approached him.

'Strangers,' he observed. 'It is not often that strangers come to this valley.'

Scáthach's eyes had taken in the contents of the smithy's workshop and her eyes widened slightly. There were rows of swords and spears, shields and helmets hung around the walls.

'Perhaps because this is a warlike valley,' she observed dryly.

The smithy flung back his head and roared with laughter; it was a deep sound like far off thunder.

'You are observant, girl.'

'You seem to be equipping people for war, rather than shoeing horses, fixing wheels and pursuing the more peaceful pursuits of a rural smith,' she went on.

The smithy grunted.

'It is true that my smithy is called open more often to provide weapons of war than implements of peace.' He shrugged. 'But that is the nature of man. He is always concerned with thoughts of war and conquest rather than living in peace at one with nature. Indeed, even when man is not seeking to conquer his fellows, he wants implements to conquer nature itself. A veritable warmonger is man.'

'A smith who is a philosopher!' sneered Flann.

But the girl shook her head disapprovingly.

'A perceptive eye is still a perceptive eye no matter in whose head it belongs,' admonished the old druid.

The smith roared with laughter again, almost shaking the earth with his giant frame.

'Well said, Ruacán.'

Flann glanced suspiciously from the smith to the druid.

'So you know each other?'

'Who does not know of Ruacán the Wizened?' demanded the smith.

'And who might you be, smithy?' pressed Flann.

'My name is Goibhniu.'

'Goibhniu is the greatest of all the smiths,' added the old druid. 'Gaze on his work, Scáthach. He has the skill to make you a sword which none could vanquish and a helmet which would present so terrible a visage that your enemies would flee the moment they beheld it.'

Flann chuckled hollowly but Scáthach moved forward into the forge and gazed upon the weapons which hung there. It was true that she had never seen such beautiful craftsmanship before; no, not even in Uibh Rathach where Eola's collection of weapons were reputed to be the best in all Éireann. She gazed upon their workmanship with undisguised admiration.

Wandering along the rows of swords she came to one whose beauty, terrible as it was in a weapon so sharp, caused her breath to catch. Its blade shone brightly silver from some strange metal; it was keen and fluted. Its handle was an intricate and bejewelled design of gold and silver, inlaid with precious stones. She reached out a hand to touch it, almost wonderingly.

'Ha!' grunted the smith. 'You have come to the most beautiful and precious of my creations. You have a fine eye for a weapon, girl.'

Scáthach wheeled round, angry at the condescension in the smith's voice.

'I am Scáthach of Uibh Rathach! I wear a warrior's torc.'

The red-headed giant stamped his foot and roared with laughter again.

'A fine name, girl. But are you entitled to bear it and that twisted gold around your neck? A warrior's torc can be picked up and placed on a neck, it does not mean to say that the wearer is a hero.'

Flann moved forward, slapping his hand to his side before realising that he did not possess a weapon. All their weapons, saving the shield and javelin which Scáthach had recovered from the underwater cave, had been lost when the *Nemhain* had struck the rocks.

'By the gods, smith, loan me but one of your swords and I will teach you how a warrior replies to an insult.'

Ruacán had taken himself to a seat by the cabin door and had seated himself, watching the proceedings with a faint smile.

The smith, Goibhniu, stood grinning at Flann, who barely came to his chest height.

'By the powers,' he chuckled, 'I have no quarrel with a boy.'

'You have a quarrel with me, smith,' intervened Scáthach, 'for you have insulted both my name and honour.'

Goibhniu turned to her, blue eyes wide, his faced creased in a broad smile.

'Ah, this is warrior's talk, girl. Are you up to it?'

'As you see, I am without a sword. Loan me but one of yours and I will show you whether I am entitled to wear a warrior's torc.'

'No!' cried Flann. 'He insulted me. I will make this ugly brute apologise.'

He rushed forward and grabbed the nearest sword and went towards the smith, swinging dangerously.

The giant stood his ground, laughing. With one sweep of his hammer, he simply knocked aside the weapon, closed on Flann and with one giant hand reached forward, grabbed the luckless warrior by his shirt front, and lifted him several feet bodily from the ground. Then he threw him several yards across the clearing.

Flann landed with a thud and lay winded for a moment.

'You brute!' cried Scáthach, grabbing at the sword nearest to her. It was the one she had been admiring. It seemed to fit into her hand as if it were made for her. The balance was perfect. But anger dominated her mind now and she did not seem to notice its perfect extension of her own right hand. She closed on Goibhniu who still stood grinning and making no attempt to reach for a sword nor shield.

She made a lightning thrust, but the smith merely swung his hammer, knocking the blade aside with a resounding clang. Scáthach felt the vibration all the way down the sword, into her arm and body.

She halted. Her anger suddenly faded. Her eyes met the wide blue orbs of the smith and she realised that here was no ordinary artisan. The man wielded his hammer as a warrior might handle a sword and shield. She approached him more carefully now, crouching low, her sword point darting about for an opening.

Goibhniu chuckled.

'Well done, girl. You learn quickly.'

He stood waiting for the attack and when it came, he turned aside and struck out with his hammer.

The sword almost flew from her grip with the ferocity of the blow.

'Excellent,' commented Goibhniu as she hung on and regained her balance.

She turned, biting her lip in perplexity. How was she to overcome this confident, lazily smiling giant?

She attacked again.

Another blow on the sword blade with his mighty hammer sent her reeling back.

It became clear to her that Goibhniu the smith was possessed of a tremendous strength and skill. Nevertheless, she renewed the attack, almost, at one point, getting through his guard.

He chuckled and again the hammer found its mark.

Her arm, indeed her whole body, began to grow weary and weak. Her head began to ache from the vibration of the hammer blows through her body. She began to stumble and her attacks grew more clumsy. She refused to give up. She became aware of Flann calling out to encourage her and she clenched her teeth and attacked again.

This time the giant dealt a powerful blow which, while she still clung to the sword, sent her reeling backwards. She stumbled and measured her length.

Face red with mortification, she crawled back to her

feet, tears welling in her eyes in anger. She rushed for the smith. Yet again she found herself on the ground staring up at the giant from a prone position.

'Enough!' Goibhniu suddenly said, casting aside his hammer and reaching one great arm forward to grip her by the hand and lift her to her feet as if she had been as light as a feather. She stood feeling dazed and puzzled. 'Enough!' repeated the smith. 'You have proved yourself worthy of a warrior's torc and of the name you bear. Welcome to my forge, Scáthach of Uibh Rathach. Accept the hospitality of Goibhniu.'

The girl stared at the smith curiously.

'Who are you?' she demanded.

'I have told you,' grinned the giant. 'I am Goibhniu the smith.'

'You are no ordinary smith,' insisted the girl.

'You may be right,' Goibhniu assented humorously.

Scáthach stared at him for a moment and then shrugged. She peered down at the sword in her hand and then smiled.

'Well, since you offer your hospitality, Goibhniu, I have a mind to take this sword.'

The red-haired smith raised an eyebrow and his grin broadened.

'You may have proved that you are warrior enough, Scáthach of Uibh Rathach, but are you worthy to take Goibhniu's sword?'

She drew herself up haughtily.

'Have I not proved that?'

'No,' replied the smith flatly and the assertion took the breath from her.

She drew her brows together and started forward angrily but Goibhniu held up his hand to stay her.

'I have said that you have proved yourself a warrior, but whoever carries that sword must be possessed of more than courage. Even a wolf has courage.'

'I will pay you for the sword,' snapped the girl.

The smith examined her speculatively.

'Indeed, you may. You shall pay me by answering three questions. If your answers are right then you shall not only have the sword but a helm as well. You may have the best helmet that I have fashioned.'

Flann came forward with suspicion on his face. He had not forgiven the smith for the easy way the giant had defeated him. It was a blow to his dignity.

'Who will judge the fairness of such questions and the veracity of the answers?' he demanded.

The smith nodded to the old druid who was still seated, an interested spectator.

'There sits our judge.'

Flann frowned at Scáthach.

'I do not trust this,' he whispered to the girl. 'Like as not the two are in league.'

Scáthach looked questioningly at the young warrior.

'But for what purpose?' she asked.

When Flann could not frame an answer she turned to the giant smith and shrugged.

'Very well. I assent. Three questions and if I answer correctly then this sword and a helmet of my choice shall be mine.'

The red-haired giant grunted.

'And, as fair is fair, if you answer wrongly, you and the boy there will remain here and work as my unpaid helpers in the forge for nine months and nine days.'

This brought forth a cry of protest from Flann.

The smith feigned surprised.

'Is it not fair, boy, that I should have some gain out of the wager if I win?'

Flann was about to protest again when Scáthach said: 'That seems fair enough. When will you be ready with your questions, Goibhniu?'

'Ready I am,' grinned the smith.

118

Scáthach turned to Ruacán.

'Are you ready to judge in fairness, old one?'

The old man did not rise but nodded his head.

'I am ready, by the will of the gods.'

'Then ask your questions, Goibhniu the smith.'

'Then first tell me this – what is swifter than the wind?'

Scáthach frowned. 'And your second question?' she asked.

'The second question is – what is sharper than a sword?'

'And the third?'

'What is whiter than snow?'

The girl stood gazing at the grinning face of the red-haired giant.

Goibhniu said: 'I cannot give you a great deal of time. You must have your answers within nine hours. That shall allow you three hours to ponder each of your three answers.'

Scáthach sniffed.

'I want little time to find your answers. Give me a drink of crystal water and you shall have the answers as soon as I have drunk of its contents.'

The smith roared and slapped his thigh.

'By the gods, I like your confidence.'

He turned to a nearby spring and brought a cup of clear water to the girl.

She drained it in one gulp.

Goibhniu looked surprised.

'Are you prepared to tell me the answers now?'

Scáthach smiled with self-assurance.

'I am. Thought is swifter than the wind, Goibhniu. Understanding is sharper than a sword. And truth is whiter than snow.'

Flann looked across to the old druid who sat smiling and nodding his head.

The red-haired giant was giving a deep throaty chuckle.

'Truly, you are well tutored of Buimech,' he said.

The girl frowned.

'What do you know of my mother?'

'You are Scáthach of Uibh Rathach,' countered Goibhniu. 'Therefore you are the whelp of Eola and Buimech. And you have answered well.'

Flann had seized the girl by the hand. His joy was apparent on his face.

Ruacán rose to his feet and came forward.

'I expected no less from you, my child,' he said softly.

'May I take the sword?' asked Scáthach.

Goibhniu the smith nodded.

'With that sword, Scáthach of Uibh Rathach, you are invincible. That sword was made with the fire from the Plain of Nia. It is called *An Chraobh Ghlasach*, the cold champion. No mortal warrior will be able to withstand you. That sword was made for you and no other.'

Scáthach could not fathom the meaning of the red-haired giant's words. She was about to press him further when Flann interrupted.

'And you owe her a helmet!'

Goibhniu turned into his forge.

'I shaped this helmet out of the fires of Hy-Falga at the hour of the birth of one fitted to wear it. Here. Take it. It is called *An Cruadín*, the hard helm. Once it is placed on your head, to the sight of your enemies you will be transformed into a terrifying vision. None shall prevail against you.'

The silver helmet with its plumes and visor was breathtakingly beautiful; the craftsmanship was that of an artist of rare talent.

Scáthach placed the helmet on her head. It fitted well and was comfortable to wear.

Goibhniu surveyed his handiwork.

'It is well, Scáthach of Uibh Rathach. Had these others harboured ill against you then the sight of you in that battle-plume would have caused them to cry out in dismay at the terrible spectacle you would have appeared to them. But they truly wish you well.'

Flann sniffed.

'It needed no conjuror's trick to deduce that I wish Scáthach well.'

Goibhniu shook his head sadly.

'One day, and that day will soon be here, you will thank the gods for such conjuror's tricks.'

Flann's face bore an expression of contempt.

'Not I.'

'We will see. And on that day you will hear a smith's hammer ring thrice to remind you of your doubt.' Gobhniu turned and waved his hand to his forge. 'And in the meantime, to show you no ill-will, young warrior, as you are without weapons, take a sword, javelin and shield from my store and let it be with the compliments of a conjuror.'

Flann stood uncertainly.

'If this is a means to try to make me feel guilty about my beliefs then you will not succeed.'

Once more the red-haired giant laughed, striking his large hand against his thigh and shaking his head.

'By The Dagda, you are a stubborn young man. But in that quality lies your strength. Soon there will be need of your stubbornness. Come, take your choice of weapons. I ask nothing in return from you.'

Still suspicious, Flann went forward and carefully made his choice of weapons.

Scáthach was smiling.

'Now we are properly accoutred for our journey,' she said. 'We can go on in confidence, Ruacán.'

The old man shrugged.

'We can go on. But never in confidence, my child. The road to Lethra is still fraught with dangers.'

Scáthach raised her shield and javelin.

'With these weapons, there is naught to fear,' she said. 'You yourself have told me so.'

'My child,' the druid said softly, 'there is more to fear than physical danger. Indeed, physical danger is a matter of small moment. The worst dangers to be feared are not in strength of arms.'

Flann came forward, once more his suspicion and cynicism displayed on his face.

'How is this so, old man? My people, the people of the Cruithne, are the slaves of a petty tyrant who has imposed his will by force. In mind they are strong and rebellious but what can they do when encountering a greater might, a more formidable strength? Would you preach to them that there are greater dangers that the strength of arms?'

'I would,' replied the druid calmly.

'Such as?'

'There is no danger as bad as that which strikes at men's minds. You may rob people of their houses, you may destroy their health and you may ruin their character. Yet so long as the mind remains intact they are still human. There is a hope that their houses may be regained, that their health may be restored and their characters vindicated. There is a hope that their persecutors may be brought to justice. But if their minds be destroyed, there is an end to all such hopes!'

'Do you tell me that the Cruithne will one day be free?' asked Flann.

Ruacán nodded firmly.

'I do so tell you. As long as their minds are not shackled, they will eventually overcome their physical constraints. That is the pattern of the world.'

'What dangers will we face on this path to Lethra,' intervened Scáthach, 'if they are not physical dangers?'

'That is not for me to say,' the old druid told her. 'I can only advise and warn. It is not for me to guide your future.'

Goibhniu, who had been watching, and listening to the interchange, now intervened.

'Come, enough of this talk of gloom and doom. Feast with Goibhniu the smith and rest here a while before continuing your journey.'

'Very well,' agreed Scáthach. 'Today has been hot and tiring.'

'Then,' said Goibhniu, 'you shall feast and rest and refresh yourselves.'

He turned and led the way into his cabin.

Scáthach and Flann paused on the threshold and stared in wonder at the room beyond. It bore no resemblance to the outside of the building. It was a long, richly decorated room in which a table stood laden with dishes of exotic quality and amphora, two-handled pitchers of wine.

'Be seated,' cried the giant, gesturing to richly upholstered chairs. 'Be seated and eat.'

Once more Scáthach gazed curiously at the red-headed smith.

'Who are you?' she repeated.

The giant roared with laughter.

'I have told you. I am Goibhniu the smith. Now eat.'

Flann needed no second bidding and was soon tearing into a dish of fowl with gusto.

It was a feast such as Scáthach had never eaten before. And, after a while, drowsiness overcame them. Goibhniu, still chuckling, led the way to couches of embroidered tapestries. Uncaring at the mystery of such fine furnishing in a poor smith's home, they fell on the beds and were soon asleep.

Scáthach awoke first. She was lying on a green sward in a clearing in the forest. Not far away, Flann was stretched out, still snoring gently, while beyond was the recumbent figure of Ruacán. She sprang up warily. There was no sign of the smith's forge nor cabin. She stared around at the silent forest hardly believing her eyes.

Then she saw, lying nearby, her weapons. The strange helmet, the exquisitely crafted sword, the javelin and shield of the ocean god, Manánnan Mac Lir. She turned. The weapons Flann had taken from the smith lay near his sleeping form.

She shivered slightly as she pondered the mystery.

Nine

The glen was dank and silent, a narrow passage between high mountains that seemed to stretch endlessly upwards, dark and remote, into the skies. The silence was oppressive. Scáthach paused, listening. There came no sound of bird song out of the surrounding woods, nor the faint scuttle of animals in pursuit of their food, nor even the soft sound of the breeze through the branches of the trees and grasses. The silence was omnipresent.

Scáthach turned to Ruacán the Wizened.

'What place is this? It is a doleful spot.'

'Yet through it lies the road to Lethra,' replied the old man.

'Is there any way around it?' asked Flann.

Ruacán smiled.

'Do not tell me that you are nervous of travelling the dark glen. I thought you did not believe in superstition nor in conjuror's tricks?'

Flann flushed.

'No more do I, old man,' he said in bad temper. 'I would prefer not to travel through this glen because it is the sort of territory where one might expect an ambush. That is all.'

'Ah.' The old druid made no further reply.

It was Scáthach who had to repeat the question.

'No,' Ruacán replied. 'There is no other way, my child. To travel to Lethra you must travel through the dark glen.'

The girl sighed in resignation.

'Then the sooner we set out the sooner we shall reach the far side of this place.'

Flann eased his sword in his scabbard.

'I still do not like it, Scáthach,' he said uneasily.

'I will go on ahead,' said Ruacán, pushing forward and striding off down the path into the glen.

Scáthach made to follow but Flann reached out a hand to her arm and stayed her.

'Neither do I like that magician,' he said softly.

'Ruacán?' The girl frowned. 'Why? He has proved a friend to us, Flann. Why are you so suspicious of him?'

'Why is he taking such pains to help us and journey with us?' demanded Flann. 'No man does anything without reward.'

'He is a druid,' Scáthach replied.

Flann twisted his features.

'They are the worst of men. All they want is power over people.'

Scáthach sighed unhappily.

'I cannot agree with you, Flann. My mother was a druidess. She was of the mystic order.'

'I cannot vouch for your mother, Scáthach, but I can tell you the tale of the druids of my own people, the Cruithne. They betrayed the people into the hands of the tyrant Aintiarna for profit. And when the people rose to throw out Aintiarna, then the druids betrayed them again.'

'Your experience cannot be denied, Flann,' the girl said sadly, 'but not all druids are like those of the Cruithne.'

'Until it is proved otherwise, I shall judge them by my experience,' replied the young warrior.

Scáthach shrugged and turned down the path after the vanishing figure of Ruacán. She felt troubled. She had come to like the impetuous young Flann Mac Fraech. She felt a closeness to the warrior which she had not felt it possible to feel for anyone other than Eola and Buimech. Yet she did her best to disguise her fondness for Flann. She was saddened that he was so suspicious of Ruacán the Wizened for she trusted the old druid implicitly. She now looked upon the old man as her mentor and guide. However, she could not deny that Flann had had a bad experience with druids. People were not perfect, not even druids who took oath to live their lives in harmony with mankind and nature. It was sad but perhaps one day Flann would come to realise that not all people could be tarred with the same brush. People were individuals.

They moved along a narrow path down into the valley and, at once, the air turned chill as the great blue granite mountains hid the sun from them. Then the giant trees enclosed them, blocking out the sky. Scáthach found herself shivering slightly.

Ahead Ruacán strode confidently as always, picking his way along the path with his oak staff, striding forward in spite of his age and curved back. Now and again he paused and seemed to listen but there was no sound. The air was still.

Behind Scáthach came Flann, one hand gripping the handle of his sword, his eyes moving quickly from side to side as if prepared for some imminent attack.

They proceeded for some hours in the utter stillness of the valley, exchanging no word between them, pausing only when Ruacán paused to listen a moment and then move on further into the dark woods. The journey was monotonous and tedious. However, they pressed on.

The unexpectedness of the sound caused Flann to halt as if poleaxed. It was several seconds before he drew his sword. Scáthach, on the other hand, though surprised, had fallen into a warrior's crouch, her javelin and shield to the fore. Only the old druid stood resting on his staff with his head cocked to one side almost as if he had half expected the terrifying screech that had split the stillness.

'What is it?' demanded Flann, his face white, as the screech became a squealing that made him flinch.

'Have you not heard a boar being slaughtered before?' asked the old man.

Scáthach recognised the death cry of a wild boar but then said: 'Indeed, Ruacán, but slaughtered by whom?'

'Let us discover the answer to your question,' replied the old man, and set off briskly in the direction of the sound.

A little way along the path they came on the carcass of the slain boar, quiet and still now. From it there protruded a great hunting spear the like of which Scáthach had never seen before. Its wood was of a type she could not recognise, highly polished and carved with strange symbols and designs. Silver metal was wound around part of its shaft while the same highly polished silver seemed to form its point, but most of that was buried in the boar.

She reached forward and tried to wrest it out of the boar but try as she could, the spear was firmly embedded into the carcass. She tried with both hands, placing one foot on the carcass and heaving with all her might. It did not budge.

'Who attempts to steal my spear?' thundered a deep voice, like the threatening of a summer storm.

They swung round to find a giant of a man standing watching them. If they had thought Goibhniu the smith was a giant, then this man was fully a head taller and broader. He wore a yellow kilt and tunic and carried a thick leather belt studded with jewels around his large midriff. From the belt hung a large sword and a dagger. The dagger was almost big enough to provide a sword for Flann or Scáthach, while the sword would have needed two hands to lift it. The giant wore a large golden hero's torc around his neck while his head was a riot of corn-coloured hair. His face was humorous and his eyes a twinkling blue. Had it not been for his larger size and the colour of his hair, Scáthach might have suspected that the man was Goibhniu in some disguise.

'Who are you?' demanded Flann, pushing forward protectively to Scáthach's side.

The giant ignored him, his gaze on the girl.

'Who attempts to steal my spear?' he thundered again.

'Not I,' responded the girl spiritedly. 'I meant to examine it for I have never seen so beautiful a hunting spear before.'

The large man grunted indifferently.

'Nor will you again, girl,' he said.

He strode forward and holding the spear in one giant hand he lifted it to his shoulder with the bleeding carcass of the boar still attached. Then he stared at the three of them.

'You are strangers in this land,' he observed. His tone implied a question.

Ruacán moved forward to act as their spokesman.

'Indeed we are. We journey the path to Lethra.'

The giant made no comment. He turned and swung off down the path with his burden across the shoulder.

'Wait!' Scáthach shouted.

The man halted and turned back.

'It is customary in my country to offer strangers hospitality.'

The giant's eyes widened and then he threw back his head and laughed.

'Boldly spoken, girl. If it is hospitality you desire then you may have it. Come, follow me.'

Without another word, the man turned and recommenced his long, striding walk. They had almost to run to keep the man within sight. After a while they reached a small wooden stockade in which stood a wooden hut. A fire was burning outside.

'Welcome to my encampment,' the big man said, throwing down the spear with the carcass still attached.

'We would be better welcomed if we knew who welcomed us,' snapped Flann, his chest still heaving from the exertion of following the giant.

'Would you now?' pondered the man, as if considering the fact. 'In that case I should know who I am welcoming to my encampment first.'

Flann snorted.

'You see before you Scáthach of Uibh Rathach, Ruacán the Wizened and Flann Mac Fraech.'

The giant looked at the young warrior slyly.

'You wear a hero's torc and carry yourself proudly, boy. Yet it is strange that you do not introduce yourself as Flann Mac Fraech of anywhere in particular. One would have thought you were some great chieftain by your manner.'

Flann flushed in anger.

'Have I transgressed some rule of hospitality to be made the victim of rudeness?' he snapped.

'No rule has been transgressed. But there is much pride in your voice, boy,' replied the giant. 'Nevertheless, we shall let it pass.' His blue eyes wandered to the others. 'Ruacán, you are welcomed by virtue of your wisdom and age. Scáthach of Uibh Rathach, you are welcomed for your ancestors' sakes. You, Flann Mac Fraech, are welcome as the companion of these two travellers.'

Scáthach raised an eyebrow at the quaintness of the method of welcome.

'And who is it,' she said, 'who welcomes us?'

'Forgive me, Scáthach of Uibh Rathach, I am named Bolga, and this is my domain, the valley of the dark pass.'

'And what do you do, Bolga,' snapped Flann, 'to sit in judgement on others?'

Scáthach reached forward and held out a hand to stay the impetuous temper of the young warrior. However, the giant, Bolga, seemed to take no notice. Instead, he bent over the slaughtered boar and began to carve it for the spit. The girl watched curiously.

'Isn't it easier to remove the spear before carving your boar for cooking?' she asked.

Bolga grinned.

'Easier but impossible.'

'Why impossible?' she pressed.

'Because this is no ordinary hunting spear. When it enters, it makes one wound but, once it penetrates the flesh of man or animal, its head opens out into thirty barbs so that it cannot be withdrawn.'

Flann whistled softly, his anger momentarily forgotten, at the wondrous spear.

'That is truly a formidable weapon,' he said. 'Can you imagine anyone facing someone armed with such a weapon? They would be too fearful of the consequence to stand and fight.'

Ruacán's lips thinned.

'You are right, my son,' he said. 'Such a weapon is a fearsome thing. In the hands of an evil person it would do great harm. Only in the hands of someone who would not abuse its power would it be a weapon for peace.'

Bolga chuckled.

'And who is to judge who that may be, Ruacán?' he asked.

'It is already predestined,' replied the old man quietly.

'The spear of Bolga will have two more owners before it will vanish from the ken of man.'

The giant's eyes widened.

'Do you seek to steal the spear of Bolga then?' he demanded.

Scáthach shook her head.

'No. But mayhap I could purchase it from you?'

Bolga made a negative gesture.

'The spear of Bolga is not for sale, girl.'

'Then I shall fight you for it,' she replied simply.

The giant chuckled humorously.

'You do not lack in courage, Scáthach of Uibh Rathach. No, you do not lack in courage.'

He examined her thoughtfully for a moment.

'I am in a generous mood,' he said eventually. 'I will tell you what I am prepared to do. You may have the spear in return for a favour.'

Flann drew his brows together.

'What trick is this? Beware, Scáthach,' he warned.

The girl smiled at the warrior.

'First let us hear Bolga's proposal. There are always two answers to a question and I can refuse equally as I can accept.'

Flann sighed.

'You have seen that this is called the valley of the dark pass?' Bolga began.

'That much is obvious,' snapped Flann.

The giant ignored his interjection.

'Once it was a beautiful valley, well lit and lush in flowers, musical in bird song. Once. For in the centre of the valley stood a small temple to the lords of light. In that temple hung a lantern and while it hung there, light exuded through the valley. Then one day an evil warlock extended his rule over this valley and stole the lantern of the lords of light. He took it to his fortress which stands on the peak of one of those high

131

mountains and hid the lantern in his dungeons, in the bowels of the mountain, so that its light would never shine again in this valley and all would be dark and still for evermore.'

Bolga turned his blue eyes to Scáthach and stared into hers.

'I believe you are sent for a purpose, girl. Go and retrieve the lantern and I will give you my terrible spear – the *gae Bolga*.'

'Why don't you go and retrieve the lantern?' demanded Flann.

The giant's shoulders dropped.

'Alas, I was the keeper of the temple of Solas, the lord of light. I allowed the lantern to be stolen. Such was my punishment that the lord of light put a *geis* on me, a prohibition which forbade me to carry out the deed of rescue. I was to wait for one who would do it in my name.'

Flann glanced at Scáthach.

'I say this is a trick.'

The girl shook her head.

'Tell me, Bolga, who is this mighty warlock who has defied your gods and made this valley dark?'

'His name is Cruitín the crook-back. He is as cunning and sly as the fox, as tenacious as the wild boar and as strong as the bear. He is not to be trifled with.'

'You paint a terrifying picture,' smiled the girl.

'He is terrible, indeed,' agreed Bolga, his face serious.

'A lamp for a spear?' Scáthach reflected. 'That seems a good exchange.'

'Scáthach!' Flann cried in protest.

'Where is the fortress of this Cruitín?'

Bolga stretched out a hand, pointing between the dark trees to the high, precipitous slopes of the granite mountain beyond.

'You will find his fortress resting on the top of that peak, Scáthach. But be warned, as your young friend has said. Cruitín is an evil man.'

'Then it is time that he is taught evil does not pay,' replied the girl.

Ruacán seemed to be the only one who was not perturbed by the events. He took himself to an oak tree and sat down with his back resting against the stump. Flann looked scandalised.

'Are you sitting there and letting Scáthach go without warning her?'

The old druid smiled thinly.

'She has had enough warnings, my son. She has made up her mind and once a mind is made up no one can change it.'

'You propose to stay here and let us proceed alone?' pressed Flann. 'Is it not your duty to come with us?'

'My son, there is little I can do at my age by way of climbing mountains. Scáthach has skills enough and, I believe, she has mental agility enough to perform this task.'

Flann bit his lip.

'Then stay, old man. I shall go with her.'

'Go or stay as you like,' replied the druid, closing his eyes.

Flann wheeled around to the girl.

'Are you set on this course, Scáthach?' he asked.

She smiled at his impetuous loyalty.

'There is no need for you to come, Flann. This task I can accomplish on my own.'

'By the gods, no!' insisted the young warrior. 'We have come thus far together. We shall go on together to meet this Cruitín.'

She sighed softly.

'Very well, Flann. Let us find a path to the black one's fortress.'

Bolga was chuckling now.

'You will find the path easy enough. May the gods protect your arms.'

Scáthach raised a hand in acknowledgement and turned away followed by Flann.

'Wait!'

Bolga shuffled forward.

'One more thing I must tell you, Scáthach of Uibh Rathach. When you reach the lamp, do not attempt to lift the visor from it. No one can gaze on the light of Solas and live. Whosoever gazes at the light will be not only blinded but utterly destroyed.'

Scáthach stared back.

'It is a powerful lantern.'

'Powerful indeed,' agreed Bolga.

'But it is safe so long as the visor is lowered over its flame?'

The giant nodded.

'And is Cruitín able to gaze upon the lamp?'

Bolga shook his head.

'He is of the darkness. He, especially, would be destroyed. But he stole the lantern when the visor was drawn and hid it in his dungeons where no one will ever gaze upon its light again.'

'Thank you, Bolga,' the girl said. 'We will go now.'

They turned back along the path through the darkened valley heading towards the steep sides of the surrounding mountains.

Flann was unhappy.

'Is it worth this hazard simply to gain the spear of Bolga?' he asked after they had gone for some distance in silence.

'You heard what Ruacán had to say. The *gae Bolga* is a dangerous weapon in the wrong hands.'

'Ruacán!' sneered Flann. 'Are you so sure that your hands are the right ones to guard this weapon? Maybe you have become so enamoured of the spear that you want it because it exists.'

He suddenly bit his tongue at the harshness of his words.

The girl did not seem upset.

'Do not think I have not asked myself that question, Flann,' she replied after a moment's hesitation. 'Yes, I have a collection of powerful weapons now – the javelin and shield of the ocean god, and the sword and helmet of Goibhniu. Perhaps, having seen that fierce weapon, the spear of Bolga, I covet it as well? Yes, that I have thought about and questioned my heart. The answer is – no. I do not want the spear for myself. I need the spear because I feel that it is my destiny to have it. Do not ask me to explain any further. I cannot.'

Flann grimaced.

'I am sorry, Scáthach. I regretted the words almost as soon as they left my mouth. I am a clumsy fool at times. I mean well, but I . . .'

She turned, raising herself on tip-toe and suddenly brushed his lips with her own.

'Hush now, Flann. You have no need to explain yourself to me.'

His cheeks reddened.

'Scáthach . . .' he began, but she had turned and was moving on.

'Come on, Flann, I would like to find this fortress of the dark one before nightfall.

'Nightfall,' Flann tried to bring his mind back to the task in hand. 'It seems that it is permanently nightfall in this place.'

They came through some trees to find themselves facing a great grey granite wall.

The girl pointed.

'There are some steps cut there. Perhaps that is the path upwards to the peak.'

'Let me go first,' insisted Flann.

She made to protest but he was already scrambling upwards.

Scáthach reached down to where her helmet, *An Cruadín*, was slung from her belt, and put it on her head. She made sure that her shield and javelin were slung easily on her back and that her sword was by her side. Then she began to follow the young warrior upwards, climbing from one step to another. Each step was chiselled into the granite at about three feet in distance so that the climb was not an easy one in spite of the steps. They had to push themselves from one step to another, following the almost vertical face of the mountainside.

After a while they were both forced to rest, lying on a narrow ledge of a step and gazing out across the dark valley.

'I wonder who this crook-back is?' Flann reflected after a while.

'We will soon discover,' Scáthach replied, sitting up and peering upwards.

Storm clouds were beginning to chase each other across a lowering dark sky. They could hear the far-off rumble of thunder. But there was no sign of lightning around.

'Let's move on. Quickly,' urged the girl.

Flann agreed. It was no place to be caught in a storm.

He began to haul himself up the granite steps again, moving upwards slowly and painfully, for by now their arms and legs ached from the exertion.

The heavens erupted without warning. Rain torrented down on them and made the granite rocks slippery and dangerous.

'Shall we halt?' cried Flann, raising his voice above the noise of the hissing rain.

Scáthach shook her head.

'Let's keep on until it is too dangerous to go further,'

she replied. 'Be careful, the rocks are as if they are covered in grease.'

'We will move slowly,' agreed Flann.

Once more they began the upward climb, carefully, slowly, step by step. It seemed a hundred years had passed since they had begun to make the precipitous journey. Then they found themselves on a granite platform sticking out from the side of the mountain, and the stairs had come to an end. There was one exit and that was into the black maw of a cavern.

'At least we will be out of the rain,' breathed Scáthach with some relief.

They sheltered for a moment or two in the mouth of the cave in order to recover their breath and wring the worst of the rainwater from their clothes.

'I suppose this cave leads on to the fortress of the dark one?' Flann observed, whispering so that his voice did not carry in the echoing cavern.

'Yes, there is certainly no other way leading upwards from here,' replied the girl.

Flann peered into the gloom.

'It is going to be dark in here. I'll see if there is anything lying about with which I can make a torch.'

There was a deal of debris around the mouth of the cave and it did not take him any great amount of time to put together a firebrand which he lit from the spark of an improvised flint and tinder.

From its flickering light it became obvious to them that the cave was well used and was, in fact, the entrance to a passageway which wound upwards into the interior of the mountain. Bric-a-brac which seemed like the discarded remnants of booty from numerous raids and forays was scattered along this path.

'Do we follow it?' asked Flann, pointing to the passage.

'Is there any other route?' asked Scáthach.

He drew out his sword and, holding it in his right hand and the firebrand in his left, he began to move slowly upwards, following the cleft in the rocks which provided the path. It was not musty and the floor, so Scáthach noticed, was well trodden as if by generations of users. Now and then, when they hit a rise which was steeper than in other parts, someone had chiselled steps in the incline, making it easier to ascend.

Twice Flann had to stop to forage for more fuel for his torch. At least there was no lack of such materials among the debris which lay scattered. Once he had bound them and the flame had grown strong again, they proceeded on their way. It seemed to take ages, and several times, as with their procedure up the granite steps outside, they had to pause to recover their breath. Scáthach wondered how long they had been in the ascent. Hours or days? She had no way of telling here in the darkness.

Then, without warning, they emerged into a large cavern. So large that not even the flickering glow of the torch could reach its vault-like roof. It was a cavern of immense proportions. They peered around in curiosity.

'I think we may be just below the fortress of Cruitín,' Scáthach said, observing that there were great piles of arms and weapons, stacks of chests and other boxes and receptacles littering the place.

'Maybe this is where he keeps the lantern,' Flann suggested hopefully.

'Perhaps,' replied the girl but without echoing the young man's expectation.

'Which way?' asked Flann.

'One way is as good as another until we have discovered exactly where we are.'

They began to move in a direct line across the room towards its far side.

Scáthach wondered where the piles of booty had been looted from and what sort of warlord was the man known as Cruitín the crook-back. By the look of the horde gathered in this vast cavern, he was successful by any standard.

They were halfway across the cavern floor when a strange screeching cry stopped them in their tracks. It was a strangled cry, like the shriek of a woman ending in a curious half bark.

'The gods between us and harm!' whispered Flann, trying to hold the lantern as high as possible to spy from which direction danger threatened.

Scáthach had unslung her javelin and brought her shield round to protect her.

The cry came again, this time close, very close.

'What is it?' whispered Flann.

In the gloom two lights blinked. A dark shape gathered. It was a moment or two before Scáthach realised that the two blinking lights were baleful eyes staring at them. The dark shape was low on the ground and seemed to be hunching itself together.

Once again there came a low growling sound which rose to a terrifying scream, ending with the coughing bark.

Then the thing had launched itself towards them.

Ten

Scáthach was aware of the dark mass of muscle launching itself straight at her. She swung her shield round and brought her javelin into position just as the shape made contact. The force of the impact knocked the girl backwards to the floor. She had the presence of mind to keep her shield in front of her and felt the screech of rending talons, hard nails raking the metal of the protective covering.

Dimly, she heard a yell of dismay from Flann. She was aware that something was weighing on her javelin so that she could not use it. She let go, grabbing for her sword while trying to scramble away from the great weight which lay on her.

'It's all right,' came Flann's reassuring tone, 'the beast is dead. You stuck it with your javelin.'

The young warrior bent down and held out a hand to her. She heaved herself up and looked down. In the darkness she could not distinguish it and so she took off her helmet to look more closely at the creature.

She had seen wild-cats before but none as big and fearsome as this jet-black creature which lay stretched on the floor, her javelin piercing its body. A dark stain of blood was oozing from it while its fighting fangs, incisors of sharp yellow, were still bared for the death grip which she had just avoided.

Flann was frowning at the beast.

'A cat of some sort,' he said.

'True enough,' replied the girl, placing one foot on the carcass and using it as a lever to draw out her javelin. 'A nice house-guard this is. I wonder if our host has other such creatures about?'

'We must be on our guard from now on.'

Scáthach peered round the great cavern but nothing seemed to be stirring. She slung her helmet from her belt.

'Let's continue this way,' she said, moving onwards again.

They walked on in silence, passing the stacks of caskets and boxes and piles of booty which lay in dust-covered heaps. At the far end of the cavern they came to some steps cut in the stone leading upwards to a great wooden door.

Scáthach led the way, ascending them quickly.

A great iron ring handle worked the mechanism of the catch. It grated as she twisted it and swung the door open. Its hinges gave a protesting shriek.

The girl hesitated and listened for a moment.

'Come on, Flann,' she hissed. 'This must lead into the fortress itself.'

Flann followed silently.

They entered a corridor, a broad stretch of stone-block passage with only one door at the far end, another door of stout wooden beams fastened with large iron strips.

Scáthach reached out her hand to take the handle. It was a similar type to that which had been on the first door.

Her hand closed on the iron ring and twisted.

There was a shrill noise behind them. They turned just in time to see an iron grating drop from the ceiling of the passageway halfway along and give an echoing clang as it crashed to to the concrete of the floor.

With an oath, Flann had run back along the corridor and flung himself on the grating with violence. It did not budge, nor could he sense any movement as he tried to raise it.

'We're trapped,' he said unnecessarily.

Scáthach shook her head.

'It may only be a safety precaution for the mechanism seemed to work when I twisted the door catch.'

'Then try the catch again,' urged Flann.

The girl did so but made no impression on the grating.

'There is no way to go but forward,' she said.

Flann compressed his lips.

'Forward it is,' he said.

She swung open the door.

They were in a large hall, lit with flickering torches slotted in holders around the high, vaulted, granite walls.

Here and there a tapestry hung to alleviate the grey stone of the walls and ceiling. There was no furniture in the hall at all.

They moved on cautiously.

'Welcome!'

They started at the unexpected sound of a shrill human voice. It echoed in the chamber like a phantom sound.

They looked about.

It was Flann who spotted the window, high up on the far wall. He pointed. About fifteen feet above the level of the floor was an aperture about three feet by two. In it a figure stood looking down at them.

Scáthach's eyes narrowed.

The figure was that of a man of indeterminable age, completely bald with a white parchment-like skin. He was bent forward slightly and they could see that he was possessed of a crook-back making one shoulder higher than the other. He was clad in a black robe with a cowl but with the cowl flung back behind him. The features were deeply etched, the eye sockets sunken and dark as if the man were ill or had not slept for some time. The eyes themselves seemed to glow red, although this must surely have been a trick of the light. They moved restlessly, as watchful as terriers at a rat-hole. The red slits that were the man's lips were a thin hostile line.

'Who are you?' cried Scáthach.

The thin lips moved.

'I am Cruitín, lord of this fortress, lord of the valleys beyond.'

Flann eased his hand nervously to his weapon. He felt a cold sensation tingle on his spine as he viewed this merciless figure.

'And who are you, who dare enter my domain?'

Scáthach glanced at Flann and smiled encouragement.

'At least he is not omnipotent,' she whispered.

'What's that you say?' shrilled Cruitín.

'I am Scáthach of Uibh Rathach,' she shouted defiantly. 'I come with my companion, Flann Mac Fraech, to restore something you have stolen to its rightful owner.'

There came a trilling sound from the black-robed figure which made them frown until they realised that it was the sound of the man's laughter.

'Stolen? Rightful owner? These are concepts that I do not know.'

'Undoubtedly,' replied the girl firmly. 'The thief has no understanding of such concepts until he is visited by a thief.'

'And you come to steal from me?'

'No. There is a difference between what one seizes and what one really possesses.'

'You speak in riddles, girl.'

'You appear to make yourself rich by theft.'

'What is wrong in that? All property is theft from someone. And possession is truly the sweetest of emotions. The spirit of possession doubles a man's strength.'

Flann gave a bark of anger.

'There is a saying among my people, the Cruithne of Éireann: where there is no property there is no injustice.'

'And no pleasure nor joy,' added the dark figure. 'Yet I presume you are not of some holy order come to sermonise me and convert me to your hypocrisy and cant? You have stated that you come to rob me.'

'We have come to retrieve . . .'

'This conversation is pointless. You have trespassed on my hospitality for too long. Now you shall pay for your effrontery.'

With that the man vanished from his vantage-point.

Flann shot Scáthach a look of puzzlement.

There was a faint noise behind one of the tapestries. It moved. Abruptly there spilled into the hall four heavily-built warriors, armed with shields and swords, vicious-looking men with close-cropped hair and body scars which denoted they had survived numerous combats.

'Let's try Goibhniu's weapons,' cried Scáthach as she reached for her helmet, set it in place and grabbed for the sword, discarding her javelin for there was no room to use it in such a confined space against four attackers.

Flann was already engaging one of the warriors, who had rushed quickly upon him, obviously believing in surprise and weight to gain an easy victory. But the young man was not so readily overcome and stood his ground, exchanging blows.

Two of the attackers turned to Scáthach and hesitated, exclaiming in fear.

The helmet of Goibhniu appeared to work its strange aura, causing them to see the girl as some threatening vision.

Scáthach seized the opportunity by rushing on her numbed opponents and despatched one with her first sword thrust. The second one, screwing up his courage, began to engage her. It was obvious that he was not an unworthy swordsman for he had a quick blade and muscles to press home the attack. Scáthach, though never in real danger from the man's dexterous sword, was hard pressed to keep the man's attack away from her.

Flann was also finding his opponent to be of equal talent and it took some time before an opportunity presented itself to slip under the man's guard with a lightning thrust.

'Two against two is a more equal figure!' yelled Flann, seeking to detach the fourth warrior from sneaking up behind Scáthach in an attempt to take her by stealth.

The man swung round and they closed just as Scáthach was able to rid herself of her opponent.

The fourth man, seeing himself alone, relaunched his attack with desperation in spite of calls to surrender from both Flann and the girl. He only desisted from his fierce onslaught when Flann finally came in under his guard with a quick lunge.

Panting somewhat from their exertions, Scáthach and Flann stood back to back waiting and watching for a further attack. There was a silence. There was no sign of Cruitín at his window. Eventually it became obvious that the dark-cowled man had gone.

'What now?' gasped Flann.

'We find a way out of here to wherever the crook-back has hidden the lantern of Solas.'

'I don't think Cruitín would allow us to take it so easily,' Flann warned. 'He will be preparing something.'

Scáthach inclined her head in agreement.

'Be wary. Now let us find out how these warriors entered this hall.'

Flann gestured towards one of the tapestries.

'There must be a door behind that,' he said.

They moved to the wall and pulled aside the tapestry. A bare granite wall confronted them.

'I am sure that they emerged from behind this tapestry,' protested Flann.

'Perhaps through some secret door,' Scáthach muttered and began to tap her way along the wall.

'There!' cried Flann as her sword hilt began to resound hollowly.

Indeed, they could hear what must be a secret entrance into the hall but, try as they might, they could find no means of opening it, no mechanism, no spring to swing it open even a crack.

'This is hopeless,' muttered the girl, turning away. 'There must be some other method of exit.'

They explored all the walls behind the tapestries but the same stark granite faced them each time.

Scáthach turned to face the window from which Cruitín had gazed down on them.

'It seems that's our only route,' she murmured.

Then again they heard the faint sound from behind the tapestry. It billowed. They turned, crouching, their weapons to the fore, ready to face more of Cruitín's burly warriors. This time, however, something else spilled into the hall: something more evil and vicious than a horde of warriors.

Flann stepped back with a gasp.

A great twisting serpent spilled forward, its giant flat head raised, two bead-like eyes staring unblinkingly at them. Its maw was partially opened, showing tiny, sharp white teeth, between which flicked a long red thin tongue. It looped and rotated in great rings across the floor towards them, hissing as it came.

Scáthach's eyes narrowed as she measured the sinuous rolls of the serpent's body, muscles that could crush its opponents without effort.

Flann's jaw dropped in surprise as he saw the girl suddenly turn and run away down the hall.

He could not believe that Scáthach's nerve would fail her against this creature, frightening as it was. After all, she had withstood so many perils and now . . .

He felt stupid and guilty as he saw her pause and pick up her discarded javelin, turning back to his side.

In slow writhing motions, the creature edged nearer. Its raised head was about six feet from the floor, so large and muscular was it. Suddenly, without any warning, the giant flat head lunged for Flann. He tried to leap sideways, tripped and fell. He scrambled away, keeping firm hold on his sword and shield; away from the open, drooling maw. The creature raised itself to strike again. It was fully thirty or forty feet in length and like no other serpent that Scáthach or Flann had ever beheld.

'Flann!' cried the girl, as she saw the beast's head poised to launch an attack once more.

Flann was still on the ground trying to get up. This time he twisted round just as the serpent's head reached his body, and smashed out with his shield, hitting it against the nose. The impact caused the shield to buckle a little and throw the young warrior backwards. However, the impact must also have caused the creature some surprise and hurt. It recoiled back a moment and in that moment Flann scampered away and rose to his feet.

'There is a strength in this beast that I fear,' he called to the girl. 'Try to keep away from its jaws.'

'Have no fear, Flann,' replied Scáthach determinedly. 'Fear is your only enemy. In fear there is death.'

She moved forward now, javelin to the ready, shield raised to protect her body.

The serpent's attention was still on Flann and it slithered towards him once more.

Scáthach moved closer and pricked at its writhing coils with the tip of her javelin in order to distract its attention. It issued a tremendous hiss and its flat head moved, its black bead-like eyes searching for what had discomforted it.

Fixing its gaze on the girl, it turned its coils towards her.

It lashed out with its tail, almost catching her. She had nearly forgotten that such a creature was able to use both ends of its obscene body as weapons. She leapt aside and the tail went crashing into the wall, shaking the building and causing dust to rise and debris to fall about them.

The girl ran round, out of the range of the tail, and went towards the head.

The maw of the beast was twisted back in an almost evil parody of a grin, yet she realised the grin was but a product of nature's whims for the pleasure of an anticipated kill was a feeling produced in one species alone . . . man. Measuring the distance with her trained eye, she watched the movements of the creature's head as it swayed now and then from side to side, its mouth open and closing, hissing as it did so.

147

She, too, began to sway her body, in rhythm with the beast, feet firmly planted on the ground, but swaying to and fro, to and fro, until Flann wondered whether the girl was being mesmerised by the creature.

Then the creature struck, mouth open, incisors ready to catch on to its intended prey.

And it was then that Scáthach struck, pulling back her javelin and launching it with all the force she possessed. It flew straight and true into the open maw of the beast, right through the upper mouth, through its tiny brain and split the upper skull so that its blade appeared through the top of the head.

The thing gave a terrifying hiss and its great coils began to writhe and twirl like a massive whirlpool of muscle.

Scáthach turned.

'Get back, Flann,' she warned.

Together they ran for the passageway entrance by which they had come into the hall. While it was useless as a means of an exit because of the iron grill which now blocked off the passage, it was useful to act as a means of protection from injury by the terrifying threshing mass of the dying beast.

They stood, breathing heavily, watching the thing in its death throes. The brain had died but the body took a longer time to accept the fact of death. It twisted and lurched, smashing against the walls, causing dust and debris to fly everywhere, tearing down the tapestries.

Finally, all was quiet.

Flann rubbed his nose reflectively.

'I wonder what other means of protection this crook-back Cruitín employs?'

Scáthach grimaced with distaste.

'Truly did Bolga call him a lord of darkness. Come, Flann, we must find this lantern and shed some light on this valley of darkness.'

Flann nodded assent.

148

'However, we still have the same problem,' he pointed out. 'How to get out of this hall. I am somewhat glad we didn't find that secret door in case we entered and found that thing lurking behind it,' he gestured to the dead serpent.

The girl pointed to the window.

'As I said, there is our means of exit.'

'It's fifteen feet above floor level. Even if you stand on my shoulders, you should not reach it nor could I come with you even if you did.'

Scáthach moved to the carcass of the serpent and, using her sword, cut the javelin out of its skull.

She measured the height of the window and then the length of the hall with her eye. Finally, she made up her mind.

'Flann, help me clear the carcass of this beast aside,' she ordered, gripping the tail and hauling. It was a strenuous job to shift the great coils to the side of the hall.

'What are you going to do?' demanded Flann.

'One of the feats that my father, Eola, taught me was called the feat of the Salmon's Leap. He made me practise it many times until I perfected it.'

'I have not heard of such a feat,' Flann said.

'It was my father's speciality when he was a young warrior and few could emulate him. May the gods give me that ability now. Stand aside.'

Flann watched her in bewilderment while she went to the far end of the hall opposite the window and stood for a moment breathing deeply. She had slung her helmet and shield on her back and her sword as well. But she held her javelin like a pole in both hands before her. Then she raised herself on tip-toe and began to take some giant strides, increasing her pace, racing towards the wall until Flann thought she was going to smash into it, but then she stamped down the shaft of the javelin onto the flag stones, twisting her body, heaving it off the ground until she went up feet first, arching up.

Flann gasped.

Incredulously he watched as the girl sped through the air with what seemed ease, letting go of the javelin and curving up through the window and landing in a crouch on the other side of it.

The young warrior blinked in amazement.

'Are you all right?' he whispered, gazing up.

Scáthach's smiling face showed at the window.

'Had it been any narrower I might not have made it,' she confessed. 'Hand me up the javelin.'

Flann picked up the discarded javelin and handed it up to her. She took it.

'I'm in a corridor,' she said. 'I'll try to find something by which you can climb up.'

Indeed, beyond the window Scáthach stood in a fairly wide corridor of the same granite stones with which the hall was constructed. Torches burnt in their holders along its walls.

She gave a quick wave to Flann and moved off down the corridor. There were no doors leading off its long stretch until it turned at right angles and ascended by means of steps into another, wider and more brightly lit, passageway. Along here several tapestries hung and suddenly an idea came to the girl. The tapestries were hoisted on the walls by means of thick cords of silk and these were tied into position on hooks protruding from the walls. She drew her sword and slashed at them, causing one tapestry to drop to the floor. It was work of a moment to cut off the silken cords and tie them into a workmanlike rope which she judged to be long enough to reach the floor of the hall behind. Then she turned back to the window.

Flann was still waiting below.

'I have a makeshift rope,' she called. 'I'll find something to fix it with.'

The obvious thing was the iron holder for one of the torches of the corridor. She tied one end of the rope to it and threw her weight on it. It held firmly. The other end she threw from the window to the waiting Flann. In an instant the young warrior was beside her.

'Where now?' he asked.

'In search of the lantern,' she replied. 'This way.'

She headed off again to the right-angled turn and led the way along this corridor.

'There are plenty of rooms leading off here,' Flann pointed out. 'Which one would Bolga's lantern be in.'

Scáthach paused and bit her lip.

Then she closed her eyes and forced her body to relax. The soft voice of Buimech seemed to echo in her mind. 'When in doubt let your innermost instinct be your guide. Instincts do not betray you.'

She opened her eyes and gazed at the doors.

'Not here,' she said. 'This way.'

She led the way down the corridor, twisting and turning until it began to lead downwards again and finally ended at a small door.

Flann gazed at her dubiously.

'Here?'

She smiled.

'I feel that it is here,' she said, reaching for the handle and turning it.

The heavy wooden door swung open on its hinges. The room beyond was in total darkness. They could not see anything.

'Get a torch, Flann,' she commanded.

The young warrior turned along the corridor and took one of the firebrand torches from the wall.

It revealed a windowless chamber, small, no more than fifteen feet square. A small table stood in the centre and there was no other furniture in the room. On the table stood a silver lantern, attractively wrought with all manner of strange beasts carved into its casing. They saw that the lamp itself was visored by a piece of silver worksmanship which was held in place by hinges.

'The lantern of the lords of light,' whispered Scáthach.

Flann whistled in wonderment at the exquisite craftsmanship of it.

'Remember not to lift that visor,' he suddenly warned as Scáthach drew nearer. 'Bolga warned that if you lifted the visor from the lamp it would not only blind us but destroy all who gazed on it.'

'I remember,' the girl replied quietly.

There came a movement behind them.

Cruitín stood there, his parchment-like face twisted in an evil smile.

'Well, you are both warriors of excellent mettle to have reached thus far into my fortress of darkness,' he piped in his thin, reedy voice. 'You have slain my cat, four of my best warriors and the beast who guarded my hearth. For that, of course, you will pay. But before you do so, warriors, I offer you my respect for your accomplishment. It is good to have opponents worthy of contest.'

Flann moved forward, sword ready, but the crook-back held out a hand to him, pointing with one long finger, its nail long and dirty like a talon. The man said nothing but looked at Flann, simply frowning.

Flann hesitated and then dropped his sword point.

'Flann!' cried Scáthach in alarm as she saw the young warrior's face dissemble into a mask of utter misery.

'Black!' cried Flann. 'Despair! Nothing! There is no hope. No future.'

He dropped onto his knees and began to wail like a baby.

'What have you done to him?' demanded Scáthach.

Cruitín gave a shrill chuckle.

'I am the lord of darkness, all things dark and evil obey my command.'

The girl saw that Flann was totally under the evil one's spell. She tried to recall the teachings of Buimech. She used the druidic technique of meditation just as she felt the first waves of chill darkness emanate from Cruitín's mind towards her. Using all her willpower she forced out the waves of black despair which began to encompass her mind.

The evil one frowned as he felt the power of her mind.

'So? You are not like this one,' he gestured to the cowering Flann. 'You are possessed of the knowledge . . . yet, yet you are not of the knowledge. You have a weakness. What?'

Scáthach fought back the probing blackness. Sooner or later the evil one would discover her fear of the Place of the Dead, of monsters conjured from the shadows, of her childhood fears which she had yet to deal with.

Dimly she was aware of Flann cowering in a corner of the room sobbing; he was kneeling, his head turned into the corner, hands over his face, like a child.

The waves of cold blackness were sweeping over her. She fought hard, knowing that the moment her guard was down Cruitín's thoughts would overwhelm her and send her into the black pit into which he had sent Flann. She must hang on.

She must concentrate on something: on the smiling face of Buimech her mother. Buimech was trying to tell her something, tell her . . .

Fighting to keep the black tide of evil at bay, she turned to the table, towards the silver lamp which stood on it.

She reached for her helmet and took it off. It was a struggle, a slow procedure against the vibrations from the evil one who stood head bowed, concentrating his whole energy on overcoming her mind. It seemed that he was so intent that he had closed his mind to what she was physically doing, concentrating solely on the possession of her mind.

She turned her helmet back to front and put it back on her head so that the metal came down before he eyes, blinding her.

She moved to the lamp, standing behind it, and suddenly dropped to her knees behind the table. Closing her eyes tightly, she reached forward, feeling for the latch and hinges. Then she held her breath and opened the visor.

A terrible light sprung from the lamp. Even cowled as she was and with eyes tight-shut she was aware of a blinding flash.

Somewhere she heard a ghastly shriek.

She waited a moment more, feeling the light as overpowering as she had felt the blackness of Cruitín. Then she slammed back the visor and waited for several long breaths.

She heard a groaning sound but nothing else. The black waves which had tried to encompass her mind were gone.

Scáthach stood up, opened her eyes and took off her helmet.

Before the table Cruitín lay stretched on his back, one arm flung backwards, his eyes wide and staring. Across his parchment-like flesh the skin was blistered as if he had been terribly burnt. He was clearly dead. The girl turned to the corner where Flann had been. He was still on his knees groaning.

'Flann!' she cried in alarm. 'Are you all right?'

She bent down and raised his head.

He blinked several times before opening his eyes and trying to focus on her.

To her relief he finally was able to focus.

'The light . . .' he mumbled. 'The darkness . . .'

'Rest awhile. You are all right now,' she smiled comfortingly.

'What happened? There was a terrible blackness . . . Where is Cruitín?'

He made an attempt to rise but she held him back.

'The crook-back is dead.'

Suddenly, far off, Flann heard the ring of metal on metal; like three hammer blows. He frowned and gazed at Scáthach.

'What was that?' he demanded.

'What?' she asked puzzled.

He was about to explain when he recalled what Goibhniu had said.

'One day, and that day will soon be here, you will thank the gods for such conjuror's tricks . . . on that day you will hear a smith's hammer ring thrice to remind you of your doubt.'

A look of understanding crept across Flann's face and he swallowed at the realisation.

'You used the lantern?'

Scáthach nodded.

'And we may now take it to Bolga.'

Shaking his head, Flann climbed to his feet and ran a hand through his hair. He felt embarrassed.

'I was of little use to you, Scáthach.'

'That is the gloom of Cruitín talking. I could not have accomplished the task without you.'

'Yet I could not withstand his . . . his mind probe, while you could.'

'I was taught by Buimech, my mother,' replied the girl solemnly.

Flann pursed his lips.

'Gobhniu said that one day soon I would have reason to be thankful for a druid's magic.'

'Not magic, Flann,' corrected the girl. 'Knowledge. To those who do not have knowledge, many things seem like magic.'

She sighed a little, saddened at the shadow of resentment

155

on Flann's face, and turned to pick up the lamp. Then she realised that he had a warrior's pride, believing that there was nothing which was beyond his understanding. What saddened her more was the thought that he had a male pride which meant he felt it unseemly that knowledge held by a woman should be denied to him. She hoped that he did not feel that way for in that pride lay a foolish vanity which was the self-esteem of ignorance.

Meanwhile, Flann recovered his weapons and distastefully gazed down on the body of Cruitín. Then he shrugged and followed Scáthach from the room.

Eleven

The day was hot with scarcely a breeze whispering in the tall trees. The sky was blue and cloudless and the sun hung still and bright, high above the horizon. There was a silence in the woods as if all the animals had wisely decided it was too hot to expend energy and had found shady places to curl up to wait for a more cool period in which to hunt or scavenge for food. Now and then a sleepy cry of a bird was heard.

Three figures on horseback moved slowly along the forest pathway.

Scáthach led the way on a large, high-spirited white mare. It was fitted with a rich saddle and brightly decorated bridle and harness. Among the weapons slung across her slim shoulders were her sword, javelin and the fearsome spear of Bolga – the *gae-Bolga*. Her helmet was slung from the pommel of her horse and her sword was at her side. Behind her, on a roan, came Flann, while behind him Ruacán the Wizened rode a quiet black pony.

Bolga had been generous indeed when Scáthach and Flann had returned from the fortress of Cruitín the crook-back with the lantern of the lords of light. Not only had he kept his word to present the girl with the *gae-Bolga*, his fearsome hunting spear which made one wound when it entered the flesh but, once penetrated, would open thirty barbs so that it could not be withdrawn, but he had offered further gifts. The gifts of horses were his to enable their journey to Lethra to continue at a faster pace. He had fed and entertained them in his encampment and they had proceeded on the next morning with his words of praise echoing in their ears.

The three rode confidently now, more sure of themselves, their ability to face adversity and danger. Even Flann, though still suspicious of the druid Ruacán, seemed more at ease in his company and smiled a little more often than he had before. Ruacán was as enigmatic as ever, however, smiling softly as with a hidden knowledge. He was content now to let the others lead, offering words of advice only when consulted; content to follow in the rear. After all, Scáthach had now proved herself as a leader, as one equipped not only to fight with arms but to fight with her mind.

As for Scáthach, she was more self-assured now that she had come through her encounters with Goibhniu and Cruitín. She began to realise that the encounters had been a necessary part of her self-development. She was more poised, more secure in her faith in her own abilities.

She turned in her saddle and called back to Ruacán.

'The path divides ahead.'

The druid stretched out a frail hand.

'The left hand path, that is the one which leads into Lethra,' he replied. 'Through the mountain pass and we will be there before midday tomorrow.'

'At last,' breathed the girl. 'So near.'

Flann nudged his horse alongside the white mare.

'Do you have a plan when you come to Lethra?' he asked.

Scáthach shook her head.

'So far I have only thought about getting to Lethra. I suppose the next step is to find out what the mysterious symbols mean.' Her hand touched the golden medallion at her neck. 'They should lead me to what I seek.'

'Travellers ahead!' came a low warning cry from the druid.

Scáthach peered forward.

Ahead on the path, coming towards them, was a large wagon pulled by two oxen. A coarse-looking fat man in rough homespuns sat on the driver's seat pulling at the reins. Behind the wagon, on a worn-looking nag rode a middle-aged man more richly dressed although his clothes seemed to have seen better years.

'I'll go first,' Flann said, 'they seem to have come from Lethra and they might know something.'

Scáthach shrugged and allowed the eager young warrior to go trotting forward to greet the travellers.

Flann could see that the two men were obviously merchants of sorts. Their wagon was piled with furs and amphora and other items of trade.

'Greetings!' sung out the man on horseback. 'Greetings travellers. You are not taking the path to Lethra, by any chance?'

Intrigued, Flann halted.

'We are, indeed, stranger. Is that where you come from?'

The rider nodded. He was a tall, languid-looking man,

with a sharp clay-face and speculative eyes. He was as tall and white as his partner, who drove the wagon, was squat, plump and pink.

'We have indeed,' replied the rotund man on the wagon, anger in his voice. 'Bad cess to it!'

Flann stared in surprise.

'Why do you curse the place?'

'You must be a stranger to Lethra,' remarked the languid rider.

'That is so.'

'Then take our advice and turn aside from this path. It is an evil land,' he went on.

'Evil indeed,' echoed his companion. 'I spit on the ground at its name.' He suited the action to the word.

'You'd best explain yourselves,' Scáthach intervened, trotting up to hear their remarks.

'Why, easy enough . . .' began the tall rider, turning his attention to the girl.

Then a curious thing happened: his voice caught in his throat as he stared at her. First, it seemed that his eyes were riveted by the gold medallion and then, unwillingly, they travelled to the girl's face. Then the eyes began to bulge and he started to stammer. His companion seemed likewise afflicted.

'Lady, forgive us . . .' stammered the fat one. 'We meant no harm . . . no harm.'

Suddenly the tall man had urged his horse aside from the path and was galloping down the trail which turned off from the main road to Lethra. Yelling and urging the oxen into a shambling trot, the fat man was almost comical in his attempts to emulate his companion.

Flann sat in his saddle staring at their departure in disbelief.

'Shall I overtake them?' he demanded, realising that his mount could easily outdistance the pair.

Scáthach shook her head, bewildered.

'They are scared. But why? Do you know what this means, Ruacán?'

The old druid trotted near.

'It means that there is some evil in Lethra which frightens merchants,' he said simply.

Flann scowled.

'That much we can deduce for ourselves. But what is the evil?'

'Ah.'

The druid hunched his shoulders and let them fall.

'Let's go on,' urged Scáthach, moving her horse forward. Flann hesitated, glanced at the bland face of Ruacán, sighed and followed. The druid brought up the rear again.

They entered a long narrow valley, as dark as the valley of Bolga before they retrieved the lantern of the lords of light. They began to near its end as night began to fall and so they agreed it was best to halt and camp before journeying further. Dark shapes of bats swooped among the forest branches uttering their piercing shrilling sound. Owls moaned softly in the trees and the rustle of nocturnal creatures disturbed the underbrush. It was not a pleasant place to camp; even the pool by which they lit their fire gave forth inexplicable splashes every now and then as if some water creature were watching them. They ate sparsely and slept fitfully. Scáthach was pleased that she had Flann and Ruacán as companions. She tried not to show her nervousness for the place reminded her of the Place of the Dead. However, the hours of darkness passed without incident. The dawn came and they were up early and moving on.

The sun made a difference, chasing away the gloom and foreboding of the night. They rode out of the tenebrous forest and across a small grassland plain away from the mountains. Halfway over this plain, on either side of the pathway, stood two poles on which appeared to be some totems or symbols. It wasn't until they came near to them that they saw that the totems were whitened human skulls.

Scáthach shivered slightly. What land would mark a welcome by setting up skulls on sharpened stakes to indicate its borders?

Ruacán said, perhaps unnecessarily for both Scáthach and Flann had realised the import of the signs: 'This is the land of Lethra.'

'We must be careful, Scáthach,' Flann said, peering around him while loosening his sword in its scabbard. 'I do not like the way the people of this land greet strangers.'

'We will follow the path and see where it leads us,' the girl replied.

They rode on, following the straight path across the short plain and ascending it as it twisted into the low hills beyond.

They were moving through a narrow defile, cut through a chalk-like hill, when three warriors came round a bend. Before they could react with a greeting, the three men had drawn their swords and, with angry cries, rode full tilt at them.

Flann, who was slightly ahead, met the brunt of their attack, his sword ready, for he had been nervously easing it in his scabbard ever since they crossed the boundary of Lethra. Scáthach had time to clamp her helmet on her head and draw her sword before she went to his aid. The two of them went into skirmish laying out left and right. The fearsome-looking helmet caused the attackers to hesitate as they beheld it but they overcame their dread and continued the attack. It took only a few moments for the three attackers to realise that they had met their match and they were soon pulling back. In answer to a cry from one of their number, who appeared to be the leader, they all turned and fled from the scene.

Flann was about to follow when Scáthach stayed him with a quick word.

She was sitting astride her mount, her helmet in her hand, frowning as if deep in thought.

'What is it?' demanded Flann.

'Did you see the triskele symbols on the shields of those warriors who attacked us?' asked the girl.

'Indeed I did.'

She held out her gold medallion. Flann realised that they were the same.

'That is the symbol that I am seeking. The symbol on this medallion. That is the symbol on the casket in which I was cast into the sea to drown when I was a baby. That is the symbol on the shields of the men who attacked Uibh Rathach and slew my father Eola.'

Ruacán rode nearer.

'Then what does that tell you, my child?' he said, smiling softly.

Scáthach frowned for a moment.

'It tells me that the mariner, Rónán Mac Méin, was correct when he estimated that Lethra was where the casket must have come from.'

'Indeed, it confirms that your search should end in Lethra.'

'But why would those warriors attack us?' demanded Flann.

'Why would the owner of the symbol they wear attempt to kill a young child and then attack the fortress of those who had fostered that child?' intervened Ruacán.

'We must track down those warriors to find out,' Flann asserted.

Scáthach agreed.

Once more they rode on, following the winding track through the hills. Now they began to come on isolated farmsteads and here and there a village. At each place the reception was the same. Those who showed themselves at their approach hung their heads in cowed or surly attitude never once raising their gaze to the faces of the three. Once, a couple working in the field through which they were riding stared up, saw Scáthach and, to their astonishment, fled just as the merchants had done.

For a moment, Scáthach wondered whether she was unwittingly wearing the helmet which Goibhniu had made which was reputed to make her enemies see a terrible vision. But she was not wearing the helmet. Why, then, were the people running from her in alarm?

Finally, they came to a tavern and halted. It was a poor enough place, not like the rich hostels of Éireann. There was an atmosphere of dreariness; many of the windows were unglazed and there was only a thin column of smoke, more like the smoke of a candle than a fire, trickling from the chimney. Still, smoke meant a fire and fire meant warmth and food. They felt the need to break their journey and, if at all possible, to gain some information.

They dismounted and entered the musty-smelling tavern room. The fire was, indeed, frugal, a few sticks of dampened wood smoking in the hearth. It seemed deserted but Flann's imperious cry brought forth an ageing man who was bent double. He was unshaved, and unkempt, his eyes never left the floor, and his manner was nervous.

'Yes, yes, masters,' his voice cackled wheezily. 'What can I do to serve you?'

'Food and ale,' demanded Flann.

'Ale we have but our stock of food is poor. Our last cow was taken to pay taxes and, alas, we have nothing but oatmeal. A bowl of oatmeal I could serve you.'

Flann exchanged a glance with Scáthach.

'This is a strange tavern, a tavern without food?' commented the young warrior.

'Indeed, master. Indeed, but our taxes are so heavy

and . . .' he shrugged. 'I do not complain, master. Do not think I intend criticism.'

'This is a soulless land,' sighed Flann.

The old man chanced a quick glance at him, immediately dropping his eyes again to the floor.

'Are you strangers in Lethra, masters?' he asked.

'This is the first time we have come to your country, old man,' agreed Flann.

'Then you do not know how things are here.' The old man sighed deeply as if with the pain of long suffering.

'Tell us,' invited Flann, 'but first bring us that ale. Three cups of your ale.'

The old man shuffled off to obey while the three sat at a dust-covered table.

'What ails this country?' whispered Scáthach to Ruacán.

The old druid shrugged.

'That, I believe, you will find out.'

The hosteler returned with the cups of ale, but it was a bitter, cheerless brew and it did not slack their thirst.

'Now, what ails this land of Lethra,' pressed Flann.

'Well, master,' began the old man, suddenly giving another of his bird-like glances at Flann, but this time his glance fell on the medallion worn by Scáthach and he raised his pale eyes to her face. He whitened, his jaw dropped. For a moment or two he started to trembled. It was with a great effort that he seemed to recover himself. Once more his gaze fell to the floor.

'Well?' snapped Flann.

'I am sorry, master,' mumbled the man unhappily.

'You were about to say what ailed this country of yours.'

The man shuffled his feet.

'Ailed it? Why, nothing ails it, master. Lethra is the greatest country under the sun. We have a glorious leader who gives us joy when she journeys among us.'

He turned and shuffled off quickly leaving them staring after him.

Suddenly his head shot out from behind the door.

'There is no charge for the ale, masters. No charge.'

Then his head disappeared and they were left alone.

'By the sons of Míle,' breathed Flann, 'now this is a curious place.'

Scáthach smiled ruefully.

'I am inclined to agree with you,' she assented. 'What do you say, Ruacán?'

The old druid shrugged.

'You will get no information from the tavern keeper. We must press on until we can find someone who will provide the information you seek.'

The girl nodded.

'Logical enough.'

Flann stared distastefully at his ale.

'This is undrinkable. If this is all that is left tavern keepers to provide for travellers after the ruler of this country takes their taxes then it is a poor place indeed.'

Scáthach stood up.

'Let's ride on then.'

For some hours they rode on until, passing by a small copse, Scáthach managed to bring down a rabbit with a quick cast of her javelin. They halted and lit a fire. A fresh, sparkling stream nearby offered them crystal cold water to drink. It was a pleasant enough meal.

They were resting when the snap of a twig announced that they were not alone. Through the underbrush came a large, red-faced man; he carried a short sword, and a bow, with a quiver of arrows at his belt.

'What is this?' he demanded, staring at them. 'Poachers on the domain of the High One?'

'We are no poachers,' replied Flann, scrambling to his feet indignantly. 'Indeed, we did not know that this copse belonged to anyone. We are three travellers wanting food and drink. The taverns of this land seem unable to provide either. A poor country for travellers indeed.'

'So you thought you would help yourself by poaching? Thieves!' sneered the gamekeeper, for they had decided that such the man must be.

Scáthach moved forward, she had been standing partially behind Flann.

'We are not thieves,' she said softly.

The red-faced man stared at her a moment. If anything his face grew redder, his eyes bulged. He opened his mouth and made some inarticulate sounds.

'What ails you, man?' snapped Scáthach.

'No ... nothing, lady,' stammered the man, his eyes dropping to her medallion and a low groan escaping his lips. 'Forgive me, I did not see you there otherwise I would not have been so bold.'

Flann exchanged a puzzled look with Scáthach.

'What do you mean, man?' he asked.

The red-faced gamekeeper dropped to one knee, doffing his game.

'Forgive me, Aífe,' he muttered.

Scáthach's frown deepened.

'Aífe?' she queried. 'What manner of address is this?'

The gamekeeper, hearing the displeasure in her voice, shied like a nervous horse.

'I did not mean offence, High One. I meant not to be so familiar nor bold. Have pity on me.'

'Fellow,' interrupted Flann, 'you are speaking in riddles.'

'Forgive me, lord,' he scrambled to his feet and began to back away nervously. 'Forgive me for disturbing your meal, the fruits and meat of the forest are yours ... indeed, yours is the right to eat freely of anything the world provides.'

166

He turned and fled as he was still speaking so that the last words were caught faintly from across his shoulder.

'Hi!' yelled Flann, astonished at the fellow's behaviour.

But the man had vanished.

The young warrior turned with a frown to Scáthach.

'Is it my imagination or are all the people in this country mad?'

'Not mad, my son,' Ruacán interrupted, 'but it seems that many mistake Scáthach for someone else.'

Scáthach smiled.

'Of course, what a slow fool I am, to be sure. But who do they take me for? This person, Aífe?'

Flann cracked his fist into the palm of his hand.

'Indeed! And this Aife seems to be a person of power. They must think all women warriors are like this Aife who rules over them. Strange, though, how they give rank to people. Never have I heard such terms spoken in such profusion before – lord, lady, master, High One. Do people truly speak in such terms to others? In Éireann no man bows his neck before another man. Why, we are all the sons and daughters of kings.'

'It is truly a strange custom, Flann,' agreed Scáthach. 'I have never known its like. Have you heard of such customs, Ruacán?'

The old druid nodded.

'Alas, I know that not all people believe as we do. Among our people, every office is open to election, from the most petty chieftain to the all-powerful High King of Éireann. Only the most worthy in our society are elected to these offices and under our Brehons, the judges, no one can become negligent or despotic. But, alas, some societies are primitive and believe that there is such a thing as inheritance, a law of primogeniture, that the first born must inherit the estate of his father, that is the office of a king or his property.'

Flann gave a grimace of disbelief.

'This I find hard to believe. How can one inherit property for a start?'

Ruacán shrugged.

'Some societies do not hold land as we hold land. They do not believe in the common ownership of land run by the clan and governed by the clan assembly and chieftains. Some societies believe that individuals can own land.'

The young warrior shook his head.

'But that is ridiculous. An individual can work the land but by the consent of the clan. No person can *own* land nor even dispose of his cattle or sheep without the common permission of the clan.'

'There are some places where this happens, my son,' the druid pressed. 'And in those places some believe that if your father was a king, then it is your right also to be king and rule the people as your father.'

'You say "father" and not "mother",' observed Scáthach.

The druid nodded.

'Indeed. In those societies, too, some believe that women are not equal to men either in office or in property. In some places women do not inherit property nor take office. Nor are they even allowed a voice at the clan assembly.'

The girl laughed.

'You are joking, old man.'

Ruacán shook his head sadly.

'No. That is the way of some societies.'

'But it is nonsensical,' Flann intervened. 'You say, because someone's father was king, then, by right, they become kings? Yet what if they are unfit to be king? What if their minds are unbalanced, what if they are not capable of pursuing the commonwealth of the people? What if they are evil or despotic? What of those things?'

Ruacán shrugged.

'Under the law of some societies, they are still allowed to be king, still allowed to rule.'

'I never heard the like,' Flann said, still disbelieving. 'No man or woman should claim such office simply because their father, or, indeed, their mother, held such office before them. To do so is to ensure that the people are poorly led by tyrants who will not strive to promote the common good. A leader can only lead when the people desire him or her to do so.'

Scáthach was reflective for a moment.

'Are you saying, Ruacán, that this land of Lethra is such a place where these forms of government pertain?'

'Look around you, Scáthach,' invited the old druid. 'See how the people cower and are fearful of the approach of strangers? Hear the language they use? It is the language of slaves.'

Flann whistled softly.

'It is a strange world where people allow such government. May the gods safeguard the freedoms we have in Éireann.'

Ruacán smiled wryly.

'So, you have prayers for the gods now, Flann Mac Fraech?'

Flann coloured slightly.

'It is just an expression of speech, old man,' he said irritably.

'We should be continuing our journey,' Scáthach intervened anxiously.

'Indeed,' Flann assented at once. 'We must also find out who this Aífe is and why you are mistaken for her.'

They saddled their mounts and set off again. The countryside was bare of crops and they saw many a field and homestead burnt, the remains charred and blackened. As before, few people who saw them in the distance stayed to welcome them, and some that did hung their heads and would not gaze on the travellers, answering their questions in monosyllables. No one would answer their questions fully or comprehensibly.

169

Finally, they stopped a child who was playing in the ruins of a stone farmhouse. It was a fair-haired boy about seven years of age, with blue eyes wide with innocence and a ready smile. He seemed out of the usual mould of children they had seen in the country and when Flann accosted him he came forward with a broad smile on his open features.

'Hello?' he greeted, staring at them solemnly, each in turn.

'Hello, boy,' smiled Scáthach, edging her horse forward to speak to him. 'What's your name?'

'I am called Dias.'

'Well, then, Dias, answer me this: why did you not run away when you saw us coming?'

The boy smiled and shrugged.

'Why should I?'

Scáthach chuckled.

'No reason. It's just that most people in this land do.'

'They are silly then.'

'Indeed they are. But do you know why it should be?'

'No. People from here are like that.'

It was Ruacán who caught this subtle inflexion in the child's voice.

'You are not from Lethra, then?'

'No. But my mother is. That is why we are here. She has been away many years and wanted to come back to see her father. I have never been here before.'

'Ah,' Flann was obviously disappointed by the information. He had been hoping to gain some news about the strange country.

'Tell me,' pressed Scáthach, 'do you know who Aífe is?'

'Of course,' replied the boy immediately.

The three exchanged a look.

'Who?' demanded Flann.

'She is the High One and . . .'

'Dias!'

A woman came from behind the ruins and grabbed at the child.

'Haven't I told you never to speak with strangers here? Come!'

She turned, and although Scáthach called to her to halt she simply shouted back over her shoulder, 'We are strangers here. We know nothing!' Then she was gone among the ruins.

Flann glanced at Scáthach.

'At least we have found out who Aífe is. But that doesn't seem to help us.'

'Let's go on,' the girl sighed.

Towards evening they came to a river which provided an ideal place to camp. A clump of trees gave shelter while the river gave fresh water and the leaping salmon were quickly speared for supper. It was a pleasant enough evening and the food was good. They sat for a while around the fire discussing the strange land in which they found themselves and asking Ruacán to expound more on his knowledge of how other peoples of the world governed themselves.

Finally they turned in and sleep overtook them immediately.

How long he had been asleep he did not know. However, Flann Mac Fraech came half awake in the darkness, bathed in sweat and with his heart beating rapidly. He wondered what had disturbed him. He lay listening for a moment or two before realising that he was listening to a low, long, sobbing moan . . . a wail of despair and desolation. It grew fainter and fainter as if someone was being carried away into the distance. Flann Mac Fraech now came fully awake.

Twelve

Flann sat up and gazed around the encampment. The first thing he noticed was that Ruacán was missing. His bed roll was still stretched beside the fire but of the old druid there was no sign. Frowning, Flann rose and reached for his sword. It was dark, very dark. The fire had died down to mere embers and cast little light. He saw that Scáthach appeared to be still sleeping soundly and he moved carefully over to her and touched her gently on the shoulder.

She did not move.

He drew his brows together and shook her, this time more roughly, and hissed: 'Scáthach!' in her ear. 'Scáthach, wake up. All is not well.'

There was no movement. Her breathing was deep, perhaps a little too deep for normal sleep? He shook her for a third time. Her body rolled limply this way and that as if she had no control over it. Not even her eyelids flickered. Truly, he realised with horror, she must have been drugged.

Compressing his lips, Flann gazed around. He could see nothing in the darkness.

Where was Ruacán? Had the old druid betrayed them in some way? But why? For what?

Once more he heard the soft moaning sound from far off.

He rose from the recumbent form of Scáthach, turned and set off in the direction of the sound.

An early morning breeze was now rising through the trees and above them the clouds were being chased across the sky. Now and then the silver disc of the moon shone momentarily through the clouds, lighting the woods and casting strange pale shadows.

Flann had not gone far before he heard whispered voices. He paused and listened, trying to catch the sense of the sounds.

'May the Fomorii take the accursed object . . .' A voice came clearly from nearby. 'How can we muffle it?'

'Wrap your cloak over it,' came another voice.

'Why should Aífe want such a thing anyway? It is unnatural.'

Flann crept closer and saw three warriors crouched around something which lay between them, something which let forth a pitiful moaning sound.

'It was your idea to rob the woman of this,' one of them was saying to a fellow. 'Let us get on the right side of Aífe, you said. She would like the shield and spear carried by the stranger woman.'

The other man grimaced.

'We would have had them earlier had you not fled when we sought to attack them.'

Flann's eyes narrowed.

So these were the three warriors who had attacked them earlier! What were they crouching over? What was it that was moaning softly. Surely it was not Ruacán? But who else could it be?

The moon shone momentarily and by its ethereal silver light he saw Scáthach's shield on the ground with the *gae-Bolga*, her terrible spear, next to it.'

For a moment he felt a strange tingling against the nape of his neck. The shield was moaning! What was it the old druid had said? This was *An Seancholl Snidheach*, the strong-ridged hazel, given to the ocean god by The Dagda, father of the gods. And it was said that the shield could shriek a warning when its owner was in danger. Could the shield truly be moaning? Or was it some odd trick of the morning breeze?

He shook his head in wonderment and then realised that whatever the magical accomplishments of the shield, the three were thieves for they must have stolen the shield and spear while Scáthach lay sleeping. Indeed, perhaps they had drugged Scáthach in order to steal the weapons from her. There seemed no other explanation.

Anger flared in him. Raising his sword, without any preamble, he made a sudden dash at them, scattering them in all directions in a sudden onslaught. They went with cries of alarm at the unexpectedness of the attack.

'Thieves!' roared Flann, swinging round, sword at the ready.

Two of the strange warriors recovered from their fright almost immediately and came back to him with drawn swords, engaging his attention. They thrust and parried his attack and, after a moment or two, Flann realised he had been foolish to attempt to engage them on his own. And, in his anger, Flann did not perceive the third warrior creeping round behind him in the gloom, moving cautiously towards his back. Only a momentary realisation of something hard striking the back of his skull registered with him before he crashed into a dark, velvet-lined pit.

When he came too his first conscious sense was of a blinding, bright light. He groaned and tried to raise a hand to ward it off. Sharp stabbing pains in his head, like tiny dagger pricks, made him groan again. He dimly heard a woman's voice say: 'He is awakening. See what he has to say, Droch.'

He blinked and tried to open his eyes.

It took several efforts to focus. He became conscious that he was lying on a couch or bed, upholstered in soft cushions covered in silk. Then he took in the fact that he was in a room. Such a room he had never seen before. It was a fairly large room, though not too large, made, it seemed, entirely of marble with multi-coloured veins running through its creamy surfaces. Here and there colourful tapestries hung and rich ornaments stood. To one side of the room, a series of arches, supported on intricately carved and fluted columns, gave access onto a patio or verandah beyond which was a cloudless blue sky and brilliant sun.

A man hovered into his vision.

Flann blinked again and stared up.

'Where am I?' he demanded.

The man was elderly, bald yet with tufts of white hair above his ears. He wore a robe of saffron colour with a silver half-moon disc, on which was inscribed a familiar triskele pattern, hanging around his neck.

'Drink,' the elderly man ordered, ignoring his question. He held out a small cup of gold towards Flann.

'What is it?'

'Something to take away the pain, warrior,' replied the man, placing a hand behind Flann's head and raising it so that he could drink. The liquid was of a syrupy consistency, tasting sweet as he drank but leaving him with a bitter taste in his mouth.

'Lie back a minute and you will feel better.'

'Where am I?' demanded Flann again. 'What happened?'

The elderly man smiled.

'You will have the answers all in good time. First things first. Who are you?'

Flann felt the little stabbing pains receding in his head.

'I am Flann Mac Fraech,' he said, reaching up to massage his brow.

'Ah. You are of Éireann?'

'I am of the Cruithne of Éireann,' confirmed Flann, wondering at the ease with which the pain had receded.

'And what brings you to Lethra?'

Memory had come back now and Flann tried to struggle up.

The elderly man reached forward and placed a hand, which was surprisingly strong, on his chest, pushing him back on the couch.

'Stay still. You are too weak to move yet.'

'Who are you?' Flann demanded.

'I am Droch, adviser to the High One.'

'High One?' Flann tried to remember where he had heard the title before but his head ached abominably and he could not remember for the moment.

The old man, Droch, did not amplify.

'What are you doing in Lethra?' he demanded.

Flann pulled a face.

'Information for information,' he replied. 'Where am I?'

'You are in the fortress of the High One, the ruler of Lethra.'

Memory came back. Of course, the High One was Aífe, the person who Scáthach was mistaken for. So Aífe was the ruler of Lethra? No wonder people were scared of Scáthach's presence. But it was strange that they had not realised that Scáthach was not their ruler when they saw her up close.

'And how came I here?' he demanded.

'You were captured by members of the bodyguard to the High One.'

'Ah! The three thieves who tried to make off with the shield and spear of . . .' the young warrior bit his tongue and stared at Droch. 'Yours is a strange land where travellers are attacked and robbed by the bodyguard of your ruler. I demand to see your ruler.'

Droch smiled thinly.

'So you shall, Flann Mac Fraech. But all in good time. Why are you travelling in Lethra and who are your companions?'

Flann's expression became stubborn.

'I want an explanation for this transgression of the laws of hospitality.'

Droch threw back his head and laughed.

'Laws of hospitality? You are not in your land of Éireann now. Here we recognise no such laws. Our law is expediency, warrior of the Cruithne.'

'Then I am come among barbarians,' Flann replied angrily. 'I will say no more until I see your so-called "High One".'

Droch sighed.

'So be it. The High One is not as patient as I am.'

He rose from the couch and stared down a moment.

'I would have more respect in the presence of the High One, warrior of Éireann.'

Flann twisted his mouth into a sneer of distaste.

Droch shrugged and left the room.

No sooner had he done so than Flann swung himself from the couch. A spasm of dizziness almost immediately overcame him. He shook his head and tried to pass it off. He was certainly weak. He reached for his belt and then shrugged ruefully. It would have been too much to ask for his captors to have left him sword or dagger. He eased himself from the couch and stood, swaying for a moment. Then he moved carefully through the arches.

The verandah beyond proved to be a balcony. It was several storeys above the ground while below, in a court-yard, warriors idled or strolled. Even if he could lower himself down, he could not contend with all of them. He frowned, noticing that all the warriors carried shields with the peculiar triskele symbol which had interested Scáthach. On all sides great buildings towered, brilliant white in the sunlight. Flann had never seen such a rich and prosperous-looking city before.

He could see great circular areas of cut grass on which white stone benches stood. There was one immediately in front of the building in which he stood and in its very centre stood a monolith, about twelve feet in height and four feet wide. It was square in section and, at first sight, plain. In colour it was golden and Flann realised, with a gasp, that the metal was gold. The artifact must be priceless. He could see dark shadows on it and realised that it was inscribed, but for what purposes he had no idea at all.

Some of the warriors stood on the circular green, weapons to hand. Yet Flann could see no women, nor children nor other people than the armed men.

Here and there, through the magnificent white buildings, he could see a glimpse of avenues, mostly deserted. It was a city that resembled no other to his experience for the lack of people, only the warriors, made it a place of mystery and sinister foreboding.

'Impressive, isn't it?' asked a familiar voice behind him.

He swung round, his eyes widening.

'Scáthach!' he cried in dismay. 'So they have captured you as well?'

The girl stood, looking momentarily unfamiliar in a gown of white silk, embroidered in golden thread and jewels. It was unlike her usually utilitarian warrior's costume. She frowned a moment, uncertainly, and then smiled at him.

'As you see, Flann.'

Flann's mind was working now, remembering his waking, of the girl being drugged and Ruacán missing.

'Was it the old druid?' he demanded, angrily, moving forward to where she stood. 'Did Ruacán betray us?'

The girl shrugged indifferently.

'You know the ways of druids,' she said.

Flann bit his lip in anger.

'I warned you I would never trust a druid.'

'No, my love,' smiled the girl softly. 'That is as it should be.'

Flann drew his brows together and stared at the girl, suddenly perplexed.

'What?'

Scáthach countered his bewildered expression with a smile which Flann could only describe as lascivious rather than alluring.

'What is it?' she asked. 'Something troubles you.'

'You called me – "my love". You have never called me that before.'

The girl shrugged as if it were a matter of no importance.

'Well, if I have not, I have thought it.'

She turned back into the room with Flann following her in bewilderment.

'Tell me, Flann, did you tell them anything?' the girl asked.

Flann shook his head.

'Nor will I. The man, Droch, questioned me and promised the ruler, whom he calls the "High One", will question me later. Remember that people we met confused you with someone called Aífe? She is the High One.'

'But you have not told him your purpose in Lethra?'

Flann was puzzled.

'My purpose? My purpose is to aid you in your quest.'

The girl nodded hurriedly.

'That is what I mean. Of course.'

'Scáthach . . .'

Flann hesitated. There was something wrong, something strange about the girl's behaviour, something odd and he could not put his finger on it.

'Yes, my love?' she smiled again at him with an alluring gesture which rang false.

He moved towards the girl. She came to him willingly

enough, reaching up and stretching her arms around his neck, her mouth eagerly searching his.

When he drew back, breathless and surprised at her forward behaviour, for the girl had always been reserved, he could not resist the strange, worrying notion that something was not right. And it was then he realised what it was. He was an absolute fool! How slow his mind must be working. No wonder Scáthach was confused by people with Aífe, the High One!

He thrust the girl from him almost roughly.

'What magic is this?' he breathed.

She placed his finger between her red lips, nibbling it gently and coquettishly.

'It is no magic, my love. Come, do not treat me so.'

Flann gazed at her realising just how different her manner was from Scáthach's. It was something about the way she carried herself. The girl seemed voluptuous, and even physically there was a difference for her figure was a little fuller, her lips pouted in a lascivious smile, there was, somehow, a gross seductiveness about her. The clear bold eyes of Scáthach were now sultry and speculative.

He swallowed hard.

'You are not Scáthach of Uibh Rathach!' he cried.

The girl raised her head and laughed.

'If I am not, who am I who looks so much like her?'

'I am not sure, but you are not her!'

For a moment the girl's eyes blazed in fury and he saw her fighting to control herself. It took a moment to win the battle. She made an attempt at an alluring smile. It seemed only a mask now.

'How can you be so cruel to me, Flann? Do you not love me?'

She pouted at him.

'I love Scáthach of Uibh Rathach!' he said fiercely, realising, as he spoke, that it was the first time he had admitted the feeling even to himself.

'And I am not Scáthach?'

'You are Aífe, the High One of Lethra. How you are able to look like Scáthach, I do not know. How you obtained her image is beyond my comprehension but this I know . . . you are not Scáthach.'

The girl frowned a moment and then shrugged with indifference.

'You are perceptive, Flann Mac Fraech.' Her voice had hardened abruptly. There was merely a trace of Scáthach's voice in it, but only a trace. This was a much harder, more calculated tone. 'But little good your perception will do you now. Droch!'

At once the elderly man in the saffron robes appeared and bowed obsequiously before her.

'How can I serve you, most High One?' he genuflected.

Flann compressed his lips in amazement.

So this was, indeed, the ruler of Lethra! Yet she was the double of Scáthach! How could this be?

The girl who looked so much like Scáthach gave an impatient wave at the man to rise.

'I have learnt the purpose of these strangers. We must prepare to travel to the fortress of my brother. The day which was foretold has come at last. We must prepare immediately.'

Droch looked concerned.

'But with this warrior caught, there is only the girl and the old druid,' he protested. 'Surely we will not fly from them? Let me send out men to capture them. Why, we can put a thousand warriors into the field against them. It is unlike you to fly from danger.'

The High One stamped her foot in anger.

'Fool! The girl is Scáthach of Uibh Rathach and you know well what was prophesied. We must seek aid from my brother. He knows what may be done.'

'Yet not only have we captured her companion, this

young warrior, but we have taken her shield and spear, the ones that you say have magic properties.'

Aífe gave a bark of laughter.

'Shields and spears are nought compared with the prophecy. Enough talk, Droch. Make arrangements for your journey to the Island of Shadows.'

Droch bowed his head.

'And what of this warrior? Shall I have him slain?'

Flann tensed himself. If he were to die he would take Droch with him. But the girl sighed impatiently.

'Have him brought along,' the High One said, a sneer in her voice. 'He may yet be helpful as a pawn to bargain with if all else fails. Come, we have not a moment to lose.'

Droch stood aside as she swept out and then signalled two warriors to enter.

'It is your lucky day, warrior,' he smiled at Flann. 'Bind him and bring him to the ship,' he ordered, before following the High One.

Flann tried to struggle but the warriors, with deft hands as ones used to performing the task, swiftly had him trussed and one of them produced a blindfold, shutting out his vision. Still attempting to struggle he was dragged across the room. A voice whispered sibilantly in his ear.

'You can go conscious, warrior, or unconscious. It matters not to me.'

Flann stopped struggling. Better to remain conscious and try to find a means of escape than not.

He heard Droch's voice ordering: 'Take him to the ship. We will catch the morning tide.'

He frowned.

Why were these people so afraid of Scáthach? Where were they taking him? How could the High One assume the exact likeness of Scáthach? What was the nonsense about a prophecy? How could he let Scáthach know what had befallen him? His mind was tumbling with questions but no answers came readily to ease his cascading thoughts. He had to resign himself to being dragged along towards whatever fate awaited him.

Scáthach came to her senses being roughly shaken awake by Ruacán. She had a terrible headache and felt her mind was clouded in a mist.

'Wake up, daughter of Eola,' cried the old druid.

She shook her head and rose on one elbow, peering around unsteadily.

It was light and, by the height of the sun in the sky, fairly late in the morning. She had never slept so late before.

'What is the matter, Ruacán?' she yawned.

'Our camp was attacked during the night,' the druid replied.

Scáthach was wide awake now, sitting up and looking round.

'Why didn't I wake? What do you mean?'

Ruacán's face was troubled.

'I awoke to find some strange warriors in the camp. One of them was bending over you, sprinkling some powder on your face. I rose to cry out but was hit on the head. I only came too a moment or so ago. I had been dragged behind some bushes away from the camp.'

'Are you all right?' asked the girl.

The druid smiled.

'I have an old skull but a thick one. But you were drugged. Let me mix you a potion to rid your head of the ache.'

Scáthach was searching the encampment with her eyes.

'And Flann? What of him?'

The girl rose suddenly realising that the young warrior was not in the camp. She was angry with herself for thinking of the young warrior last. But as she rose, the pain in her head was so great that she would have fallen had not the old druid caught her and forced her to sit down again. While he prepared a potion, mixing some herbs with hot water from the pot on the fire, he spoke.

'I think he must have tried to stop the warriors and they took him away as a prisoner. I found signs of a struggle a little way away. Also, your shield and the spear, the *gae-Bolga*, are missing.'

Scáthach peered round, checking the truth of the druid's statement.

'Who could have done this thing?' she demanded.

Ruacán pursed his lips.

'In Lethra you have enemies, Scáthach of Uibh Rathach. That is why you have come to this place, to seek them out and the meaning of your birth.'

'That is true,' agreed the girl. 'But if the enemies be mine, why would they be content to steal some of my weapons, a spear and shield, and leave me unharmed. And why take Flann captive?'

'That is a mystery for you to solve, my child.'

'Are there tracks that we can follow?'

'Your eyes are sharper than mine.'

She drank of the druid's mixture and rested awhile at his orders before feeling fit enough to move. As soon as that was possible the girl went to the spot which the druid had indicated. The old man was right. There were signs of a struggle. Her trained eye saw how the grasses were bent, the trees disturbed. Nearby she saw that three horses had been tethered, obviously while the three thieves had left them to sneak up on the encampment.

She observed that tracks coming to the spot had left even depressions in the ground but returning in the direction they had come she noticed that the hoof marks of one animal were much deeper as if it carried a heavier burden.

'Two men rode this beast,' she observed to the druid who stood watching her.

'Your eyes are as clear as your mind, my child,' he nodded with approval. 'Flann's horse is left behind, so it is clear they took him prisoner and mounted him on one of their horses.'

'The tracks are clear and will be easy to follow,' she said. 'That is something to be thankful for.'

'Indeed.'

'Let us follow then,' Scáthach said, turning back to the camp with the intention of fetching the horses.

'Wait!'

'For what reason?' demanded the impatient girl, turning back to the old man with a quizzical stare.

The druid held up a hand, palm outwards.

'Patience, child. Firstly, and most importantly, you should know, as a warrior, that it is not wise to set off on a pursuit without food in your stomach. Then, secondly, you have a choice to make, daughter of Eola.'

'The first reason is easily dealt with,' Scáthach said. 'And you are right to rebuke me about it. We shall break our fast and then follow the tracks.'

'But the second matter of choice?' persisted the druid.

'I know of no other choice to make,' replied the girl, frowning.

'Then let me make it plain. The loss of a shield and a spear are but little things in the scheme of life. But what catches in your heart is the abduction of Flann Mac Fraech.'

The girl coloured and was about to deny it but she realised that Ruacán was right. She was worried about the safety of Flann. She bit her lip and waited for the druid to continue.

'I see you do not deny it,' smiled the old man. 'Well, you can follow Flann in an attempt to rescue him or you can continue your journey to seek the truth of your birth and the reason for Eola's assassination. You have a choice of two paths.'

185

Scáthach stood and stared for a long while into the bright eyes of the druid.

'There is no choice in that, Ruacán,' she said. 'My quest can wait awhile. I must go in search of Flann.'

The druid smiled gently.

'Then so be it. You have chosen your order of precedence wisely, my child. In the end the two choices are but one and the two paths of choice will be synonymous.'

They returned slowly to the encampment. There was a quiet between them for a while and then the girl asked:

'Ruacán, do you know more than you will say? I sometimes have the feeling that you know the future.'

The old man sadly shook his head.

'I can only advise as things appear to me and perhaps you may accept my advice. It is not for me to predict events or divine your fate. You are in control of your destiny, my child. At times there come choices and sometimes one needs wise counsel. But even wise counsel cannot determine what path you will tread, only advise you.'

Scáthach bent to buckle on her weapons and then turned to stirring the fire to prepare breakfast.

'Sometimes I have the feeling, Ruacán,' she half repeated as she worked, 'that what you know is greater than the sum of our existence. That you truly know what is to be. Do you have the ability to divine auguries or read the signs of predestination?'

Ruacán chuckled softly.

'Is anything predestined?'

'I believe so.'

'Not so. Nothing is predestined if we do not wish it so. For those who predict the future have as much power to shape it as those who merely ride on the tide of events.'

The girl smiled in puzzlement.

'I thought the druids believed that all things were predestined?'

186

'Will you denigrate the free will of humankind?'

'No. But isn't it taught that our lives are already charted at our birth?'

'Indeed, there are many things which can ordain the path we follow: whether we are born weak or strong, whether we are born to those parents or these, whether we are fair or dark, whether we are knowledgeable or lack the ability to understand. Many such things chart our path in life. But when all is said and done there is, in all of us, an inner force which must make us finally responsible for our fate. We are given choices; in the final analysis, my child, we cannot rely on any influence except our own.'

'I thought I was following my own destiny?' observed the girl dryly.

'You are shaping it,' replied the druid. 'There is the difference, daughter of Eola. Never sit back and say whatever happens is destiny. That is the excuse of failure and the authority of a tyrant.'

The girl shook her head and sighed.

'Then let us eat, Ruacán, and then set out in search of Flann for, if I am in control of the future, I will succeed in finding those who abducted him and punish them.'

Ruacán chuckled.

'Well spoken, daughter of Eola. If you are not afraid of the future then you will be confident of the present.'

Thirteen

They stood on the shoulder of a hill gazing out across a low fertile green plain through which a broad river ran, a river so wide and majestic that it could only be crossed by boat. Several sea-going ships were anchored along its banks and they could see that to the west the river spread outwards into a great estuary emptying into the sea. But it was the city which held Scáthach's gaze for she had never before seen such a great metropolis. The city stood on the river bank and was unwalled. Yet its buildings towered into the sky and were built of white marble on which the bright sunlight danced and reflected, dazzling them from time to time.

'What place is this?' whispered the girl.

'This is the principal city of Lethra,' replied Ruacán.

'What gods built this place?'

The old druid smiled.

'Not gods but men. Gods have the world for their temples, only men feel the necessity to build such constructions to flatter their vanity.'

'But you must admit that it is beautiful,' whispered Scáthach.

'There is more beauty in a forest, or in a lake at the foot of the mountain,' said the druid. 'I find little beauty in man's constructions.'

Scáthach shrugged and looked towards the city with its gleaming buildings.

'Those who abducted Flann must have gone to the city,'

she reflected. They had been following the tracks for half a day; tracks that were easy enough to follow. 'We will go down and try to find out where they have taken him.'

Ruacán sighed.

'You may meet enemies in the city, Scáthach,' he warned.

The girl put on her helmet, *An Cruadín*, and eased her fearsome sword, *An Chraobh Ghlasach*, the cold champion, in its scabbard. Then she took her javelin and shield and smiled at the druid.

'I am Scáthach of Uibh Rathach,' she said firmly. 'Let the people of Lethra try my anger.'

The old druid pursed his thin lips.

The girl was confident now; fully confident in her ability. But perhaps she was too confident. Well, she must learn.

She turned her horse down the pathway which led onto the plain towards the outskirts of the city and the old druid followed leading Flann's abandoned horse behind. Scáthach observed that while the plain was green and fertile, and in many places was cultivated, there seemed little sign of life. It was a sunny day and the crops seemed ready for the harvesting yet there were no workers going to the fields.

Along the road there were a few warriors who stared curiously at her and her fierce visage but made no move to challenge her or the old man.

At the gates of the city, where the road led between two great buildings which served as portals to the unwalled place, two warriors stood nodding drowsily on their spears, shields slung on their backs, and they barely acknowledged Scáthach as she passed through.

'This is a city that does not fear strangers,' the girl said to the druid.

'A city which does not fear enemies,' corrected the old man.

Scáthach saw the point.

'Where shall we begin our search?'

Ruacán grinned.

'Where else but at the door of the ruler of the city.'

Scáthach hailed one of a group of warriors who was strolling by.

'Where is the *dún* of the chieftain of this place?' she demanded.

The man stared at her in fearful bewilderment, his wide eyes upon the ghastly image of her helmet.

'Who rules this city?' pressed the girl.

'Why,' the man's face suddenly broke into a nervous smile of understanding, 'Why we are ruled by the High One, Aífe.'

Scáthach raised an eyebrow disdainfully.

'High One, indeed?' she muttered. 'And where does this Aífe dwell?'

The warrior pointed along the roadway through the buildings.

'If you follow along the road here you will come to a large circular green. Beyond that is the Palace of Bleeding Stone and it is in that the High One dwells.'

Scáthach was about to turn away when a thought prompted her to ask: 'Have you heard tell of a prisoner brought to the city this morning?'

'Many prisoners come to the city,' the warrior replied indifferently.

'This was this morning,' pressed the girl. 'A young warrior from Éireann.'

'It could be so. I am not aware of it.'

He turned and walked hurriedly away, thankful to be out of her presence, but leaving Scáthach suppressing a sigh of annoyance.

'Come on, Ruacán, let us find this High One . . .'

She trotted her horse along the paved streets wondering that in so large and magnificent city there seemed so few people and they only warriors. There were no children, no women and no sign of any workers other than warriors. And another thing, she realised curiously: everyone seemed to move around morosely, as if without purpose to their lives. They came to the large circular green on which a great monolith stood. It dwarfed them, being twelve feet in height and some four feet wide, but it was the material from which it was made that caused both of them to pause and stare in amazement, for the construction seemed to be of solid gold. Slipping from her mount, Scáthach moved forward to inspect it more closely and found that it was, indeed, the case. Solid red-gold on which was inscribed the curious triskele motif which she had come so far to trace the meaning of. Yet again her hand went to the golden medallion and fingered it nervously as she contemplated the similarity of the design. Below was a curious writing, nothing like the simple strokes of the Ogham script of Éireann; more decorous, more devious.

'Ruacán, do you know the meaning of this writing?' she asked.

The old druid shook his head.

'Alas, few are privileged to know this language for it is the secret speech of the gods themselves.'

The girl frowned.

'Then why is it inscribed on this monolith for all to see?'

The old man smiled softly.

'It is not for me to say, yet it is for you to find out.'

The girl frowned in impatience and turned towards the towering marble palace buildings beyond.

'Let us find out from this High One,' she commented dryly.

A warrior stood regarding them with nervous curiosity at the head of the steps leading to the palace.

Scáthach was wearing her helmet and he was clearly uncomfortable at the grim visage.

'What do you wish, warrior?' he asked softly, anxiously tugging at the handle of his sword.

'Take me to your High One.'

He shrugged and spread his arms.

'Impossible!'

The next second he found the girl's sword point at his throat.

'Nothing is impossible, warrior,' she said in a pleasantly even tone.

The warrior was clearly unhappy.

'This request is,' he stammered. 'For the High One has left here.'

'Left?' snapped Scáthach.

'Just before noon, the High One left the palace to go on a journey.'

'Where?' demanded the girl.

'I know not,' replied the warrior and added, with a flash of spirit, 'The High One does not confide in me.'

'Then in whom does the High One confide?'

The man shifted uncomfortably.

'Who would know the confidences of the High One? Perhaps Droch but he has gone with the High One. Perhaps Maor the Steward . . .'

'But he has gone with her also?' sneered the girl.

'Oh no, he is in the palace.'

Scáthach brightened.

'And would this Maor know if a prisoner was brought here this morning?'

'He would know everything that happens here, warrior,' replied the man. 'He is the Steward.'

'Then take us to this Maor.'

The warrior hesitated.

'I am not supposed to leave the entrance unattended . . .' he began but a gentle pressure of her sword point against his throat made him obey the girl's order.

Maor the Steward was a pudgy, pale-faced individual

with shifty eyes and flabby lips. He stared up with pale, devious eyes, as they entered the room in which he sat; apparently he was examining accounts spread on a table before him. He half started from his chair and then, seeing how well armed the girl was and that she held one of the palace guards at sword point, he sunk back. He was also clearly alarmed by the sight of the fierce headgear of Scáthach.

'What does this mean?'

The girl smiled.

'It means, Maor, that you will tell us if a prisoner was brought to this palace this morning? A young warrior of Éireann.'

Maor's eyes narrowed more in cunning than any other consideration.

'Will I?' he muttered.

'Indeed,' nodded the girl, swinging her sword point towards him. 'And quickly.'

The pudgy steward's eyes batted for a moment and he swallowed.

'True enough. A prisoner was bought here this morning early.'

The girl gave a smile of relief.

'What was his name?'

'Flann was the first name, I think. I know nothing more.'

'Take us to him.'

The bulbous lips sneered.

'That I cannot.'

Scáthach's sword point moved dangerously.

'Wait!' the pudgy man almost shrieked. 'It is true. I cannot. The High One and Droch, her advisor, have taken the young man with them and left the palace.'

The girl bit her lip in disappointment.

'Where have they gone?'

'They left on the noon tide in the High One's fastest ship.'

The girl leaned closer with her sword point at the Steward's neck.

'Where have they gone?' she demanded again, raising her voice a tone.

The Steward's eyes moved as if seeking some escape.

The sword point pricked his skin and a pinpoint of blood showed.

His mouth fell open, his white face began to colour.

'Please,' he said. 'Please . . .'

'Tell me!' snapped the girl.

'They have gone to the court of Darcon.'

Scáthach frowned and glanced at Ruacán.

'Do you know of this Darcon?'

The druid nodded.

'Darcon the Tyrant rules the Island of Shadows which lies in the northern regions.'

Maor cast a disapproving look at the old man.

'Darcon is brother of the High One,' he said with an air of rebuke.

Scáthach ignored him for the moment.

'Where is the Island of Shadows exactly?' The question was directed at Ruacán.

The old druid paused for a moment and then grimaced.

'Three to four days' sail to the north. It is an island off the coast of Alba.'

'Then we must go there.'

The girl's chin came up determinedly as she made the statement without thought or hesitation.

'You will not find it so easy to deal with Darcon or the High One,' sneered Maor. 'Go there and you will be killed.'

Scáthach turned back to him and eased the sword point again at his throat.

'I might just kill you, kitchen rat.'

The pudgy-faced man winced.

'Killing me will not alter your future,' he replied with some degree of spirit.

'True,' laughed the girl after a moment's reflection, 'but it may bring me satisfaction.'

'Do not play with him,' interposed Ruacán. 'It is a long journey to Dún Scáith.'

'What is that?' asked the girl.

'That is the fortress of Darcon in the Island of Shadows.'

The girl turned back to Maor.

'And where might we find a ship to take us to this land of Darcon?'

The steward shrugged indifferently.

It was the warrior who had stood mute since they had entered the room who replied.

'Down by the river are ships, ships from several lands which trade with us.'

'Thank you, warrior,' said Scáthach gravely.

'No need to thank me. I am going there myself to seek passage away from here. After what I have done this day I am a dead man in Lethra.'

'But you could not help yourself,' pointed out the druid.

'The High One makes no allowances,' replied the warrior. 'I will go to the land of . . .' He paused and glanced at Maor. 'I will go away from here.'

'Begone then, warrior. May your gods go with you,' said Scáthach. The warrior saluted her and was gone in a thrice.'

'The vengeance of the High One is terrible and stretches everywhere,' warned Maor. 'He will not escape punishment and neither will . . .'

He stopped as his eyes focused on the point of her sword moving towards his throat.

'Silence.'

He was silent.

'Now tell me, as well as the warrior from Éireann, was anything else taken by Aífe?'

Maor pursed his lips.

'Speak quickly,' whispered the girl, pressing the point gently.

'Yes, yes,' grunted the steward. 'I saw the High One examining a shield and spear which were brought in with the warrior. She was especially interested in these weapons.'

'And did she take the shield and spear with her?' demanded Scáthach.

'She did.'

Then she ordered him not to move and, with rapid motion, quickly bound the pudgy steward into his chair and gagged him. She stood back a moment and critically surveyed her handiwork before turning to Ruacán.

'That should hold him for a while. We must go down to the river and find a ship sailing for the Island of Shadows.'

The old man sniffed.

'Easier said than done, my child. Few ships sail for those waters. It is an evil place. Darcon is said to be the son of the Mórrígú, goddess of death and battles. He is not called Darcon the Tyrant for no reason. An evil one.'

'Then all the more reason to follow and rescue Flann,' said the girl determinedly. 'Anyway, I was originally told no ship would sail to Lethra, yet here I am. Now you say that no ship will sail to this Island of Shadows. Yet I say we will soon be there.'

The old man sighed.

'What is to be, will be,' he said with a shrug.

'Come, then.'

She turned and preceded him from the great, silent palace of the High One, back into the graceful, though empty, thoroughfares of the city. Remounting their horses, they walked them through the deserted streets towards the area which lined the river. Here the city lost its well-laid avenues and tall buildings and carefully attended monuments. With an almost startling abruptness they moved into a shanty town of wooden buildings, mainly rotten and ill-kept, with narrow streets piled high with rubbish and debris. Here for the first time they began to see the citizens of Lethra, dirty, ragged children, playing in the refuse of the street, women of all ages, backs bent under burdens, old men, begging bowls in hand and young men minus limbs, some on crutches, wandering with seeming purposelessness, eyes blank and dead.

Scáthach drew in her breath sharply.

'What does this mean?' she whispered to the druid.

'It is the price of the city,' replied the old one. 'This is Lethra's glory. Look well on it, my child. When you hear someone preach of the greatness of a place, of a city or a country, then remember the suffering and mangled flesh which went into creating that greatness. Ask yourself whether such suffering truly means greatness.'

The girl stared about her at the poverty and misery with distaste. Never had she seen such a sight before. In Éireann the old and impoverished were not allowed to suffer thus. The sick and ailing poor were provided for by the laws of the Brehons; the clans supported the welfare of all its members. To allow people to suffer thus was immoral — criminal! Her heart burnt with a consuming rage as she stared at the suffering around her. And for what purpose? To raise the marble halls of Lethra for the glory of the so-called 'High One'.

Eventually they found themselves on the narrow quaysides of the river where half a dozen ships of varying sizes were moored. Groups of sailors were loading and off-loading cargoes watched by sullen groups of people held at bay by warriors with drawn swords. Scáthach could feel the discontent and anger seething among the people.

Ruacán caught her gaze and smiled grimly.

'You are right, my child. One day all this will erupt. It is the law of nature.'

'The sooner, the better.'

She turned her gaze speculatively on the ships, not forgetting the main purpose of their being there.

The old druid laid a hand on her arm.

'If you are inquiring for a ship, better to name your destination as Alba rather than Dún Scáith, for the very name of the Island of Shadows will put fear into the bravest man.'

'Very well.'

She paused and hailed a burly sailor overseeing the loading of a cargo.

'Where is your ship going?'

The bearded man gazed up at the slightly-built girl, her head clad in the fierce war-helmet, and with the accoutrements of a warrior, and frowned.

'We go to the land of the Cantii, in southern Britain.'

Scáthach was disappointed but she pressed: 'Do you know of a ship heading for Alba?'

The bearded man raised a gnarled hand and ran it through his tangled black beard.

'They say that Bracan takes his ship there,' he said after a moment or two. 'He is from the land of Alba.'

'Bracan? And where might I find this Bracan?'

The burly man turned and indicated a nearby tavern with a wave of his arm.

Scáthach raised a hand in acknowledgement and nudged her horse over to the quayside tavern. She and Ruacán dismounted and found a boy willing to take charge of their mounts for a few coins.

Inside, the tavern was noisy as it was crowded but the sailors inside fell silent at her appearance and begrudgingly made way for the slight figure of the girl in warrior's harness, helmet still on her head, hiding her countenance.

Just as Goibhniu had said, in battle it gave a terrible vision to her enemies; and still it gave to those who gazed on her without battle-fever a formidable appearance. They moved away from her as she, followed by the old druid, marched to the bar where a sweating and nervous-looking host watched her coming.

'What can I do for you, warrior?'

'I seek Bracan.'

There was a murmur among the sailors and the silence which had fallen at her entry was gone. Having ascertained the object of the strange warrior's coming, and realising it was not for them, they fell to their talking and laughter again. Only one man, a tall, thin, red-haired man, moved forward. He wore a permanent scowl on his thin face which proclaimed his profession by its tanned and weather-beaten skin.

'I am Bracan,' he said stiffly. 'What business have you with me?'

'I hear you sail to Alba.'

'Then you have heard correctly.'

'I am in mind to take passage there with my companion,' Scáthach nodded towards Ruacán.

Bracan glanced at the old man and turned back to Scáthach speculatively.

'It might be arranged,' he conceded after a moment or so.

'Where do you travel in Alba? To what port?'

Bracan did not answer immediately but motioned to the host to fill his mug again.

'I go to the seaboard of the Gael on the western coast of Alba,' he said when the mug had been handed back with a frothy head of beer crowning it.

Scáthach glanced towards the druid who nodded imperceptibly.

'That is good. We would go there.'

Bracan's eyes narrowed.

'It is a voyage of three, maybe four days.'

'We will pay.'

'Ah . . . ' the thin lips of the captain drooped a little. 'But how much will you pay? It is a hard voyage, a rough voyage.'

'What is your price?' asked the girl.

'A gold coin per day for each of you,' said the sailor.

Scáthach knew that the price was a reasonable one for had not Goll demanded nine gold pieces for her passage alone from Éireann to Gallia?

'That is agreed.'

Bracan raised his eyes in surprise for obviously he had been expecting some protest and bargaining.

'When do we sail?' demanded Scáthach.

'With the evening tide,' replied Bracan. 'Our ship is the *Feannóg*.'

Scáthach hesitated.

'What cargo are you carrying?' she asked abruptly.

The sailor looked at her blankly and was clearly puzzled by the question. Then he said quietly: 'Little cargo comes out of this place and we were beaten to that which there was. Why do you ask?'

'Have you room to take three horses?'

'Ah. That will cost more.'

'How much more?'

'Three horses? Food for them during the voyage? Another gold piece per day per horse.'

'That is expensive.'

'It is my price. And the voyage money must be paid before we set sail.'

Scáthach hesitated and then shrugged.

'I agree.'

Once more Bracan looked surprised at how easily the girl gave in to his demands.

'You must wish to reach Alba in a hurry, warrior,' he observed.

'That is my business.'

'Agreed.' He put down his empty mug and turned. 'If you want to bring your horses on board now and settle.'

'Very well.'

They followed the tall man from the tavern and collected their horses from the boy who had been looking after them. Bracan led the way along the quays to where a sleek-looking ship was moored. Even Scáthach had to admire the low black racing lines of the *Feannóg*. It was a clean vessel, obviously well crewed and well looked after. It was not like Goll's *Nemhain* which had been ill kept, its decks unscrubbed, the sails needing repair and with an atmosphere of dirt and desolation.

'A good choice,' muttered Ruacán, as his eyes travelled around the vessel. 'This Bracan runs a professional ship, at least.'

At Bracan's orders, planks were raised in place from the quayside onto the vessel alongside so that they could walk their horses onto the ship, and then by means of pulleys and stays a group of sailors lowered the unprotesting animals into the hold and made them comfortable for the sea voyage ahead.

Scáthach counted her dwindling collection of coins and handed several to Bracan who took them and recounted carefully before announcing himself satisfied with the deal.

'My mate is currently ashore trying to round up extra hands which we need for the voyage,' explained Bracan. 'We will not delay when he returns and will be on the open sea before nightfall.'

He left them to their own devices and they found an easy seat in the stern of the ship, on the raised quarter deck by the great tiller.

Scáthach, with a sigh, was about to remove her helmet, when Ruacán put out a hand to stay her.

'What is it?' she demanded.

'Have you forgotten how people reacted when they saw your face on our journey through Lethra?' he asked.

'Yes,' replied Scáthach, 'but no one has since behaved so peculiarly.'

'That is because your face has been disguised by your helmet. Best keep it on until we reach the shores of the Gael in Alba.'

'But why?' demanded the girl. 'Why should people fear my face?'

'Why indeed. We have yet to learn that mystery. Until we do, it would be better not to imperil our journey.'

Scáthach shrugged.

'Very well, Ruacán. I will accept your guidance for you have proved a good friend and guide.'

The old man grinned, somewhat cynically.

'That is not what your friend Flann thinks. He suspects that I am engineering some devious plot.'

'Flann has many qualities,' replied the girl. 'He is brave and steadfast. But . . .'

Ruacán smiled softly.

'He is not at one with the world and seeks to fight that which he does not understand.'

Scáthach bowed her head in assent.

'Well, no crime to that,' went on the druid. 'In that he shares the fault with most of mankind. They are fearful creatures not opening themselves to the fact that they are part of creation, at one with creation. Instead, in their fear of it, they seek to dominate it. Until they learn to live in harmony with it, indeed with themselves, then they will be unable to make progress.'

The old man raised his eyes and glanced at the quay-side.

'Ah, I think Bracan's mate is coming aboard now.'

Scáthach followed his gaze to where a seaman was coming aboard the vessel. He was a swarthy complexioned man with a shock of black hair which almost covered his face. He wore an eye-patch over his left eye.

Her blood ran cold as she stared at him.

His sharp, almost ugly features and sneering mouth had been burnt into her memory.

Ruacán frowned.

'What is it?' he demanded.

'Goll!' she whispered. 'That man is Goll of the *Nemhain*!'

Fourteen

The low, dim coastline of mist-shrouded Alba lay on the port bow. The seas were grey and restless and the sky was mirrored in its slate-coloured surface. The winds were fresh and blustery and cold. For three days the *Feannóg* had ploughed through the waters from the more pleasant coastline of Gallia towards the colder northern waters. And now, after what seemed an age, the ship was nearing the seaboard of the Gael which lay through the narrow sea-passage which divided Alba from the land of Éireann.

At Ruacán's instigation, Scáthach had made no move to contact Goll or make her presence known on board the ship. Bracan had not asked her name and so she had never volunteered it. And whenever she appeared out of her cabin, she wore her visored helmet to prevent the evil former captain of the *Nemhain* from recognising his erstwhile passenger whom he had attempted to rob and kill. It was, in fact, Ruacán who managed to learn the story from Goll's own lips of how his own ship struck a rock and foundered off the coast of Gallia. Goll had been carried to the coast on a spar and eventually found himself in Lethra where he had persuaded Bracan to take him on as a mate. Bracan's own mate had died of a fever on the voyage to Lethra so the captain was willing enough to take on extra hands.

Goll was surly and angry at the loss of his own ship and crew. Ruacán warned the girl to stay out of his way as much as possible.

'The man tried to murder Flann and me for gain,' the girl told the druid. 'He has barely begun to pay his debt.'

'If you desire retribution,' replied the druid, 'wait until we get to the shore of Alba.'

She had agreed. And now here was the shore of Alba off their beam. The *Feannóg* was turning its bows towards the rocky coastline.

'An hour before we anchor,' smiled Bracan agreeably from the tiller where he was instructing his helmsmen.

'Excellent,' the girl replied. 'At what point do we land?'

'That headland there is called Aird nan Murchan. That is where we land for it is our home port.'

'And how far is that from Dún Scáith?'

Bracan's face turned pale. He jerked around to stare at the girl.

'Dún Scáith? Why do you want to know about that place?'

The girl smiled under her helmet.

'Is that not my business?' she said softly.

'Dún Scáith is the domain of Darcon the Tyrant, the son of the goddess of death, who rules the Island of Shadows. It is an evil place; the gods of light between it and me!'

Scáthach was bemused by the fear in the red-haired sea-captain's voice.

'Is it far?' she insisted.

The man hesitated a while and then shook his head sullenly.

'Not far,' he said slowly. 'A short distance northwards, but if you are going there, you must encounter many dangers before you see the ramparts of Dún Scáith.'

'Dangers?' the girl swung round to Bracan. 'What dangers?'

The seaman bit his lip.

'I have said too much.'

'You have not said enough,' replied the girl sharply.

'Tell me what business you have with the Island of Shadows first,' insisted Bracan. 'Is it right that I put myself in danger even to speak about the land of the son of the goddess of death without knowing to whom I speak? Since you have come aboard you have been visored behind that fierce helmet. Why, you might be the Mórrígú herself for all I know.'

Scáthach shook her head.

'No fear of that, Bracan. I go to Dún Scáith in search of a friend who was kidnapped and taken there by the High One of Lethra.'

The sailor's eyes widened.

'You mean to rescue your friend from Dún Scáith?' he asked in a tone of incredulity.

'I do.'

'But the High One of Lethra, Aífe, is the half-sister of Darcon. You have no hope against them.'

'Yet how do I get to this place?'

The sailor shook his head stubbornly.

'You will be killed . . . or worse.'

'And what of my friend?'

'Your friend is as good as dead.'

'I do not think so. And if . . . if he is, then there shall be a price to pay.'

205

The sailor looked at the girl with some degree of awe creeping into his eyes.

'Truly, you must be a great warrior or a greater fool if you would seek vengeance against Darcon.'

'How do I reach Dún Scáith?' she insisted.

'Northward, across the Plain of Ill-Luck and through the Perilous Glen and the Valley of the Shadow to the Bridge of Leaps. On the far side you will find Dún Scáith.'

'How many days' journey?' she pressed.

'If any have succeeded in making it then they have not returned to tell,' replied Bracan.

Scáthach's chin came up firmly.

'I will succeed and I will return.'

'And the old one . . . ?' asked Bracan, indicating the druid. 'He goes with you?'

'We go in search of our friend.'

'Then the gods go with you.'

'Set us ashore and you need have no more fear for us,' replied the girl.

'Tell me who you are so that our bards may at least compose laments at your hopeless endeavour.'

Scáthach squared her shoulders.

'Should your bards compose verses at my endeavour then they will be songs of the downfall of Dún Scáith. And they will remember Scáthach of Uibh Rathach.'

There was a sharp intake of breath.

'So it is you!' grunted an ugly voice.

Scáthach swung round to see that Goll had moved quietly near them, close enough to have heard her thoughtless and proud declaration of her name.

Bracan stared at his mate.

Goll's ugly face was creased in anger.

'I thought there was something familiar about you, girl. And the way you kept your face visored . . . I should have realised.'

206

'What does this mean?' demanded Bracan.

'It means that Goll was the captain of a ship which brought me and my friend to Gallia,' explained the girl facing the evil-looking mate. 'He took our gold and then, observing we had more, tried to kill and rob us. In the struggle, his crew lost control of their ship and it foundered. We were saved, and so was this sea-vermin.'

Goll's face was terrible.

He moved forward a pace with a threatening gesture. Scáthach laughed.

'You don't like to hear the truth?' she sneered.

'Is it the truth, Goll?' demanded Bracan.

Goll shook his head vehemently.

'No,' he blustered. 'She lies, captain. She is the pirate who tried to take over my ship. She killed a passenger named Éccneid and tried to take control of the ship . . . I shall kill you for the loss of my good ship and crew, the loss of my livelihood.'

'You brought that on yourself, pirate!' snapped Scáthach.

Goll reached towards his sword but the girl's hand was already defensively on her sword's hilt.

Bracan looked uncertain as he gazed from one to another.

'There must be a judgement on this matter,' he muttered. 'I cannot let you or your companion go on your way, nor can I let Goll go on his way, until the matter is brought before the Brehons of Alba.'

Ruacán moved forward and nodded approval.

'A wise decision, captain. It is according to the law,' he said.

Scáthach raised an indifferent shoulder and let it fall.

'It shall be according to their judgement.' She glanced at Goll, who stood glowering at her. 'What do you say, Goll? Do you dare accept the judgement of the Brehons?'

'No!' he cried, suddenly drawing his sword and swinging it at the girl. 'You will not escape my vengeance.'

Scáthach had been given a split second warning of the other's intent by a slight narrowing of the eyes and clenching of the muscles. She leapt aside as Goll's blade swung and her own sword was drawn in a moment.

'Stop!' cried Bracan.

But Goll was seething with anger and flaying at the girl with his sword. His face was a mask of hatred as he tried to close with her.

Bracan moved to intercept him but Ruacán laid a hand on his arm.

'I think Goll has demonstrated the truth of the matter by his fury and hatred,' he said quietly. 'Let them decide the matter.'

'But that is not right,' protested the sea-captain.

In spite of himself, he stood back and watched the two combatants circling each other.

It became obvious that Goll lacked the finesse and training of the girl in weapons although his strength and cunning were of equal match. It was inevitable, however, that he could not sustain his attack against the agile mastery of the sword displayed by Scáthach. Soon he was tiring; and, in tiring, he became desperate. He made several lunges that a more discerning mind would have kept him from. Once or twice the girl actually drew back to allow him to recover instead of finishing the bout there and then.

Finally, Scáthach moved forward and with seeming ease engaged him in such a way that Goll's sword went flying out of his hand and into the air, and stuck into the deckplanks, quivering from the impact.

With her sword held a few inches from his throat, Goll stood gasping, his eyes still blurred in fury.

'Do you surrender, Goll?' Scáthach demanded.

He stared at the girl blankly.

She had to repeat the question and this time the point of her sword pressed close against his chest.

'Yes,' he grunted.

She lowered her sword.

'Then the judgement is still with the Brehons,' she said, half turning towards Bracan.

The warning came from the shadowy reflection in Bracan's eyes, a slight movement. Scáthach leapt aside, twisting round on one foot as a dagger hissed passed her head and embedded itself into the nearby masthead. Before she had come to a halt, Scáthach had brought her sword into a defensive position with a swift wrist-action, its point aimed firmly towards the chest of Goll. The one-eyed seaman hesitated only a moment, his eyes wide and staring at the girl with such malignancy that it seemed that he was unaware of the sword aimed at his chest. Then he jumped sideways, staggered, recovered his balance and launched himself across the rail of the ship and into the turbulent waves beyond. Bracan moved forward with Scáthach and Ruacán at his shoulders and stared at the white-crested waves. They saw a black bobbing head for a moment or two and then nothing. For a long while they stared, trying to catch sight of the man.

'Drowned,' Bracan said laconically. 'A stupid man.'

Ruacán sighed.

'He has convicted himself.'

Bracan bit his lip.

'Aye, so he did,' he assented and then repeated: 'He was a stupid man. While the channel is narrow here, this is the Caol Muile, the seas run swift and fierce. There was no hope of him swimming ashore. A wasted life.' The sea-captain hesitated. 'You still want to be put ashore at Aird nan Murchan?'

'Yes,' said Scáthach.

'Very well.' Bracan turned and went back to the helmsman to give his full attention to the course changes to bring them through the surging channel of Caol Muile, a sea channel between the low hills of the island of Muile to the west and the high mountains of the mainland of

Alba to the east. At the end of the channel lay the heights of Aird nan Murchan.

Scáthach turned to Ruacán, sheathing her sword. She felt no sorrow for the death of Goll. He had been an evil man, a man with much blood on his hands. At least he had chosen his own path to the fate which awaited him in the Otherworld.

'And so to the next part of our journey,' she said quietly.

The druid nodded.

'Across the Plain of Ill-Luck, with its mires and bogs, and through the Perilous Glen, where monsters and ravening beasts and serpents lay in wait for the unwary,' he recited softly. 'Through the Valley of the Shadow to the Bridge of Leaps which spans a deep ravine above a boiling sea. Once you have passed these obstacles then, only then, will you come to Dún Scáith.'

The girl gazed at him with a frown.

'Do you know these places?'

Ruacán smiled enigmatically.

'I would make a bad guide and advisor if I knew nothing of these places.'

She stared hard at the old man.

'Tell me, old one, as you are of the knowledge. Do you know if Flann lives? Is he well? Can we rescue him?'

The druid shrugged.

'That is too much to ask and for you to know, daughter of Eola. Sometimes I can see shadows of what might be but that is not to say they will be. Nothing is preordained. There are possibilities written in the heavens at our birth but, like the gods, mortals are possessed of free will and what they do can change the path they tread if they use a firm step and do not wish to be the prisoners of fate. However, I can tell you this, my child: Aífe, the High One, has no plans to kill Flann Mac Fraech yet.'

Scáthach's eyes narrowed.

'Yet? What do you mean by that?'

'Nothing that you are not able to work out already, my child. Stay a while and meditate on events . . . so far you have been too busy reacting to events to seek to understand them and by so understanding to control them. Think about them, for most of what you need in order to reason out their mysteries is before you.'

Scáthach made a gesture of impatience.

'Do not speak in riddles, old one.'

'I do not,' replied Ruacán calmly. 'Think.'

Scáthach frowned and then shrugged.

'I cannot understand.'

The druid smiled softly.

'That is because you are trying too hard, my child. Let yourself relax. Do not tense your thoughts. Relax and soon all will become clear to you as it is to me.'

Still frowning, the girl turned away to lean by the rail of the ship, staring at the approaching shoreline. Sometimes she could curse the equivocation and smoothness of a druid's tongue. She tried hard to fathom the old man's meaning, turning events over in her mind, but no explanation came to her. All she knew was that Flann, with her new-won shield, the ocean god's own 'hard ridged hazel' – *An Seancholl Snidheach* – as well as the *gae-Bolga*, the fearsome spear of Bolga, had been taken. According to the druid, they had been taken for a purpose by Aífe, the High One, ruler of Lethra. The reason was there to see, so the old man had told her. But there was no reason that she could understand. She thought about the matter a little more before, with a sharp sigh of impatience, she gave up and concentrated on watching the *Feannóg* approaching the shore of Aird nan Murchan, the gateway to the route to Dún Scáith.

Bracan edged the ship towards a wooden quayside underneath the shadow of tall mountains, the heights of Machan after which the place was named. It was a tiny settlement which reminded Scáthach of some of the coastal settlements in Mumhan. The dwellings were built of stone against the harsh winds and there was a circular *dún* or fortress which stood above the settlement and guided it.

Groups of people had come down to the quay to greet the *Feannóg* as it docked. Cries of greeting were exchanged between some of the sailors and those on the quayside. This was the ship's home port and Scáthach gathered it had been some months away on a trading cruise. Among the people hurrying down to the quay she saw a tall, fair-haired man; he was ruddy of cheek and well muscled, yet his weather-tanned face had humorous creases and the eyes shone with a hidden laughter. He was dressed in the accoutrements of a warrior. His gold torc around his neck gleamed dully in the cloudy daylight and his multi-coloured cloak denoted his high position in the settlement.

'That is our chieftain, Laoch,' observed Bracan.

The fair-haired man swung aboard and saluted Bracan.

'What news, Bracan,' he asked, coming forward from the well of the ship.

'Not good,' replied the sea-captain. 'We lost Each and three of the crew in a storm off Gallia. A man named Goll, from Éireann, who replaced Each as mate, was drowned on the way here.'

The chieftain's face clouded.

'Bad news, indeed.' He suddenly glanced at Scáthach with Ruacán at her shoulder. His eyes asked a question.

'These are travellers. They took passage with us in Gallia,' explained Bracan.

The chieftain frowned.

'Travellers, eh? Where do you travel to? Aird nan Murchan is not on the route of most travellers.'

Scáthach smiled.

'Greetings, Laoch. I am Scáthach of Uibh Rathach and this is Ruacán. We travel to Dún Scáith.'

Laoch took an involuntary step backwards in surprise.

'A place of evil! What can you seek there?'

'We go to rescue a friend of ours who was taken there as a prisoner by Aífe of Lethra.'

'Better lament your friend as one dead,' replied the chieftain of Aird nan Murchan. 'If he has been taken to the Island of Shadows then he is already beyond hope.'

Scáthach stuck out her chin.

'That I shall never believe until it is a fact, Laoch.'

The chieftain gazed at the girl for a moment or two.

'You speak bravely, Scáthach of Uibh Rathach; as brave as your name is a proud one. Oh yes, even here in Aird nan Murchan the bards sing songs about Uibh Rathach and of the might of Eola.'

'I am the daughter of Eola,' replied the girl.

The chieftain nodded.

'I thought that might be. And by the way you name yourself, I believe that the grave of your father has been measured.'

Scáthach inclined her head.

'It is so. And he was slain by those bearing the symbol of Lethra. From Éireann to Gallia has my search led me in pursuit of his slayers and those who forced my mother, Buimech, into an early grave. I will not be put off from my search until it is completed.'

Laoch looked at the girl with respect.

'Then I will not attempt to,' he replied simply. 'Instead, allow me to extend to you the hospitality of Aird nan Murchan for this night and on the morrow I shall accompany you across the pass through the heights of Murchan,' he waved to the mountains beyond, 'and set your feet firmly on the path which leads to your destiny.'

Scáthach smiled.

'We accept the hospitality of you and your people, Laoch.'

'Excellent.' The chieftain turned to Bracan. 'I will conduct our guests to my *dún*. Join us there also, Bracan, when you have finished here.'

Bracan nodded assent.

'I will have your horses disembarked,' he said to the girl, 'and bring them to Laoch's fortress.'

'And here is the rest of the money I owe,' returned Scáthach, reaching into her purse and extracting the remaining gold pieces.

Bracan looked uncomfortable. He took the coins as if unwillingly.

'If it were not to pay my crew, Scáthach of Uibh Rathach, I would refuse these coins. Alas, we were unable to take on a cargo at Lethra and we have four widows and their families to feed in Aird nan Murchan.'

The girl smiled.

'You are an honest man, Bracan. I do not grudge you as we made a fair bargain.'

She turned with Ruacán and followed the chieftain, Laoch, from the ship onto the quayside.

People gathered round curiously, and the girl, for the first time in days, was able to take off her helmet and sling it at her side.

Laoch gazed at her attractive features in open approval.

'Tell me, daughter of Eola,' he said, falling in step with her, 'why is it that you carry a war-helm the like of which I have never seen before; so fierce and yet so beautiful? Why is it that you carry a sword that might have been made by the gods? Why is it that you carry a javelin that warriors might fight over for possession of such a weapon. Why do you carry such weapons and yet do not carry a shield?'

Scáthach smiled ruefully.

'The answer lies in Dún Scáith,' she replied. 'When Aífe took my companion, Flann Mac Fraech, a prisoner, she also stole my shield and my battle-spear.'

Laoch had pursed his lips in surprise.

'Did you say that your companion's name was Flann Mac Fraech?'

Scáthach inclined her head in assent.

'You know him?'

Laoch shrugged.

'I know that there is a man who calls himself chieftain of the Cruithne of Éireann, one Aintiarna, who has sent envoys along the seaboard of the Gael with news of a reward for the head of Flann Mac Fraech. A reward of one hundred gold pieces.'

The girl bit her lip. She had almost forgotten the reason why Flann Mac Fraech had left Éireann.

Laoch smiled grimly.

'Have no fear for most people along this coastline know that Aintiarna is a cruel tyrant and that Flann tried to free his people. There will be none who will accept Aintiarna's reward . . .'

'Except?' prompted Ruacán as the man hesitated.

Laoch grimaced.

'Except those who now hold him prisoner.'

'You mean Darcon of Dún Scáith?' pressed the girl, her face pale.

'Aintiarna and Darcon are two of a kind,' replied the chieftain of Aird nan Murchan. 'They are both spawned from the same egg; evil and powerful men who seize power and wield it for their own ends, not for the good of the people.'

Scáthach turned to Ruacán.

'Then we must press on immediately,' she said. 'Flann is at their mercy.'

The old druid smiled.

'The greater the haste, the less speed we will make, my

215

child,' he admonished. 'Food and rest is what is required before we set out on this journey. Without food and rest we have no chance in facing the perils before us.'

'In that there is wisdom,' Laoch added. 'Let me and the chosen of my warriors come with you for you will not be able to storm the ramparts of Dún Scáith alone.'

It was Ruacán the druid who shook his head.

'While an army has to storm ramparts, Laoch, a single person can walk through the gates. While your offer is a sign of your bravery and honesty, it cannot be accepted. We must continue our journey alone.'

Laoch glanced uncertainly at Scáthach.

The girl smiled.

'The old man is right, Laoch of Aird nan Murchan. Our task is better fulfilled alone.'

Laoch looked worried.

'How can a girl and an old man hope to reduce the fortress of Darcon the Tyrant?' he demanded.

Scáthach bridled.

'Why, do I hear prejudice in your voice, Laoch? I can outfight any warrior, or any three warriors you care to send against me at the same time.'

Laoch raised a pacifying hand.

'I do not doubt your ability, Scáthach of Uibh Rathach, but it is said that Darcon is the son of the Mórrígú, the goddess of death and battles. He can raise legions from the Otherworld to defend his ramparts.'

The girl eyed him steadily.

'Knowing this, you still want to enlist yourself in my cause?'

Laoch shrugged expressively.

'Can I let you go forth to face such odds alone?'

Ruacán intervened again.

'Yes,' he said shortly.

The girl glanced at him.

'Would it not be better to have Laoch and his men to help us?'

The old druid's brows drew together.

'Have I let you down with my counsel yet, daughter of Eola?'

Scáthach thought a moment and shook her head.

'Then we will continue our journey alone,' said the old man firmly.

The girl sighed.

'I am in your hands, Ruacán.'

The druid's face relaxed.

'That is so. Now let us feast and rest and tomorrow, as the sun rises over the eastern mountains of Alba, Laoch will show us the pass across the heights of Murchan to the Plain of Ill-Luck.'

He turned and strode firmly before them up the path to Laoch's fortress.

Laoch watched him for a moment, hesitated and sighed.

'Who can know the mind of a druid?' he said diffidently.

Scáthach smiled thinly.

'This druid has stood me in good stead with his wisdom until now.'

The chieftain inclined his head.

'May he continue to do so,' he said softly.

Fifteen

Whoever had named the place the Plain of Ill-Luck had named it well. Since Scáthach and Ruacán had parted from Laoch at the top of the mountain pass on the heights of Murchan, they had entered another world. Twisting down from the brilliant lit mountainside, they had descended onto a plain which was shrouded in mist, a thick, swirling green vaporous cloud which stretched from the feet of the mountains as far as they could see which was not far.

'Do not wander from the road,' Laoch had warned, 'for it stretches through mires and bogs which will swallow you and your horses within moments.'

In fact, after a mile or so, Scáthach realised that the only way forward was to dismount and lead her horse, with Ruacán following behind leading both his own mount and Flann's horse which they had brought with them. The pathway was so narrow that two could not go abreast upon it. It was a restricted strip of stone-laid pathway which twisted and turned like a serpent. On either side, in spite of the green vaporous clouds which wafted over it, the girl was aware of steamy, muddy boglands, belching with gasses and filled with strange noises which made her shiver in spite of herself.

'This is truly an evil place,' she called to the old druid.

'It is a place of testing,' replied Ruacán.

'Testing?' queried the girl. 'Testing of what?'

'Of oneself, daughter of Eola.'

The girl sniffed disdainfully and turned her attention back along the path. The swirling mist seemed to distort sounds in the eerie gloom. Now and then she would pause and listen as a strange noise caught her attention. What creatures inhabited the boglands? Once she was so intent on listening to curious noises, an odd chirping cry, that she slipped from the path and had she not been holding the bridle of her horse would have fallen into its cold, eager, soft hands which clawed at her legs almost vice-like in their embrace.

Ruacán came shuffling forward along the pathway to

help extract her. The smell of the green-black mud which clung to her body was putrid. As the old druid helped pull her out of the sticky mess, the mud let her go with a sound almost like a human sigh.

For a moment or two Scáthach sat on the pathway, shivering a little.

She raised her eyes to the old man and her thanks were silent.

'We should not remain here longer,' advised Ruacán.

She nodded and climbed to her feet.

Once more they moved off slowly through the swirling mist.

It was an hour later that the thickness of the mist began to dispel, becoming more low lying and patchy. But the sky above, when they had a glimpse of it, was grey, almost black, and offered little cheer. They were still passing through swampy bogland from which the gnarled fingers of dead trees poked, black and gaunt, from the stagnant waters. The path twisted on through the perilous swamp.

Once or twice Scáthach had the feeling that they were being watched. Once she thought she saw a movement beyond the trees of some vast dim form from the nightmare-spawning shadows. Her hand went to the hilt of her sword and her mouth pressed into a thin grim line.

Her thoughts began to fill with a chill fear.

'This is the place of testing, daughter of Eola,' came Ruacán's whisper as if he felt her fear.

'I am not afraid of anything which is real and of this earth,' replied the girl.

'Nor must you be afraid of shadows,' responded the old druid. 'Clear your mind. Clear it as your mother, Buimech, taught you, and do not fear the unseen. If you fear, then you have lost.'

Scáthach frowned. Her greatest fear, as a child, was of creatures from the world of shadows. She had hoped that she had been able to dispel such fears but she knew that they were being dredged into her mind once more.

'How can I not be afraid of that I do not see?' she demanded.

'How can you be afraid of it when it does not exist?' countered the old man.

She bit her lip. Across the bogland, with its swamps and mires, she could feel hostility, a hostility to her and humankind such as she had never felt before. The misty plain swarmed with entities which were inimical to her, semi-sentient things which were an ever-present danger to her physical and spiritual wellbeing. There was no logic in this. No gods of lightness had set foot here. This was not their domain. Here the world was dying or dead, and in its gloom there crouched creatures of darkness and evil, waiting to pounce and strike, attracted by the humans as they moved through the frightening vista, for whom only spiritual integrity was their armour.

Scáthach suddenly halted and smiled.

She half turned to Ruacán.

'I think I understand now,' she said. 'I will try to make my spirit worthy of this test.'

From the surrounding murkiness there came the terrifying roaring of creatures in rage and anger.

'Yes. I understand,' she repeated with a soft smile.

Ruacán nodded slowly.

'That is good, daughter of Eola. For those who smile at the darkness will not succumb to it dangers.'

They pushed on through the chill swamps, the quiet of their journey punctuated now and then by the shrill cries of rage and disappointment, by the splash of unseen things sinking into the muddy depths of the mires through which they picked their way.

Three times they halted as they came to the remains of whitened bones – human bones, with skeletal hands clutching vainly at rusting swords and shields. They marked the places where others had succumbed to their fears. The girl stepped carefully over the grim remnants that strewed their path and proceeded without a backward glance.

Then the ground started to rise, away from the swampy lowlands. The pathway began to grow broader and more easy to travel. It rose gently, rose away from the Plain of Ill-Luck and pushed its way through the mist into clearer air. They followed the pathway over another range of mountains but, Scáthach noticed, the sky was almost black, like night. Dark storm clouds scudded low in the sky and now and then came an occasional ominous rumble of thunder, but they could see no flash of lightning. By the time they reached a fork in the peaks through which the path took them into the valley beyond it the world was as black and chill as night.

'Where is this place?' demanded Scáthach.

Ruacán smiled gravely.

'We have emerged from the Plain of Ill-Luck and now we must traverse the Perilous Glen.'

'What manner of evil shall we encounter?' demanded the girl.

The old druid shrugged.

'What manner of evil do you fear, daughter of Eola?'

She frowned, was about to press him for a further explanation, and then shrugged.

They moved on down the pathway into the valley beyond. There was no sun. Now the sky was so black with low storm clouds that the visibility was limited. Threatening thunder rumbled constantly and ice-cold rain began to patter on them chilling their bones. All around the glen the mountain sides rose steeply with high ragged tops that were like shadows in the gloom. There was no colour in the glen, no vegetation; the earth was burnt like a wasteland. No trees nor flowers carpeted the muddy flats and where the gnarled branches of a tree stretched imploringly to the heavens it was as if the wood was rotten and crumbling. Here and there a pool of stagnant water lay with foul-smelling odours. It was a scene of utter desolation.

Unlike the swamp and its mires, the path was fairly visible in spite of the blackness of the day and they mounted their horses. However, in case of danger they walked them slowly along the pathway, Scáthach keeping a careful watch in the chill gloom for any menace which might emerge.

'This is well named, Ruacán,' she smiled. 'The Perilous Glen.'

'But we have yet to see its perils,' replied the old druid.

As if in reply there was a sudden flash of lightning. So close did it strike to them that Scáthach was momentarily blinded. She blinked her eyes for a moment and opened them just in time for the crash of thunder to shake the ground around them. Her horse shied nervously, and she bent forward to coax it and quieten its skittishness.

It was then that she saw the beast.

It stood to a height three times that of a tall man, a great creature sitting on its haunches on two powerful legs. Its great body tapered from its huge thighs upwards to a tiny snake-like head with serpent eyes and flickering tongue. Its forelimbs were short, much shorter than the muscular hind feet, yet with talons that could obviously tear its prey without effort. It squatted on the road ahead, its black eyes watching them with malevolence.

Scáthach swallowed hard as she took in the powerful beast.

When she was a child, listening to the stories of the bards, she had heard of such creatures which dwelt in the grim, dark lands of the Fomorii, the lords of evil. Heroes had gone forth to do battle with such creatures and never returned. For some time, as a child, she had nightmares of

222

such creatures, of being alone and unarmed as they moved down on her. Now the nightmare was a reality.

She swung her war-helm from its thong and placed it on her head, and then she took the *Corr-Bholg*, the javelin which The Dagda, Father of the Gods, had given to his son Manánnan Mac Lir, the ocean god. It was light and quivered in her hand. Yet she wished she had the more powerful *gae-Bolga* which would enter with one wound and open out into thirty barbs once it had penetrated the flesh. With that she could face this fierce beast which barred their path.

'Stay back, Ruacán!' she called, making ready to meet the beast.

'What manner of evil do you fear, daughter of Eola?' cried the old druid.

Scáthach frowned, not understanding why the old man repeated the question. Then the giant beast was charging down on her. She stayed her mount until the great creature was almost upon her and then she dug her heels in and yanked upon the bridle. The horse responded, moving sideways, so that the creature went lumbering by.

Strangely it halted, not moving on to attack the old druid, who sat calmly on his horse watching the encounter as if he were safe, one hand holding the reins of Flann's roan mare. The beast turned, as if perceiving that its antagonist was Scáthach and not the old man.

The girl raced her horse in a semi-circle in order to place herself between it and Ruacán again.

'Get away from here, Ruacán,' she cried. 'Reach safety while I try to stay this creature.'

The flat serpent head of the beast lashed out at her, its flickering long tongue slashing against her helmet. She realised, with grim horror, that had she not been wearing her helmet then the tongue, razor sharp, would have lopped off her head like a sharp sword slicing through butter.

Dimly, out of the corner of her eye, she noticed that

Ruacán was not moving. He was quietly sitting astride his horse watching without fear on his ancient features. And Flann's roan stood quietly beside them, gently nuzzling at the grass as if unaware of the contest.

Once more the girl cried out to him to fly to safety as she spurred her horse into another manoeuvre to escape the flickering tongue of the terrifying creature. Vainly she examined the shining, yellow-green hide of the thing, searching for some vantage point of attack, some area of weakness in the glossy plating of its toughened hide.

The flickering tongue lashed out again, smashing against the side of her helmet and causing her to nearly lose her balance. She sprawled momentarily from her saddle, clinging on only by a tightening of her thighs against the back of her steed. Then she was upright again and urging the horse away from the reach of the creature.

She realised that, for whatever reason, the creature was not interested in attacking the old druid yet, so she need not concern herself with Ruacán's stupid behaviour in not withdrawing out of the danger zone. But how could she overcome this vile nightmare from her childhood? There seemed no weakness in the beast's great hide, no point at which the thing was not armoured. And all she had was her javelin and sword. Once cast, she would not be able to retrieve her javelin unless some incredible piece of luck presented itself to her. The idea of being able to get close enough to the beast to use her sword was unimaginable. The flickering tongue was as sharp as a sword itself and only pure luck had prevented her being cut in two, for twice the tongue had caught against her war helmet, *An Cruadín*, which was well named 'the hard helm'. Silently, she uttered a prayer of thanks to the skill and craftsmanship of Goibhniu the smith who had shaped the helmet.

224

She had halted her mount now on a small knoll to examine the creature as it cautiously moved towards her, its great tongue flickering from its flat serpent head. Perhaps there was a way to kill it. If she could cast the javelin into its mouth, upwards so that it went through the roof of the mouth, then it might penetrate its brain.

She was aware of the nervous tension of the horse under her; aware that the cast of the javelin had to be precise and that if the horse shied or even rippled its muscles, then her aim would be a fraction off and prove useless.

Fear was drenching her in sweat as she watched the creature edging nearer, rising on its great hind legs as it approached. Yet, trying to control her fear, she slipped from her horse and gave it a slap across the flank to send it out of danger. Ah, if only she had her shield and the *gae-Bolga*!

She stood, trembling a little, body tensed for the cast of her javelin, right hand stretched back behind her clasping the shaft, the left hand before her to steady her aim. Her mouth was compressed in a thin line, eyes narrowed as she focused on the terrifying maw of the creature as it edged nearer.

Then, when she judged the moment to be right, she cast the javelin with as much force as she could summon.

Straight and true the javelin headed for the gaping maw of the beast but, as its impact seemed inevitable, the flickering black tongue came forth and swept it aside as a man might swat a fly, dashing the weapon into the ground a hundred yards or more away.

Cold fear swept over the girl now. She stood trembling, unable to run, indeed unable to move. Fear froze her to the spot. She gave a cry of despair as she realised the inevitability of her fate. Once more she was the little girl with the nightmare of the great devouring beast.

'Oh, mother! Mother!' she whimpered, a little girl's voice echoing in her ear.

'Why, what are you afraid of?' came Buimech's soft tones, soothing and caressing her.

'What manner of evil do you fear, daughter of Eola?' she heard Ruacán asking.

She stood shivering, awaiting the cutting strike of the beast's long tongue.

'It is but a nightmare, daughter,' whispered Buimech's voice. 'A shadow on the wall, without substance, without form. It is a dream. Not what is but what you fear might be.'

'What manner of evil do you fear, daughter of Eola?' came Ruacán's voice more urgently.

Scáthach, with closed eyes, bit her lip. She knew what manner of evil she feared: the nightmare creature come to haunt her. And here it was . . . here in reality . . .

'It is but a nightmare that will pass,' whispered Buimech's voice, as she had heard it years ago as a young child, starting from her bed of fears with the creations of the Fomorii at her heels.

'I know what manner of evil I fear,' Scáthach whispered fiercely to herself.

'All that we are, or seem, is but a dream within a dream,' came Buimech's voice.

It was then that the girl suddenly came to an understanding. She knew what Ruacán had been trying to tell her; why he had not been afraid of the creature and why he had made no attempt to flee. This was her own nightmare, her own particular fear and evil. It had no existence outside her own mind.

Her eyes flickered open to stare at the creature now towering threateningly above her. Yet her fear was now gone. She was of the knowledge. She understood. She threw back her head and cried:

'I abjure you. I do not believe in you. Begone to the dark depths of the mind and do not come forth again!'

She flung back her head defiantly.

226

The creature seemed to hesitate and then it seemed to dissolve, becoming opaque, then transparent, before disappearing as if in a cloud of mist.

Scáthach stood looking at the place where a moment before the creature had stood in frightening reality. Her eyes were wide, her lips trembling a little.

Ruacán trotted up on his horse. He had rounded up Scáthach's mount and led it as well as Flann's horse beside him.

His ancient face was set in grim lines.

'Sometimes you worry me, daughter of Eola,' he confessed.

She stared up at the old druid.

'Why do you have need to be worried, old one. You knew that this creature was not real.'

He smiled.

'Oh no, it was real enough. You believed in it, so it was real.'

The girl frowned.

'I do not understand.'

The old druid shrugged.

'Maybe one day you will understand completely. But it seems that day is a long time coming.'

'Explain now,' demanded the girl, 'that I may understand the quicker.'

The old man smiled softly and shook his head.

'That is no way to understand.' He glanced up. 'The day grows late and as the perils have gone from this place we may make camp here for the night. Tomorrow we must continue our journey. Go and retrieve the *Corr-Bholg* while I make camp.'

He slid from his horse and tethered the mounts to the stump of a gnarled tree.

Scáthach hesitated, staring in annoyance at the druid, then she sighed and went off to retrieve the javelin from where the make-believe creature had cast it. She was frustrated with the old man's ambiguous and enigmatic sayings. Better if he just came out with what he meant than hiding behind cryptic and baffling statements. She sniffed. Could it be that the oracular obscurity hid the fact that the old one had no knowledge? She felt guilty even as the thought entered her mind because the old druid had showed his knowledge many a time. But what was the point of knowledge if one did not pass the knowledge on?

For a long while she sat silently watching the old man preparing a meal before a fire he had put together from the dry, rotten wood that lay strewn about. He was boiling eggs which Laoch had given them, with bread and some of the local wine of Aird nan Murchan – a sharp-tasting brew which they called 'the water of life'. Finally the girl could no longer hide her irritability.

'How may I face the dangers to come, old one, if you do not teach me?' she demanded.

Ruacán grimaced.

'Wisdom is something that cannot be taught, my child. In the dangers that face you, you need only wisdom.'

'Was it wisdom which taught me that the beast just now was not real?'

'Yes. And when you reflected properly you found it so. I did not teach you that.'

'But . . .'

'Child, be reflective. That is all I ask. You can gather facts like a farmer gathers hay. Yet if you simply gather the hay and leave it in a pile, the hay rots and is unusable. Wisdom lies in how one uses the hay. The knowledge of that is more important than gathering the hay.'

Scáthach sighed impatiently.

'I need not a lesson in farming, old one.'

'No,' replied Ruacán, 'you want someone on hand to explain things to you instead of perfecting your mind to reason out explanations for yourself.'

'That is not so,' the girl was stung to reply. 'I can reason as well as most . . . better than most, I warrant. It is just that there are some things beyond understanding which only a druid knows.'

Ruacán had taken the eggs from the cooking pot and suddenly handed the girl one.

'See that flat stone? If you have reason then you will be able to stand the egg upon it.'

'Stand the egg upon it?' queried the girl, puzzled.

'Yes. If it is reason you have then you will be able to stand the egg upright so that it doesn't fall over.'

The girl took the egg in her hand and frowned at the smooth flat surface of the stone to which the druid pointed. Half-heartedly, she tried a couple of times, but the egg fell over each time.

'It is impossible,' she snapped. 'What druid's trick is this?'

'No trick,' smiled the old man. 'It is simply a matter of reason and you say that you have reason enough and merely want an explanation of facts.'

The girl bit her lip.

'It cannot be done,' she said sharply.

The druid took the egg from her and then, turning to a bag of salt, he poured a quantity onto the flat stone; then, with a gentle turn, he stood the egg up on its end in the salt so that it did not fall.

'Trickery,' scoffed the girl. 'Anyone can do that.'

The old man smiled softly.

'Ah yes. Anyone can do it after being shown the way.'

The girl bit her lip, her cheeks reddening. She bowed her head and thought a while before making further comment.

'I have much to learn,' whispered the girl. 'There is much knowledge that should be stored in my mind.'

'Child, the fuller the ear of grain, the lower the stalk bends; empty of grain, the stalk grows tall and strong. Don't clutter your life with facts unless you have the wisdom to use them.'

229

'I should be more humble in your presence, Ruacán,' sighed the girl.

For a moment the old druid flashed a look of anger at her.

'Humble? No! Humility is as much the child of pride as exaltation. Those who humble themselves only wish to be exalted, child. Humility is often feigned submission, a subterfuge of pride which persuades others to lower themselves so that the humble render others submissive. No, child. You must be neither humble or proud but at one with everyone.'

The girl looked uncertain.

The old man reached forward and touched her arm.

'My child, flow with life. Do not fight the currents. Merge with life. Do not seek to move the mountain from your path but climb it or pass round it.'

The old man stood up and stretched, drawing his cloak more tightly round him.

'And now it is time for rest for we must continue when the sun rises.'

'And will we reach Dún Scáith tomorrow?'

'We have yet to travel by way of the Valley of the Shadow and the Bridge of Leaps.'

He turned and went to his bed roll and she could ask him no more.

Only a perceptible change of light across the gloomy valley announced the dawn. There were no bird songs to hail the coming of the light and they rose in quiet to break their fast and saddle their horses. It was not long before they were ascending out of the Perilous Glen on a road which took them through foothills and across mountains before descending again in zig-zag motion into a valley even more dark and gloomy than the previous one.

'Is this the Valley of the Shadow?' asked the girl.

Ruacán grunted assent.

'What need I be afraid of here?' pressed Scáthach.

'Of yourself, daughter of Eola,' replied the old man.

The valley was crowded with a dark wood in which strange birds flitted and called, sometimes moving so close that their damp wings brushed her face. The air smelled musty, like the earth of burial grounds. She had been taken to the ancestral burying grounds as a child by her mother in order to bring flowers as tokens of remembrance. It was a visit she had come to fear for she feared the graves and places of the dead. Indeed, she came to fear death itself. Death was the ultimate thing to fear and this place, this Valley of the Shadow, was a place of the dead; a fearful place. Cobwebs spread from tree to tree and across the path so that their coldness suddenly spread across her face.

She snatched at them with anger, brushing her cheeks. She would not show fear again and yet she hated the silken webs of spiders and the high-pitched cry of night bats. Then, she abruptly heard a sound of flapping and something struck her in the face. She felt tiny pin-pricks in her scalp and forehead, and something like a wet, chilly tissue covered her face, preventing her from breathing. She gave a choking cry, raising both hands to claw at the thing on her face. Her heart pounded in fear and revulsion. Her flesh crawled as she felt the small, bloated body beating against her hands, felt the wings flapping. She tore the creature from her and flung it to the ground.

The creature lay stunned on the path. To her horror she saw that it was a fairly large species of bat, its flapping wings were nearly two feet in length, and its body almost a foot long. It had large ears, broad at the base but narrowing abruptly to sharp, recursive tips. It also had thick woolly fur extending onto its wing membranes, which appeared ash-grey in colour.

With a cry of distaste, she drew her javelin and spiked it as it lay stunned on the ground. It gave a high-pitched, penetrating squeak, flapped its great wings for a moment or two and then lay still.

'Not all one's fears can be so easily dismissed,' remarked Ruacán.

The pathway had narrowed through the trees so that only a single horse could move through the great avenue of dark wood. Wolves started to howl from far away yet their voices seemed to grow nearer and nearer.

'I dislike this place,' she whispered apprehensively. 'But I will not be afraid of it.'

'If you are not afraid of it, then it will not exist,' she heard Ruacán say behind her.

'Then I command it not to exist!' she cried in sudden anger.

She bit her lip in annoyance as there was no change in the spectacle of the grim forest.

'You still fear it,' observed the old druid.

The girl hesitated and then nodded agreement.

'Since I was a child, I have feared death,' she admitted. 'And this is how I visualise death.'

'And these are the shadows you fear?'

'If this is death, this is what I fear.'

'Yet what is death? It is as much part of life as birth. Rather should we fear birth, daughter of Eola. If a baby had a glimpse of its trials and travails during its life, would it ask to be born? Death is no different from life. It is simply another door through which we must go. If we fear to enter that door then we must fear every second, minute and hour of each day we live, and our lives will be that much poorer. Do not fear death any more than life.'

'Yet I fear it.'

'You fear the moment of death, you fear pain?'

'I think that is what I fear,' agreed the girl hesitantly.

'Did you fear the moment of your birth?'

Scáthach shook her head.

'I had no control over the moment of my birth.'

'Neither have you control over the moment of your death,' replied the druid. 'If you are at one with life you will not fear death. If you have lived a full life at peace with yourself then you will not fear death, my child. Death is as natural for us as life, it is the other side of the coin. This valley is not death, these shadows are your own fears which you have conjured.'

The girl sat thinking for a moment and then she sighed and nudged her horse onwards. After a moment she suddenly peered forward eagerly.

'I see a light ahead, the end of the forest.'

Ruacán chuckled softly.

'Then you have lost your fear of death.'

The girl swung round, her face a complex expression of surprise and bewilderment.

'I have understood it,' she said in wonder.

'And in understanding there comes a realisation that there is nothing to fear.'

'Perhaps.'

'It is so,' replied the old man firmly. 'Fear, which also leads to hate, is born from ignorance. Cast aside ignorance and you will cast aside fear and hatred. See, you have passed through the Valley of the Shadow.'

They emerged from the tall, dark, silent woodlands and into a bright countryside over which hung a canopy of azure and the sun, a bright golden disc, shining with a dazzling heat.

Scáthach paused to wipe her brow and gaze back upon the black forest.

'I am beginning to understand,' she said to Ruacán. 'Most dangers that we fear reside only in our minds. I do not fully understand but I believe I begin to understand.'

The old man smiled.

'Maybe one day you will be of the knowledge, daughter of Eola.'

They rode slowly along the pathway, out of the valley

233

and once more over foothills and through mountain passes. Now there was a brightness in the sky and the tall mountains rose blue, with white snow caps, on all sides, their lower skirts crowded with purple heather and yellow broom.

The girl was more relaxed now, having passed the dangers of the Plain of Ill-Luck, the Perilous Glen and the Valley of the Shadow. Soon they would reach Dún Scáith.

Sixteen

It was early afternoon when they came through a cleft in the mountains to pause on a broad ledge of rock overlooking the sea which moved restlessly one hundred feet below them. Before them stood the tall impressive grey ramparts of Dún Scáith, the fortress of Darcon the Tyrant, reputed son of the goddess of death and battles. It was an austere construction of great granite blocks with hardly an opening or window in its bleak walls. It rose as part of the granite outcrop on which it stood so that it was almost impossible to see where nature's building had left off and where the hand of man had constructed the rest. It rose grimly against the heavens, thrusting upwards as if in challenge to the surrounding world.

Scáthach's eyes narrowed as she surveyed the construction. Only one great set of doors gave entrance and these were shut tight and there was no sign of life anywhere within the vicinity.

As she walked her horse forward onto the rocky ledge

she realised that the fortress was separated from it by a chasm of some thirty feet or more at the bottom of which, a hundred feet below, boiled a turbulent white-foamed sea. There was no bridge to connect the mainland on which they stood with the rocky island on which stood Dún Scáith . . . the Island of Shadows.

The girl turned to the old druid, who sat astride his horse watching her, still leading Flann's roan horse behind him.

'I thought you said there was a bridge here?' she demanded.

Ruacán shrugged and smiled thinly.

'Bridge? I said that we would come to the Bridge of Leaps.'

'Then where is this bridge?'

The druid pointed further along the chasm.

'If you want to bridge the gorge, there is only one way forward.'

Further along the ledge, almost hidden by a jutting rock, she now saw a wooden construction. She dismounted, tethered her horse and moved forward to examine it. There was no doubt that it was a bridge but it was a bridge such as she had never seen before, a bridge of strange craftsmanship, made of wood but wood interlocked in curious joints and angles.

Scáthach examined it curiously from a distance.

It was unguarded and invited the traveller to move across unimpeded.

Yet there was something wrong; she felt it instinctively.

Frowning, she turned back to Ruacán who had also dismounted and stood watching her with an expression of curiosity, as a person sometimes stands and watches the behaviour of an animal, bemused by what it will do.

'This is a strange bridge, old one,' observed the girl.

The old man did not answer.

'Why is it unguarded?' pressed Scáthach.

'That you should be able to work out for yourself, daughter of Eola.'

She bit her lip in annoyance.

'Why is it called the Bridge of Leaps?'

Again the druid was silent.

The girl sniffed.

'So this is another of your tests, old one?'

The old man smiled.

'*My* tests?' he said gently. 'I make no tests for you that are not of your own choosing.'

The girl scowled and turned to re-examine the bridge.

She saw that the bridge formed a small apex in the middle where there appeared a joint. She wondered what all the hinges and joints were and what their function was. Then a faint suspicion filled her mind. She looked around and searched the stony ledge. There were some small boulders lying nearby. She picked up one of them and weighed it carefully in her hands, but then discarded it for its lightness. Then she picked up another, which was so heavy that it needed both hands to carry it.

Walking to the head of the bridge she stood, feet apart, raising the boulder in both hands until she brought it up first to chest height and then above her head. Her face was red and her muscles groaned at the effort. She stood, swaying for a moment. Then she cast the boulder from her so that it fell almost in the centre of the bridge.

Although suspicious, Scáthach was not prepared for what happened next. There was a snapping sound, the slap of planks on planks and, so it seemed, the entire bridge suddenly drew itself together like a concertina, the planks recoiling like a mighty spring so that the boulder was thrown off and cast into the chasm below. It bounced down the smooth granite sides of the gorge and finally

236

disappeared into the frothy, boiling seas below. If the boulder had represented a person then they would not have survived the fall let alone immersion into the fierce waters which gushed along the ravine.

For a moment Scáthach stood staring in disbelief and then, as if by some unseen hand or some miracle, the bridge unfolded itself, its springs slapping the planks back into place so that once again it stood innocently inviting travellers to cross in order to lure them to their doom in the abyss below.

'You knew of this!' the girl cried accusingly, as she faced the old man.

Ruacán shrugged.

'Let us say that I suspected something of the sort.'

'And you did not warn me?'

'On the contrary, daughter of Eola, you warned yourself.'

'If I had set foot on the bridge, I would have been killed,' snapped Scáthach.

'But you didn't,' the old man pointed out patiently.

'If I had done so, would you have let me?'

'You must work out your own salvation, I can only advise.'

The girl sniffed and turned back to the bridge.

'Is there any other way across the ravine?'

'None,' replied the druid.

'And there is certainly no way to cross by this bridge if we want to survive.'

'That is true.'

She turned and sat down on a boulder, chin resting on an upraised fist, and stared moodily at the chasm while she considered the situation.

'What name did you say was given to this bridge?' she asked abruptly. 'Didn't you call it the Bridge of Leaps.'

The old man nodded.

'That is what I have heard it called.'

A slight smile crossed the girl's face.

'A curious name for a bridge.'

Ruacán was silent.

The girl stood up and went to her horse where she had left her javelin. She picked it up and gazed at it and then, holding the shaft with both hands, pressed her full weight on it, feeling its strength and flexibility.

Then she walked back to the chasm and measured the distance with her eye.

'If I don't cross this place, Ruacán, then I will have failed. But fail I won't.'

'How so, daughter of Eola?' the old man was smiling.

'Because I shall obey the name of the bridge,' she replied with firm decision in her voice.

Once again she tested the staff of the weapon and then turned to the old man.

'It seems that we must part here for a while, Ruacán. I am going to enter Dún Scáith and rescue Flann. If I am successful, we will return here. Take care of the horse. Watch for us.'

The druid nodded slowly.

'It will be as you say, Scáthach of Uibh Rathach,' he said softly.

The girl walked to the chasm and stared down for a moment, then she measured with an eye the stretch of the gorge. Firmly, head high, she walked slowly back across the ledge as far as she could go. Then, holding the shaft of the javelin just under the spearhead with both hands, the butt uppermost, she began to run towards the edge of the ravine. Her long legs strode the distance, accelerating the motion of her body. Then she was within a yard. Down came the butt of the javelin, hard on the rocky ledge, and her lithe body was being pulled upwards into the air, slowly, as if time were suddenly standing still, upwards and over, muscles tightening in her shoulders and neck. Her body reached the apex of the curve, arching and twisting over like a salmon in mid-leap. Then she was falling feet first and landing in a crouch on the far side of the gap.

She remained for a moment squatting on her haunches as she recovered herself. She had not let go of the javelin and she now stood and hauled it across. Upright, she turned to the druid on the far side of the ravine and smiled.

'Now I see why it is called the Bridge of Leaps,' she smiled.

The old druid nodded.

'Never was there such a hero's leap,' he assented.

The girl shook her head.

'Oh yes, yes there was. A greater hero than ever I shall be taught me the Salmon Leap. Eola of Uibh Rathach was my teacher.'

'But his pupil has outshone him this day,' replied Ruacán. 'May the gods go with you into this fortress of shadows, daughter of Eola.'

She raised her arm in acknowledgement and turned towards the grey forbidding walls of the fortress.

The great wooden gates were shut tightly. There was no chink nor crack in their thick planking, nor even a sight of any means of opening them.

Scáthach paused before them and examined them with critical eye.

There was no means at all of gaining entrance which she could see. The tall granite walls of the fortress were unscaleable. She gave a mental shrug. Well, if there were no way in but through the doors and these were barred against her then there was only one thing to do.

She raised her javelin in both hands and brought the butt once, twice and thrice against the wooden doors. The sound went booming into the inner recesses of the fortress.

For a while there was no response. Only silence greeted her. Impatiently she raised the javelin to strike again.

'Stay, little girl! No need to make such a din.'

The voice was a hideous high-pitched cackle.

Scáthach frowned and peered around but could see nothing.

'Who speaks?' she demanded.

'I speak, little girl,' came the voice.

Peering upwards, above the gate, she saw a block of granite had been swung to one side, making an aperture of about a foot square. From this dark recess a hideous gargoyle of a face was grinning down from under matted dirty-white hair. The one eye stared down which was uncannily bright and burnt with a curious red glow.

'And who are you?' demanded the girl.

There came a peel of high-pitched laughter which caused her blood to run cold for a moment or two, and a tingling at the nape of her neck.

'Who am I? Why, I am Eis Enchenn. I am the door keeper of Dún Scáith. And who stands so proudly before that door?'

Scáthach threw back her shoulders, sticking her chin out defiantly.

'I am Scáthach of Uibh Rathach.'

'Are you now?' the voice was a little sharper, the head stuck quickly forward, reminding the girl of the action of the head of a snake.

'I demand entrance,' cried the girl.

Again came the cackle of the harridan.

'Do not be so high and mighty here, little girl. This is the fortress of Darcon, son of the Mórrígú, goddess of death and battles, ruler of the Island of Shadows.'

'And is he afraid of me, which is why he must bar his gates to me?' sneered Scáthach.

The old hag gave a shriek of outrage.

'Rather you should be in fear and trembling, mortal, for if you looked upon Darcon's countenance your soul would flee from this world and seek refuge in the Otherworld.'

'Is he so ugly?'

She thought that she would provoke another shriek of anger but the old hag suddenly began to croon, her head moving from side to side as if she were rocking to and fro.

'My, my. We have heard of the coming of Scáthach of Uibh Rathach. There are those among us who did not think that you would reach here. But you have met your tests well. You are a worthy opponent.'

'And not one prone to flattery,' the girl said shortly.

Eis Enchenn, the one-eyed hag, chuckled softly.

'Perhaps not. Perhaps not.'

'Will you let me in?' the girl pressed, growing impatient. 'Or do I have to force my way in?'

'Why have you come here?'

'If you have known of my coming, and of my name, you will know of my purpose.'

The harridan shrieked with laughter.

'The young one, the handsome young warrior. That is why you have come. My, my, girl. But there are many more like him in the world just as there are fish in the sea. He is not worth your attentions. He is not worth your love.'

Scáthach found herself flushing crimson.

'Who said I loved Flann Mac Fraech?' she demanded hotly.

'You do not? Why then are you here?' shot back the crone.

'Because he is my friend,' retorted Scáthach.

Eis Enchenn wheezed with laughter, rocking back and forth again.

Scáthach's patience vanished. She drew back her javelin, aiming it at the face of the old woman.

'Do you let me in or do you die?'

'No, no. Do not give way to anger, little girl,' admonished the harridan. 'If you were lucky enough to kill me then who would let you in?'

'My patience is not infinite,' replied Scáthach. 'I will not ask again. Beware of my anger if I have to force my way inside.'

'Well, well,' mused the crone. 'Indulge an old woman. I have no quarrel with you, Scáthach of Uibh Rathach. I will let you in if you answer me three riddles.'

The girl fumed with impatience. Nevertheless, she lowered her javelin and stared back. Her threat to find another way into the fortress was a bluff and she knew it. It would take a long time to scale the great walls and even then she did not know if she could do so.

'Three riddles and you will open these doors?'

'That is the bargain.'

'What three riddles?' demanded the girl.

'Do you agree to answer them?'

'And if I do, who is there to judge that the answers are correct?'

'Would I deny the truth?'

'You might.'

'Shame be your portion, little girl. I'll not deny the truth if your answers are correct.'

Scáthach sighed restlessly.

'Very well. I will answer your questions, Eis Enchenn, and woe betide you if you do not concede the truth of the answers.'

'Very well. The first question is – you see the chasm behind you. How deep is the water there?'

Scáthach half turned to the ravine and then shrugged.

'As deep as the bottom,' she replied.

The harridan gave an angry squeal which caused the girl to realise that she had given the right answer.

'That was too easy,' snapped Eis Enchenn. 'Too easy.

242

Now let me think. Yes . . . yes. Tell me how many types of tree grow on the Island of Shadows?'

Scáthach glanced around, drawing her brows together in thought.

The harridan began to chuckle wheezily.

'Ah, you have no answer for that one, do you, little girl?'

Scáthach suddenly smiled as an answer occurred to her.

'Yes, I do. Two types of tree grow here – the green and the withered.'

Eis Enchenn gave a yell of anguish and began rocking back and forth.

'Come now,' Scáthach pressed. 'I grow tired of this game. Let me in or demand of me the last of your riddles.'

'You will not answer this question, little girl. I have been too soft on you so far but this riddle you will not be able to answer. Tell me . . . what is blacker than the raven's wing?'

Scáthach pursed her lips as she stared upwards at the mocking face of the crone.

'Come, come,' called Eis Enchenn, mockingly, 'have you no answer? You must answer all three questions to be allowed in. You have accepted the rules of the contest and you must answer.'

She went into a fit of shrieking laughter.

'When you have ceased choking yourself to death, old woman,' called Scáthach, 'I am ready to reply.'

The harridan was still at once.

'What is your answer?' she wheezed.

'Death is blacker than the wing of a raven, and black death will be your lot unless you open these portals and let me in.'

Once more the girl raised her arm and readied her javelin to throw.

'Wait, Scáthach of Uibh Rathach. Wait. I will open the portals and admit you. You have answered all three questions well. I cannot deny that.'

The gruesome head disappeared from the small dark aperture and the granite block slid noiselessly into place.

After a few moments there came a great creaking and the soft scream of wood over stone. The great doors seemed to break apart in the centre and move inwards. The opening was as black as pitch and from the interior of the fortress came the vile smell of corruption, of dank rotting earth, which caused the girl to take an involuntary step backwards.

This was truly one of her childhood fears but, to her surprise, she found her fear gone. Instead her blood tingled with excitement at the nearness of her journey's end. Flann was within reach. She would rescue him. Her journey to this place had dispelled her fears, as Buimech had foretold it would. She was no longer afraid of corruption, no longer afraid of the shadows and monsters conjured from them. She was Scáthach of Uibh Rathach and she bowed her knee to no one.

She took her helmet from its thong at her waist and placed it upon her head, then she slung her javelin on her back and drew forth her sword.

The doors drew inwards, opening as if to a yawning maw of malignancy and decay, but it did not bother her. Sword in hand she strode forward.

The crouching figure of Eis Enchenn huddled in the darkness before her.

'Welcome, Scáthach of Uibh Rathach. Welcome to Dún Scáith,' the crone cackled.

'I need no welcome,' snapped the girl. 'Where are you holding Flann Mac Fraech? And where is the *gae-Bolga* and *An Seancholl Snidheach* which Aífe of Lethra stole from me?'

'Come, come, my girl, this is no way to answer the hospitality of Darcon,' wheezed the old woman. 'Surely you will respect the custom of hospitality?'

'As much as it was respected when Flann was kidnapped from our encampment and my weapons stolen.'

Scáthach moved further down the dark granite corridor into which the doors had opened, wrinkling her nose against the putrid smells that pervaded the place. At the far end of the corridor she saw other doors open leading into a courtyard, equally as grey and dank as the rest of the fortress.

There was a squeal of wood over stone behind her. She wheeled round, sword in hand. The great doors of Dún Scáith were closing.

She swung on the harridan. For the first time she could see the old one clearly. Eis Enchenn was of indeterminable age; that she was elderly there was no doubt, but she seemed more like an emaciated corpse than a living person, an animated skeleton. Her crouching bony body was wrapped in smelly, dirty animal skins. Her filthy, unwashed hair was matted and her burning single eye glared malignantly at the girl. Around her scrawny neck she wore a necklace of animal teeth and she held a huge thigh bone in one hand.

'What are you?' demanded Scáthach in disgust as she viewed the old woman. 'Are you human?'

Eis Enchenn shook the thigh bone towards her, screeching angrily.

'You have no call to heap insults on me after I have opened the doors of Dún Scáith to you, girl!'

'Perhaps not,' agreed Scáthach, 'but I have not seen such an ill-kept person as you before.'

The old woman spat towards her and piped in her thin piercing voice: 'You have the haughty arrogance of youth, girl. Wait until you have lived as many summers as I have before you sneer . . .'

She paused and cocked her head to one side and started to cackle again.

'But I speak foolishly. It is written that Scáthach of Uibh Rathach will not live another summer.'

The girl, hearing the inflection in the other's voice, tensed her muscles, her hand gripped tightly on the sword.

'Speak plainly, hag,' she hissed. 'What do you mean?'

Suddenly the harridan began to move in a swaying motion left to right, right to left, like a snake, in a curious, mesmeric, twisting motion. Scáthach stared at her in distaste, watching the skeletal figure moving, increasing the motion until she started to quiver and until she began to work herself into a frenzy of excitement. The foam flew in flecks from her gnashing jaws. The fierce red eye seemed to start from her head, and she moved forward holding the great thigh bone towards the girl. It was not until then that Scáthach realised that the bone was actually a human thigh bone. She shivered slightly and drew back in disgust.

'Stop, old woman, before I strike you dead where you stand,' she cried and raised her sword.

The thigh bone gestured towards her, the crone shrieked loudly and then there was a blinding flash. Scáthach blinked rapidly and took a pace or so backwards. She had no idea whence had come the fierce streak of light nor what had caused it. Everything before her eyes had dimmed. She raised a hand to massage them, blinked again and tried to focus.

Eis Enchenn was chuckling and still performing her weird swaying dance. It was a sickening sight seeing the old creature bent with extreme age, swaying and chanting, like some animated skeleton covered in a leather taut skin, her horrid eye gleaming with its red unholy lustre.

'Foolish girl!' she squealed. 'Did you think I would let you into my lord's domain without hindrance? You have managed to come thus far but you will go no farther. I have promised my lord that you will be brought before him . . . but as a prisoner.'

Scáthach rubbed her eyes and gasped.

'You dare break your word?'

'What word?' sneered the obscene crone. 'I only promised to open the gates of the fortress. I have done so. Now they are closed and you are my prisoner, girl.'

'Not yet!' cried Scáthach, raising her sword again and attempting to rush on the harridan.

Once more she saw the awesome thigh bone pointing towards her and sensed, rather than saw, the flash of blinding light. She shut her eyes but a fraction too late for when she tried to open them everything was dim and out of focus again.

She suddenly felt something wet and slippery enmesh her like a net, but it was a fine net, a cobweb of immense strength. It fell over her and immediately wrapped itself around her body so tightly that she could not move. She could not even move her wrist to use her sword to cut her way out. The sticky mesh enclosed her like a tightly wound shroud.

She could hear Eis Enchenn shrieking with laughter and she cursed herself for her stupidity. How dim-witted she had been to think that she had no need of the wisdom of Ruacán. She wished he was with her now.

She felt the mesh tightening, driving the breath from her body. She could do nothing but attempt to fight for breath. So tight it became that she fell to the ground, gasping.

Then Eis Einchenn slithered over to her.

'Proud child, stupid child. Did you think it would be easy to gain victory over the Island of Shadows?'

Then she raised her thigh bone and brought it crashing down onto the head of the bound girl. For a split second Scáthach was aware of the impact before losing herself into a black, bottomless pit.

Seventeen

Scáthach came to consciousness still cursing herself for her stupidity. She opened her eyes to darkness and had to wait a moment for her eyes to grow accustomed to the dank gloom. That she was in some dungeon, probably below Dún Scáith, was obvious. She did not move, in case she was being watched. She wanted as much time as she could to examine her surroundings before making her captors aware of her return to consciousness.

Some light must have been penetrating from somewhere, perhaps the flickering glow of a torch or candle, for she was able to discern the main features of her surroundings. She was in a cell-like room which seemed to have been tunnelled out of granite. It was no more than ten feet long by ten feet in width and probably the same in height. She saw that instead of a door, iron bars spread across one end of the cell. On looking more carefully, she observed that the iron bars themselves constituted a door.

She lay on a wooden cot on which rotting straw had been placed. There appeared to be nothing else in the cell.

Having made her inspection, her mind turned to her own welfare. Her head ached but the suffocating mesh which had caused her downfall was gone. Someone had removed her helmet and war harness and of her weapons there was no sign. All she had left was the gold medallion which was still in place on its chain around her neck. She tried to lick her lips and found her tongue rasping and her mouth dry.

248

That the harridan, Eis Enchenn, had tricked her comfortably was obvious. She was a prisoner at Dún Scáith. That much was certain. She wondered if Flann was a prisoner in a similar cell nearby.

Having spent as much time as she could assessing what information she could discern with her eyes, she decided she should move. She sat up, with a slight groan, for her head ached fiercely, and swung her legs over the edge of the cot. She noticed a jug by her cot and reached down a hand to dip her finger in the liquid, licking at it suspiciously. It was water. It seemed fresh and uncontaminated. She decided to chance her fate and picked up the jug, sipping a little and wetting her face with it.

There was a movement in a corridor outside.

She stood up expectantly. Apparently, someone had been monitoring her movements.

A figure emerged in the gloom outside.

Scáthach caught her breath sharply. A wizened-faced, hunchbacked dwarf emerged into the gloomy light and stood grinning at her from behind the bars.

'So?' His voice was a high-pitched, sing-song tone. 'You are awake, my pretty?'

The girl shrugged.

'As you can see, little one.'

She tried to keep her tone light.

The hunchback's thin lips drew back over yellowing fangs.

'Don't seek to provoke me, Scáthach of Uibh Rathach. Better people than you have tried and failed. That is why I am chief jailer to my lord, Darcon.'

'Why should I provoke you, chief jailer?' the girl forced a smile. 'Are you worthy of the effort?'

The hunchback scowled.

'You will not be so impertinent when I have questioned you, my pretty. I am Cuár and these dungeons are my domain.'

'Well, Cuár, I wish you joy of them. You are welcome to have dominion over such a place.'

Cuár chuckled.

'You sound brave, my pretty. Have you forgotten that *you* are in my domain? That I have power over you?'

'If there were not bars between you and me, little man, I would show you just how much power you have,' replied Scáthach evenly.

The hunchback hissed angrily and drew something from his belt.

Scáthach's eyes narrowed as she saw that it was a whip.

The little man cracked it against the stone flagging.

'Not even your whip can give you power, little man,' sneered the girl, deliberately turning her back on him and moving back to the cot, where she sat down.

Cuár stared at her uncertainly but there was anger deep in his dark, smouldering eyes. He hesitated a moment and then turned and scuttled away.

The girl waited a while, listening to the quiet of the subterranean world in which she was now plunged. It was a fetid-smelling world. She shivered slightly for it reminded her of her childhood nightmare of the putrid smell of death and corruption. She was glad that Ruacán had made her face that fear and overcome it. She wondered whether the old druid had realised by now that she had been taken captive and, if so, whether he would be able to do anything? She thought not, for there was no way the old man could span the ravine which separated Dún Scáith from the mainland. She bit her lip in perplexity as she wondered what she should do.

She stood up and went to the bars that constituted the door. She had no real expectations as she tried them and found them solidly rooted in the granite and with the door section firmly locked. There would be no way through except for someone who had the key.

She pressed her head against the bars and tried to see up and down the corridor. The angle of the bars were such that all she could see was the opposite wall of granite.

'Hello!' she called, deciding to risk shouting into the darkness in an effort to make contact. 'Flann Mac Fraech! Hello!'

There was no answer to her echoing voice.

She raised it again.

'Hello?'

Somewhere down the corridor something moved.

'Who calls?' came a male voice, echoing sepulchrally.

'I am Scáthach of Uibh Rathach,' called the girl. 'Who is that?'

'I am . . . I am . . .' the voice hesitated and a long sigh resonated in the gloom. 'Alas, I have been here so long . . . so long . . .'

Scáthach frowned. It was hard to estimate the age of the speaker. The voice was weak and the man could be elderly.

'You must know who you are,' she pressed.

'I was . . . was a chieftain once . . . I can't recall. I have been a prisoner of Darcon . . . Darcon . . . I can't recall. They call me Twenty-Seven, for that is the number on my cell.'

The girl shuddered slightly.

Could anyone have been incarcerated in this tomb so long that they had forgotten who they were?

'Why are you here?'

'I can't recall,' the voice echoed back. 'Something . . . I would not obey Darcon . . . I . . . I was a chieftain once.'

The girl leant forward against the bars.

'Twenty-Seven,' her voice was low and urgent, 'do you know anything about the other prisoners here?'

'Other prisoners?' The voice seemed puzzled.

'Yes, yes,' the girl said, trying to suppress the tone of exasperation. 'I am looking for a young warrior of Éireann, Flann Mac Fraech. Is he imprisoned down here?'

There was a pause.

'Twenty-Seven? Are you there?' called the girl.

'Yes. I was thinking. What did you say?'

'I am looking for Flann Mac Fraech who was brought as a prisoner to this place. Have you seen him?'

'I have seen no one but Cuár the hunchback for many years now,' the voice came softly. 'And as for this place . . . I have heard that there are many prisoners on other levels. They work for Darcon.'

Scáthach bit her lip.

'Have you never tried escaping?'

'Escaping? How and to where? There is no escape from Dún Scáith.'

The man's voice was resigned; it was a flat statement of fact.

'There is no place from which a person's ingenuity cannot work out a means of escape,' replied the girl. Yet even as she spoke she knew she doubted what she said. She spoke only to bolster her morale.

'Brave words!'

It was the sibilant hiss of Cuár that echoed down the corridor. She heard a sudden crack of his whip and a cry of pain and alarm from the unseen 'Twenty-Seven'. Hot anger flushed Scáthach's cheeks.

'Come here, little man, with your whip and I will teach you to strike defenceless old men!' she yelled.

The voice of the hunchback rose in a vicious chuckle.

'Still brave, my pretty? You won't be for long. I hear that Darcon's sister, Aífe of Lethra, is coming to look at you. Then your gods will not help you.'

Scáthach drew a sharp breath.

So. Finally she would see this mysterious Aífe of Lethra.

Would she know the secret of the triskele mystery and of her birth?

'Send her to me quickly, little man!' she yelled back defiantly.

There was no answer.

Time hung heavily. She had no means of knowing the passing of the hours for everything remained in permanent gloom. She sat in silence for a while, trying to compose her mind and body until some opportunity presented itself on which she could act. It was useless trying to fight against her imprisonment for there was no way she could achieve anything. Buimech had taught her that when the body is made prisoner the personality is still free through the mind. So far as a person was still able to think then they were free. And even if a person was in isolation, thought provided them with companions. No jailer could make thought a captive. And so Scáthach fell to meditation for nowhere could a person find a more quiet or untroubled retreat than in their own mind.

How long she passed in contemplating, she did not know. That she must have fallen into a restful sleep was obvious for she came awake, sweating slightly, with her mouth dry again. She blinked her eyes and stared around.

A figure stood behind the bars watching her.

She started up.

The figure was that of a woman; no, a girl of her own age, build and height. She wore a silver helmet which covered her face entirely and a long black cloak fell from her shoulders to the ground, showing her black leather war-harness, her workmanlike sword and dagger. There was a golden hero's torc at her neck. Even though her face was not revealed, Scáthach could see that the girl was attractive, her limbs supple and body lithe. She carried herself as one trained to combat.

For a while both girls stood staring at each other through the bars, each weighing the other up.

'Ah so . . .' the long breath of a sigh escaped the helmeted woman. 'So you are Scáthach of Uibh Rathach?'

Scáthach's chin came up defiantly.

'I am.'

'I am Aífe of Lethra.'

Scáthach raised an eyebrow disdainfully.

'I have heard some call you the High One.'

Beneath the silver visor of the helmet, the other's red lips turned upward in a smile.

'Some have called me that,' she admitted.

'Why do you fear me, Aífe?' demanded Scáthach.

'Fear? Fear you?'

'Yes. Why did you flee from Lethra when you knew of my coming? I have travelled long to find you.'

Aífe did not deny the girl's charge.

'Your coming was prophesied some time ago.'

'Yes?' prompted Scáthach.

'I was warned of your coming and the harm you could inflict on me.'

Scáthach grimaced.

'Prophecies sound better when they become histories,' she said dismissively. 'I have no wish to harm you and yet you have already harmed me and those close to me. Where is Flann Mac Fraech?'

The other shrugged indifferently.

'He is a prisoner here and soon will be handed to Aintiarna of the Cruithne by my brother Darcon.'

'Why did you take him captive? How has he harmed you?' demanded Scáthach.

'He served you,' retorted Aífe. 'That is more than harm to me.'

'Why do you hate me so? Simply because of some prophecy? I do not understand it.'

'Hate? Hate you?' Aífe's voice was reflective.

'There must be something more than a prophecy which caused you to hate me,' observed the girl.

The other stared at her.

'You are truly beautiful, Scáthach of Uibh Rathach. All that has been said about you may well be true.'

'Why did your warriors steal my spear and shield?' the girl demanded, switching subjects.

'I had need of them.'

'You will not reveal to me the mystery that lies here?'

'Mystery?'

Scáthach summoned her energies to control the impatience she was feeling.

'Aífe of Lethra, tell me what mystery lies between us. Why should you seek to harm me?'

'Knowledge is a weapon as deadly and finely honed as any sword, Scáthach of Uibh Rathach. I will not arm you lest you seek to destroy me. I will not present to you any weapon.'

Scáthach bit her lip in annoyance.

'Then if you will not tell me what it is I have done, or what reasons cause your hatred of me, then answer me one question – what do you intend doing with me? Is there no way that I can purchase the freedom of Flann Mac Fraech and myself?'

The other girl chuckled sourly.

'No way you can purchase Flann Mac Fraech's freedom. My brother Darcon seeks service from Aintiarna of the Cruithin and by giving your boy-warrior to the chieftain he will secure that service.'

'It means Flann's death,' cried Scáthach.

'Yes,' admitted the other calmly.

It was no use wasting time pleading with Aífe.

'And what is my fate?'

'Your fate?'

'Am I to be imprisoned for ever?'

The girl with the silver helmet shook her head.

255

'So long as you are alive you are a threat to me, Scáthach.'

'But how?' cried the girl in exasperation.

'Know that and you would know all . . . and know my weakness,' responded the other.

'So you plan to kill me?'

'Yes.'

'Am I to be allowed to know how and when?'

The High One of Lethra shrugged.

'I must think about it.'

Scáthach took a step forward.

'You are clad in the accoutrements of a warrior. Is that for show and can you wield a sword?'

The other responded sharply.

'No man nor woman can gain victory over me,' she said.

'Then give me my weapons and let me meet you in fair fight,' Scáthach cried. 'Let us end whatever it is between us by honest and fair means. Let us try the matter in single combat.

Aífe held her head to one side and examined the girl.

'It would surely be an interesting sport,' she conceded after a while. 'I will give some thought to the matter. It would be stimulating to match one's mettle with a worthy opponent.'

'Then meet me, if you do not fear my sword,' pressed Scáthach.

'You seem anxious to throw away your life so quickly.'

'Perhaps. But if I win . . . do you promise that I shall go free with Flann Mac Fraech?'

Aífe hesitated.

'You will not win. I am Aífe the High One of Lethra and no one has ever bested me in single combat.'

'There is always a first time,' countered Scáthach. 'Anyway, if I win I shall have my freedom and the freedom of Flann Mac Fraech. Is it agreed?'

Aífe was quiet.

'I shall give the matter thought,' was all she said. For a moment or so she stood looking at Scáthach as if weighing up her character and physical prowess and then she turned and vanished down the corridor.

With a deep sigh, Scáthach flung herself back on the wooden cot. She felt annoyed at the lack of response she had provoked in Aífe. If only the woman had been provoked, perhaps she could have escaped from this tomb like imprisonment. It was so hard to tell what the woman thought when her face was hidden behind the mask of her helmet. Many thoughts now flew through the girl's mind. Why was Aífe of Lethra scared of her? What was the prophecy she had mentioned? What was Scáthach's connection with Lethra? Why had Aífe lured her to this Island of Shadows? Just to kill her? Why not have her captured and killed in Lethra? She felt frustrated that her mind produced so many questions and no answers.

Angrily she stood up and went to the bars.

'Twenty-Seven,' she called urgently. 'Are you there?'

There was a pause and then the tired, elderly voice of the prisoner came echoing back.

'I am here.'

'It is I, Scáthach of Uibh Rathach. I am in a cell not far from you.'

'I know. Cuár has said he will punish me if he catches me talking with you again . . .' there was a hesitation and then the voice said firmly: 'I do not care. I hate Cuár.'

'Good man,' replied the girl. 'Tell me, Twenty-Seven, what do you know or remember of this place?'

'This place?'

'What do you know of Dún Scáith, of Darcon and Aífe, his sister.'

'Ah,' there was a long pause.

'Are you there, Twenty-Seven?' called Scáthach after several moments of silence.

'I am here.'

'What do you know?' pressed the girl.

'Darcon is the son of the Mórrígú, goddess of death and battles. He is the spawn of darkness and evil and leads his life accordingly. He seized this island from its people and constructed Dún Scáith to exploit and oppress them.'

'And Aífe of Lethra?'

'She is Darcon's half-sister. They do not share the same father but their mother is the Mórrígú, the same evil one. Aífe rules in Lethra and a miserable place she makes it, so they say. Anyone who stands against them perishes or is incarcerated, just as I have been all these years . . . so many years that I cannot remember. I am . . . I am . . . Twenty-Seven!'

The crack of a whip ended the frail voice's recitation with a cry of pain.

'Dog! Spawn of a dog!' came the harsh cry of Cuár, the hunchback. 'Did I not warn you? Now I will peel the skin from your bones with my whip to show you that you cannot defy me!'

'Stop, little man!' cried Scáthach, pressing forward. 'If you harm that man I shall kill you before another day passes.'

There was a silence and then the evil hunchback came scuttling down the shadowy corridor, his lips drawn back in an evil grin.

'What's that you say, my pretty?'

Scáthach drew back from the range of the threatening whip.

'Unlock the door and step in here, little man, and I will repeat what I have to say to you. You spawn of a maggot!'

Cuár blinked, holding his head to one side as if he had not heard correctly.

'I think that it is time you were taught a lesson, my pretty,' he hissed venomously.

258

'Are you man enough to try?'

Scáthach was deliberately provocative, stepping back into the shadows, her muscles tensing. So much depended on what reaction Cuár had.

With a sudden stream of curses, the hunchback had seized a key from his belt and was unlocking the cell door.

He was still fumbling when Scáthach launched herself at him, throwing herself from the ground and landing feet first on the chest of the vicious little man. The dwarf staggered backwards, dropping the key, his tiny malignant eyes blazing in anger at being knocked off his guard.

The girl was on her feet again, springing upwards, both hands reaching towards the handle of the whip he held.

She was surprised at how strong the little man was. She tried to twist the whip from his grasp but his short arms were full of hardened muscle. To and fro they struggled for mastery of the whip and then, with an explosion of strength, Cuár flung the girl from him so that she landed on the far side of the cell.

Back went his arm to bring the whip into play, but before he could strike, the girl was bounding towards him once again, twisting her body into the air and smashing down with both feet against his chest.

This time it was his turn to sprawl backwards, landing full-length on the stone paving, yet still holding tightly to his whip.

Scáthach was up in a thrice. There was no time to conduct this fight with the honour code of a warrior. She stamped one foot firmly into his ugly face. He cried aloud in agony. As she made to stamp again, he grasped her ankle in one powerful hand and twisted it aside so that she lost her balance. For a moment or two she tottered, struggling to regain her balance and then fell crashing down. One of his short legs kicked out, catching her in the side of the head.

She grunted and rolled away, not a moment too soon, for the whip smashed down, cracking like a serpent on the floor where she had been a split second before.

Once more she rolled upwards, onto her feet.

Cuár was prepared, holding his whip and grinning fiendishly.

Scáthach glanced round desperately and snatched the wooden cot as a shield. She raised the wooden frame just as the leather tongue of the whip smashed towards her, cracking so hard against the wooden planks that one of them splintered immediately.

'I'll teach you a lesson, my pretty,' breathed the dwarf, chuckling hoarsely.

He lashed out again.

Once more the girl used the wooden cot as a shield and once more the tip of the whip bit so strong at the wood that more splinters broke away.

Then, with a cry, the girl went charging towards the little man, trying to time her run while he was recovering from his stroke. She crashed the wooden frame against him, driving him backwards.

This time he was driven against the bars of the cell.

Scáthach dropped her hold on the wooden cot and once more caught his whip hand, bending it backwards through the bars, using them as a fulcrum in order to wrest the whip from his grasp. He cried out in pain but the little man's wrists and arms were very strong. They struggled determinedly but the girl realised that for all his smallness the dwarf possessed the strength of several men. It was a matter of time before he would overcome her.

There was only one way out and that was to try to trick him, gain time enough to seize the key from where he had dropped it on the floor and shut him into the cell.

She glanced round, her eyes anxiously searching the floor for the key. She saw it near the doorway. How could she divert Cuár's attention long enough to gain the key, slam the door and lock it?

She was holding onto his whip hand for dear life, while the little man, grunting and groaning in the effort, was slowly pushing her hold back.

She moved her head forward and sunk her teeth into the little man's wrist, biting with all her might into the stinking, putrid flesh.

The little man gave a squeal of agony and suddenly his hand opened, in an attempt to shake her off, and the whip dropped from it.

In an instance, she had seized the chance, bounding away from him and scooping up the key.

But as fast as Scáthach was, the little man was faster.

With a yell of rage, he rolled after her, grabbing at her ankle and jerking it with such force that the girl went sprawling, her hand a good yard from the precious key. Not loosening his grip on her leg, the hunchback drew her painfully across the stone floor. Then, chortling with a malignant glee, he jumped to his discarded whip and gathered it up.

Scáthach, desperate now, scrambled up.

Cuár, however, had placed himself between the open doorway of the cell and her, forcing her back against the rear wall of the cell.

He was smiling and cooing, like a mother to a baby, as he gathered the long, leather thong of the whip in his hand.

The girl glanced round desperately. She was being pressed back against the wall.

She made a move to one side but the length of rawhide shot out, its black tongue striking at a spot just inches from her eye and dislodging the plaster. She darted in the other direction to be met with a similar warning.

'Now, now, my pretty,' breathed the little man. 'We

261

have played enough games, haven't we? And soon you will beg me to put an end to your misery.'

He moved backward, his close-set eyes measuring the distance, the whip straight and ready for the cut.

Scáthach set her mouth in a grim, determined line. She was not going to cry out nor beg mercy of this evil little creature. She had made up her mind on that score. She tried to gather her remaining strength for one final onslaught on the hunchback jailer.

Back went the whip.

She closed her eyes, prepared to meet its painful sting.

'Stop!'

The voice was a familiar high-pitched wheeze.

She opened her eyes. In the doorway of the cell crouched the harridan, Eis Enchenn, her thigh bone thrust out towards Cuár as if indicating her authority. Behind her stood half a dozen black coated warriors, their swords drawn.

Cuár stood uncertainly. He made no move to put down his whip.

'I said, stop!' the crone demanded again.

'The girl needs punishment,' the hunchback said sullenly.

'She will get it, but by another hand than yours,' the crone snapped waspishly. 'Now put down your whip unless you want to find yourself whipped to death.'

Muttering sullenly, the little man gathered his whip and hung it on his belt. Then he suddenly reached towards the girl's neck and snatched the chain and gold medallion with a flick of his wrist, causing a red weal to appear on her flesh where he dragged it from her.

She could not repress a cry of pain.

Cuár smiled.

'This will go towards paying me for the trouble you have caused me, pretty one,' he sneered, placing the medallion around his own thick neck. Then he turned to Eis Enchenn. 'Is she to be executed?' he demanded, gesturing to Scáthach.

The crone wheezed with laughter.

'She might wish that was her fate after a while. No, she is to be taken to the great hall to face Darcon and Aífe.'

Eighteen

Scáthach stood in the centre of the great hall of Dún Scáith. While she had not been bound, two warriors with drawn swords stood at her side, slightly behind her. The hall was lit with innumerable glowing torches, and its size and magnificence had caused the girl to catch her breath in awe. Great pillars of stone stretched upwards, supporting the roof which was so high that it was shrouded in gloom for the light did not penetrate so far above. The walls were covered in hanging tapestries of exquisite workmanship, many bearing designs and symbols the like of which she had never seen before. The floor itself was of large stone flags polished by constant use to a curious sheen in which the torchlight was reflected. However, in spite of the torchlight, the atmosphere was one of gloom and dankness. And in spite of the fact that the hall was filled with people, there was an oppressive quiet permeating the place, a sense of despondent, joyless melancholy among those grouped around the edges of the great hall who stared nervously at the girl as she entered with her guards and stood waiting.

At one end of the hall there rose a dais to which a series of stone steps lead. This platform was covered in rugs and placed on it was a great chair of carved oak, inlaid with what appeared to be gold and silver. It was an imposing chair. A smaller chair of similar design stood a little to one side. Behind the chairs stood a row of grim-faced warriors, shields and javelins in hand. Before the larger chair, squatting on the steps, crouched the grinning harridan, Eis Enchenn, clad in her stinking animal skins and crooning softly to herself as she gazed on the girl with a speculative expression in her one malignant eye. She stroked the giant thigh bone with her skeletal hand as she made a weird humming noise in her scrawny throat.

There was a movement behind the dais and in came the lithe figure of Aífe, clad as Scáthach had seen her in the dungeons, her face covered by her visored silver helmet, her long black cloak flowing from her shoulders but not disguising her long-limbed attractive figure clad in her warrior's harness. She walked to the smaller of the two chairs and lowered herself gracefully into its comfortable embrace. Scáthach could see her full red lips under the visor, drawn back and smiling.

Standing a little to one side of Aífe was a plump man of middle-age, wearing rich robes and jewellery which seemed to indicate that he carried the office of a druid.

There was a shuffling movement among the people now, a slight increase of tension and then a tall man entered. He was clad from neck to ankle in black, a black tunic, kirtle and cloak fastened with trappings of black leather. His face was thin and swarthy and his hair matched the blackness of his dress for its was almost blue-black and shone like a raven's wing. His eyes were black and restless, his lips thin and red. Under his left eye there appeared a nervous tic, causing his face to twitch every so often like a horse shying. There was only one relief to his black garb and that was a silver half-moon which hung on a silver chain from his deck. Scáthach's eyes narrowed as she saw the strange druidic symbols on it. The man was not old, nor could it be said he was young. Even before he sank into the great chair, Scáthach had realised that this was Darcon the Tyrant, reputed son of the Mórrígú, goddess of death and battles.

She gazed on him in curiosity; openly, defiantly. At once she detected in his features a meanness of character and a cruel streak which supported the stories she had heard of his tyranny. In turn she found him staring at her with a inquisitive look, a look akin to amazement. Twice he glanced at Aífe by his side and turned back with a shake of his head.

For a long while no one spoke and then Eis Enchenn raised her thigh bone, shaking it in the air, and cackling in her shrill voice.

'Woe to the enemies of the great king, Darcon. May they wither and perish at his glance. All powerful is the king. Avert your eyes lest his magnificence blind you. Woe to those who would think evil of him.'

Darcon turned his brooding dark gaze from the girl to the crone and his face grimaced with annoyance.

'Is there any here that would question my power?' he said slowly, his voice an ominous growl.

Eyes were turned on Scáthach. She remained silent.

Darcon waited a moment, his eyebrows rising as if in surprise.

'You do not speak, woman.'

He addressed the remark directly to the girl.

'Should I?'

'Do you not question my power?'

Scáthach smiled.

'Your power? No. I do not question that you have power.'

The subtlety of her response escaped him and he sat back frowning in perplexity.

'Why did you come to my fortress?'

'I came in search of that which was stolen from me,' replied the girl, gazing steadily at Aífe who was continuing to sit back with a smile on her face.

'What was stolen from you?'

'My friend and companion, Flann Mac Fraech, my shield and my hunting spear.'

Darcon gave a dry chuckle.

'You must value these things highly to cross the seas in search of them.'

'I do. I have no quarrel with you, Darcon, save that you give shelter to she who took Flann prisoner and stole that which belonged to me. I have no quarrel with you, Darcon, save when I came to your fortress your doorkeeper took me captive by stealth and your jailer used me ill. For this, I now have a quarrel with you.'

Darcon stared in surprise at the defiant tone of the girl. He frowned in anger and then Eis Enchenn started to cackle shrilly.

'Darcon must crouch in terror before this slip of a girl,' she cried. 'Darcon the powerful is challenged by a girl without weapons, a slip of a girl who is an unarmed prisoner in his hall.'

A nervous ripple of laughter at the wit of the crone came from those gathered.

Darcon sat back, nodding.

'You frighten me, indeed, Scáthach of Uibh Rathach,' he sneered. 'But, out of your own mouth, you have convicted yourself of actions that are antagonistic to me. For that you must die.'

The girl's jaw came up but she said no more.

Then Aífe leaned forward and whispered something to Darcon. The dark man frowned and appeared to disagree with her but the High One of Lethra spoke more insistently. Darcon finally shrugged and turned back to Scáthach.

'My sister tells me that you have pretensions to being a warrior?' he spoke scornfully.

'I am Scáthach of Uibh Rathach,' replied the girl simply.

'Then I am in mind for some amusement. So is my sister, Aífe of Lethra. She tells me that earlier you challenged her to single combat. She accepts that challenge and will fight you.'

There was a gasp of astonishment around the hall. The man who stood just behind Aífe bent forward and whispered urgently to her but she waved him away.

'Enough, Droch!' Scáthach heard the girl say.

Even Eis Enchenn stared up in surprise as Aífe rose from her seat and threw off her black cloak.

Scáthach felt her heart leap in a surge of hope.

'If I am defeated, I shall die,' she said, controlling her emotion. 'What if I win?'

Darcon chuckled.

'That will not be,' he assured her.

'But if I do?' insisted Scáthach.

Darcon raised his arms and let them fall. There was a broad smile on his face.

'Then you shall go free.'

Instinctively, the girl did not trust him. Her eyes narrowed. At least combat provided her with a chance where she had no chance before. But if she defeated Aífe then she would have to get to Darcon's side before he turned his guard on her for she knew he would not honour his promise. Her only hope would be to force him to keep it.

'And that which was stolen from me, my shield and spear?'

'They shall be returned,' Aífe assured her, cutting in before Darcon could reply.

'And Flann Mac Fraech? Will you release him?'

Darcon was growing angry now.

'No. He is mine to sell to Aintiarna of the Cruithne. Enough of this bargaining. Let the combat commence.'

Scáthach bit her lip. It was useless pressing further. Anyway, promises made by Darcon and Aífe were worthless. She would have to rely on her own cunning to extract herself should she win the combat.

Aífe walked slowly down from the dais and came to stand within a few feet of Scáthach, examining her with a strange probing gaze.

'Shall it be swords and shields, Scáthach of Uibh Rathach?'

The girl shrugged indifferently. She knew the extent of her prowess with all weapons and had no preference.

'Very well,' Aífe smiled. 'Swords and shields.'

She turned to one of the guards.

'Bring us weapons.'

A moment later a warrior came forward holding the weapons which he proferred to both women.

Scáthach frowned as she examined the weapons which she had been given.

'I would prefer my own weapons,' she said.

Aífe chuckled.

'Doubtless. I have heard that they possess magic propensity. No, Scáthach. You will fight with these weapons. You would not claim advantage over me, would you?'

The girl shrugged and took the shield, balancing it for weight before putting it on her arm. Then she took the sword and, once again, weighed it in her hand.

'I am satisfied,' she said.

Aífe took her weapons indifferently and stood ready.

Darcon raised his hand to quiet the murmur which had been running through the onlookers as they bunched around the walls of the great hall.

'Let this be a combat to the death,' he called. 'No quarter must be asked nor given.'

'Agreed,' responded Aífe, smiling at her opponent.

'Agreed,' echoed Scáthach hollowly.

'Then Eis Enchenn will ensure that the combat is conducted by the rules of such engagements.'

The old woman came forward, croaking with glee and waving her thigh bone totem above her shaggy grey head.

'Are you ready?'

Both women nodded and brought their weapons to the guard position, crouching in preparation for the combat.

'Then . . . to the death!'

The other woman's voice was raised in a scream and she brought the thigh bone down as if it was a cudgel on a head.

Both women did not move for a moment, eyeing each other warily. They were frozen into their crouching pose.

It was Aífe who made the first feint, taking in a deep breath and thrusting forward, stamping her right leg before her to give force to her action. The blow was easily parried by Scáthach with an upward turn of her shield, causing the sword point to slither harmlessly up and over her shoulder. Before she could counter, Aífe had jumped backwards beyond reach.

It was clear to Scáthach by the movements her rival demonstrated that Aífe had been trained well in the art of combat and that the fight would not be a foregone conclusion.

The girl decided to test her opponent's skill to the limit.

With a sudden flurry, she moved forward briskly, shield to the fore, sword swinging in rapid motions, the smashing of metal against metal causing the great hall to reverberate with noise. No sooner had Aífe parried one blow than Scáthach struck the next. Backward in a circle was Aífe driven as Scáthach smashed blow after blow against her, so quickly that many of the spectators could not even see them before they struck. Yet Aífe parried them all with either sword or shield, her teeth barred at the effort of countering the onslaught.

Eis Enchenn watched the fight with her one tiny red glowing eye full of venom, hissing angrily each time Scáthach appeared to take the advantage and smiling and chortling each time Aífe took command.

The druid, Droch, watched with a frown and, not being a warrior and thereby understanding the nature of the combat, he let forth a wail of despair as he saw Aífe apparently being pushed back around the hall by the fierce attack of Scáthach.

Darcon, too, was watching with a worried frown as the two girls fought. His face was concerned and it was obvious he was wondering whether his sister had taken on more than she could handle in accepting Scáthach's challenge. Once he rose in his chair and raised a hand as if to summon the guards.

Scáthach saw the movement from the corner of her eyes and knew what to expect even if she won the combat. She would have to move swiftly and ensure that Darcon was in her power before he had time to act against her.

She had paused in her onslaught against Aífe. The purpose of the attack had been to discover just how skilled her opponent was. Now she had ascertained that Aífe was as skilful as she was. It would be no easy task to bring the combat to a quick close.

Suddenly, it was Aífe who was attacking, moving forward viciously with quick, slashing strokes, her full body-weight behind the effort. Now Scáthach was hard pressed to defend the weighty blows from landing; only one blow need land and the contest would be over. With shield first, then sword, she countered the flashing steel. Now it was the turn of Eis Enchenn to chuckle and shrill in delight, waving her thigh bone totem in encouragement. Darcon had sunk back into his chair, nodding approval

270

and grinning as his sister seemed to be gaining the upper hand. Droch, too, was smiling broadly in pleasure. It was, indeed, the turn of Scáthach to be driven backward and appear to be in trouble. But only a trained warrior would notice that in spite of the fierce onslaught of Aífe's blows, Scáthach was not over-reaching herself in her defensive counter measures.

Deep in the dungeons of Dún Scáith, Cuár the hunchback jailer spat on the floor in disgust. A guard had informed him of the combat going on above.

'The girl should not have been accorded the privilege and honour of being slain in combat,' he muttered. 'I would have given her the slow death, peeled her skin piece by piece from her body.'

He patted his whip and smirked.

The warrior who had brought the news gazed at the little man uncomfortably for, like many in Darcon's fortress, he held the little hunchback in fear.

'I was also to tell you that a ship from Aintiarna of the Cruithne has dropped anchor in our harbour and you are to prepare the man from Éireann, Flann Mac Fraech, for embarkation.'

Cuár sniffed.

'Am I to be left no pleasures?' he whined, protestingly. 'Are there no prisoners with whom I can have some sport?'

The warrior shrugged and, having delivered his message, he turned and scuttled away, out of the gloom of the dungeons and up into the bright sunlight above the ground, thankful to be gone from the vicious little dwarf.

Cuár turned down the passageway and then hesitated outside a cell door.

'Are you still there, Twenty-Seven?' he called.

There was a rustling within the pitch black cell and then a tired voice said: 'What is it that you want?'

271

Cuár chuckled grimly.

'You do not sound happy, Twenty-Seven. Perhaps it is because I have not given you enjoyment today. Perhaps you need exercise . . . to dance, dance at the end of my whip, eh?'

There was no sound of reply.

The hunchback cursed. Sometimes it was not fun when the prisoners did not respond. Well, he would . . . his hand was halfway to the cell door when he remembered his errand and sighed, turning on down the passageway until he came to a small flight of stairs which led to a lower level. It was dark as a tomb at this level and he was forced to pause and light a torch. By its light he continued down to a cell at the foot of the stairs.

At the sound of his key in the lock a voice called out.

'Who is there?'

Cuár smiled and drew his whip, cracking it in the darkness.

'I am Cuár the jailer, man of Éireann. Remember that. I hold you in my power.'

'What is it you want?'

Flann Mac Fraech blinked in the light of the torch. It was the first time he had seen light since he had arrived in this awesome place several days ago. In fact he was not sure how long he had been entombed in the lower dungeons of the fortress.

'Why should I come with you?' he demanded, rubbing his eyes with the backs of his hands and blinking to adjust to the light.

Cuár's whip cracked out and Flann yelped in pain, catching at his shoulder where the weapon had cut through his jerkin.

'Because I say so, whelp of a dog!' hissed the hunchback.

He prodded Flann from the cell and pushed him, stumbling in his weakness, up the steps to the upper level.

'Your companion arrived today,' the hunchback said slyly.

Flann frowned.

'What do you mean, little man?'

'Why, Scáthach of Uibh Rathach, she called herself.'

Flann's mouth opened in surprise, a wild hope gleamed in his eyes. He half turned. Once more Cuár's whip cracked and the young warrior felt the pain of the lash.

'Keep walking, scum,' snapped the jailer.

'Where is she?' Flann demanded.

The jailer laughed harshly.

'Dead or dying by now,' he said shortly.

Flann halted, a feeling of despair and sadness sweeping over him.

'Move!' cried the jailer.

Flann whirled round, the despair turning to anger. He moved towards the jailer, his hands outstretched as if to throttle him. Cuár sprang backwards and struck out with his whip. Flann halted; for a moment or two he did not feel the sting of the whip, so great was his anger and sorrow at the news. Then he moved backwards, a step or two.

'Back, you dog!' hissed the little jailer, 'or else I shall carve you into pieces.'

'Better to do that if Scáthach is no more,' muttered Flann.

Cuár bit his lip.

He knew it was hopeless to control a prisoner if that prisoner had no desire to live.

He fumbled for a key and opened the door to the nearest cell; it was the cell of Number Twenty-Seven.

'Get in there!' he commanded, lashing the air above Flann's head with his whip.

Flann moved automatically, head hanging as he contemplated a world without Scáthach of Uibh Rathach.

The jailer swung the door shut and turned the key.

'You will wait there until I send warriors for you,'

273

smiled the little man. 'A ship has been sent for you from your friend Aintiarna of the Cruithne.'

'It makes no difference to me,' replied Flann. 'It makes no difference to me what happens now.'

'Then it should,' smirked the hunchback. 'For your friend Scáthach is fighting a single combat in the hall above with your freedom as the prize.'

'You said she was dead!' Flann cried out, angrily gripping the bars of the cell.

'I said she was probably dead or dying. And so she might be. She is matched against Aífe. No one can best Aífe of Lethra. And if they do . . . why Darcon will have her slain. She is doomed anyway.'

Flann cursed the hunchback with all the fluency he could muster.

The little man went on his way chuckling. He would call the warriors from Aintiarna's ship to escort him. Flann was their responsibility now.

Flann paused for breath.

A tired voice said: 'That is no use, my friend. I, too, cursed the little one night and day when I was first brought here. Now it is as much as I can do to move across the cell to get my food.'

Flann turned into the darkness. All he could see was a shadowy form at the back of the cell.

'Who are you?' he demanded.

The man shrugged.

'I have been here so long that I have forgotten. I am known only as Number Twenty-Seven.'

'Have you no idea of your identity, of where you came from?' Flann said in disbelief.

'I recall I was a chieftain in my young manhood. That I came from a far-off sunny land. I came in peace to trade on behalf of my people who were sore afflicted by drought and was taken prisoner by Darcon the Tyrant. I have been a prisoner here for many, many years.'

274

Flann moved forward.

'Then you may be lucky, my friend. I am soon to be taken back to my own country, the land of the Cruithne, ruled over by my arch-enemy, Aintiarna. I am being taken there to be killed.'

'Then it is you who are lucky, my friend. For that means that soon your troubles will be ended. I exist here in a living death.'

Flann hesitated and realised that what the other said was true. Better to die in freedom than live in slavery.

He felt his way to the cot on which the other man sat and in the darkness held out his hand.

'You are right, my brother. You suffer the heavier fate. Ah, but if there was a way to escape from this place.'

The other man sighed softly.

'Twenty years ago I would have jumped at those words. I have sought escape for so long that I have despaired of it. There is nothing to do, my friend, except to wait for the resolution of one's destiny.'

In the great hall, high above the dungeons of the fortress, Scáthach and Aífe crouched, facing each other. Their movements were a little more sluggish now as their bodies weakened from the exertions of the combat. Sweat poured freely from their faces and their lunges and parries were slower and more cautious.

Darcon, sitting on his chair, began fretting with impatience. Once he cried out: 'Come, Aífe; cease playing with her and finish the combat.'

It was easier said than done, for every manoeuvre and stratagem Aífe started was encountered and parried by Scáthach. Time and time again she struck forward, sometimes in cunning attack and at other times in a desperate attempt to overwhelm her opponent by sheer swiftness and strength. Time and again, her moves were countered.

Then came attacks from Scáthach, as fast and as furious as her own, but the girls were so evenly matched that Aífe was able to stop them pressing home.

The combat was a stalemate. Had it not been for the determination of the combatants, for the hostility of Darcon and Eis Enchenn, then the combat would have been stopped and the contest declared a draw. But it was to be a combat to the death.

Slowly they circled, warily watching for an opening, a chance to rush forward.

It was a slow business and the crowds gathered in the great hall were growing restless as they saw that the contest could continue for ever.

Just as it seemed that no progress would be made at all, Aífe suddenly lunged forward, her sword point aiming for Scáthach's midriff, left unguarded by a change of position. Swiftly Scáthach brought her shield down to ward off the blow and, had it landed, the shield would have easily deflected it. But the blow did not land. Somehow Aífe's foot slipped and she toppled and lost her balance.

A great gasp went up from those gathered in the hallway as they saw the High One of Lethra go down.

At once Scáthach moved to take advantage of the position.

Aífe, however, swung to one side just as the other girl raised her sword and brought it down with a fierce crushing blow. The effect of her moving was to miss the swinging blade, which passed no more than a hair's breadth from her cheek and nicked the leather thong which held the girl's helmet in position.

Once again Scáthach drew back her blade and struck at her opponent, who tried to slide out of reach. The blade crashed against the helmet and sent it rolling across the floor.

For the first time Scáthach stared at the face of her

opponent. Her sword hand dropped and a look of amazement crossed her features, her mouth dropping, eyes bulging as if she could not believe her eyes.

She was staring back at a mirror image of herself. Aífe was her twin, even more than her twin for there was not a jot of difference between them.

'This is not possible,' whispered Scáthach, dropping her sword and taking a step backwards.

Aífe's face hardened its features and she seized her sword and took the opportunity while Scáthach's guard was down to raise it ready to strike.

Scáthach was so stunned that she made no effort to defend herself. Her wide eyes were on the image of herself . . . on Aífe, the High One of Lethra. She was poleaxed.

Aífe's lips were drawn back in a smile of triumph. She knew the contest was won; knew the victory was hers. Her sword was already moving for the vital spot, for the kill.

'Hold your hand, Aífe of Lethra!'

The voice, loud and commanding, rang out clearly across the hall.

It stayed the girl's hand in mid-air.

Heads turned to identify who had the impertinence to issue an order to the High One of Lethra.

Darcon had started from his chair, frowning.

'Who makes such a demand in my hall?' he demanded.

Scáthach had come out of her daze and made a belated move to cover herself. She brought up her shield and sword to the ready.

Aífe had also recovered from her surprise at being so peremptorily ordered and swung back to her opponent, but saw the element of surprise was no longer with her. She mouthed an obscenity and turned to discover who had dared to stay her hand.

Everyone was looking round.

An elderly man in the robes of a druid suddenly made his way between the rows of the people who parted to let him through.

'Did you dare give orders in the hall of Darcon?' thundered Darcon as the old man came to a halt before the dais.

'I did,' replied the druid.

Scáthach gasped in astonishment.

It was Ruacán.

Nineteen

The old druid strode forward into the shocked and silent hall. His stooping figure and white hair seemed oddly commanding. Darcon, brows drawn together, moved forward a step or two, but Ruacán raised a hand and he paused at the old man's quiet authority. Aífe, her sword now at her side, was glaring at the druid with a face distorted in anger.

Scáthach stared from her mirror image to the old druid in bewilderment.

'What does this mean, old man?' demanded Aífe, cutting into her thoughts.

'It means that what you do is against the law and well you know it, Aífe of Lethra,' replied the old druid, his voice strangely harsh and authoritative. 'Ask your advisor, Droch, there. Did he not mention you transgress the law? Or has Droch forgotten that once he took a druid's vow to maintain the law?'

Droch, the advisor, reddened and shuffled his feet.

Darcon summoned a sneer to his tightly-stretched features.

'I am the law here, old man.'

'Not here, nor anywhere,' snapped Ruacán, with a shake of his white head. 'The law stands above kings and chieftains and well you know it.'

'What is against the law?' Scáthach asked, perplexed by the turn of events. 'What does this mean?'

The old man smiled gently at her.

'The law of single combat forbids a sister to kill a sister as it forbids brother to kill brother.

'Sister?'

Scáthach turned to stare at the glowering Aífe.

Ruacán pointed his hand towards her.

'This is your twin sister, Scáthach. This is the reason behind your quest.'

'I do not understand,' replied the girl once more in bewilderment.

'In good time,' replied the druid. 'Do you put up your weapon, Aífe of Lethra, or do you tempt the anger of the gods?'

Aífe hesitated and glanced at Eis Enchenn, who squatted on her haunches, her malevolent eyes full of venom on the broad face of Ruacán. The druid turned his eyes on the harridan. Nothing was said, but after a long while the crone finally dropped her gaze. Aífe sighed and shrugged as if Eis Enchenn's lack of challenge to the old man had decided the issue.

'My sword is sheathed.'

'You must never raise it against your sister's person,' Ruacán added.

Aífe grimaced.

'It is the law,' pressed the old druid. 'And by my authority I pronounce a *geis* on you. You can never meet your sister in mortal combat.'

'You dare utter a sacred prohibition in my presence?' stormed Darcon.

'I have the power,' Ruacán replied blandly, turning to the ruler of the Island of Shadows. 'Do you doubt that?'

Darcon glanced at Eis Enchenn. The crone hesitated once more and then spread her thin arms in resignation.

'He has the power, lord,' she squeaked sullenly.

The old druid turned back to Aífe.

'The *geis*, the sacred taboo, is pronounced. Do you accept it?'

The girl bit her lip, hesitated a moment and then nodded.

'You have my word, old man. My sword will never be raised against my . . . my sister's person.'

Ruacán turned to Scáthach.

'And do you sheath your sword, Scáthach? Sheath it never to raise it against your sister's person? The *geis* is on you, too.'

Scáthach was gazing on her new-found sister.

'It is done.'

Ruacán inclined his head.

Darcon took a step towards the druid.

'You may come here preaching the law, old man, but my will prevails here. Guards . . . seize the girl!'

Two warriors moved hesitantly forward to Scáthach's side, one of them taking her sword and shield from her.

'Take her back to the dungeons to await my judgement.'

Ruacán raised his head and drew back his shoulders.

'Scáthach must be released, Darcon.'

'I rule here, old man!' snapped the king of the Island of Shadows. He turned and signalled the warriors to carry out his orders. They pushed Scáthach from the hallway.

'You must not harm her,' Ruacán admonished.

Darcon chuckled.

'You have told us some of the law, old man. But must I remind you of all the law?' he sneered. 'Aífe may not touch the girl because she is her sister, but I am only half-brother to her and it is not stipulated in law that I can suffer her no harm. You cannot pronounce your sacred prohibition on me. Nor will you. Now seize the old man and take him below to the dungeons!'

The last Scáthach saw was guards descending on the old druid and then she was hurried through the door which led down to Cuár's domain in the dungeons. Poor Ruacán, she thought. He had risked everything to protect her by proclaiming the law and now he had become a prisoner as she was. She sighed, puzzled by the turn of events. It was more than enough to find that she had a twin sister, but a twin sister who apparently hated her . . . that she could not understand. Nor the reasons why that hate was so venomous. What had she done that Aífe was full of such poison? How had Ruacán known this? Indeed, how had Ruacán been able to cross the chasm and enter, unobserved, Dún Scáith?

The thoughts raced through her head as she was led down the stone steps into the dark, cold atmosphere of the dungeons.

The hunchback looked up as the warriors entered his domain pushing the girl before them. His face was a picture of incredulous surprise.

'What has happened?' he demanded in his high-pitched, squeaky voice, as he stared in wonder at Scáthach. 'Surely she has not slain Aífe of Lethra?'

One of the guards sniffed.

'They are twin sisters. In the fight Aífe's helmet was knocked from her head and everyone saw.'

Cuár stared in wonder.

'Few have ever seen Aífe unhelmed before. And she is this one's twin?'

281

'That's right. An old man suddenly appeared in the hall and stopped the contest by reciting the law.'

'But Darcon is the law.'

'The old man was persuasive. Aífe had to swear that she would not harm her. So Darcon has returned her to the dungeons while he considers her fate. And they are bringing the old man down too.'

The hunchback chuckled.

'Well, we will make their stay comfortable while they wait to hear what Darcon will do to them. It will be something special, I'll warrant, for upsetting his pleasure.'

The ugly little man turned, and taking a bunch of keys led the way to the cells.

'In here, my pretty. I would not hold out any false hopes because Darcon has no mercy in his soul.'

Scáthach said nothing but allowed herself to be pushed into the dank, dark blackness of her prison once again. She went to the wooden cot and sank down, as the cell door banged shut on her and the hunchback turned the key with a rasping laugh.

Alone the girl sat, the thoughts still racing through her mind. She could make no sense at all out of the events. She closed her eyes as she tried to clarify her reasoning.

A movement at the door of the cell caused her to start forward.

Her eyes widened in surprise as she beheld the shadowy stooped figure of Ruacán within her cell. As she opened her mouth, the old man raised a finger to his lips to bid her be silent. Then he turned, head to one side, listening, before moving back into the cell and standing before the astonished girl.

'How . . .?' she began in a whisper.

The old man smiled.

'I eluded my captors, that is all, and doors never hold back people of the knowledge.'

Scáthach shook her head in total bewilderment.

'I do not understand,' she began.

'Then listen, my child, for we have little time and you must act quickly.'

He glanced towards the cell door, paused for a moment and then turned back to the girl.

'My child, you and Aífe are twins, born of the same mother and father.'

Scáthach grimaced wryly.

'This much I have gathered, old man.'

Ruacán smiled.

'Then listen to the story of your birth. Your father was Ard-Geimne, the king of Lethra. Though Ard-Geimne was a mortal, he fell in love with the Mórrígú, the goddess of death and battles who had visited his kingdom disguised as a beautiful maiden. Ard-Geimne was a handsome man and the goddess decided to use him for her own ends for she saw a chance for her offspring to rule the mortal world causing death and destruction among the peoples of the earth. She already possessed a half-mortal son, Darcon, who was growing to manhood here, in the Island of Shadows. An evil, profligate young man born of an evil father who was suitable to mate with the goddess of death and battles. But Ard-Geimne was a good man.'

The old druid paused.

'What was he like, this father of mine?' whispered Scáthach.

'Ard-Geimne? He was an honourable, wise and just chieftain of his people but his infatuation with the Mórrígú was his undoing. The goddess of death and battles gave birth to his daughters – twins. Aífe and yourself, Scáthach. At the birth it was prophesied that one twin would inherit the evil and ambition of her mother but the other would inherit the goodness, wisdom and justice of her father. it was further prophesied that only one of the twins would ever rule in Lethra but that the other would contain her evil and, further, would destroy the Mórrígú's only son.'

283

Scáthach shivered abruptly.

'Tell me, Ruacán,' she asked slowly, 'need I ask which twin was which?'

'Aífe was the inheritor of the goddess's ambition,' answered the old druid.

'Go on,' whispered the girl.

'The Mórrígú ordered that you be put to death, Scáthach, in order to thwart the prophecy. Furthermore, as a token of his loyalty to her, she ordered your father personally to cast your body into the sea that you may be drowned. But, as I have said, your father was a kindly and loving man, a man of goodness. Instead of casting you into the waves to your doom, he took a wooden casket and had it waterproofed, and he placed you into the casket, which bore the sacred symbols of Lethra. Then he cast you upon the sea on a tidal current, praying wholeheartedly to the ocean god, Manánnan Mac Lir, to take you into his safe keeping. Your father then returned to the Mórrígú and, with a clear conscience, was able to tell her that you had been cast into the sea as she had instructed.'

The girl sighed softly.

'And the ocean god brought me to the hands of Eola and Buimech.'

Ruacán nodded with a smile.

'That he did. Eola and Buimech took you from the sea and raised you as their own, teaching you what skills they knew for, in their hearts, they knew that one day you would have to set out to discover the secret of your birth.'

'And Ard-Geimne?'

'The Mórrígú eventually had him slain in order that her daughter, Aífe, could rule in Lethra.'

'But,' frowned Scáthach, 'the Mórrígú is a powerful goddess. How did she not know that I had survived through the intervention of Manánnan?'

'Easy enough to tell,' smiled the old man, 'the power

of Manánnan, who is the son of The Dagda, father of the gods, was able to maintain the secret from the knowledge of the goddess of death. It was not until Ard-Geimne was dying that she read his final thoughts . . . in those last few moments, your real father reached out to you . . . praying that you would come to Lethra to fulfil the prophecy . . . and she realised that you were alive. She told your sister, Aífe, and Aífe told her half-brother Darcon. It was Darcon's idea that Aífe should order the warriors of Lethra to fit out a vessel and go sailing to the coast of Éireann in search of you. They found Eola's fortress, sacked it and killed him but you were away hunting.'

Scáthach nodded sadly.

'And this was all the doing of my . . . my mother?'

'You were born from the womb of the Mórrígú, my child,' acknowledged Ruacán, 'but you have inherited your father's wisdom and goodness and the skills of your foster parents, Eola and Buimech.'

Scáthach shook her head.

'How can I fight a goddess . . . how can I fight my mother?'

'It is foretold, child,' replied the old druid. 'You have been given the power, and you must use it, otherwise the world will become enchained to her evil whims.'

'I cannot fight Aífe,' she pointed out. 'You have made me accept the sacred taboo. How can I fight her?'

'Not with a sword,' replied Ruacán, 'but are there not other means of fighting?'

The girl sat, once more her thoughts racing.

'Even now in the great hall above, the Mórrígú sits with Darcon and Aífe, plotting the best way of killing you,' observed the old man.

Scáthach stood up, her shoulders squaring.

'How can I escape from here and find my weapons?'

The druid chuckled.

'There speaks Scáthach of Uibh Rathach. Come, follow me.'

He turned and made his way to the cell door, pausing to listen a moment or so before swinging the door gently open.

'We must find Flann,' the girl whispered, following at his heels.

'We will,' Ruacán assured her.

They moved down the darkened corridor to where some steps ascended. Without hesitation, the old druid clambered upwards. On a second level was a broader corridor, lit by flickering torches. Several doors led off the passage and the old man paused before one of them.

'Here,' he said softly.

The girl reached for the handle and turned it. Inside was a room filled with armaments. There on a table she saw her weapons. There was *An Cruadín*, the hard helm; there was her shield, *An Seancholl Snidheach*, the hard ridged hazel; there was her sword, *An Chraobh Ghlasach*, her javelin, the *Corr-Bholg* and her fierce spear, the *gae-Bolga*.

She gave a gasp of delight.

'Hurry now, my child,' whispered the old man, 'array yourself for battle.'

The girl nodded and quickly put on her battle harness and took her weapons.

'With these, I feel invincible.'

The druid chuckled.

'Armour and weapons are only as good as the one who uses them, child.'

'Can you tell me where Flann is held?' demanded the girl, suddenly calm and clear-headed again. She felt in complete control now.

'Below in the dungeons. I will lead the way.'

Ruacán turned and led the way back into the dungeons, down dimly-lit corridors, to halt before a cell door.

The girl paused hesitantly.

'Flann?'

There was a gasp of astonishment and then Flann's voice, nervous and full of suppressed excitement, came back: 'Who speaks?'

'Don't you know me?' laughed the girl.

'They told me you were dead,' cried the young warrior coming forward from the shadows to stand with his face pressed against the bars.

'I still live,' she grinned, 'and so does Ruacán here.'

Flann swallowed.

'You came to rescue me?'

Scáthach grimaced.

'It is a long story, Flann Mac Fraech. First we must rescue you from this cell.'

'Wait,' the young warrior's eyes were troubled. 'How do I know that you are Scáthach of Uibh Rathach and not Aífe. I was nearly fooled once before.'

Scáthach saw the suspicion in his eyes and frowned, wondering how she could reassure him.

Then, on impulse, she leant towards him and kissed him softly on the mouth.

He started, staring deeply into her eyes and then a slow smile spread across his features.

'That is no kiss that Aífe is capable of giving,' he whispered.

Scáthach chuckled.

'I am glad you can feel the difference, otherwise you are not the man for me, Flann Mac Fraech.'

Then she stepped back and gazed at the cell door. She frowned at the lock and glanced at Ruacán.

The old man smiled.

From his robe he took a piece of wire and inserted it into the lock, twisting this way and that until there was a soft click. Then the door swung to and Flann pushed out, clasping Scáthach in a fierce embrace.

'By the gods . . .' he began.

Laughing, the girl disentangled herself, but her eyes were soft and kindly.

'We have much to do, Flann, before we can be so selfish.'

'Lead the way,' replied Flann, firmly. 'I have a debt to pay to the people in this fortress.'

'And I,' echoed a familiar voice.

Scáthach peered at the shadows, recognising the tired voice.

'Twenty-Seven?'

From the shadows a tall, grey-haired man emerged. In spite of his age and long years of imprisonment the man was still muscular, nearly seven feet tall, a giant of a man, who must have once been possessed of amazing strength. His skin was black, his face strong and handsome, although it bore the years of his confinement in lines. His lips were fixed in a determined line.

'I am . . . Twenty-Seven.'

Flann turned to the tall man.

'We have shared a cell these last few hours, he cannot remember who he was, yet he must have been a powerful chieftain.'

'Will you come with us to test the mettle of the evil which governs this fortress?' asked Scáthach.

The black man nodded.

'With all my heart.'

Ruacán leant forward suddenly, reaching up with a frail hand and brushing the man's forehead.

The man who called himself Twenty-Seven frowned in surprise.

'There,' smiled Ruacán. 'There, my friend, your memory should return.'

The man blinked, his face bewildered and then his expression suddenly cleared.

'I am . . . I am,' his features suddenly stretched in a

288

broad smile. 'I am called Dubh and I was . . . I was ruler of Ophir. Twenty years have I been a prisoner here.'

'How did you become a prisoner?' demanded Flann.

Dubh rubbed his forehead.

'The details are as yet vague. I came trading from my land of Ophir, bringing valuable stones from the mines we quarry. I came to Darcon . . . and rather than trade honestly with me, he took the precious stones and threw me in prison where my people and I were enslaved. I alone have survived of my people. I, alone.'

Scáthach reached forward and laid a hand on the giant's broad forearm.

'You will be revenged and compensated, Dubh of Ophir.'

The ruler of the far-off land of Ophir smiled at the girl.

'Your soul shines in honesty, Scáthach of Uibh Rathach.'

Ruacán sighed impatiently.

'We must be on our way before our escape is discovered. Surprise is our greatest weapon before Darcon can plot our end.'

Flann nodded.

'You are right, druid. But before we go, let me give you my hand. I have long been suspicious of you and your intentions. I am sorry for thinking ill of you. You were right: I must not blame the song on the singer. There are good druids and bad for they are but mortals.'

Ruacán brushed the young man away, almost embarrassed.

'Had I been you, Flann Mac Fraech, I would have been suspicious also. Now let us move, quickly.'

'Not so quickly, scum!'

The high-pitched voice of Cuár caused them to freeze.

The hunchback came sliding forward at the far end of the corridor, unwinding his whip as he came, a grotesque smile on his ugly features.

289

'Well, well, well . . . thinking to escape from Cuár's domain? Well, you answer to Cuár first, my friends. And this is the opportunity I have been waiting for. Now there is no one to stop me from slicing the flesh from your putrid bodies.'

He cracked the air with his whip and began to chuckle.

Scáthach slid the visor over her face and said: 'I will deal with the little one.'

But to her surprise, Dubh of Ophir pushed her gently aside.

'He is mine, lady,' he whispered. 'For twenty years he has been mine.'

The giant moved forward.

For a moment or two Cuár frowned and then, recognising the giant, his features took on a fearful expression for a moment before he regained his look of confidence. He slashed at the air once again.

'Why, Twenty-Seven! So they have released the sewer rats?'

'I am Dubh of Ophir, jackal's spawn,' hissed the giant, moving forward. 'Remember that name when you go shrieking down to the underworld of the Fomorii who will feast on your immortal soul.'

Cuár's eyes widened and he drew back his whip.

'Back in your cell, dog!' he shrieked.

But Dubh moved forward still.

Back went the whip hand. They saw the whip flashing through the air at the giant but, astonishingly, it did not seem to land. The next moment Dubh had the whiplash held in a vice-like grip in his hand and he jerked the hunchback towards him, as if the grotesque little man was a feather-weight. The hunchback let out a piercing shriek. Then Dubh reached forward and picked the struggling manikin up. One giant hand grasped the other's throat, cutting off his wind, the other was held against the base of

Cuár's spine. The little man's legs waved helplessly. Then, with his muscles rippling, Dubh raised the sadistic jailer to the full height of his arms and threw him head first against the stone walls.

There was an ominous crack and Cuár's body slithered to the floor and lay still, his head twisted at an awkward angle.

The giant gazed indifferently at the carcass.

'His death was too merciful for what he inflicted on others,' he said disdainfully.

Ruacán sighed softly.

'Blood cannot always wash out blood, my friend.'

Dubh's eyes narrowed.

'In my country we have a saying, wise one. The gods will not punish the man who makes return for injury.'

Scáthach had moved to the dead body of Cuár, bent down and removed her golden medallion, which he had taken from her. She placed it around her neck once again and turned to the others.

'Come,' she called urgently. 'Let us find our way out of these dungeons.'

She led the way, followed by Flann and Ruacán with Dubh taking up the rear, now carrying Cuár's whip.

They surprised three warriors sitting playing the board game of *brandubh*, 'black raven', in the outer chamber of the cell complex. Before they had time to fight or sound the alarm, they had been overcome and bundled into a cell. Flann availed himself of the opportunity to arm, while Dubh picked up a sword and shield.

The girl found a spiral stone staircase leading upwards and seemed to recall it was this passage that led into the great hall of Dún Scáith. She turned and motioned to the others to follow her quietly.

They encountered no one as they climbed up and finally reached a long gallery which was curtained at the far end.

Moving softly forward, Scáthach reached the curtain and found the join, moving it gently aside so that she could see through a crack.

Whereas before the great hall had been filled with people, now it was empty save for two figures seated on the dais: Darcon sprawled in his seat, his pale face anxious, while seated slightly forward in the other chair, her features dark and brooding, was Aífe. Scáthach cast an anxious look around the hall. There was no one else revealed in the glow of the numerous torches which lit it.

'Why did you give your word to that old man?' Darcon was demanding of his half-sister.

Aífe shrugged.

'It is the law and well you know the fact, Darcon.'

'The law,' sneered the other. 'Our mother is all-powerful. She makes the law for these mortals to obey, the mortals do not make laws for the obedience of the gods.'

Aífe bit her lip.

'Yet we are all under the law, immortals and mortals alike. It must be so.'

'You may choose that it is so, but not I. Let us have no more of laws. The prophecy must not come to pass. I will send Cuár to silence her.'

At that moment, Scáthach chose to push aside the curtain and enter the hall.

Aífe saw her first and came swiftly to her feet.

'Cuár is dead, Darcon,' said Scáthach evenly.

Darcon's mouth hung open a moment in surprise. Then he rose from his chair.

'Well, then, we must finish the job ourselves.'

He gestured to Aífe.

'Destroy her,' he cried.

Scáthach's twin sister hesitated.

'The law,' she protested. 'I am under the sacred *geis* not to raise my sword against her.'

'Droch!' cried Darcon angrily.

From behind the curtaining at the back of the dais Aífe's wily adviser came forward.

'Since your mistress will not kill her sister, you must do it,' snapped Darcon.

Droch nodded; drawing a slim throwing-knife from the sleeve of his robe, he moved forward grinning.

It was then that Ruacán, followed by Flann and Dubh, moved out from behind the curtain to stand behind Scáthach. Droch paused, staring unhappily from one to another.

Darcon uttered a profanity.

'Kill her!'

Droch's eyes moved speculatively. Then, before anyone could guess what he was doing, his throwing arm came up, and the knife was speeding with unerring accuracy toward's Scáthach's throat. It was Flann who reacted with speed, leaping forward and throwing up his shield so that the knife impacted into it. A split-second later, Dubh's sword embedded itself into the chest of Droch, who fell gasping onto his knees, blood pouring from the wound. The servant of Aífe groaned and slipped sideways and was still.

'A wasted life,' Scáthach murmured softly. She raised her eyes and gazed questioningly at her twin. 'Would you also waste your life, Aífe?'

Aífe held her arms outward from her body, her hands open.

'I will not break the sacred *geis*. No mortal may do so with impunity. I can never meet you in single combat for I was raised in obedience to the will of the gods as were you, my sister. No, I will not break the law. But, my clever sister, there is one who has been washed upon our shores who will quite happily serve the purpose.' She half turned her head over her shoulder and called: 'Goll! Now is the time you seek your vengeance.'

293

For a moment Scáthach stared in surprise at the figure of the sea-captain, as he emerged from behind the dais. It was obvious that the sailor had been well rested and fed and recovered from his leap overboard from the *Feannóg*. He had been more than lucky to survive the tempestuous seas. He wore a warrior's harness now, bore a shield and carried a javelin.

'Quick, man! Throw!' yelled Aífe, realising that Goll was no trained warrior to meet the girl in single combat. She had staked everything on the man surprising everyone and killing Scáthach by a swift cast of his spear.

However, Goll was stupid enough to want to savour his revenge and came forward grinning, his javelin raised to take better aim.

Dispassionately, Scáthach seized the weapon nearest at hand, the *gae-Bolga*, and before Goll knew what she was about, she had drawn and cast it with a movement which left everyone surprised by its swiftness. The terrible spear point entered Goll's chest, sending him flying backwards across the hall with surprise on his evil face. Then his one eye widened, he opened his mouth and gave out a soundless scream before collapsing. The terrible thirty sharp barbs had opened in his body and send his soul speeding to the Otherworld.

Darcon stared at the body indifferently.

'I knew the man was a fool. He had not skill in facing a trained warrior.' He glowered at Scáthach and her companions. 'Where is Eis Enchenn?' he asked Aífe. Scáthach's twin looked worried now.

'She went to find Cuár.'

'Get the guards!'

Flann stepped forward.

'Signal the guards and you are dead,' he said evenly.

'By the gods of Fomorii!' cried Darcon, reaching forward and drawing his sword. 'If no one else has courage to rid me of this girl,' he shot a malevolent glance at Aífe, 'then I will do so myself!'

Flann started forward to meet him, sword in hand, but Scáthach motioned him to stand to one side.

'No, do not shed his blood, Flann. This is my destiny.'

'But the sacred law,' protested Flann. 'If Darcon is Aífe's brother, then he is your brother also, and the law applies . . .'

'We are not bound by any law,' cried Darcon. 'We may have shared the same mother's womb but our fathers were of different stock. The law does not apply. And no sacred *geis* binds me.'

'Then prepare to defend your life, evil one,' cried Scáthach.

'And prepare to have your life taken!' returned Darcon, moving forward, his sword blade swinging.

Twenty

Scáthach divested herself of her javelin, which she gave to Flann, and drew her sword, moving forward to meet Darcon in a fighting crouch. She was aware immediately that Darcon was no mean swordsman, which could have been expected from a son of the Mórrígú. He had decided to make his attack a fierce and immediate onslaught and for a moment or two sheer weight drove the girl backwards across the great hall while her companions looked on anxiously.

Aífe, her sister, sat back on her seat on the dais, a curious thin smile on her lips as she watched her sister and half-brother battle it out.

Flann and Dubh stood anxiously, weapons in hand, ready to intervene if Darcon's warriors came spilling into the hall.

Only the old druid, Ruacán, seemed unperturbed and stood watching the contest with a critical eye.

Scáthach's mind was full of cold anger as she matched her skill with the tyrant of the Island of Shadows. He, she felt, was the evil behind the events which had led to Eola's death at Uibh Rathach, and who had made countless others go to unhappy ends or live in perpetual slavery to his will.

Sword blade clanged against sword blade, shield smashed against shield as the two fought in ever tightening circles across the great stone-flagged floor of the hall of Dún Scáith.

Finding the girl no easy victory, and his craft of swordsmanship matched by one as knowledgeable as himself, Darcon's volatile nature began to display itself. His face was flushed with anger and he began to take chances. His attacks took on a more wild form rather than considered moves to outwit his opponent. At one point, moving forward, and swinging his sword, he was met by a strong counterattack and, with a sudden back-handed thrust, Scáthach smashed the sword out of his grasp and sent it flying across the hallway.

Desperately, Darcon backed, as if seeking escape, and collided with the body of Goll.

At once, Darcon's face twisted into a grin of triumph. He whirled round and, with both hands, gripped the *gae-Bolga* and made to tug it from the body. Had he succeeded, he would have turned to cast it at Scáthach, taking advance of her. But Scáthach stood and watched him, smiling in her knowledge.

Darcon wrenched at the spear, his grin of evil triumph turning to puzzlement as he could not wrest the spearhead from the body.

'Do not waste your efforts, Darcon,' said Scáthach softly. 'That spear will not leave his body without being cut out. When it enters, the blade opens into thirty great barbs; each one must be cut out in order to leave the body.'

Darcon whirled round desperately, searching for a weapon.

'Help me!' he cried to Aífe.

'Don't worry,' Scáthach intervened. 'I would not kill you as an animal would be butchered. Flann, throw him his sword ... gently, Flann. Let him have a chance to defend himself before I despatch his soul to the Otherworld ... or to the land of the Fomorii!'

Flann hesitated, then shrugged. Picking up Darcon's sword he flung it towards the tyrant so that the man could catch it hilt first. Darcon caught it and, without pausing, came running back to Scáthach, striking with vicious savagery. He struck with rapid blows which told the girl that her opponent was full of anger and fear, striking almost without thinking, hoping that the weight of his attack would win the day for him.

It was then that Scáthach knew she had the upper hand, and in that moment she smiled at the knowledge.

Seeing the smile, fury ripped across the features of Darcon and he drew his sword back, letting forth a cry of intense ferocity which would have poleaxed many an opponent. Not so Scáthach. She saw his sword arm go back, leaving his right side undefended, and then she dropped to her knee, thrusting her sword forward just as Darcon ran in to make his cutting stroke.

For a moment or two Darcon stood stock still, sword still poised. No one moved. Then Darcon, his eyes wide and staring in disbelief, lowered his rigid gaze to the blade which protruded from under his rib-cage, spurting blood. His sword dropped from his nerveless hand, yet summoning his remaining reserve of strength he gave vent to a cry which froze the limbs of the onlookers. Before its echoes had reverberated through the great hall, Darcon of Dún Scáith toppled forward and fell dead on the stones.

Dispassionately, Scáthach knelt by his body and pressed her fingers to his pulse.

'He is dead, Scáthach.' It was Ruacán who spoke. He had no need to examine the body.

The girl rose and nodded.

Aífe, still sitting in the chair on the dais, seemed indifferent, sunk into her own thoughts.

'The prophecy has been fulfilled, my child,' went on the old druid. 'The Mórrígú's son is dead. Darcon will no more extend his tyranny in this world and may his soul be damned in the Otherworld.'

Slowly Scáthach drew her sword from Darcon's body, wiping it on his clothes before replacing it in its sheath.

'It means we are free,' whispered Dubh. 'Free!'

Flann was grinning from ear to ear.

Scáthach was about to speak when a terrible shrill-shrieking cry reached them, causing them to stare in horror as the fierce noise resounded through the rooms and halls of the fortress.

The great wooden doors of the hall smashed inward and the revolting harridan, Eis Enchenn, came scuttling in, her one red eye blazing, her dirty yellow-white hair flying about her head. She came forward in a crouch, keeping so low to the ground it was impossible to tell whether she moved on all fours. Her stinking skins made her seem animal rather than human and she still clutched her human thigh-bone totem. Her mouth gaped wide and from it there came the terrifying despairing shriek which rooted them to the floor.

She paused but a moment before her red eye saw Darcon's body, and with a renewed screech the old woman flung herself on the dead ruler of Dún Scáith. She gathered his head and shoulders to her and rocked to and fro, like a mother holding a baby, crooning in her shrill voice, pausing now and then to wail and lament in such tones that Scáthach tried to suppress the shiver which tingled along her spine up to the nape of her neck. Even Flann and Dubh took a step back as they gazed in disgust at the old woman.

To and fro the ancient crone rocked the dead Darcon's body, alternately lamenting and cursing him. Lamenting his death and cursing his stupidity in allowing himself to be outwitted.

Scáthach stood in horrified disbelief at the scene before turning away, sickened by it.

'Get someone to remove the old woman and Darcon's body,' she ordered Ruacán.

'You have not succeeded yet, Scáthach of Uibh Rathach!' came Eis Enchenn's shrill voice.

Scáthach turned back to the crone.

'You have killed him but you will repay his life one-hundred-fold.'

The girl smiled sadly.

It was clear that the old one was deranged.

'Go, old woman. There is nothing for you in this place,' she said softly. 'Go and end your days in peace far away from this land.'

Eis Enchenn's face spat venom at her, a scrawny hand raised the thigh-bone and shook it like a weapon.

'You have killed Darcon; you have outwitted Aífe and constricted her with your druid's *geis*, but you have yet to deal with me.'

'I have no wish to deal with you, old one. There is nothing for you here,' replied the girl.

'I will avenge my son!' cried Eis Enchenn.

Scáthach stared at her in astonishment.

'*Your* son?'

The implication of the crone's words registered in her mind.

Suddenly, Eis Enchenn stood up, stood up and grew tall. Her form began to change hideously. As if from nowhere, three black ravens began to circle her head. The hair changed to a raven blackness, held at the temples by a silver band. The face took on an angular, though ageless, form, with two large black staring eyes, so black that it was impossible to discern if they had pupils. The mouth was a sneering gash of red, the face was hard and merciless. The body was tall, it towered over them. A long flowing black robe cloaked it. Around the neck was a chain of bloody severed heads with lolling tongues and wide staring eyes and from each of their mouths there came forth hideous moaning noises. Around the feet of this awesome image it seemed as if a pool of red blood was boiling. In her hand this terrible being still held the human thigh-bone.

Ruacán was the first to move.

'The Mórrígú!' he gasped. 'Goddess of death and battles!'

Aífe had fallen to her knees and covered her eyes.

The awesome vision drew back her red gash of a mouth and gave forth a piercing, hideous peal of laughter.

The old druid made to move to Scáthach's side but the thigh-bone was extended towards him. It was as if the old man had become frozen to the spot.

The deep black eyes of the being turned back to Scáthach.

'Vengeance is mine!' came a long shuddering whisper.

Scáthach tried to reach for her sword but her limbs were like stone.

In her mind she heard a voice calling her. Buimech's voice. And realisation flooded her mind. It was useless to challenge one of the gods with mortal weapons. She must rely on her knowledge, but what knowledge would help her?

She glanced at the others, who stood staring at the being as if mesmerised and unable to move.

'You have thwarted my will,' hissed the terrible image. 'In spite of my precautions you have slain my son and rendered my daughter impotent. Yet I am the power and it is my right to punish.'

Up came Scáthach's chin defiantly.

'I am told that you are my real mother. Would you destroy your own offspring?'

Again came the maniacal peal of laughter.

'Yes, if my offspring thwarted my plans. I planned to bring chaos and destruction into the world of men. I planned to set nation warring against nation. For in death and battles I thrive and grow strong. Soon I would have the entire world worship at my feet. Man is a petty, stupid creature who, with only a little prompting, would bathe in blood for me.'

Scáthach shook her head sadly.

'Mankind may worship at your feet from time to time when madness is upon it but its aspiration for good will always draw it back from the abyss you envision.'

The human thigh-bone in the gruesome phantasm's hand rose towards the girl.

'What images of hell can you conjure, Scáthach?' hissed the voice. 'For whatever terrifying things you can imagine, your fate will be worse!'

The girl tried to keep calm, trying to reason how she could overcome this vile creature which had been her mother.

It was as if Ruacán's voice was whispering in her ears.

'Yes, she was your mother. There is weakness in that.'

Weakness?

'Remember the lessons you have learnt, my child. Seek the answers within yourself. Remember the Plain of

301

Ill-Luck, the Perilous Glen and the Valley of the Shadow. Do all these things mean nothing?'

Scáthach brought her gaze up to the blazing fury of her mother's gaze and suddenly smiled.

Yes she had learnt lessons; she had learnt to accept that things were not always what they seemed and perception was merely a matter of one's own thought. If one perceived something as terrifying it did not always follow that it was terrifying to others. And this being before her, the awesome goddess of death and battles, was but her mother. Her mother. A wave of sadness overwhelmed the girl. Her fear and anger became edged with pity.

The awesome brows of the vision drew together uncertainly.

'Why do you smile?' it hissed.

'There is sadness in you,' replied Scáthach.

'Sadness?' sneered the voice.

'Sadness in your motherhood.'

The Mórrígú's black eyes widened.

'Speak not to me of motherhood, you who have slain my son.'

'It is your daughter who speaks, mother.'

'You! You are come from my womb but you are no daughter of mine!'

'Therein is the sadness of your motherhood.'

The being frowned again, not sure of the girl's meaning.

'Dare you talk to me of sadness and motherhood? You should be quaking in fear before me knowing what I shall do to you.'

'How can I be fearful before my own mother?' demanded Scáthach. 'I can only feel pity for you.'

'Pity?' the voice rose to a shriek.

The girl nodded.

'You are what you are and I can only grieve for it. You

302

thrive on hate and hostility. Malice and vindictiveness are all that you know. Yet within you there must be some humanity. Did you not lament the loss of your son? What stirred you to that emotion? Is there some hope for you yet, some compassion lurking within you that was born of your motherhood?'

The being gnashed its teeth.

'Speak not to me of compassion. You stand on the brink of destruction!'

Scáthach paused. It seemed to her that the thunderous tones were not as strong as they were; the figure was no longer as horrific as before. No longer as tall and awesome.

'I must be charitable to you, for you are my mother,' she said softly.

'You must fear and hate me,' stormed the spectre, 'for that is the lot of all mankind.'

'Not I. I can only weep for you. You are my mother and yet you pretend you have no feelings.'

'Hate me!' shrilled the voice, yet the voice was weak and fearful, almost imploring hate.

The frightful vision seemed to be undergoing a metamorphosis. Even as Scáthach stood, smiling sadly and pityingly at it, the tall image began to wither and grow frail; it began to shrink and turn into an elderly woman – not the gruesome frame of Eis Enchenn, but simply a frail old woman. The face changed from malevolence to fear and suddenly, screeching piteously, the being faded and disappeared.

Scáthach stood staring for a long time at the spot where it had vanished.

The old druid suddenly touched her arm and smiled.

'Your wisdom and self-knowledge prevailed, my child.'

Scáthach returned his gaze without speaking.

Flann, recovering from his frigid inactivity, moved forward uneasily.

'What happened? How did it disappear . . . it was the goddess of death and battles and could have withered us at a look?'

Scáthach smiled softly at the young warrior.

'It was my mother, Flann.'

The old druid nodded.

'The goddess of death and battles can only thrive on the fear and hatred of mankind. Pity, especially the pity of her own daughter, whom she had wronged, could not sustain her in this world. She has fled to the Otherworld.'

Dubh came forward smiling.

'You are truly a wise woman, Scáthach. How did you know how to use the weapon of pity against her?'

Scáthach's face was sad and her mouth turned down.

'The truth is, I did not. I really do feel pity for her. In truth, she was my mother and that fact I cannot deny. Just as I cannot deny Aífe there as my twin sister.'

Aífe had risen to her feet and was standing with her head hung sullenly on her chest.

'What punishment have you in store for me, Scáthach?' she whispered.

The girl paused and then shrugged.

'Punishment? Should I punish the lame for being lame? Your weakness is not of your own making. You may go, Aífe. Remember there is now a *geis* between us. We may not harm each other in battle.'

Her twin looked at her in disbelief.

'But where should I go?' she whispered.

'Go back to Lethra and continue to rule there, but rule in wisdom and for the good of your people, not for the good of yourself. For if I hear of any despotism in Lethra, if I hear you continue to rule with fear and hate in the tradition of our mother, then I shall come again. The *geis* between us shall remain but you will no longer rule in Lethra.'

Ruacán smiled broadly.

'Here is wisdom, indeed.'

Aífe stood hesitating.

'You are truly possessed of great wisdom or great stupidity, Scáthach of Uibh Rathach.'

'Then we shall find out which it is in the coming years,' replied her sister.

'Scáthach!' It was Dubh who shouted the warning.

Warriors were pushing into the great hall, uncertain and irresolute, gazing curiously at the slain body of their ruler.

Scáthach leapt upon the dais and held up her hands.

'People of Dún Scáith! Darcon the Tyrant has been slain. Cuár the jailer lies dead and Eis Enchenn has been despatched to the Otherworld. The tyranny and evil that has lain like a fog over this fortress and this land is gone, evaporated like the morning mist when the sun comes up.'

There was a murmur of voices, debating, questioning, unconvinced. They stood, unsettled and undecided.

'You have two choices, people of Dún Scáith,' continued the girl. 'You can leave this place, or you can stay and I will lead you, if you desire it.'

They faltered again, unsure, and then one of the warriors came forward and drew his sword.

Flann's hand snaked to his weapon and Dubh moved a step forward, growling menacingly in his throat.

But the warrior placed the sword at Scáthach's feet.

'You may command my sword, Scáthach of Dún Scáith!' he said.

At once there rose a cheer of acclamation from the others.

'Hail to our new chieftainess! Hail Scáthach of the Island of the Shadows!'

After a time, when Scáthach had despatched the warriors to remove the bodies of Darcon and Droch and ordered food and drink to be brought for herself and her companions, Ruacán said: 'What do you mean to do as chieftainess of this place, my child?'

Scáthach smiled.

'I am still the daughter of Eola of Uibh Rathach. And Eola's martial academy was famed throughout the world. What should his daughter do but follow his example?'

Flann leant forward across the table, as they sat feasting. He raised his eyebrows in surprise.

'You would make Dún Scáith an academy of martial arts?'

'The greatest in the world, Flann,' smiled the girl. 'For here, I would teach not only skill with weapons but, more importantly, skill of the mind. For here would the teachings of Buimech and, above all, of Ruacán the Wizened, be taught. Yes, I will use my skills to teach warriors and champions so that they may set forth to make this world a better place.'

Flann paused a moment and then he grinned.

'Would you need an instructor? I am told that I have a fair hand with the sword.'

Scáthach leaned forward and impulsively gripped his hand.

'Dear Flann, I would need both instructor, friend and companion.'

There was a long pause and Ruacán broke it by turning to Dubh.

'And what of you, Dubh of Ophir? Will you stay?'

The giant shook his dark head and smiled.

'I have been twenty years away from my land of Ophir and much has happened in that time. I must return lest my people have suffered in my absence.'

Scáthach smiled.

'We will fit you out with the best ship to be found in Dún Scáith and a crew to handle her.'

Dubh bowed his head.

'Future generations will hear, in the stories and legends

of Ophir, how Scáthach rescued their ruler and safely returned him.'

A warrior entered and bowed to the girl.

'Your sister, Aífe, is ready to bid farewell.'

Scáthach rose, and accompanied by Ruacán, Flann and Dubh, followed the warrior to the quayside that lay beside the fortress. A ship, with the markings of Lethra, was preparing to sail.

Aífe stood by the gangplank, waiting to embark.

'Well, sister,' she said warily.

Scáthach halted at arm's length and smiled at her mirror image.

'Well, sister,' she replied.

There was an uncomfortable pause between them.

'It is sad that the *geis* stands between us,' Aífe sighed. 'Alas, I shall never know which of us is the greater warrior.'

'Isn't it better that such a thing never be known?' asked Scáthach.

'Perhaps; perhaps not. Still, the prohibition has been pronounced. And I shall return to be the High One of Lethra and rule as you have ordained. But one day . . .'

She smiled enigmatically.

'Farewell Scáthach of Uibh Rathach.'

'Farewell Aífe of Lethra.'

They did not touch each other, did not clasp each other's hands. There was still much between them. Then Aífe turned and walked onto the ship. The mooring ropes were soon parted, the sails set and the vessel began to draw away from the stone jetty.

For some time Scáthach stood on the quayside watching the sail of the ship dipping and bowing until it disappeared out of sight behind a headland.

When she turned from the quayside back to her companions, Ruacán detected the tears in the girl's eyes.

307

'It is sad to find a sister and to lose her,' he said softly.

She sniffed and made no reply for a moment. Then she reached forward and took Flann's hand.

'Ruacán,' she said, 'I shall soon have family enough to occupy my thoughts. I have developed the gift of prophecy, the gift of Buimech. Before the year is out I shall bear Flann a child.'

The young warrior gazed at her astounded.

'The child will be a daughter ... I shall call her Uathach. She will grow in beauty and her lover will be the greatest champion ever to come out of the land of Éireann.'

Ruacán nodded thoughtfully.

'Truly, my child, you have developed the gift of fore-knowledge. You no longer need a druid to guide you on the path for you are possessed of the gift of the *imbas forasni*, the light of foresight. Now you are the greatest warrior in the world, the one to whom great champions and warriors from all the corners of the world will come to learn their art. You have no need of my skill any longer. I must be on my way.'

Scáthach gazed at him sadly.

'I did not mean to chase you away with my stupid boasting, Ruacán,' she said.

The old man laid a hand on her arm for a moment.

'I must go.'

'But we have been through so much together, old man. I may still need your companionship and advice.'

The old druid chuckled.

'What need have you for an old man when you have Flann Mac Fraech for your companion?'

'We would like you to stay,' pressed Flann, colouring a little. 'I know that I had suspicions about you in the past but I hope you will forgive me. Do not leave on my account.'

Ruacán placed a hand on the young warrior's shoulder.

'I do not do so, my son. Take advantage of your happiness while you can. Mortal lives are short.'

He turned and pointed to one end of the quayside.

'My *curragh* waits. I must go.' He smiled from one to another, bidding farewell to Dubh, to Flann and then to Scáthach. 'We have come a long way together. Now you must continue on your road alone. I can give you nothing but this, my child: when you are in pain and doubt, examine your heart and be true to it. Learn what you are and be such. If you ever become a stranger to yourself then you will lose all you have gained.'

The girl bowed her head to the old man and he reached forward and touched her lightly in the centre of the forehead with his hand.

Then he turned and made his way down the stone steps of the quayside and climbed into his *curragh*.

Dubh turned away to seek others to organise his ship in preparation for his voyage home to Ophir but Scáthach and Flann stood on the quayside, hand in hand, watching the old druid rowing away from the Island of Shadows. Abruptly, without warning at all, and even though the sky was blue and without cloud, a wind rose across the sea, and it became blustery. They strained their eyes anxiously across the great troughs and billows.

'Oh!' cried Scáthach, 'why did we let the old one go? He will be drowned.'

But Flann was staring with a curious frown.

'I do not think so. Did you ask yourself why his *curragh* was suddenly at the quayside when he wanted it? Did we not leave his *curragh* on the shores of Gallia when we made our journey to Lethra?'

Scáthach frowned, realising that it was so. Once again she wondered how the old man could have crossed the chasm to get into the fortress to effect her rescue?

'I do not understand,' she said softly.

309

Out to sea the foam-flecked waves rose and fell across the troughs.

'Look!' cried Flann. 'By the gods, look!'

They stared into the spraying sea.

For a moment they saw old Ruacán resplendent in brilliant white robes edged with gold, his white hair streaming behind him; it was as if he were sitting on a great white charger and riding across the waves. The vision lasted only for a split second. Then it was gone. The sea was suddenly calm again and there was no sign of Ruacán.

'Did we see that?' whispered Flann shaking his head in disbelief.

Scáthach smiled gently. It was suddenly clear to her now.

'We saw it. And now I understand everything. Your suspicions about Ruacán were partly right, Flann. He was not simply a druid. He was Manánnan Mac Lir, the ocean god, obeying the prayers of the father I never knew.'

The sea was calm and blue around the bright green island, reflecting the cloudless sky in which the sun rode high in the heavens. Even the grey walls of Dún Scáith seemed friendly and not as threatening as they had seemed before.

'Come, Flann,' chuckled Scáthach. 'Let us turn this Island of Shadows into an Island of Light.'

Author's Afterword

The story contained in Compert Scáthach Buanand (*The Begetting of Scáthach the Victorious*) survives only in fragmentary texts and allusions in other works from the medieval period.

Scáthach is best known to readers of Irish mythology from her appearance in the 'Red Branch Cycle' (or 'Ulster Cycle'), a series of tales which culminate in the famous Táin Bó Cualigne (*The Cattle Raid of Cualigne*), sometimes hailed as the Irish equivalent of the Greek Iliad. The earliest complete version of this text dates back to the 12th century. This has been translated into English and retold many times. Ireland's greatest mythical hero, Cúchulainn, the Hound of Ulster, was sent to Scáthach to finish his training at her famous academy of martial arts. For a time he became the lover of Scáthach's daughter, Uathach. Then he took part in the war between Scáthach and her sister Aífe. Having defeated her, Aífe became Cúchulainn's lover and bore him a son, Conlaí, who he eventually killed in combat, not recognising him. It was Scáthach who gave Cúchulainn his most famous weapon – the gae-Bolga, the spear she had been given by Bolga, god of lightning.

The story of Cúchulainn's training by Scáthach occurs in the tale Tochmarc Emir (*The Wooing of Emer*) which is thought to have been written down for the first time in the 7th century. A partial manuscript of the tale survives from the 10th century while a full text is given in the

311

12th-century Leabhar Laighnech *(Book of Leinster). A different version of the tale is given in the 9th-century text* Aided Aenfir Aífe *(The Death of Aífe's Only Son). The text was edited and published in* Béaloideas, The Journal of the Folklore of Ireland Society, Vol. IX, No 57, 1930. *It was also the subject of a study in* Compert con Cúlainn *(The Begetting of Cúchulainn) by Professor A. G. van Hamel, Dublin Institute of Advance Studies, 1933. The same basic text occurs in a 13th-century copy entitled* Foglaim con Cúlainn *(Cúchulainn's Training).*

Scáthach, whose father was the mortal king of Lethra, must not be confused with another Scáthach who appears in Irish mythology. The other Scáthach is the daughter of Énna, a lord of the Otherworld, who was claimed as wife by the champion Fionn Mac Cumhail. Fionn had forced his way into the Otherworld to claim this Scáthach as she 'was more beautiful than any mortal woman' but, on their wedding night, Scáthach played magic music which sent Fionn to sleep and when he awoke he was back in the mortal world with no way of returning. This story survives in a 13th-century text Feis Tighe Chonáin *(The Feast at Conán's House), included in* Acallamh na Senórdacht *(Discourses of the Ancients) edited by Dr Whitley Stokes, Leipzig, 1900 (Irische Texte 4), and treated at length in* Feis Tighe Chonáin *by Maud Joynt, Dublin, 1936.*

As a result of the popularity of my previous fantasy titles based on tales from Irish mythology, I have received several requests from English and American readers to give them some guide as to the pronunciation of Irish names and the occasional words which come into the text.

Obviously, there are many sounds in Irish which do not exist in English. There are 18 letters in the Irish alphabet and an accent called the fada (= long) which is written like the French acute over a vowel: eg – é. This makes the vowel long, and sometimes indicates stress. Accents are of enormous importance in Irish for they change not only the sound of the word but its meaning. Hence, the name Seán (Irish equivalent of John) written without an accent becomes Sean (old) and with the accent on the first vowel becomes séan (an omen). Two things to remember are that the letter 'h' following a consonant changes the sound, these being called aspirated consonants, while eclipses are formed by replacing an initial letter with another sound. The original letter is written but not spoken. These forms help to produce the 60-odd sounds that form Irish.

Rather than attempt to provide a complete lesson on Irish pronunciation (there are four dialects in Irish), I am providing a glossary of the words and names that occur in this book with an approximation of English phonetics. The following are given under the chapter in which they first occur.

Pronunciation

chapter one

Rónán Mac Méin: Row'nawn Mak Main
Cáoc: Kay'ok
Mumhan: Mo'wan
Éireann: Air'rin
grian-tairisem: gree'an taw'ris'sem
Buimech: Bew'meck
Eola: Yo-lah
Uibh Rathach: Eev Ra'ach
Fianna: Fee-an-nah
Ablach: Ab'lach
Baitin Mac Tigernma: Bay'ten Mak Tee'gern'ma
Teamhair: Taw'rah
brandubh: bran'doo'v
Tuath Dé Danaan: Too'ah Day Dan-awn
Manánnan Mac Lir: Man'awn-nan Mak Leer
Scáthach: Skaw'ach

chapter two

minn n-óir: minn n'oar
criss: chris
bossan: boss'an
Os: Os
Fionn Mac Cumhail: Finn Mak Cool
Sadhb: Sy've

Oisín: Osh-sheen
Mórrígú: Mor'ree'goo
fuat: foo'at
fé: fee
Ogham: Og'ham
nuall-guba: nool gub'ah
caoineadh: kween-ach
Fomorii: Fo'mor'ee

chapter three

Dún na Séad: Doon nah She-ad
Éccneid: Ak'ned
bruden: brew-den
faitche: faht-cha
Bruden na Rialtais: Brew-den nah Re'al-tash
Brosc: Brosk
Eidersceoil: Idir'skol
Durbhola: Derv'oh'la
Búanann: Bew'ah'nan

chapter four

Lethra: Leh'rah
Vercanrix: Ver'can-rix
Míl: Meel
Brehon: Bre'hon

chapter five

Flann Mac Fraech: Flann Mak Fray-ach
Cruithne: Krew-nah
Aintiarna: Ayn-teer'nah
Ulaidh: Oo'la
Alba: Al-a-pa
Airer Ghàidheal: Ay'ah Gay'al

Goll: Gull
Nemhain: Knee-wan

chapter seven

Ruacán: Roo'ah-kawn
Míle Easpain: Mee'la Eesh'pawn
Dana: Dah'nah
sciathrach: ske'ah'rak
An Seancholl Snidheach: Un Shan-col Snee-ack
(The) Dagda: Dawg'dah
Corr-Bholg: Cor-Vol'ug
curragh: cur'rah

chapter eight

Goibhniu: Gov'noo
Nía: Nee'ah
An Chraobh Ghlasach: Un Krave Glass'ack
Hy-Falga: Hi Fal'ga
An Cruadín: Un Kre'ah-deen

chapter ten

Bolga: Bol'ug'ah
gae-Bolga: gay-Bol'ug'ah
Solas: Sol-ash
geis: gay'sh
Cruitin: Krew'it'teen

chapter eleven

Aífe: Ee-va
Dias: Gee-ash

chapter twelve

Droch: Drock

316

chapter thirteen

Maor: Mawer
Darcon: Dah'con
Dún Scáith: Doon Ska'h
Bracan: Brak-an
Feannóg: Fahn-ohg

chapter fourteen

Aird na Murchan: Ard nah-Mur-chan
Caol Muile: Kyle Mew'la
Muile: Mew-la
Laoch: Lay-ack
Each: Eek

chapter sixteen

Eis Enchenn: Eesh An'cheen

chapter seventeen

Cuár: Koo-er

chapter nineteen

Ard Geimne: Ard Gem'nah
Dubh: Doo'v
Ophir: Oh-feer

chapter twenty

imbas forasni: eem-bash for'ash'nee
Uathach: Oo'ah'ack

MORGAN LLYWELYN

On Raven's Wing

He can break your bones or break your heart.
Cuchulain. Wolfhound of Cullen.
The name no warrior has borne before.

The small boy who arrives at the royal stronghold of Emain
Macha has only one desire. To join the legendary Red Branch,
the reckless, flamboyant warriors pledged to king and kingdom.
And he is still only a child when he unwittingly accepts the
terrible Morrigan, battle raven and goddess of war, as his
talisman.

From the moment he is brushed by the raven's wing, Cuchulain
becomes the greatest warrior in the kingdom – loyal to
comrades, fascinating to women, but possessed in battle by the
all-consuming rage that terrifies friend and foe alike. . .

'A panoramic sweep of love and jealousy and war'
Barbara Erskine

'Vivid, vital and victorious . . . magnificent'
Anne McCaffrey

Morgan Llywelyn's *Lion of Ireland* is also available in
Mandarin.

A Selected List of Fiction Available from Mandarin

While every effort is made to keep prices low, it is sometimes necessary to increase prices at short notice. Mandarin Paperbacks reserves the right to show new retail prices on covers which may differ from those previously advertised in the text or elsewhere.

The prices shown below were correct at the time of going to press.

☐	7493 0003 5	**Mirage**	James Follett	£3.99
☐	7493 0134 1	**To Kill a Mockingbird**	Harper Lee	£2.99
☐	7493 0076 0	**The Crystal Contract**	Julian Rathbone	£3.99
☐	7493 0145 7	**Talking Oscars**	Simon Williams	£3.50
☐	7493 0118 X	**The Wire**	Nik Gowing	£3.99
☐	7493 0121 X	**Under Cover of Daylight**	James Hall	£3.50
☐	7493 0020 5	**Pratt of the Argus**	David Nobbs	£3.99
☐	7493 0097 3	**Second from Last in the Sack Race**	David Nobbs	£3.50

All these books are available at your bookshop or newsagent, or can be ordered direct from the publisher. Just tick the titles you want and fill in the form below.

Mandarin Paperbacks, Cash Sales Department, PO Box 11, Falmouth, Cornwall TR10 9EN.

Please send cheque or postal order, no currency, for purchase price quoted and allow the following for postage and packing:

UK   80p for the first book, 20p for each additional book ordered to a maximum charge of £2.00.

BFPO   80p for the first book, 20p for each additional book.

Overseas   £1.50 for the first book, £1.00 for the second and 30p for each additional book
including Eire   thereafter.

NAME (Block letters) ....

ADDRESS ....

....

....